LITTLE, BROWN
AND COMPANY

NEW YORK
BOSTON

SPIRIT

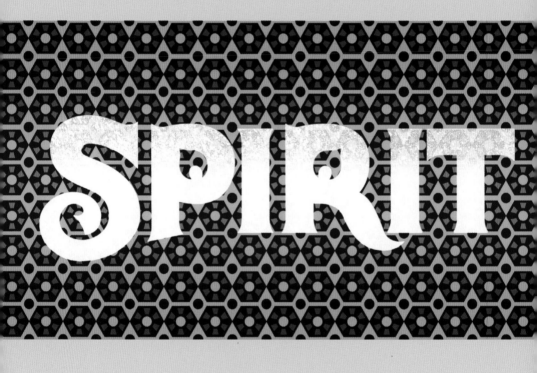

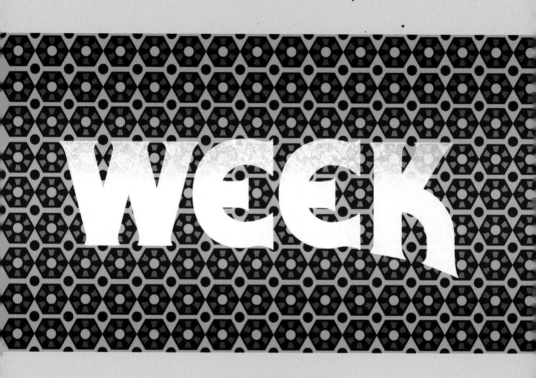

WEEK

by IRA MARCKS

Colors by Addison Duke

About This Book

This book was edited by Andrea Colvin and designed by Megan McLaughlin. The production was supervised by Bernadette Flinn, and the production editor was Jake Regier. The text was set in Amity Island, and the display type is Linotype Typo American.

Little, Brown and Company
Hachette Book Group
1290 Avenue of the Americas, New York, NY 10104
Visit us at LBYR.com

First Edition: October 2022

Little, Brown and Company is a division of Hachette Book Group, Inc.
The Little, Brown name and logo are trademarks of Hachette Book Group, Inc.

The publisher is not responsible for websites (or their content) that are not owned by the publisher.

Images of Snoopy on pages 171 and 230 © 2022 Peanuts Worldwide LLC

Library of Congress Cataloging-in-Publication Data
Names: Marcks, Ira, author, illustrator.
Title: Spirit week / by Ira Marcks.
Description: First edition. | New York: Little, Brown and Company, 2022. | Audience: Ages 12 & up. | Summary: Two people, aspiring filmmaker Elijah and thirteen-year-old tutor Suzy, are invited to a largely deserted hotel in Estes Park, Colorado, to make a film about reclusive horror author Jack Axworth and tutor his son, Danny; but the situation is not as expected: Jack is suffering from early onset dementia and, convinced that his books have released evil, is trying to buy up and destroy them as well as the hotel he lives in—but nobody is quite what they seem, and soon the whole project starts to resemble one of Jack's horror novels.
Identifiers: LCCN 2021041039 | ISBN 9780316277945 (hardcover) | ISBN 9780316278065 (trade paperback) | ISBN 9780316278218 (ebook)
Subjects: LCSH: Graphic novels. | Horror tales. | Novelists—Comic books, strips, etc. | Novelists—Juvenile fiction. | Motion picture producers and directors—Comic books, strips, etc. | Motion picture producers and directors—Juvenile fiction. | Secrecy—Comic books, strips, etc. | Secrecy—Juvenile fiction. | Estes Park (Colo.)—Comic books, strips, etc. | Estes Park (Colo.)—Juvenile fiction. | CYAC: Graphic novels. | Horror stories. | Secrets—Fiction. | Estes Park (Colo.)—Fiction. | LCGFT: Graphic novels. | Horror fiction.
Classification: LCC PZ7.7.M3378 Sp 2022 | DDC 741.5/973—dc23
LC record available at https://lccn.loc.gov/2021041039

ISBNs: 978-0-316-27794-5 (hardcover), 978-0-316-27806-5 (pbk.), 978-0-316-27821-8 (ebook), 978-0-316-33290-3 (ebook), 978-0-316-33299-6 (ebook)

Printed in China

1010

Hardcover: 10 9 8 7 6 5 4 3 2 1
Paperback: 10 9 8 7 6 5 4 3 2

To Dad

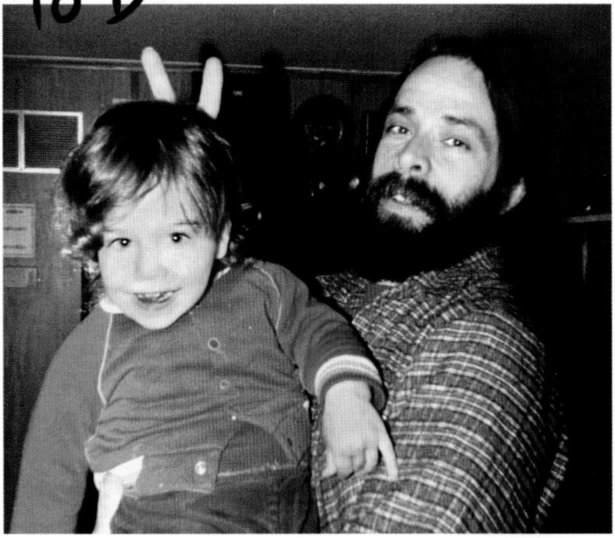

who gave me
A ROOM WITH
A VIEW.

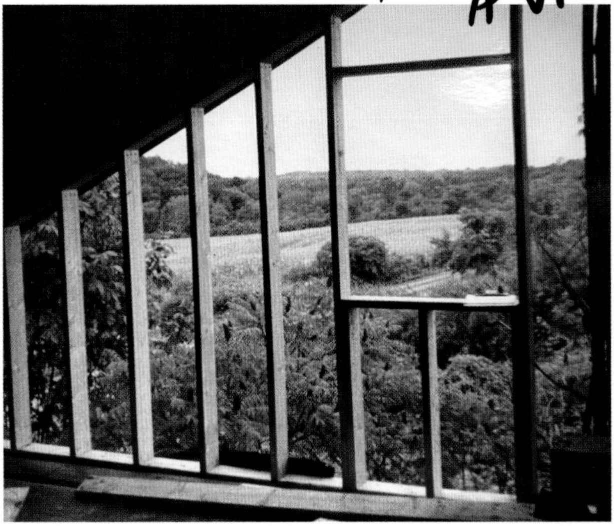

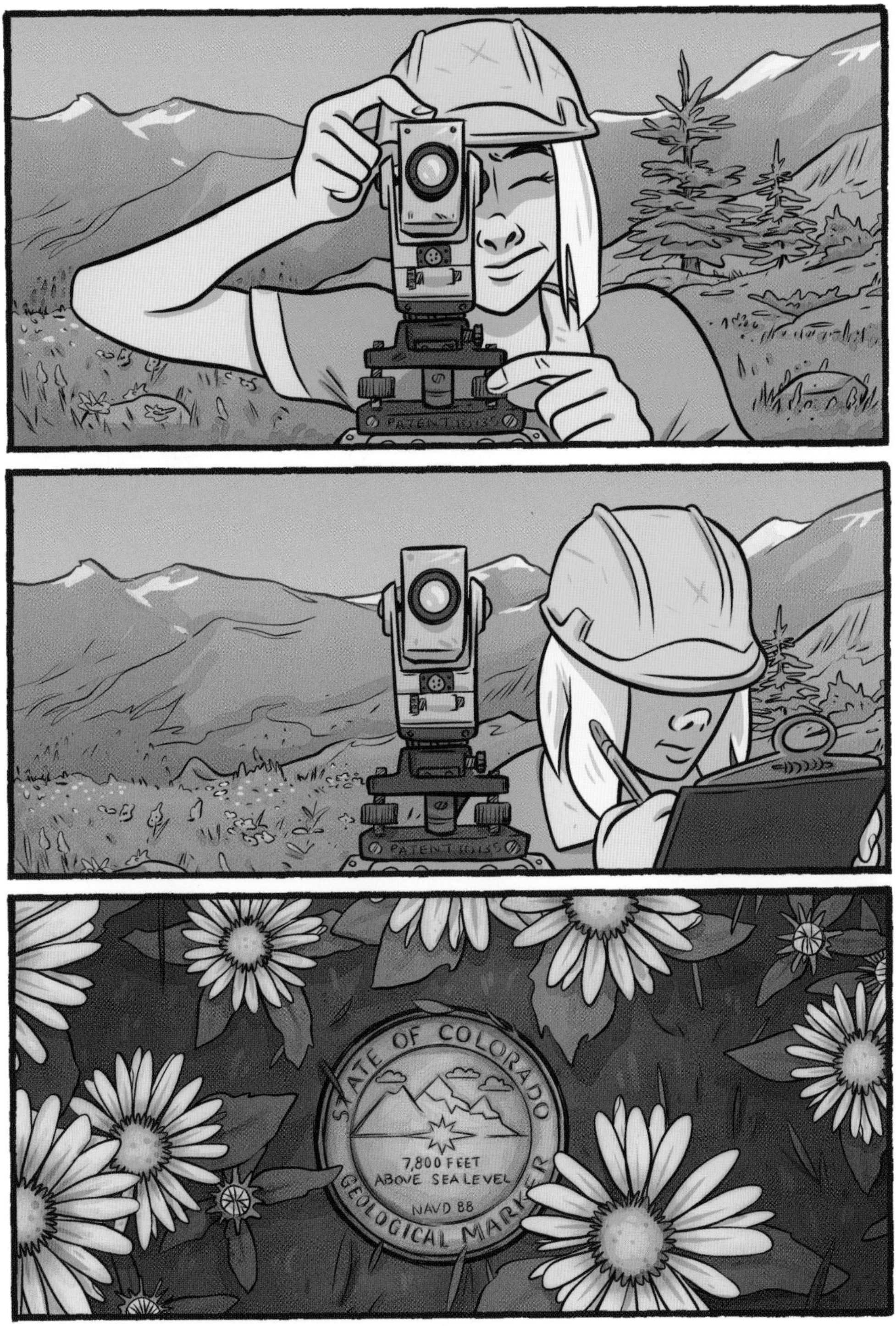
STATE OF COLORADO
7,800 FEET
ABOVE SEA LEVEL
NAVD 88
GEOLOGICAL MARKER

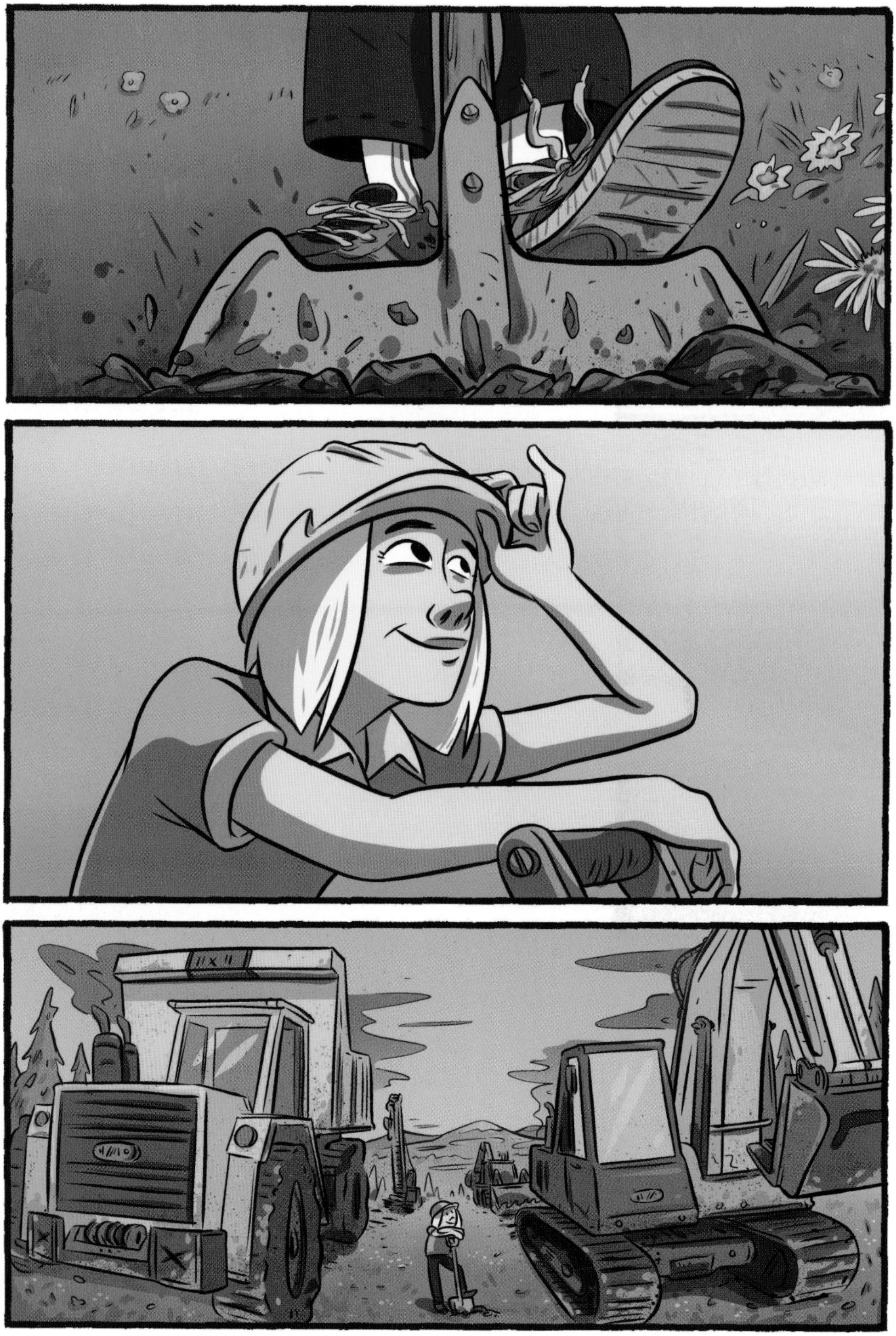

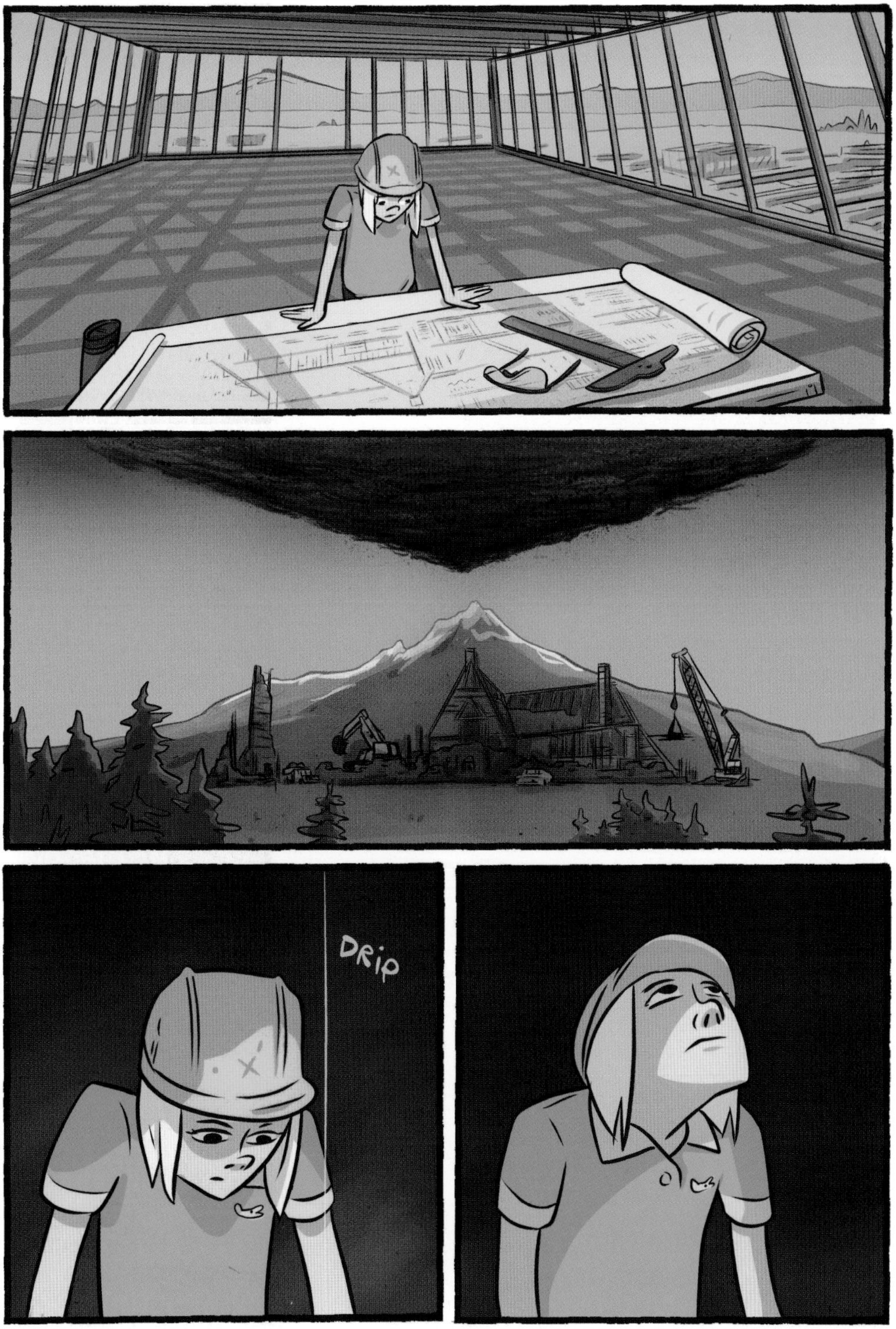
DRIP

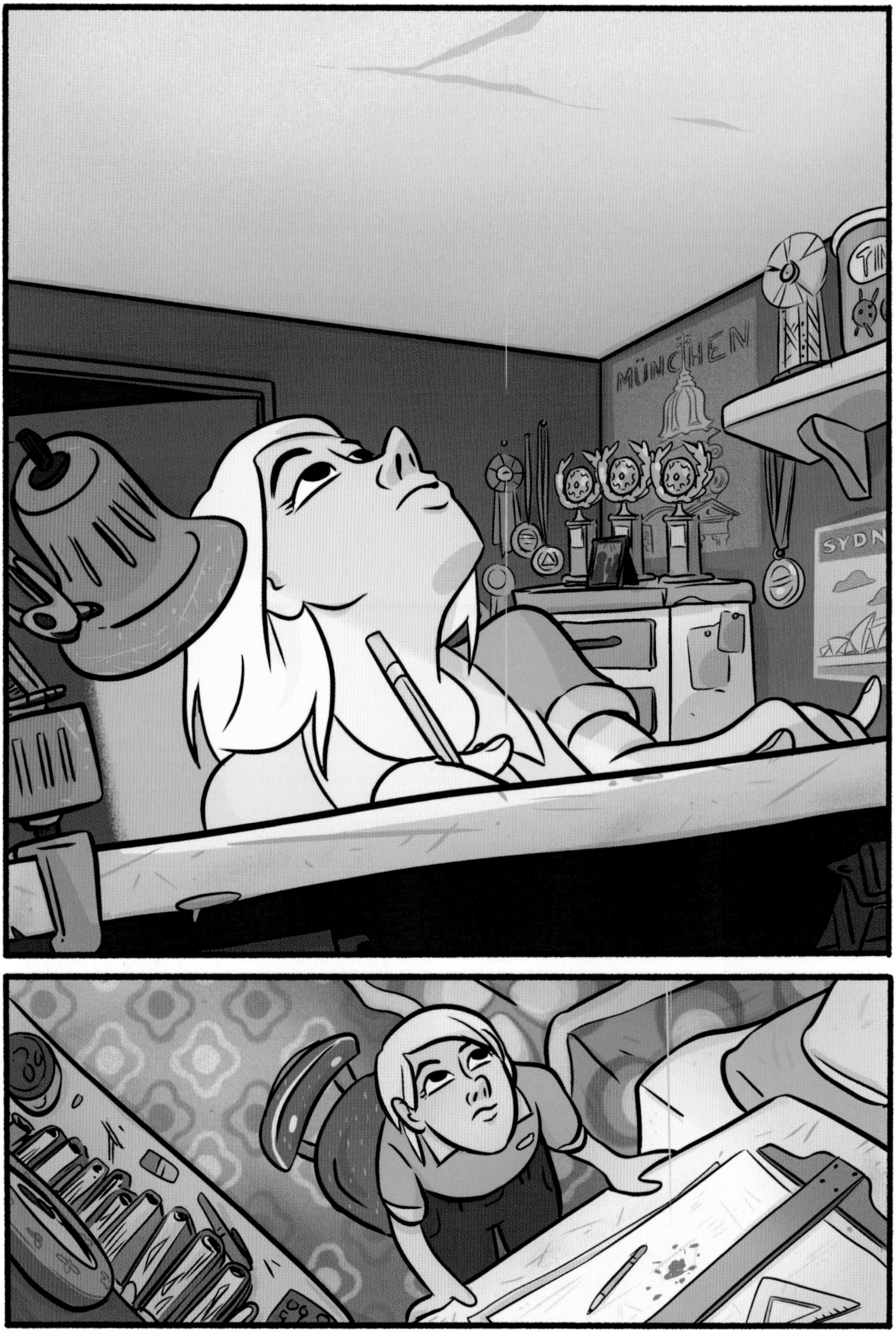
MÜNCHEN

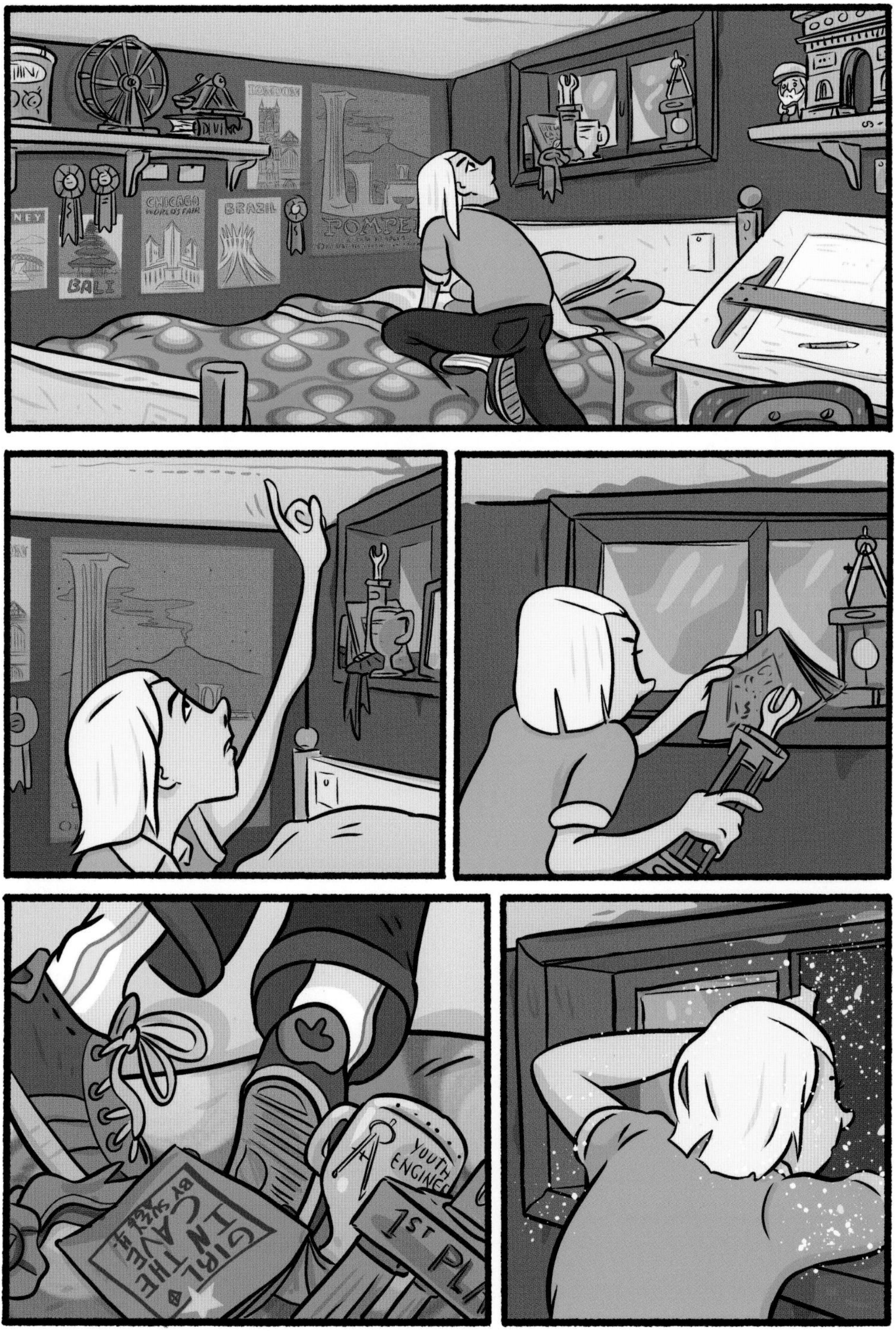
LONDON
CHICAGO WORLD'S FAIR
BRAZIL
BALI
GIRL IN THE CAVE

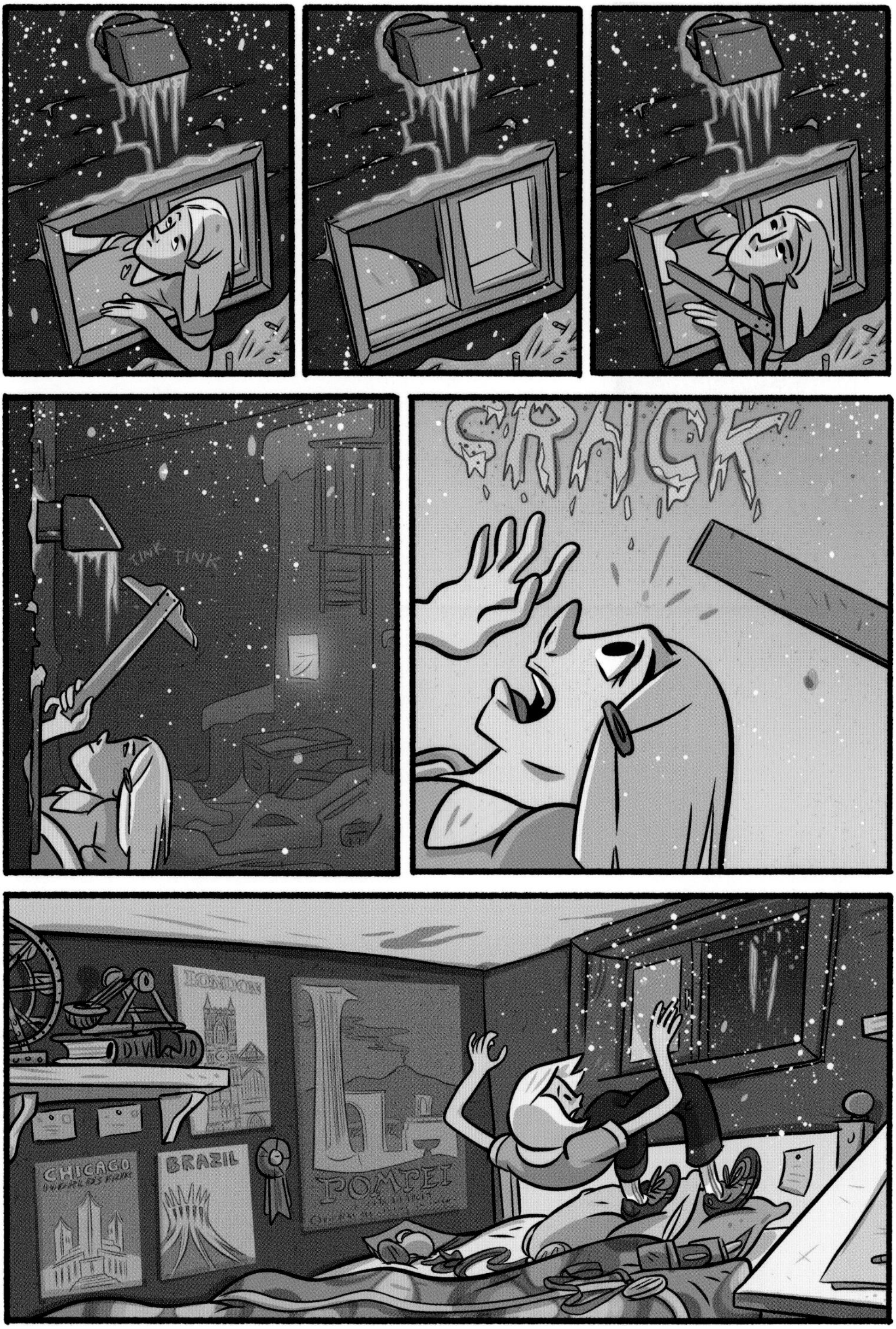
TINK TINK
SRACK
LONDON
CHICAGO
WORLD'S FAIR
BRAZIL
POMPEI

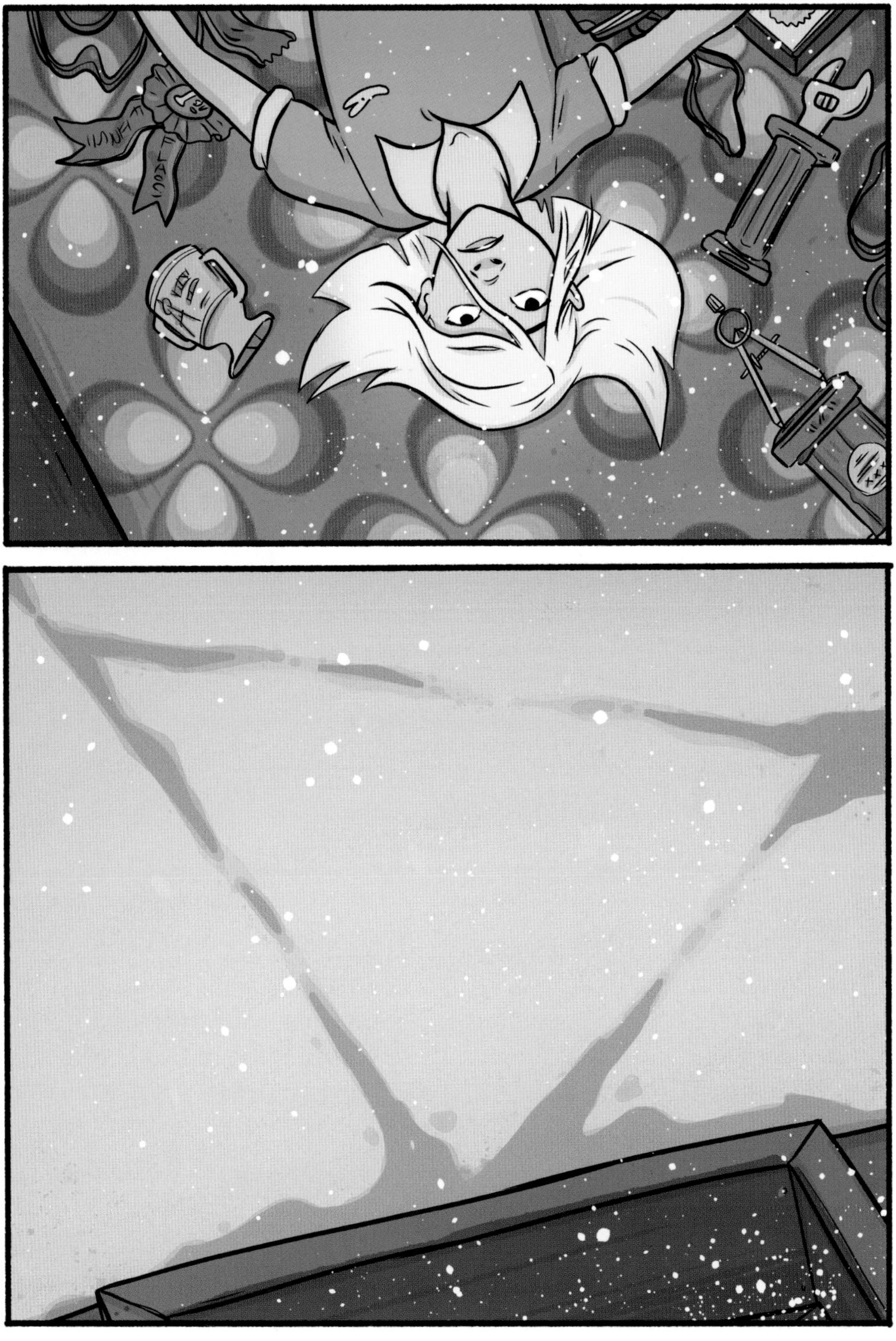

THE
UNDERLOOK HOTEL
ESTES PARK, COLORADO

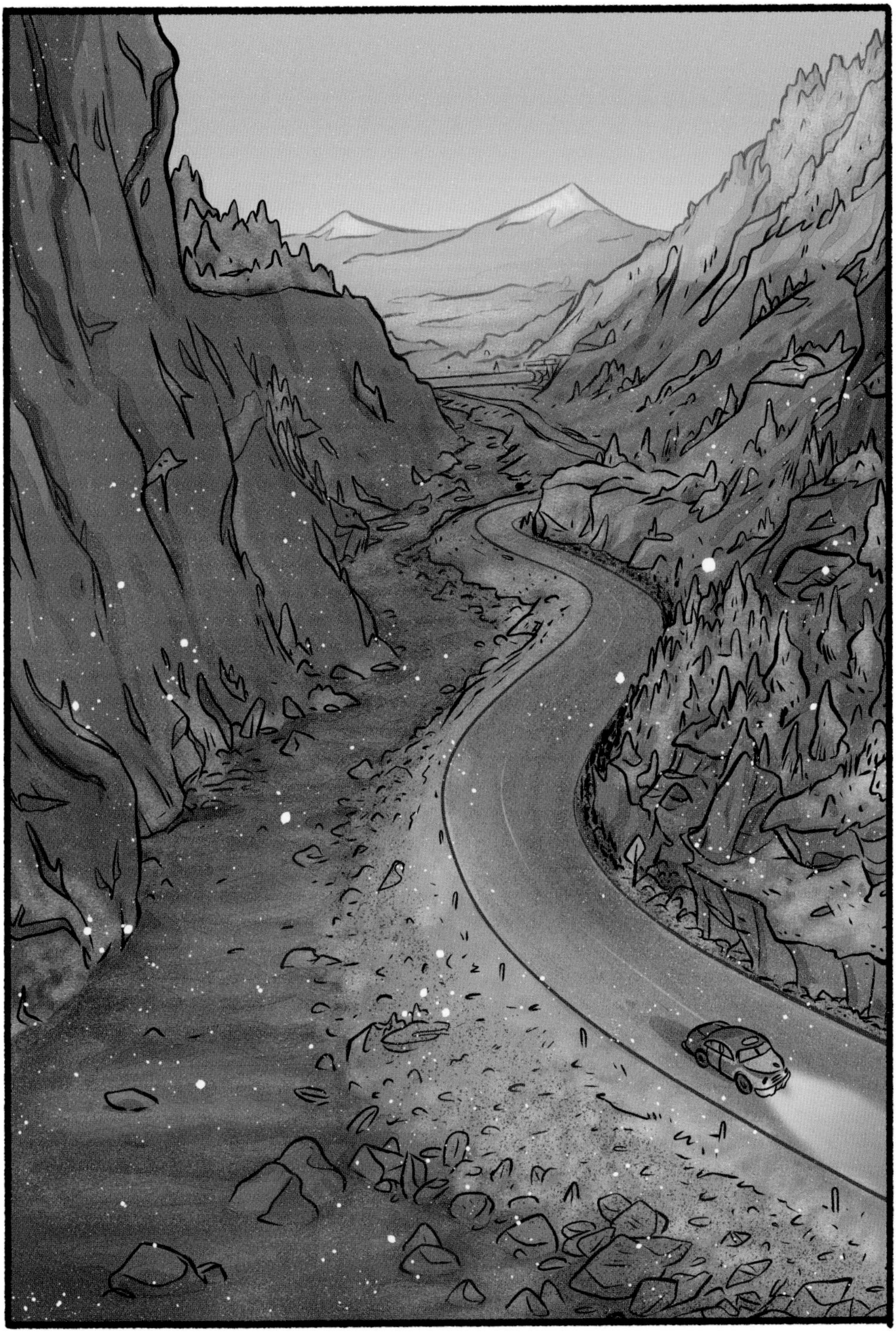

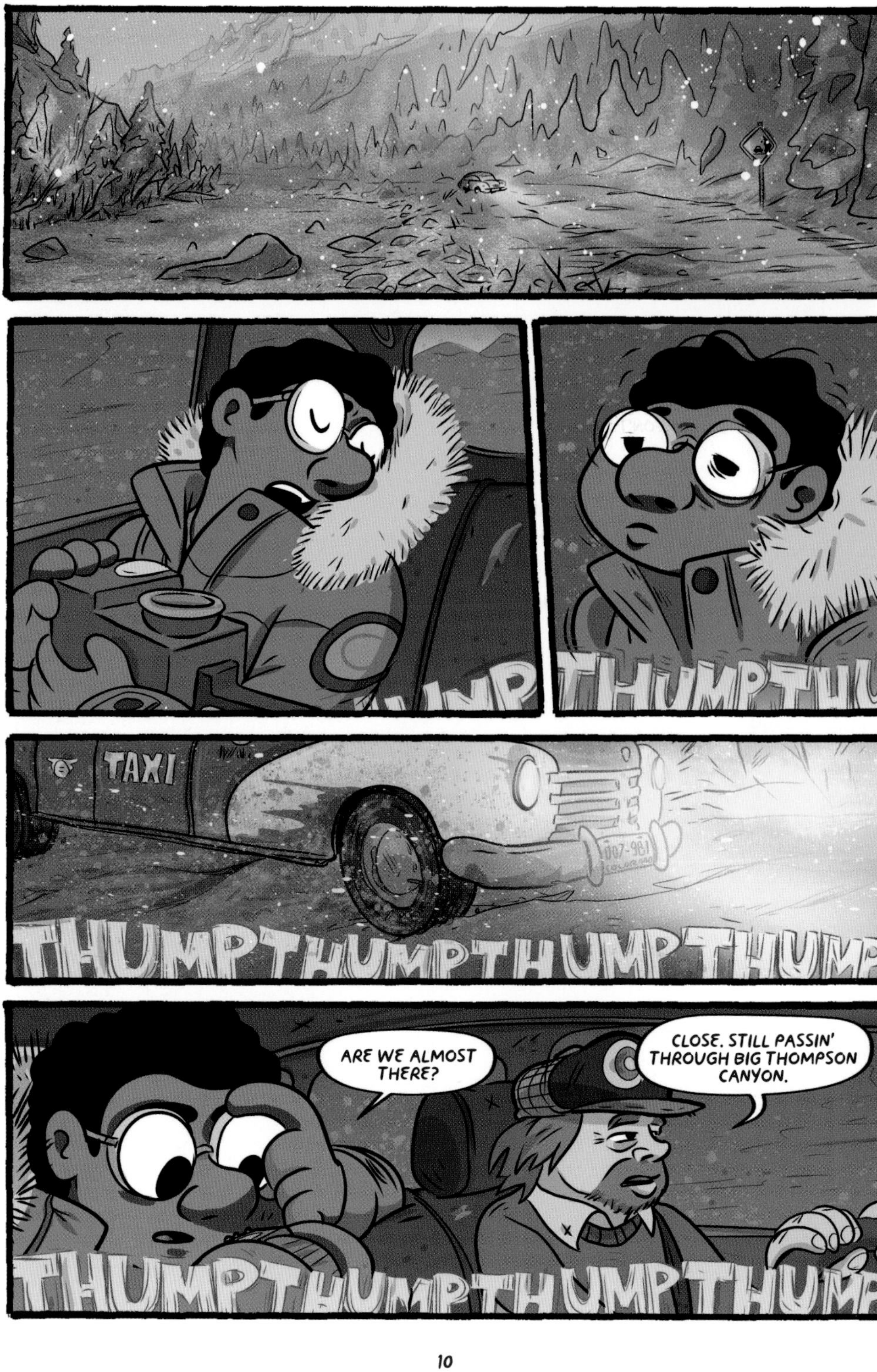

UMP
THUMPTHU
TAXI
THUMPTHUMPTHUMPTHUMP
ARE WE ALMOST THERE?
CLOSE. STILL PASSIN' THROUGH BIG THOMPSON CANYON.
THUMPTHUMPTHUMPTHUMP

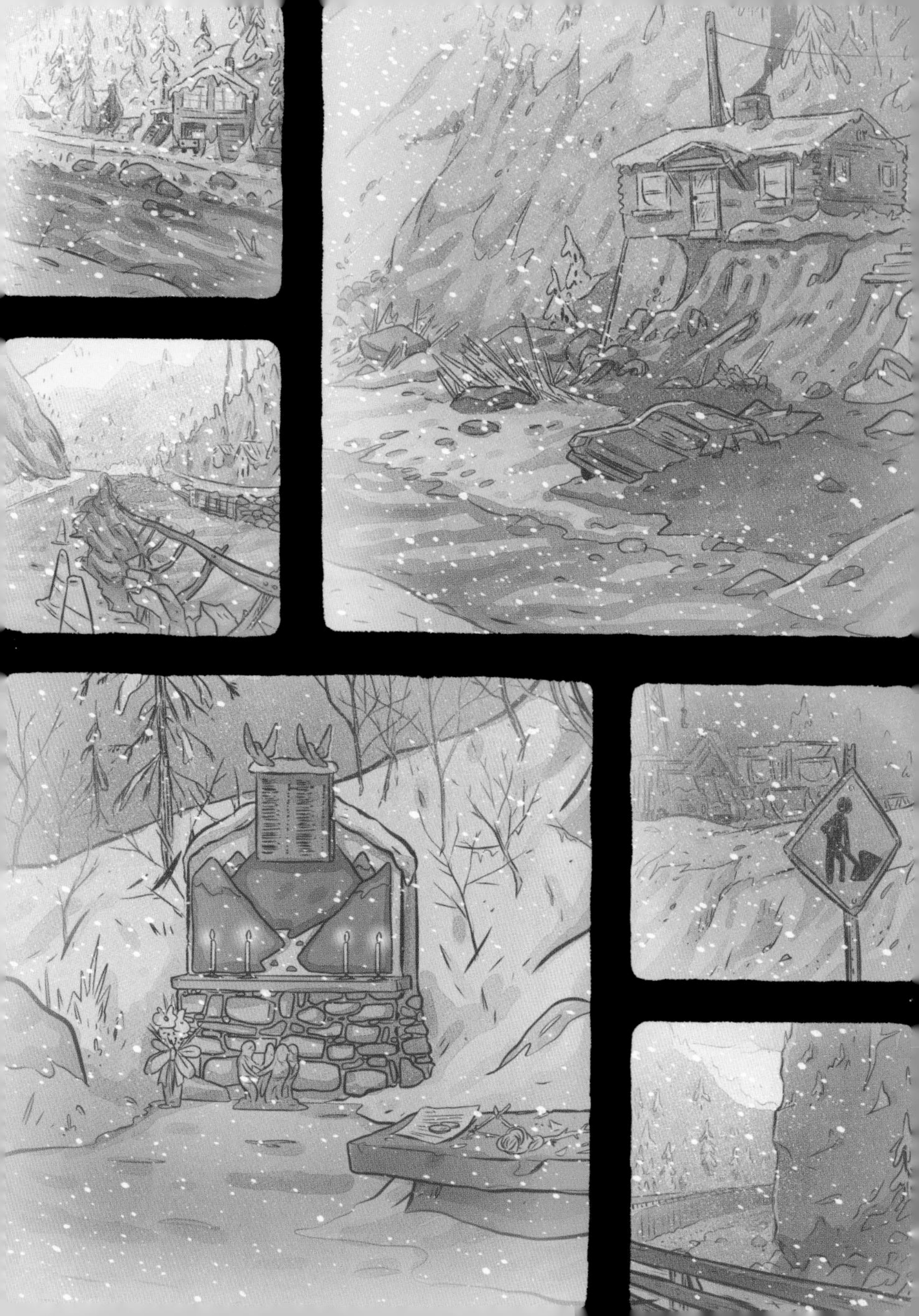

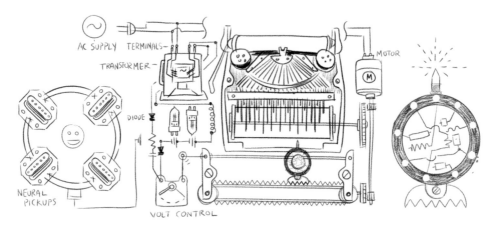

ALL RIGHT, ALL RIGHT!

DON'T BLOW A FUSE!

I TELL YA, SUZ, SOMEDAY WE'RE GONNA LIVE IN A BUILDING WIRED FOR THIS CENTURY.

HM.

LOWER THE VOLTAGE. IT'LL WORK.

WHERE'D YOU GET THE TYPEWRITER, ANYWAY?

PAWNSHOP.

IT BELONGED TO JACK AXWORTH! GUESS HE'S OFFICIALLY RETIRED NOW.

HIS TYPEWRITER WAS JUST SITTING IN A PAWNSHOP?

I GOT IT FOR A STEAL. GUY DIDN'T KNOW WHAT HE HAD—

BUT I'D RECOGNIZE JACK'S OLD AKLER ANYWHERE.

THOUGHT I'D GIVE IT A SECOND LIFE. TURN IT INTO SOMETHING FUN FOR THE TOURISTS, YOU KNOW?

15

YOU MEAN THE **UNDERLURKERS.**

WHATEVER WE CALL 'EM—

THEY PAY THE BILLS.

I'M GOING TO BE UP AT THE HOTEL ALL WEEK.

MAYBE I CAN DIG UP SOME OTHER JACK AXWORTH ARTIFACTS FOR THE SHOP.

YOU'RE GOING THERE TO TUTOR HIS SON, NOT TO SNOOP AROUND.

RELAX, MOM, I'M KIDDING.

IT BUGS YOU THAT I TOOK THE JOB, DOESN'T IT?

YOU KNOW I DON'T LIKE THAT OLD HOTEL.

AND YOU KNOW I NEED THE MONEY FOR THE COMPETITION.

I HAVE TO DEFEND MY TITLE!

SEE, THIS IS WHY I DIDN'T SAY ANYTHING.

YOU'RE ALWAYS CHASING TROPHIES!

IT'S WINTER-BREAK WEEK. WHY DON'T YOU TRY BEING A KID FOR A WHILE—

OUCH!

DARN DIODE!

OK, FINE. I WAS GOING TO DO SOME READING TONIGHT—

BUT WE CAN, I DUNNO, WATCH A MOVIE.

REALLY? CAN WE MAKE POPCORN?

WHATEVER YOU WANT, MOM.

FLIP!

OH, LET'S WATCH *GONE WITH THE WIND.* IT USED TO BE YOUR FAVORITE!

TOO LONG. I HAVE TO GET UP EARLY.

FLIP!

SUSANNA HESS— YOU DON'T KNOW HOW TO HAVE FUN.

I AM HAVING FUN.

HONK

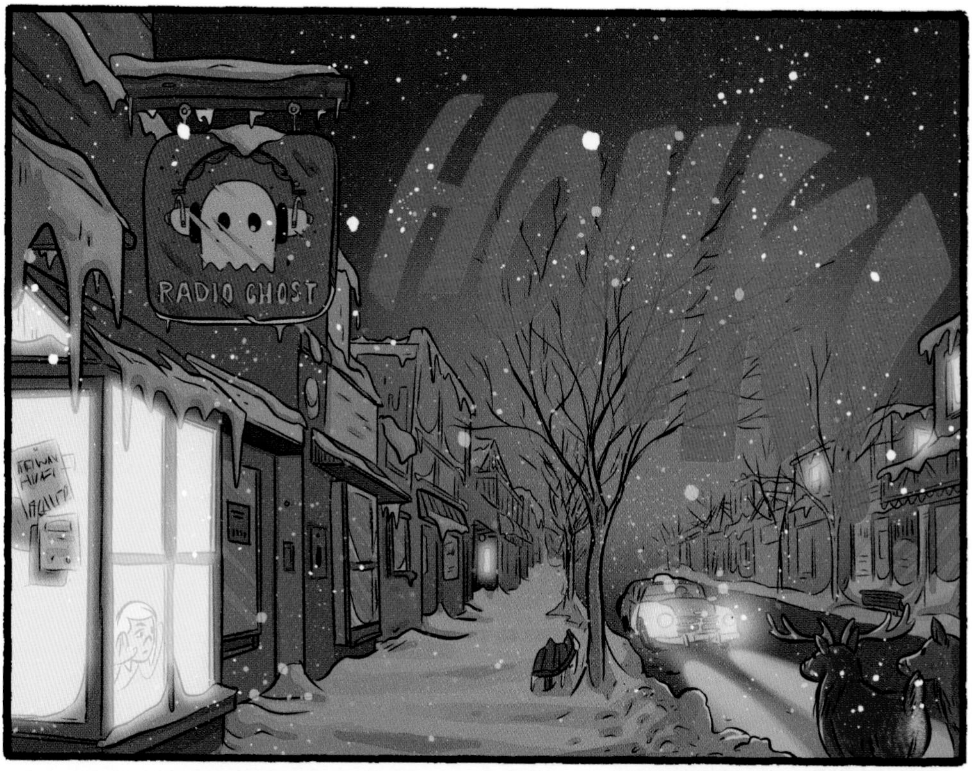
HONK
RADIO GHOST

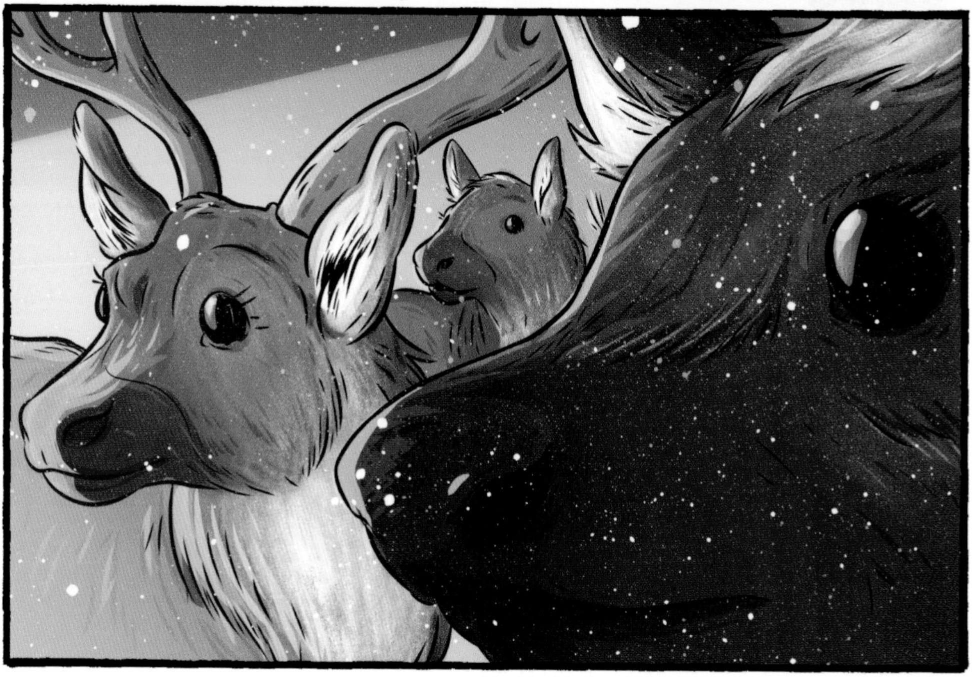

HA HA. THIS IS AWESOME!

YER ALL LUCKY IT ISN'T HUNTING SEASON.

HEY, IT'S BEEN A FUN RIDE! I GOT SOME REALLY COOL FOOTAGE.

LOOKS LIKE I CAN WALK FROM HERE.

WALK? WHERE ARE YA STAYING, ANYWAY?

THE UNDERLOOK HOTEL!

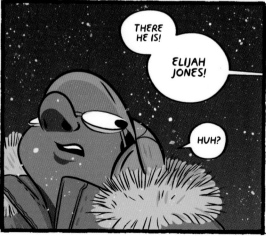

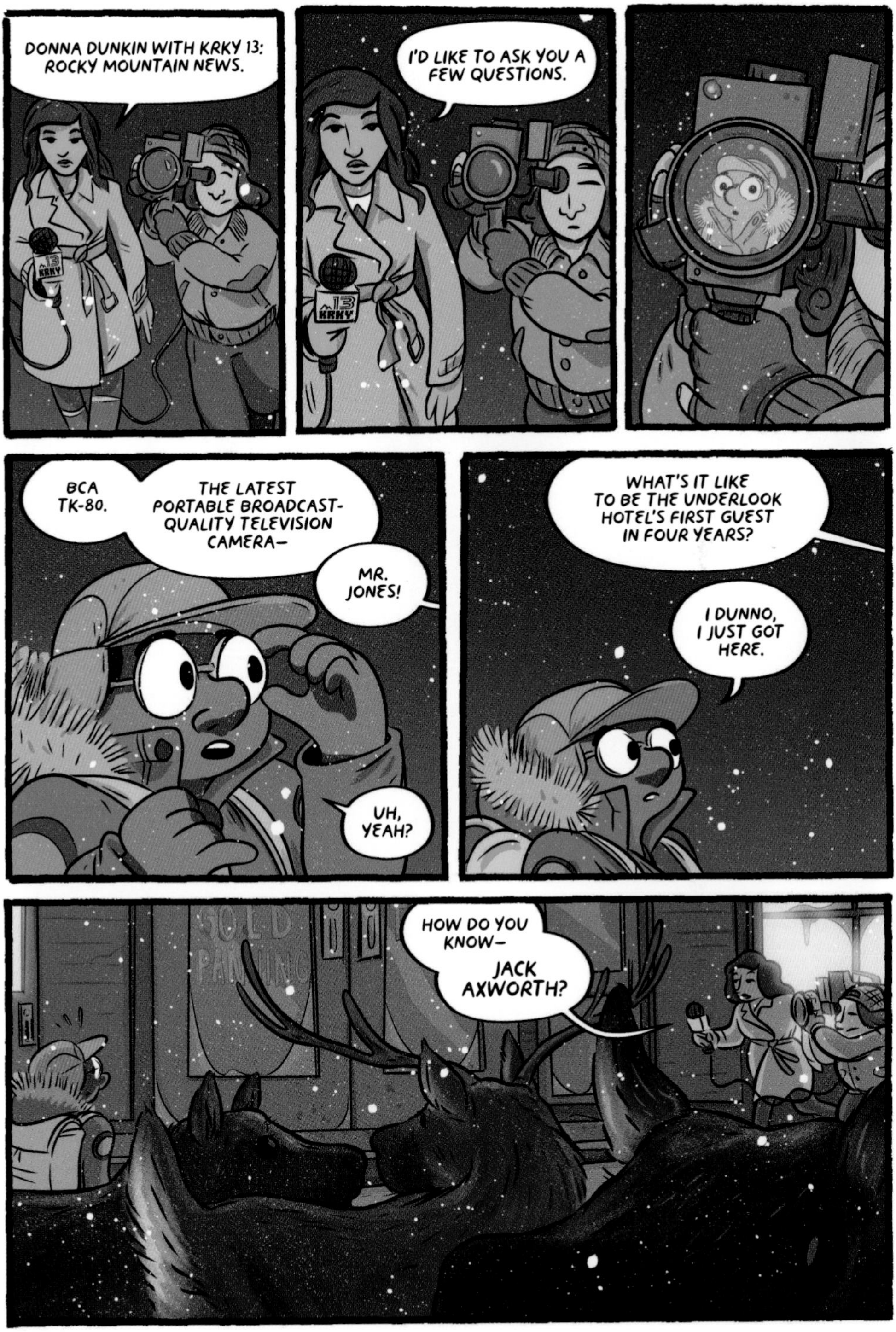
DONNA DUNKIN WITH KRKY 13: ROCKY MOUNTAIN NEWS.
I'D LIKE TO ASK YOU A FEW QUESTIONS.
BCA TK-80.
THE LATEST PORTABLE BROADCAST-QUALITY TELEVISION CAMERA–
MR. JONES!
UH, YEAH?
WHAT'S IT LIKE TO BE THE UNDERLOOK HOTEL'S FIRST GUEST IN FOUR YEARS?
I DUNNO, I JUST GOT HERE.
HOW DO YOU KNOW–
JACK AXWORTH?

IF IT'S THAT REPORTER AGAIN, TELL 'EM TO BUZZ OFF.

IT'S HER, ALL RIGHT. BUT NOW SHE'S CHASING AFTER SOME BOY.

UH-OH, HE SAW ME.

HI, HELLO?

ARE YOU OPEN?!

I'M SORRY, WE'RE CLOSED ON SUNDAYS.

GEESH, SUZY. GIVE HIM A BREAK— HE'S A KID.

WHAT? I'M JUST FOLLOWING THE RULES!

DING!

THANK YOU!

23

WITH THE IMMINENT DEPARTURE OF ESTES PARK'S RECLUSIVE AUTHOR, THE "KING OF HORROR" JACK AXWORTH, LOCALS ARE REFLECTING ON HIS LEGACY.

DONNA DUNKIN
EYEWITNESS NEWS

I SAY GOOD RIDDANCE; AXWORTH'S A CURSE ON OUR TOWN.

AND HIS BOOKS STINK, TOO.

WITH THIS NEWS, QUESTIONS ARISE ABOUT THE FATE OF THE UNDERLOOK HOTEL, OF WHICH AXWORTH HAS BEEN THE CARETAKER FOR NEARLY FOUR YEARS.

DONNA DUNKIN
EYEWITNESS NEWS

HE USED TO WORK AT THE HOTEL, YOU KNOW.

HOSPITALITY SERVICES.

I WAS A REAL CHARMER.

ONCE A DESTINATION FOR VISITORS FROM ACROSS THE WORLD, THE LUXURY RETREAT HAS STOOD QUIET FOR YEARS. THE SILENCE HAS CAST A SHADOW OVER THE STRUGGLING TOURIST TOWN.

13 KRKY

13 DONNA DUNKIN EYEWITNESS NEWS

NOT A LOT OF WORK LEFT IN A GHOST TOWN.

'LESS YOUR BUSINESS IS GHOSTS.

BUT THE UNDERLOOK MAY STILL HAVE MORE TO SAY; A YOUNG FILMMAKER NAMED ELIJAH JONES HAS JUST ARRIVED WITH A PERSONAL INVITATION FROM AXWORTH HIMSELF.

13 KRKY

13 DONNA DUNKIN EYEWITNESS NEWS

HE TALKED ABOUT MOVIES A LOT.

GOOD TIPPER, THOUGH.

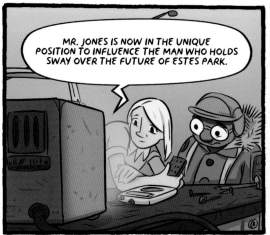

MR. JONES IS NOW IN THE UNIQUE POSITION TO INFLUENCE THE MAN WHO HOLDS SWAY OVER THE FUTURE OF ESTES PARK.

I'M DONNA DUNKIN. STAY TUNED TO KRKY 13 FOR MORE ON THIS STORY.

SEE? FAMOUS.

UHHHH.

THE FUTURE OF THE PARK HANGS IN THE BALANCE? WHAT NONSENSE!

ELIJAH, YOU NEED TO FORGET ALL OF THAT.

HERE, I'D LIKE YOU TO HOLD THIS CRYSTAL.

WHAT IS IT?

GALENA.

THEY USED TO MINE IT RIGHT HERE IN THE PARK. IT WILL TUNE YOUR FREQUENCY TO OUR QUIET LITTLE TOWN.

MAGICAL!

IT'S NOT MAGIC; IT'S A CONDUCTIVE MINERAL. IT'S PRETTY COMMON IN OLD COMMUNICATION SYSTEMS.

AND TOURISTS BUY THIS STUFF?

WE CALL 'EM **UNDERLURKERS.**

MOST COLORADO TOURIST TOWNS OFFER FISHING, SKIING, HUNTING—BUT NOT ESTES PARK.

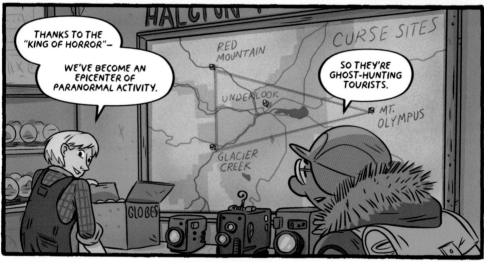

THANKS TO THE "KING OF HORROR"—

WE'VE BECOME AN EPICENTER OF PARANORMAL ACTIVITY.

SO THEY'RE GHOST-HUNTING TOURISTS.

CURSE SITES

RED MOUNTAIN

UNDERLOOK

MT. OLYMPUS

GLACIER CREEK

GLOBES

PARTLY. THERE ARE TWO THINGS THAT LET YOU KNOW YOU'RE TALKING WITH AN UNDERLURKER.

FIRST, THEY'VE GOT AN OBSESSION WITH CUSTOMIZED RECORDING EQUIPMENT.

OH, YOU NOTICED MY ZODAK PRO-MATIC! THAT'S A DAS ZOOM-OBJEKTIV LENS.

IT'S A LIMITED EDITION FROM GERMANY.

SECOND— THEY'RE OBSESSED WITH JACK AXWORTH'S BOOKS.

ACTUALLY, THAT'S A FIRST EDITION . . .

HEY! I'M NOT AN UNDERLURKER!

LEAVE HIM ALONE, SUZY.

NO JUDGMENT! YOUR KIND KEEP US IN BUSINESS.

OK! I ADMIT HE'S MY FAVORITE WRITER—

BUT I'M NOT OBSESSED.

YOU KNOW, JACK AXWORTH HAS BEEN A TOTAL RECLUSE FOR YEARS.

STILL, IT DOESN'T STOP 'EM FROM SNEAKING UP THERE TO GET A CLOSER LOOK . . .

AH!

IF I WAS ONE OF YOUR CREEPY UNDERLURKERS, WOULD MR. AXWORTH HAVE INVITED ME HERE? I THINK NOT.

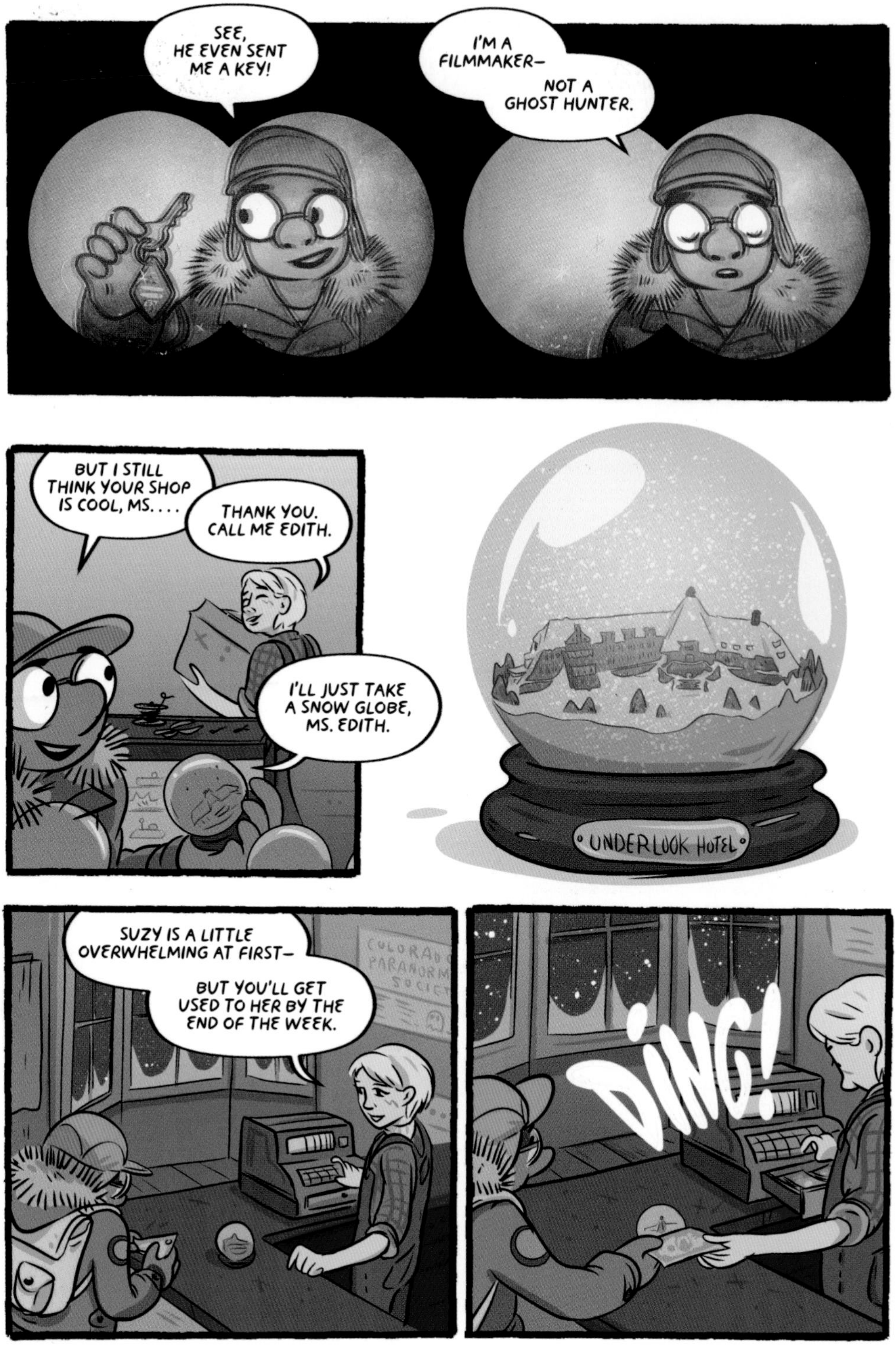
SEE, HE EVEN SENT ME A KEY!
I'M A FILMMAKER—
NOT A GHOST HUNTER.
BUT I STILL THINK YOUR SHOP IS COOL, MS. . . .
THANK YOU. CALL ME EDITH.
I'LL JUST TAKE A SNOW GLOBE, MS. EDITH.
UNDERLOOK HOTEL
SUZY IS A LITTLE OVERWHELMING AT FIRST—
BUT YOU'LL GET USED TO HER BY THE END OF THE WEEK.
DING!

END OF THE WEEK?

SUZY IS STAYING AT THE UNDERLOOK, TOO.

YOU ARE?

I'M TUTORING JACK'S SON, DANNY.

FREQUENCY ENHANCING QUANTUM CRYSTALS

WHOLESALE IN BULK!!

BAGS

DANNY AXWORTH?

THAT'S THE DANNY.

ANCING

OH, WOW.

SO I'LL HAVE A FRIEND?!

WE JUST MET FIVE MINUTES AGO.

NCING

I KNOW!

I MAKE FRIENDS REALLY FAST!

FREQUENCY ENHANCING QUANTUM CRYSTALS

GALENA RESTOCK

HEY, SUZY, CAN I INTERVIEW YOU? I WANT TO GET SOME LOCAL FLAVOR FOR MY DOC!

NO WAY. DOCUMENTARIES ALWAYS MAKE LOCALS SEEM TOTALLY WEIRD—

I'LL DO IT!

MOM!

IT'LL BE GOOD FOR BUSINESS!

OH NO!

WHAT?

MY FILM STOCK IS GONE!

IT MUST HAVE FALLEN OUT IN THE CAB!

DON'T PANIC.

WE CARRY FILM.

MISC FILM

SOLDER WIRE

AAA+YPICAL BATTERIES

EXTRA PLANCHETTES

TAROT

SPEAKER WIRE

CINE-BRITE, ZOE-SCOPE, BANAVISION . . .

NO, NO, NO.

MY CAMERA ONLY SHOOTS ON ZODAK COLOR FILM!

HOW ABOUT A CUSTOM AURA-MATIC?

SNAP!

IT'S FUN!

HEH.

I'M RUINED.

FLOP.

WHAT'S HIS AURA COLOR?

MAGENTA.

YIKES. THIS IS A DESPERATE SITUATION.

I'M GOING TO HAVE TO GET OUT THE PHANTA-SCOPE.

CLEARANCE

PHANTA...

...SCOPE?

IT'S AN OLD EXPERIMENT OF MINE. ONLY THING IN THE SHOP THAT SHOOTS ON COLOR MOTION-PICTURE FILM.

IT WAS TOO STRANGE FOR MOST UNDERLURKERS.

BUT THE PARK HAS NO NORMAL CAMERA SHOP, SO YOU DON'T REALLY HAVE A CHOICE.

FOUND IT AT A GARAGE SALE YEARS AGO. IT WAS A WORTHLESS ANTIQUE, SO I ADDED SOME NEW FEATURES.

HM. INTERESTING.

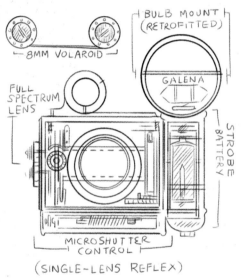

8MM VOLAROID

BULB MOUNT (RETROFITTED)

GALENA

FULL SPECTRUM LENS

STROBE BATTERY

MICROSHUTTER CONTROL

(SINGLE-LENS REFLEX)

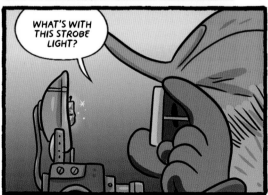

WHAT'S WITH THIS STROBE LIGHT?

AH, YOU MEAN MY CUSTOM QUANTUM REALM CRYSTAL FILTER.

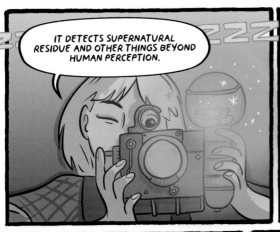

IT DETECTS SUPERNATURAL RESIDUE AND OTHER THINGS BEYOND HUMAN PERCEPTION.

THAT'S KINDA SPOOKY.

THAT'S JUST GALENA.

IT'S OUR SECRET INGREDIENT.

THIS CAMERA IS TOTALLY IMPRACTICAL. BUT I'LL TAKE IT.

OF COURSE YOU WILL, UNDERLURKER.

OK, ONE MORE PHOTO.

OH, COME ON.

SNAP!

HOW'S OUR AURA?

MOM, YOU DON'T HAVE TO WORRY ABOUT OUR AURA.

IT'S NOT JUST THAT.

THAT DARN HOTEL HAS ITS WAY OF DECEIVING PEOPLE—AND NOT JUST UNDERLURKERS. I'VE SEEN IT.

GEESH, MOM, YOU'RE SCARING ELIJAH!

NO SHE'S NOT!

I JUST NEED TO KNOW YOU'RE SAFE. CRIPES, EVEN THE UNDERLOOK PHONES HAVE BEEN DOWN FOR YEARS.

FINE! THEN WE'LL BRING A WALKIE.

AND WE'LL CALL IF WE NEED ANYTHING, OK?

HMPH.

I JUST WANT YOU TWO TO WATCH OUT FOR EACH OTHER THIS WEEK, OK?

YOU GOT IT, MS. EDITH.

YOU GOT IT, MOM.

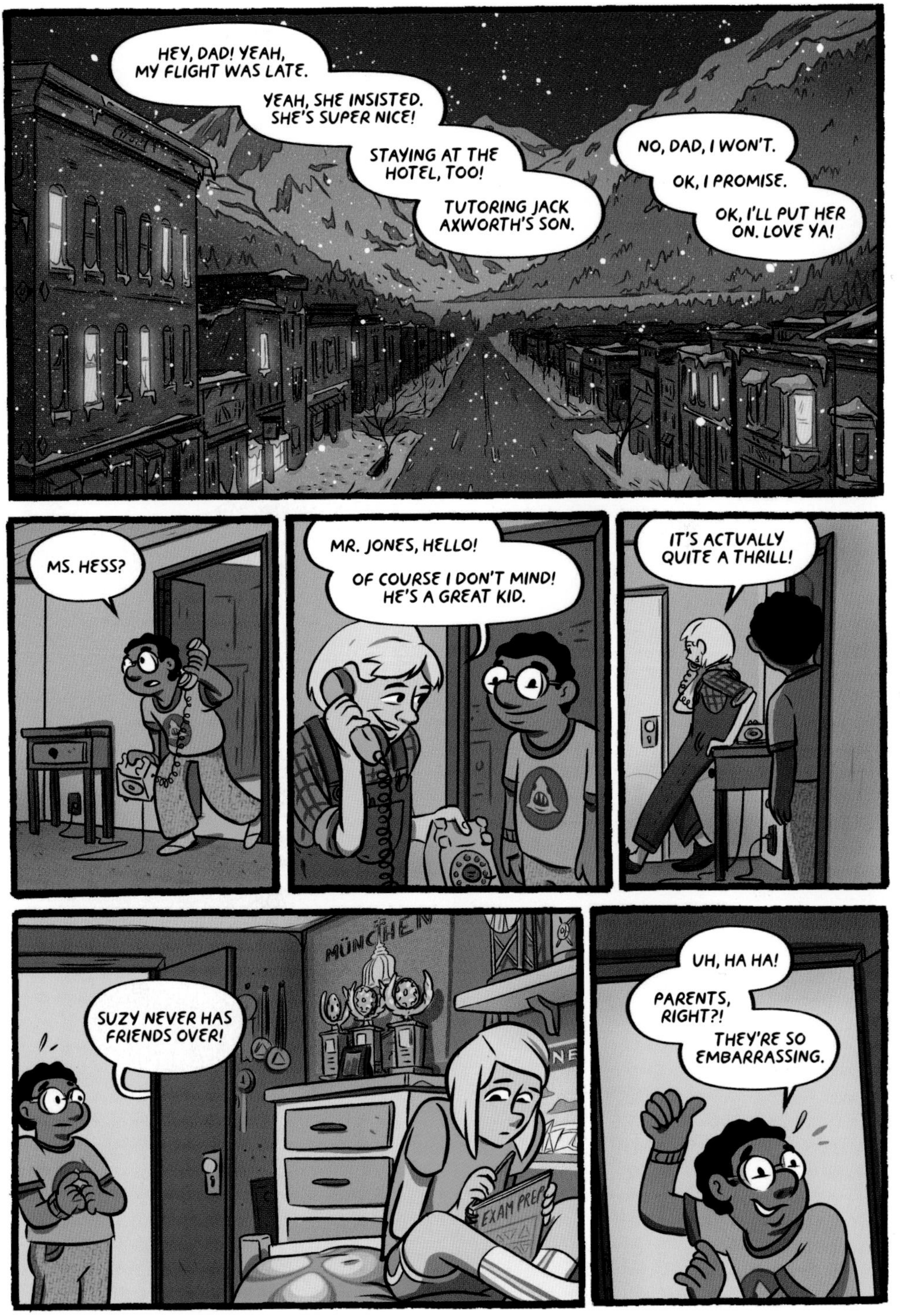
HEY, DAD! YEAH, MY FLIGHT WAS LATE.
YEAH, SHE INSISTED. SHE'S SUPER NICE!
STAYING AT THE HOTEL, TOO!
TUTORING JACK AXWORTH'S SON.
NO, DAD, I WON'T.
OK, I PROMISE.
OK, I'LL PUT HER ON. LOVE YA!
MS. HESS?
MR. JONES, HELLO!
OF COURSE I DON'T MIND! HE'S A GREAT KID.
IT'S ACTUALLY QUITE A THRILL!
MÜNCHEN
SUZY NEVER HAS FRIENDS OVER!
EXAM PREP
UH, HA HA!
PARENTS, RIGHT?!
THEY'RE SO EMBARRASSING.

SOOOO . . . UM, WHAT ARE THESE GIANT TROPHIES FOR?

CIVIL ENGINEERING.

IT'S PRETTY COMPETITIVE.

I'M AWAY AT EVENTS ALMOST EVERY WEEKEND, SO I DON'T REALLY HAVE TIME FOR FRIENDS.

YEAH, I TRAVEL A LOT, TOO.

WHO'S THIS GUY? HE LOOKS IMPORTANT.

THAT'S THE GOVERNOR OF COLORADO.

MY TEAM HAD JUST WON THE STATE CHAMPIONSHIP FOR THE THIRD CONSECUTIVE YEAR.

THAT'S AMAZING, SUZY.

WHERE ARE THE REST OF YOUR TEAMMATES?

OH . . .

IT'S JUST ME.

38

TECHNICALLY, I'M STILL A TEAM.

YOU KNOW, I'M ON EVERY SPORTS TEAM AT BOSTON INTERNATIONAL ACADEMY.

BUT I'M NOT IN ANY OF THE PICTURES. KNOW WHY?

BECAUSE I'M THE ATHLETIC DEPARTMENT'S VIDEOGRAPHER!

HA HA HA!

WHAT I WOULDN'T GIVE TO LIVE IN A BIG EAST-COAST CITY.

I COULD USE SOME REAL COMPETITION.

I GET THAT. BIG CITIES ARE COOL,

BUT IT'S EASY TO GET LOST IN THE CROWD.

MUST BE NICE TO BE, LIKE—

THE ONE, YOU KNOW?

TO HAVE EVERYONE REALLY JUST SEE WHO YOU ARE.

HEY, ELIJAH.

SORRY I HASSLED YOU. I'M JUST SO SICK OF HEARING ABOUT JACK AXWORTH. I CAN'T WAIT TILL HE'S GONE.

IF YOU DON'T LIKE HIM, WHY ARE YOU SPENDING A WEEK AT HIS HOTEL?

FOR THE MONEY. AND I GUESS I'M KINDA CURIOUS WHAT THE FUSS IS ABOUT.

ALL HE EVER DID WAS WRITE A FEW DUMB GHOST STORIES.

SPEAKING OF GHOST STORIES . . .

WHO'S THE GIRL IN THE CAVE?

GIRL IN THE CAVE BY SUZY H.

GIRL IN THE—

OH GOD.

GIVE ME THAT!

"BY SUZY H, AGE SEVEN."

THIS. IS. ADORABLE.

LOOK! YOU EVEN GOT A GOLD STAR!

WHAT CAN I SAY? I'VE ALWAYS BEEN A WINNER.

WOW. I HAVEN'T THOUGHT ABOUT THIS STORY IN FOREVER.

IT LOOKS SCARY.

WELL, THE GRAMMAR IS TERRIFYING.

SO, WHAT'S IT ABOUT?

A GIRL DISCOVERS A MAGICAL CAVE... AND INSIDE, SHE'S CHALLENGED TO A GAME OF RIDDLES

WELL, THIS GIRL DISCOVERS A MAGICAL CAVE...

...AND INSIDE, SHE'S CHALLENGED TO A GAME OF RIDDLES BY AN EVIL SPIRIT.

BY AN EVIL SPIRIT.

41

USING HER WITS, THE GIRL BEATS THE SPIRIT AND WINS ITS TREASURE.

WHEN SHE RETURNS TO THE KINGDOM, THE PEOPLE MAKE HER THEIR QUEEN.

THE GIRL BEATS THE SPIRIT, WINS A TREASURE, TAKES IT BACK TO HER KINGDOM, AND THEY MAKE HER THE QUEEN.

HAPPILY EVER AFTER AND ALL THAT NONSENSE.

CAN I READ IT?

I JUST GAVE AWAY THE ENDING.

COME ON!

HAVE AT IT, THEN.

YES!

YOU KNOW...

JACK AXWORTH FAMOUSLY HATES JOURNALISTS AND HORROR FANS.

SO WHY INVITE ME, RIGHT?

I HONESTLY HAVE NO IDEA.

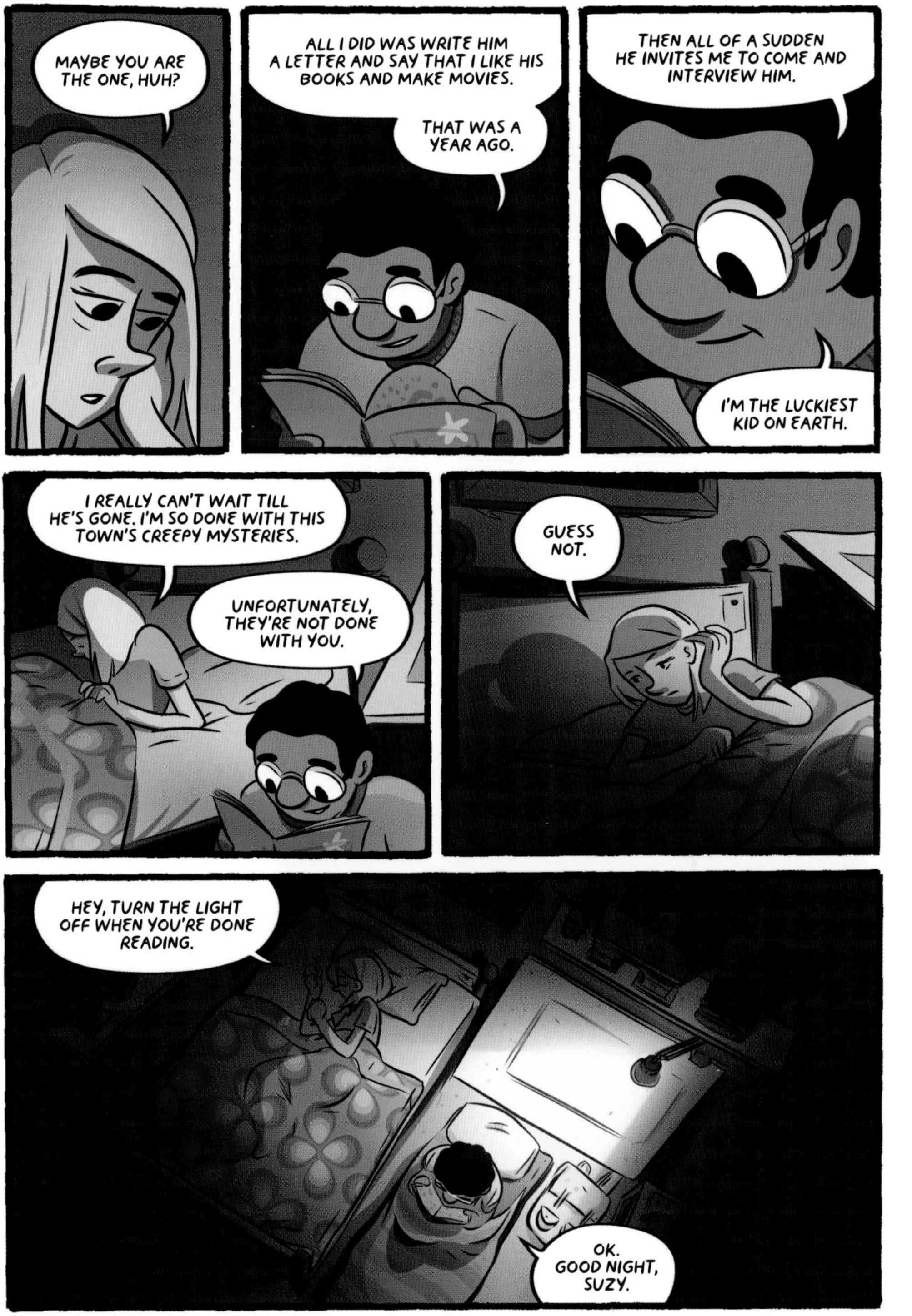
MAYBE YOU ARE THE ONE, HUH?
ALL I DID WAS WRITE HIM A LETTER AND SAY THAT I LIKE HIS BOOKS AND MAKE MOVIES.
THAT WAS A YEAR AGO.
THEN ALL OF A SUDDEN HE INVITES ME TO COME AND INTERVIEW HIM.
I'M THE LUCKIEST KID ON EARTH.
I REALLY CAN'T WAIT TILL HE'S GONE. I'M SO DONE WITH THIS TOWN'S CREEPY MYSTERIES.
UNFORTUNATELY, THEY'RE NOT DONE WITH YOU.
GUESS NOT.
HEY, TURN THE LIGHT OFF WHEN YOU'RE DONE READING.
OK. GOOD NIGHT, SUZY.

THE
UNDERLOOK HOTEL

ESTES PARK, COLORADO

MONDAY-M
Y-MONDAY
AY-MONDA
DAY-MOND
NDAY-MON
DNDAY-MO
MONDAY-M
Y-MONDAY
AY-MONDA

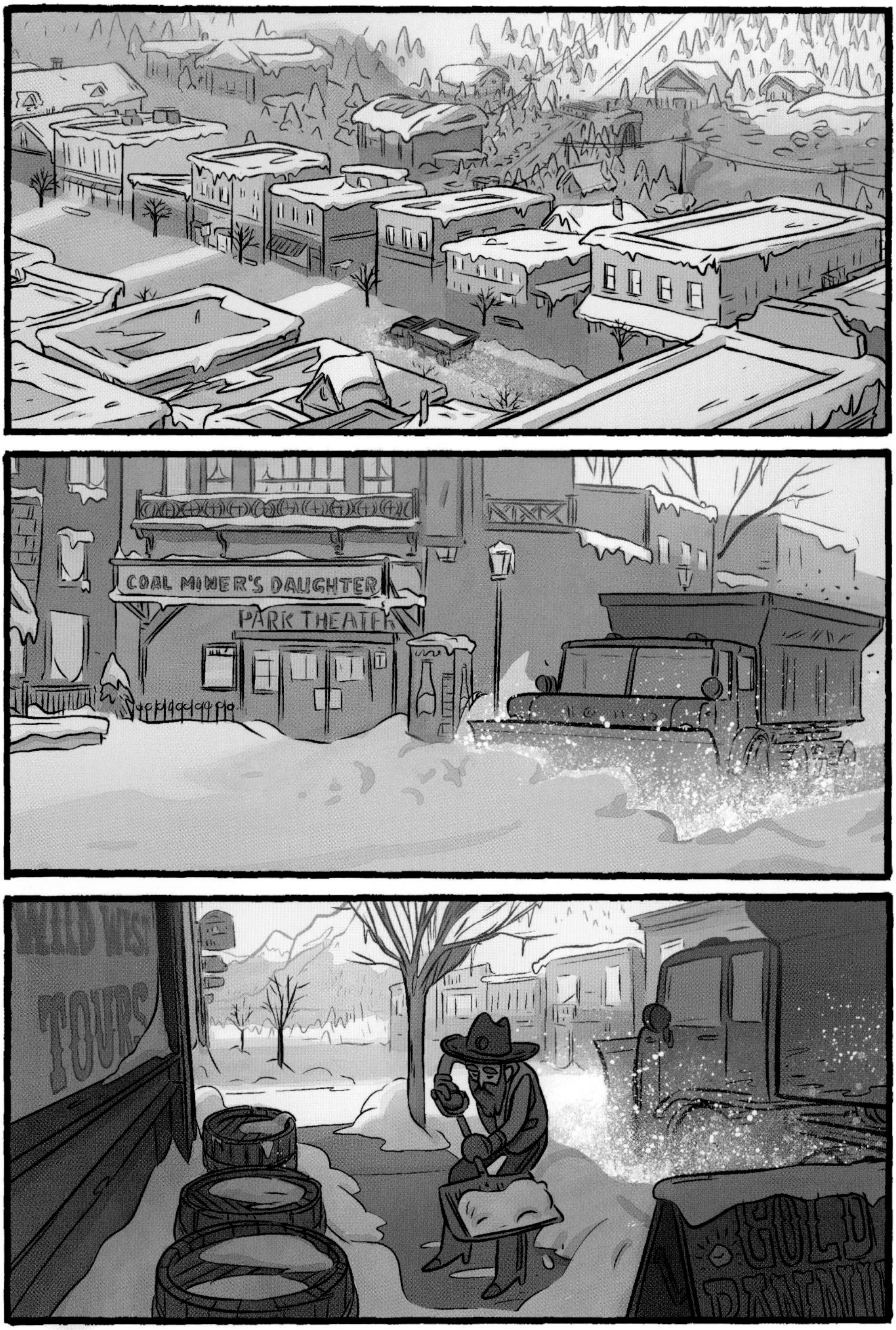
COAL MINER'S DAUGHTER
PARK THEATER
TOURS

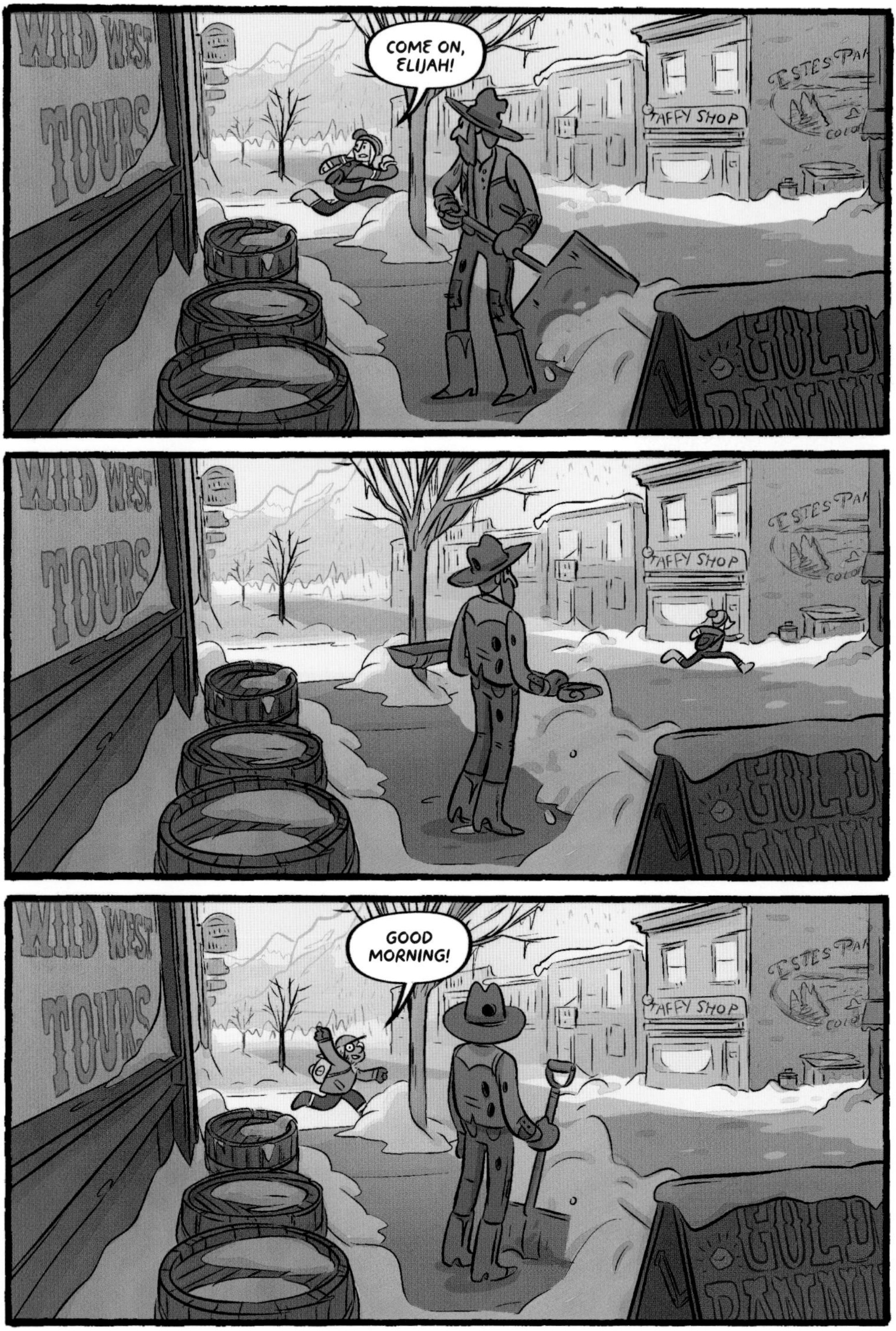
WILD WEST TOURS
TAFFY SHOP
COME ON, ELIJAH!
GOOD MORNING!

HEY, IT'S THE JONES KID!

NED—

GET ME MY MICROPHONE.

UH-OH, DUNKIN SPOTTED ME!

WE HAVE TO GET TO THE FUNICULAR!

IT'S THE ONLY SAFE WAY UP THE MOUNTAIN!

48

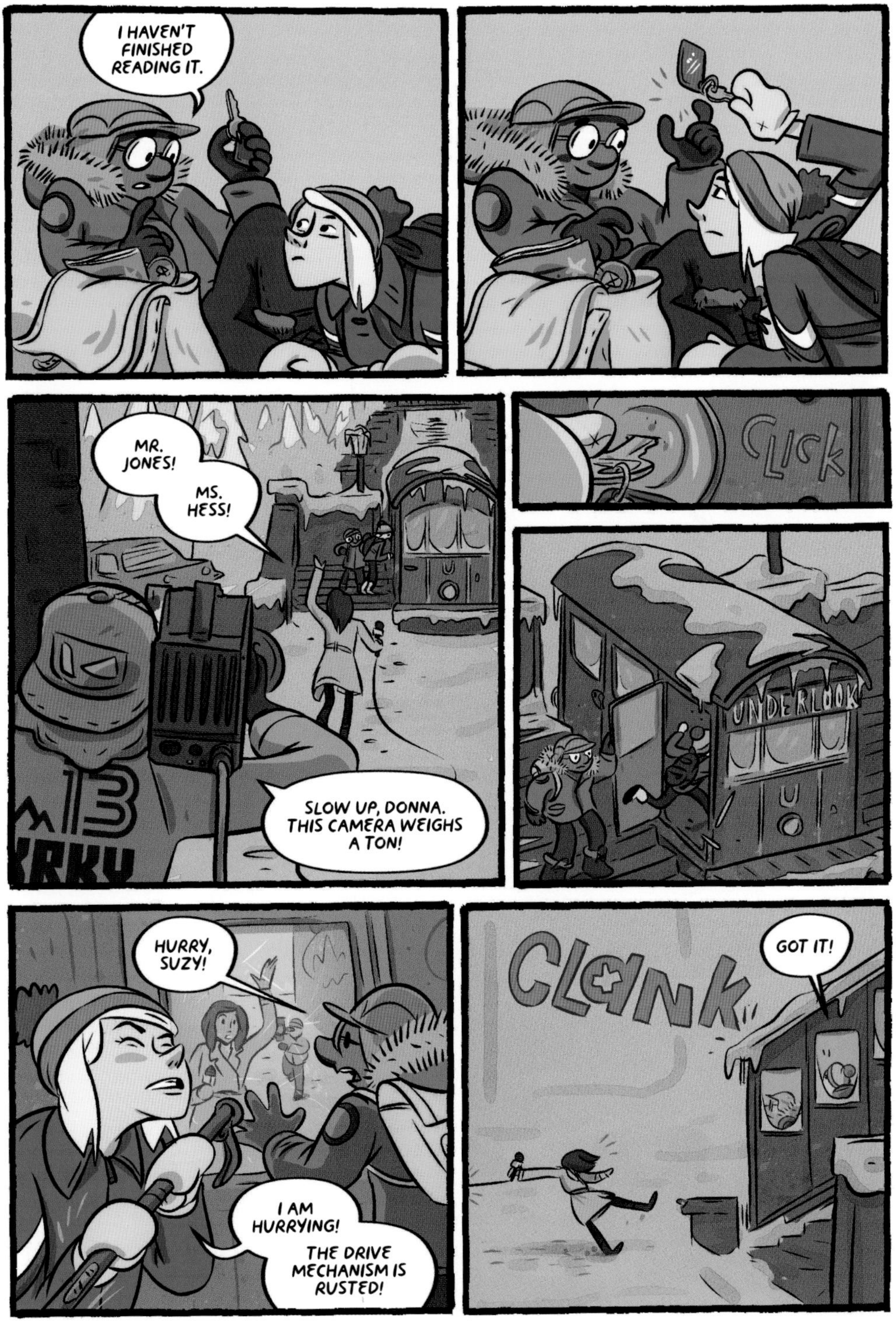
I HAVEN'T FINISHED READING IT.
MR. JONES!
MS. HESS!
SLOW UP, DONNA. THIS CAMERA WEIGHS A TON!
13
KRKU
CLICK
UNDERLOOK
U
HURRY, SUZY!
I AM HURRYING!
THE DRIVE MECHANISM IS RUSTED!
CLANK
GOT IT!

DON'T WORRY, THESE OLD STEEL CARS ARE MADE TO LAST 200 YEARS.

HEY, YOU'RE THE ENGINEER.

BOY, IS SHE DESPERATE FOR A STORY.

YEAH, YOU'RE THE BIGGEST THING TO HAPPEN TO THE PARK SINCE THE FLOOD.

YEAH, MY SCHOOL FLOODED ONCE. SOME KIDS PUT A CHERRY BOMB DOWN THE—

NO, I MEAN A *REAL* FLOOD.

LIKE A YEAR'S WORTH OF RAIN FALLING IN AN HOUR AND THEN FUNNELING THROUGH BIG THOMPSON CANYON, DESTROYING EVERYTHING IN ITS PATH.

OH. THAT KIND OF FLOOD.

THE DAY STARTED AS COLORADO'S CENTENNIAL ANNIVERSARY . . .

. . . AND ENDED UP BEING THE WORST NATURAL DISASTER IN THE STATE'S HISTORY.

THAT WAS FIVE YEARS AGO THIS JULY.

WE REBUILT, BUT THE TOURISTS NEVER CAME BACK.

WELL, THEY'RE MISSING A GREAT VIEW.

THERE'S ONLY ONE THING PEOPLE COME OUT HERE TO SEE.

51

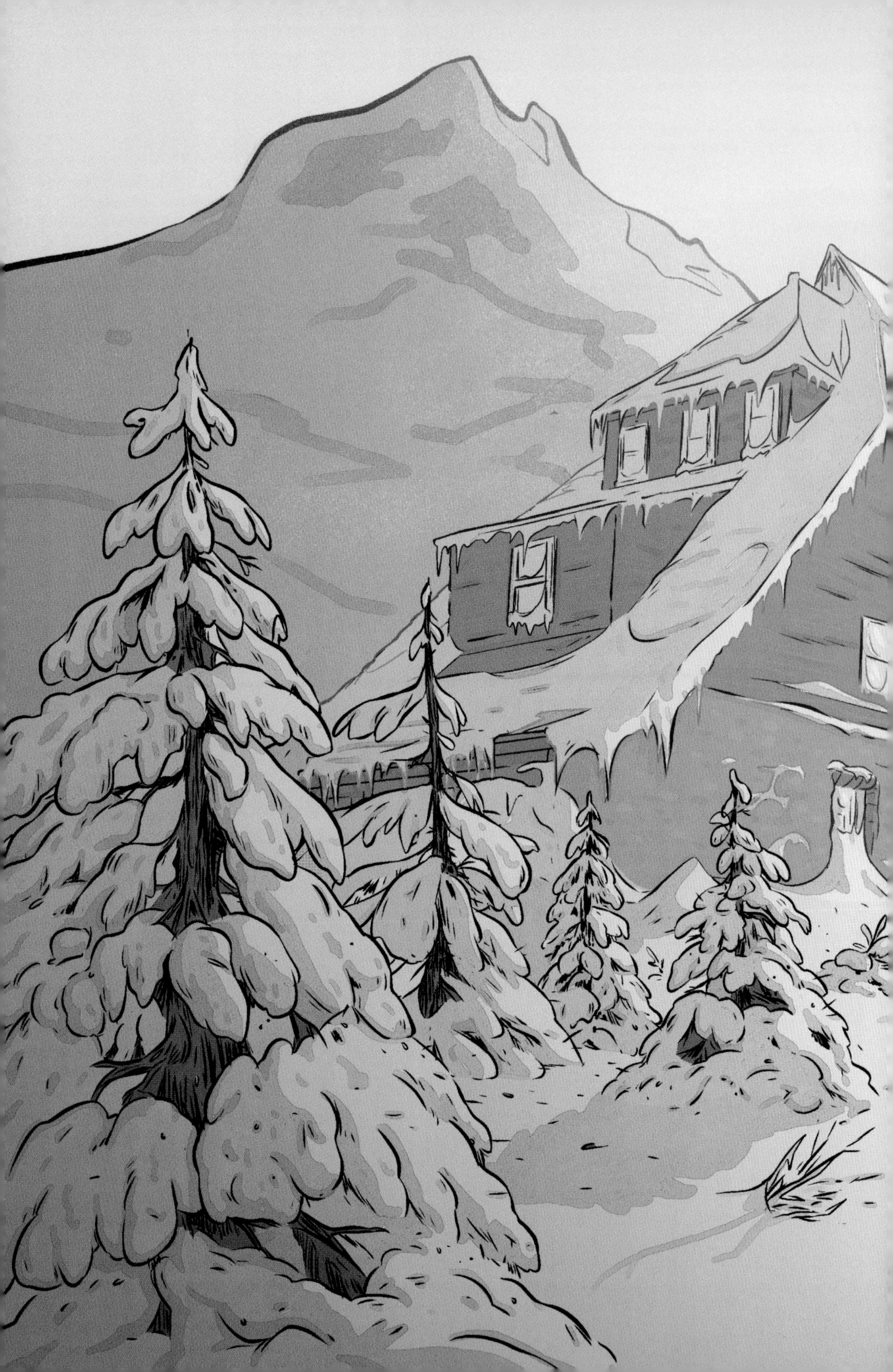

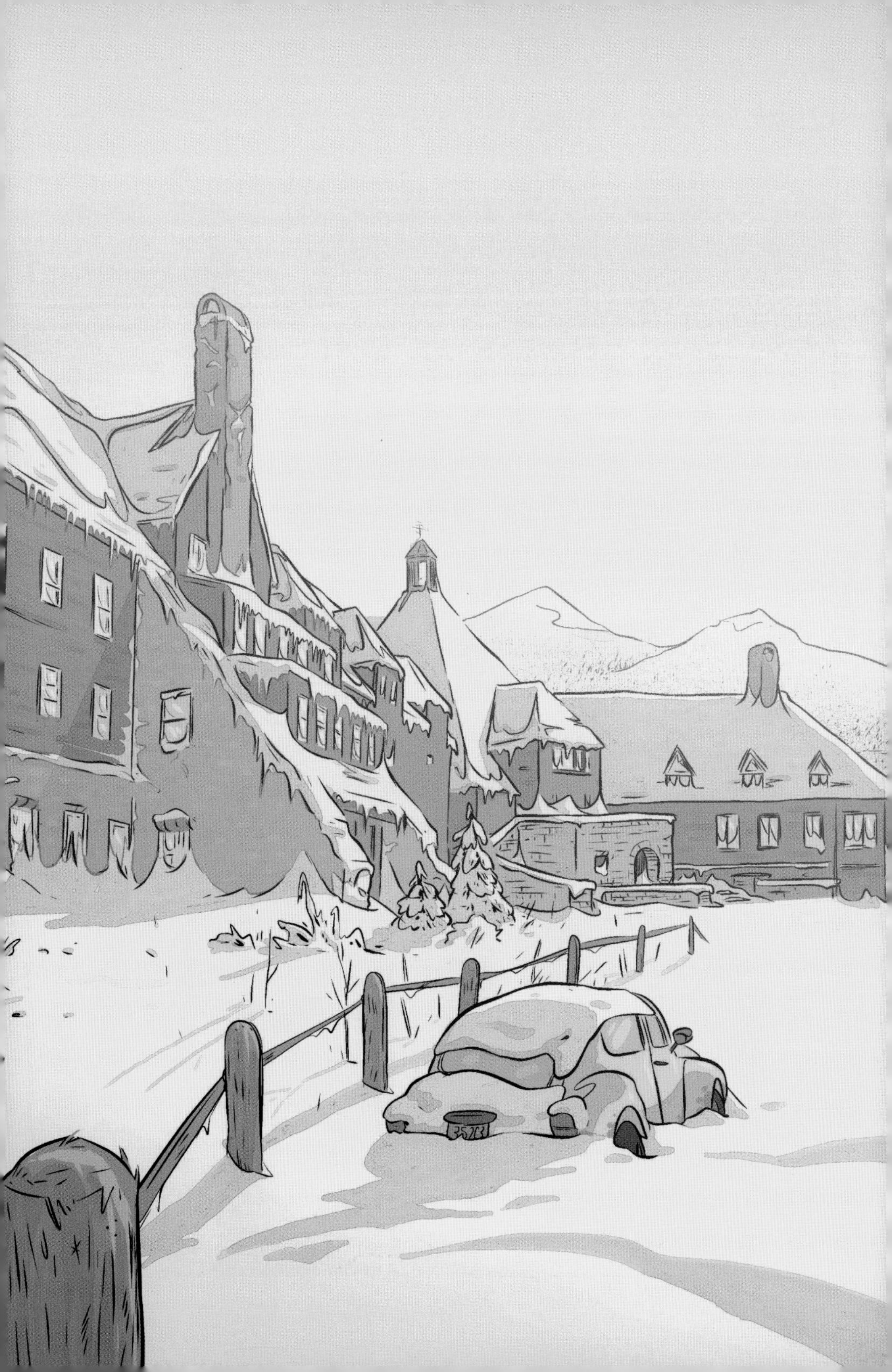

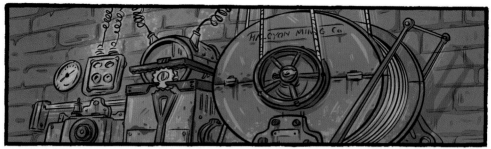

THERE YOU ARE, ELIJAH JONES!

I WAS OUT ALL NIGHT LOOKING FOR YOU!

OH! YOU'RE RENA, RIGHT? SORRY, MY FLIGHT WAS LATE, SO I STAYED IN TOWN.

I THOUGHT YOU RAN INTO ONE OF THE MOUNTAIN GOATS I'VE SEEN WANDERING THE PROPERTY.

AW! I'D LOVE TO FILM A CUTE MOUNTAIN GOAT.

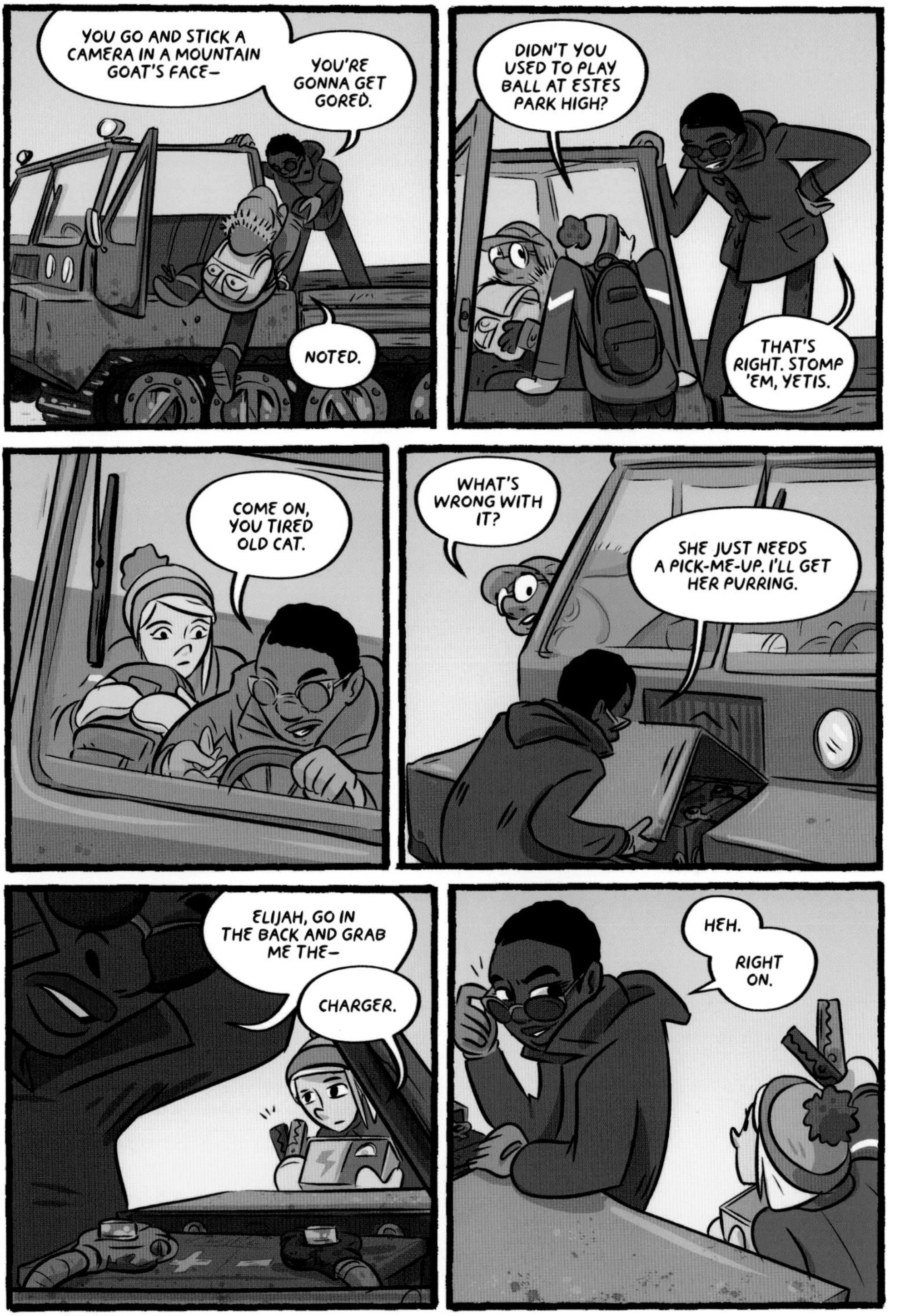
YOU GO AND STICK A CAMERA IN A MOUNTAIN GOAT'S FACE—
YOU'RE GONNA GET GORED.
NOTED.
DIDN'T YOU USED TO PLAY BALL AT ESTES PARK HIGH?
THAT'S RIGHT. STOMP 'EM, YETIS.
COME ON, YOU TIRED OLD CAT.
WHAT'S WRONG WITH IT?
SHE JUST NEEDS A PICK-ME-UP. I'LL GET HER PURRING.
ELIJAH, GO IN THE BACK AND GRAB ME THE—
CHARGER.
HEH.
RIGHT ON.

SORRY TO MAKE YOU WAIT, RENA.

EH, I HAD TO MAKE THE ROUNDS ANYWAY.

IT'S NOT JUST WILDLIFE THAT LIKES TO TRESPASS ON THE PROPERTY.

YOU MEAN **UNDERLURKERS!**

HEH, EXACTLY.

IT'S A HASSLE, BUT WE GOTTA KEEP EVERYTHING LOCKED UP AROUND HERE.

OH, SPEAKING OF KEYS—

OW!

NOT MUCH OF A PROMOTION, IS IT?

CLUNK!

IT'S SUZY, RIGHT?

HEY, REMEMBER WHEN THE YETIS WENT TO STATE?

PRND

SNOW-CAT

WE WERE DOWN BY THREE IN THE SEVENTH INNING OF THE FINAL CHAMPIONSHIP GAME.

THAT'S WHEN I STEPPED UP TO THE PLATE.

OH! OH! IS THIS A COME-FROM-BEHIND SPORTS STORY? I LOVE THOSE!

click!

NO, WE LOST. IT WAS BRUTAL.

STOMPE

BUT YOU KNOW WHAT? WE PLAYED THE BEST INNING OF OUR WHOLE SEASON.

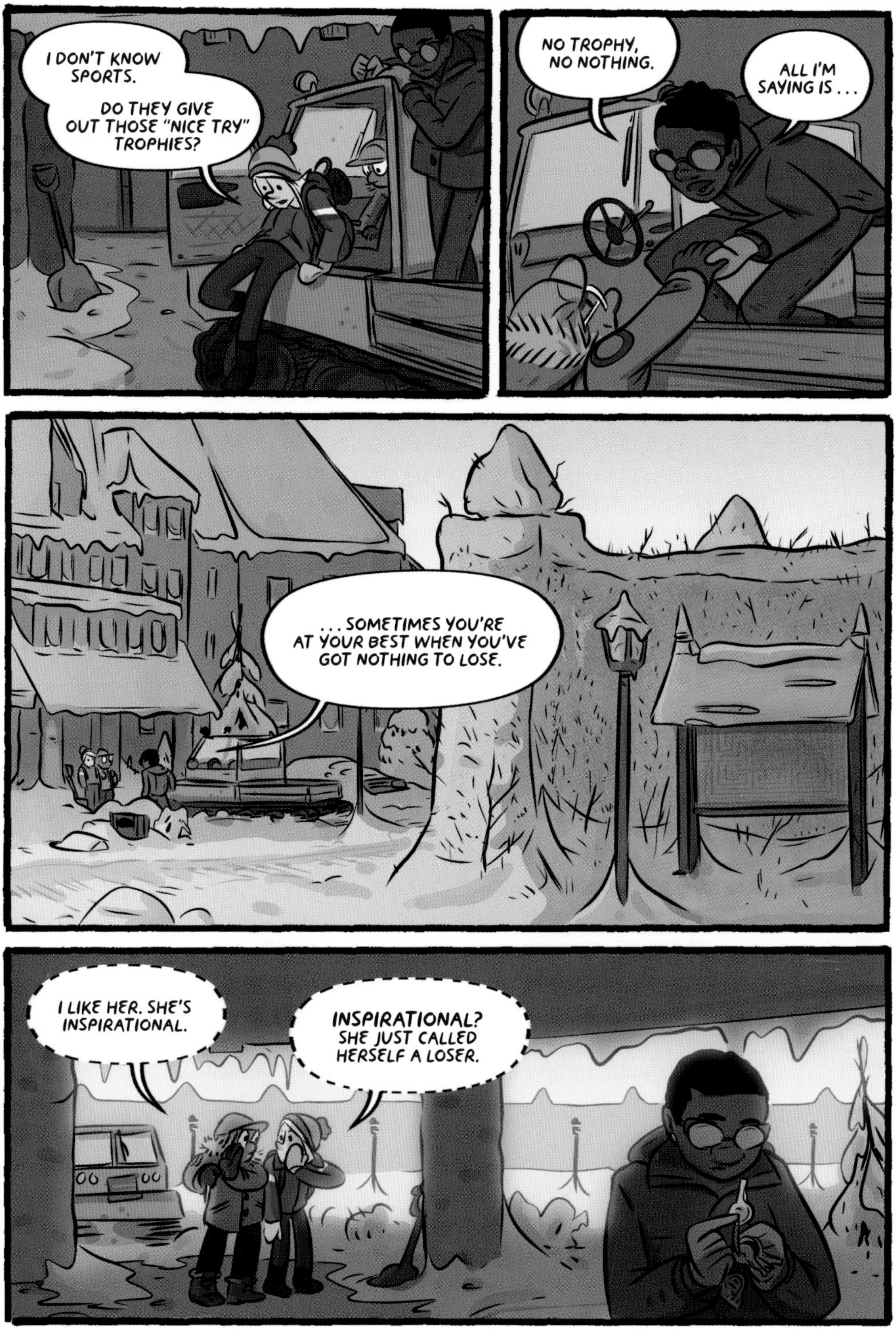
I DON'T KNOW SPORTS.
DO THEY GIVE OUT THOSE "NICE TRY" TROPHIES?
NO TROPHY, NO NOTHING.
ALL I'M SAYING IS . . .
. . . SOMETIMES YOU'RE AT YOUR BEST WHEN YOU'VE GOT NOTHING TO LOSE.
I LIKE HER. SHE'S INSPIRATIONAL.
INSPIRATIONAL? SHE JUST CALLED HERSELF A LOSER.

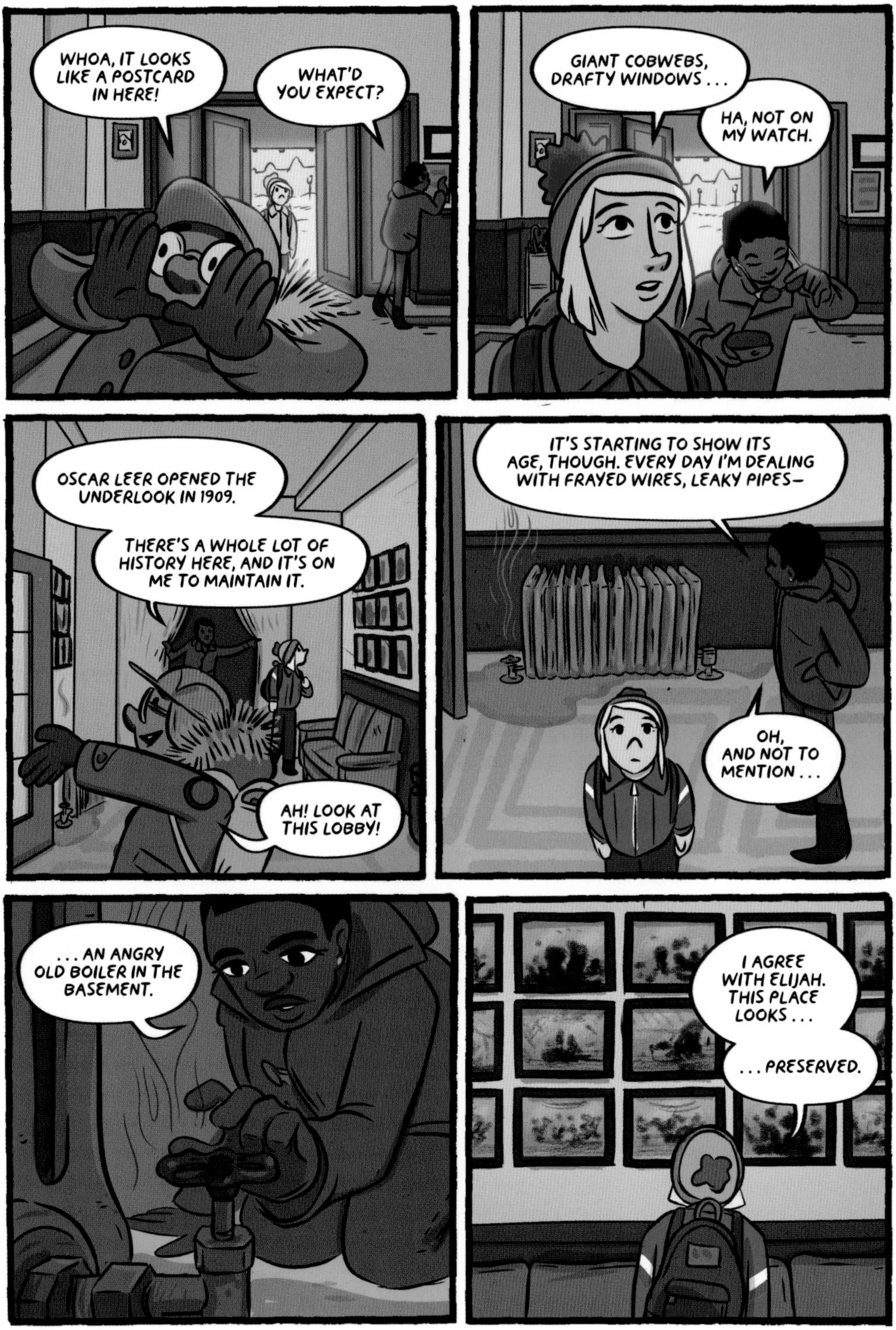
WHOA, IT LOOKS LIKE A POSTCARD IN HERE!
WHAT'D YOU EXPECT?
GIANT COBWEBS, DRAFTY WINDOWS . . .
HA, NOT ON MY WATCH.
OSCAR LEER OPENED THE UNDERLOOK IN 1909.
THERE'S A WHOLE LOT OF HISTORY HERE, AND IT'S ON ME TO MAINTAIN IT.
AH! LOOK AT THIS LOBBY!
IT'S STARTING TO SHOW ITS AGE, THOUGH. EVERY DAY I'M DEALING WITH FRAYED WIRES, LEAKY PIPES—
OH, AND NOT TO MENTION . . .
. . . AN ANGRY OLD BOILER IN THE BASEMENT.
I AGREE WITH ELIJAH. THIS PLACE LOOKS . . .
. . . PRESERVED.

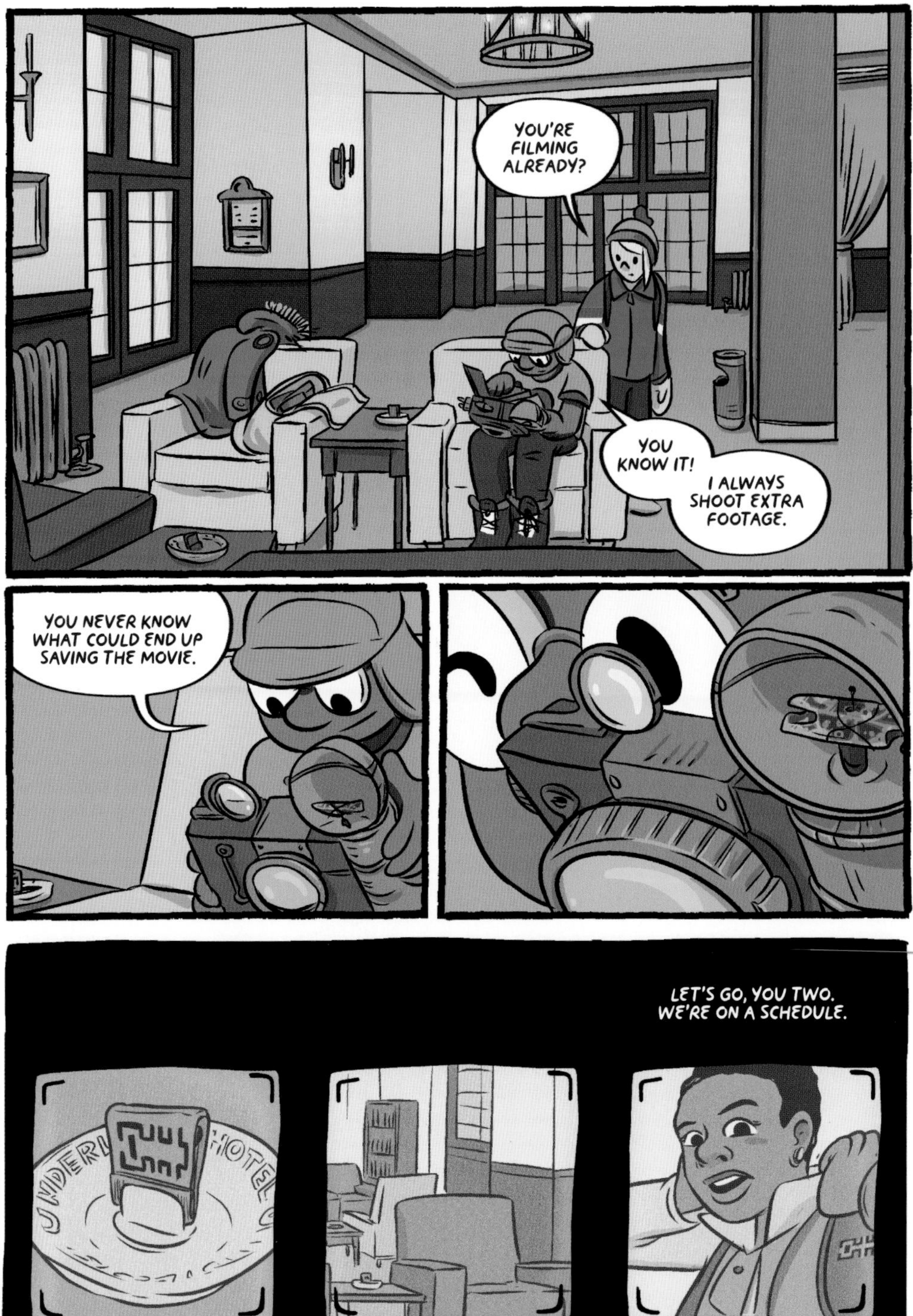
YOU'RE FILMING ALREADY?
YOU KNOW IT!
I ALWAYS SHOOT EXTRA FOOTAGE.
YOU NEVER KNOW WHAT COULD END UP SAVING THE MOVIE.
LET'S GO, YOU TWO. WE'RE ON A SCHEDULE.
HOTEL

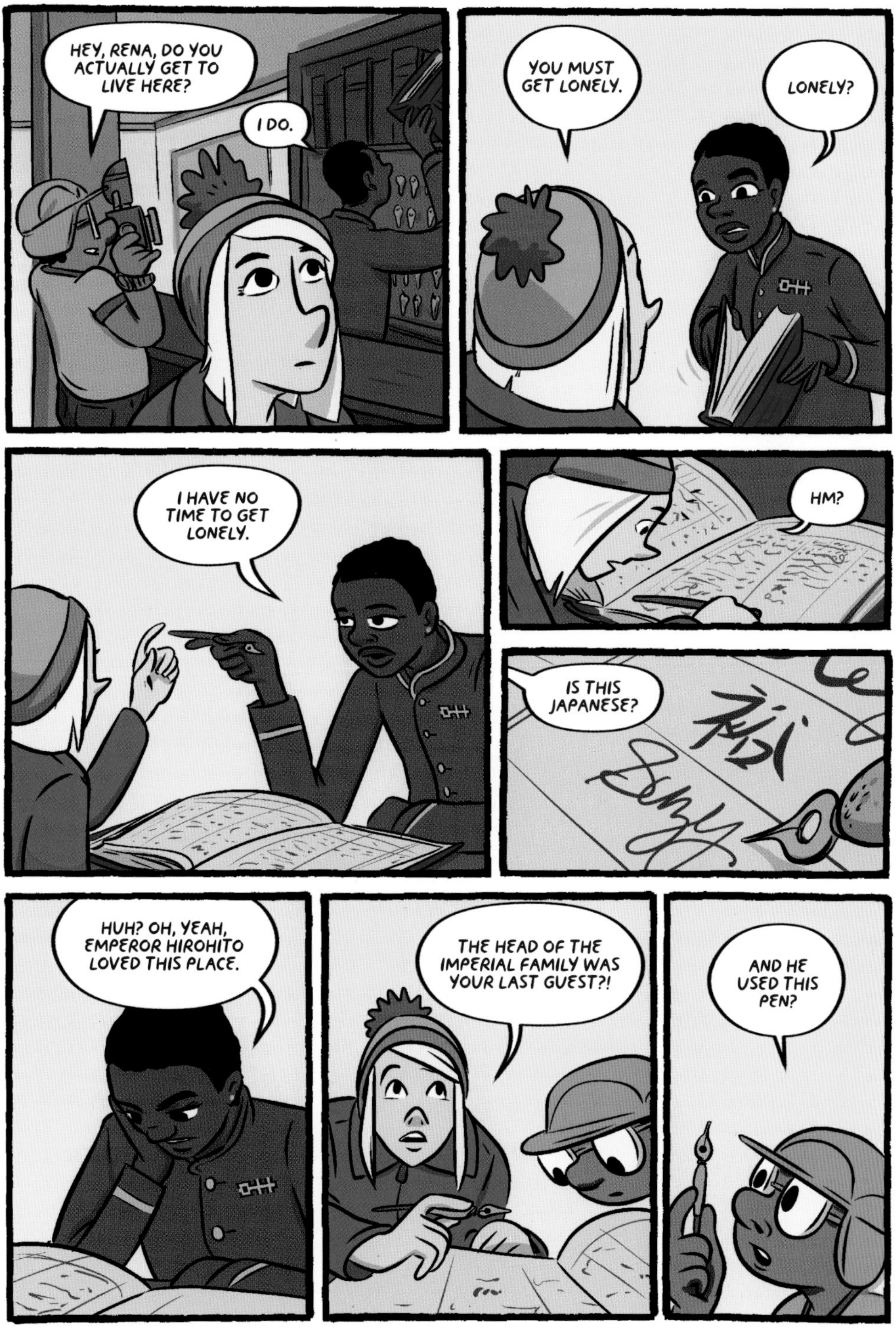
HEY, RENA, DO YOU ACTUALLY GET TO LIVE HERE?
I DO.
YOU MUST GET LONELY.
LONELY?
I HAVE NO TIME TO GET LONELY.
HM?
IS THIS JAPANESE?
HUH? OH, YEAH, EMPEROR HIROHITO LOVED THIS PLACE.
THE HEAD OF THE IMPERIAL FAMILY WAS YOUR LAST GUEST?!
AND HE USED THIS PEN?

AW!

COME ON, IT'S JUST A SOUVENIR!

THIS ISN'T A GIFT SHOP, ELIJAH.

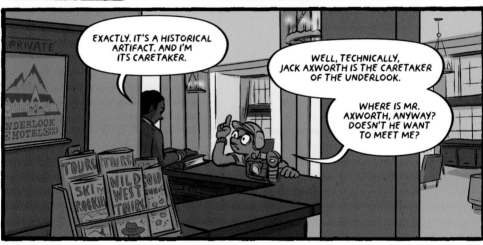

EXACTLY. IT'S A HISTORICAL ARTIFACT. AND I'M ITS CARETAKER.

WELL, TECHNICALLY, JACK AXWORTH IS THE CARETAKER OF THE UNDERLOOK.

WHERE IS MR. AXWORTH, ANYWAY? DOESN'T HE WANT TO MEET ME?

JACK AXWORTH DIDN'T INVITE YOU HERE; I DID.

YOU?!

HE'LL BE DOWN SOON.

BETTER STEP INTO MY OFFICE.

THE THING ABOUT A PLACE LIKE THIS—

IT'S NOT DESIGNED TO BE EMPTY.

AS SOON AS THE GUESTS WERE GONE—

IT STARTED TO FALL APART.

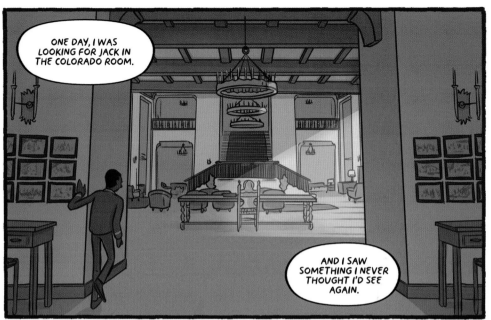

ONE DAY, I WAS LOOKING FOR JACK IN THE COLORADO ROOM.

AND I SAW SOMETHING I NEVER THOUGHT I'D SEE AGAIN.

JACK HAD GOTTEN OUT HIS OLD TYPEWRITER.

I COULDN'T BELIEVE IT. HE WAS FINALLY STARTING TO WRITE A NEW BOOK.

BUT IT WASN'T A BOOK.

IT WAS SOMETHING ELSE.

Dear Linda,

I must explain to you how all this mistaken idea of denouncing
pleasure and praising pain was born, and I will give you a complete account

THEY'RE LETTERS.

WHO'S LINDA?

LINDA LEER. SHE'S JACK'S WIFE.

asure itself, because it is pleasure, but because those who do not know how

WHERE DID SHE GO?

SHE DIED.

IT WAS FOUR YEARS AGO THIS SATURDAY.

and praising pain was born, and I will give you a complete account of the

HE'S DESCRIBING HIS DAILY ROUTINE...

JUST NORMAL, EVERYDAY LIFE...

I DON'T UNDERSTAND. WHY IS HE WRITING TO HER ABOUT THIS STUFF?

THE LETTERS AREN'T REALLY FOR HER.

HE'S USING THEM AS A WAY TO COLLECT MEMORIES.

ars, dislikes, or avoids pleasure itself, because it is pleasure, but because of
one of the most perfect days I could have hoped to live.

Love, Jack

68

I WAS FREAKED OUT WHEN I FOUND THEM, SO I TOOK AWAY HIS TYPEWRITER.

BUT MR. AXWORTH ISN'T OLD ENOUGH TO BE LOSING HIS MEMORY . . .

IS HE?

IT'S CALLED YOUNG-ONSET DEMENTIA. I LOOKED IT UP.

AND IT'S NOT JUST MEMORIES HE'S LOSING.

IT'S HIS RECOLLECTION OF THINGS WE TAKE FOR GRANTED. LIKE . . .

. . . WHAT'S BEHIND A CLOSED DOOR IN HIS OWN HOME.

AND IT'S GOTTEN EVEN WORSE.

LAST MONTH I FOUND HIM STANDING OUTSIDE BY THE OLD HEDGE MAZE.

IT WAS THE MIDDLE OF THE NIGHT.

HE WAS BAREFOOT AND IN HIS PAJAMAS.

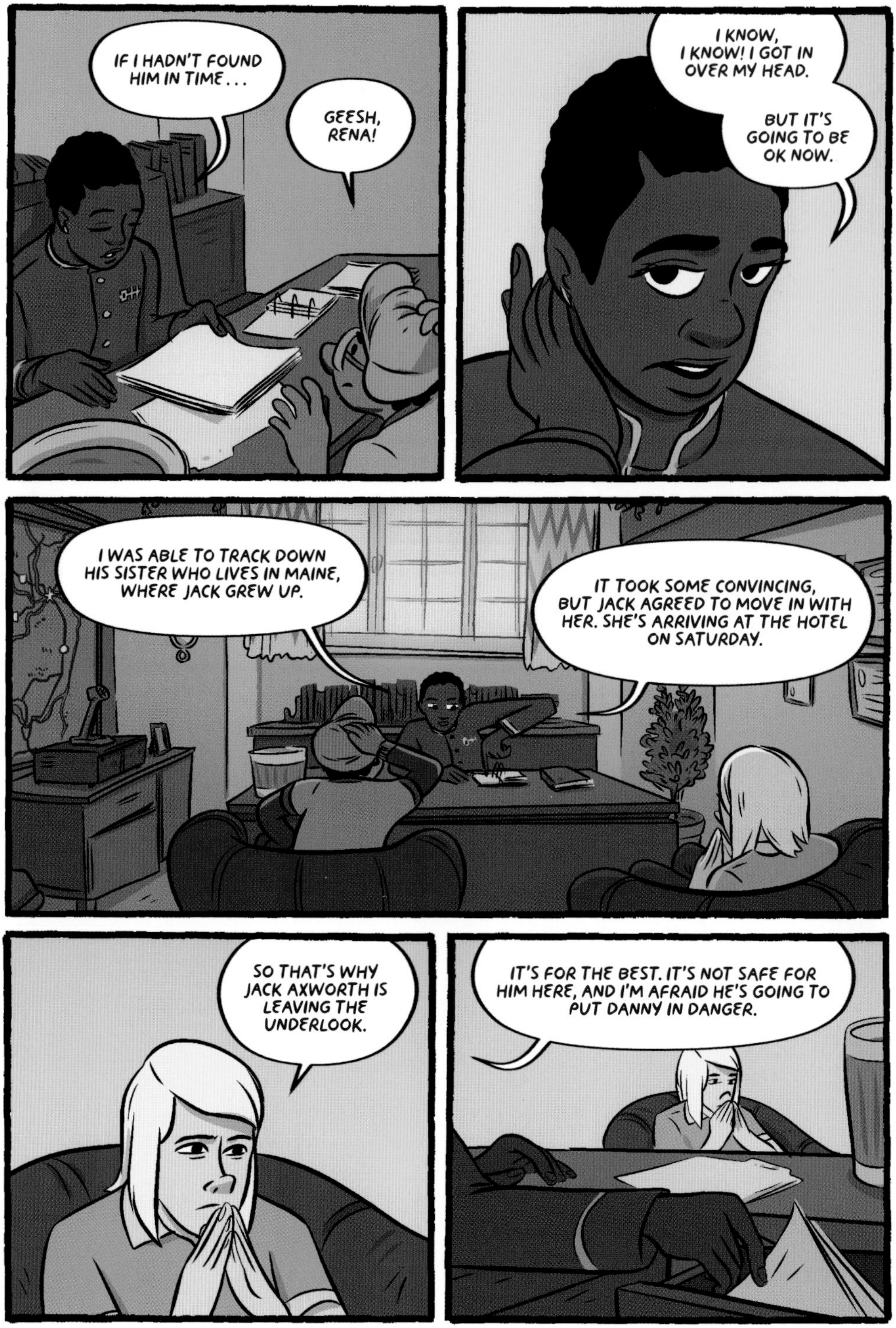
IF I HADN'T FOUND HIM IN TIME . . .
GEESH, RENA!
I KNOW, I KNOW! I GOT IN OVER MY HEAD.
BUT IT'S GOING TO BE OK NOW.
I WAS ABLE TO TRACK DOWN HIS SISTER WHO LIVES IN MAINE, WHERE JACK GREW UP.
IT TOOK SOME CONVINCING, BUT JACK AGREED TO MOVE IN WITH HER. SHE'S ARRIVING AT THE HOTEL ON SATURDAY.
SO THAT'S WHY JACK AXWORTH IS LEAVING THE UNDERLOOK.
IT'S FOR THE BEST. IT'S NOT SAFE FOR HIM HERE, AND I'M AFRAID HE'S GOING TO PUT DANNY IN DANGER.

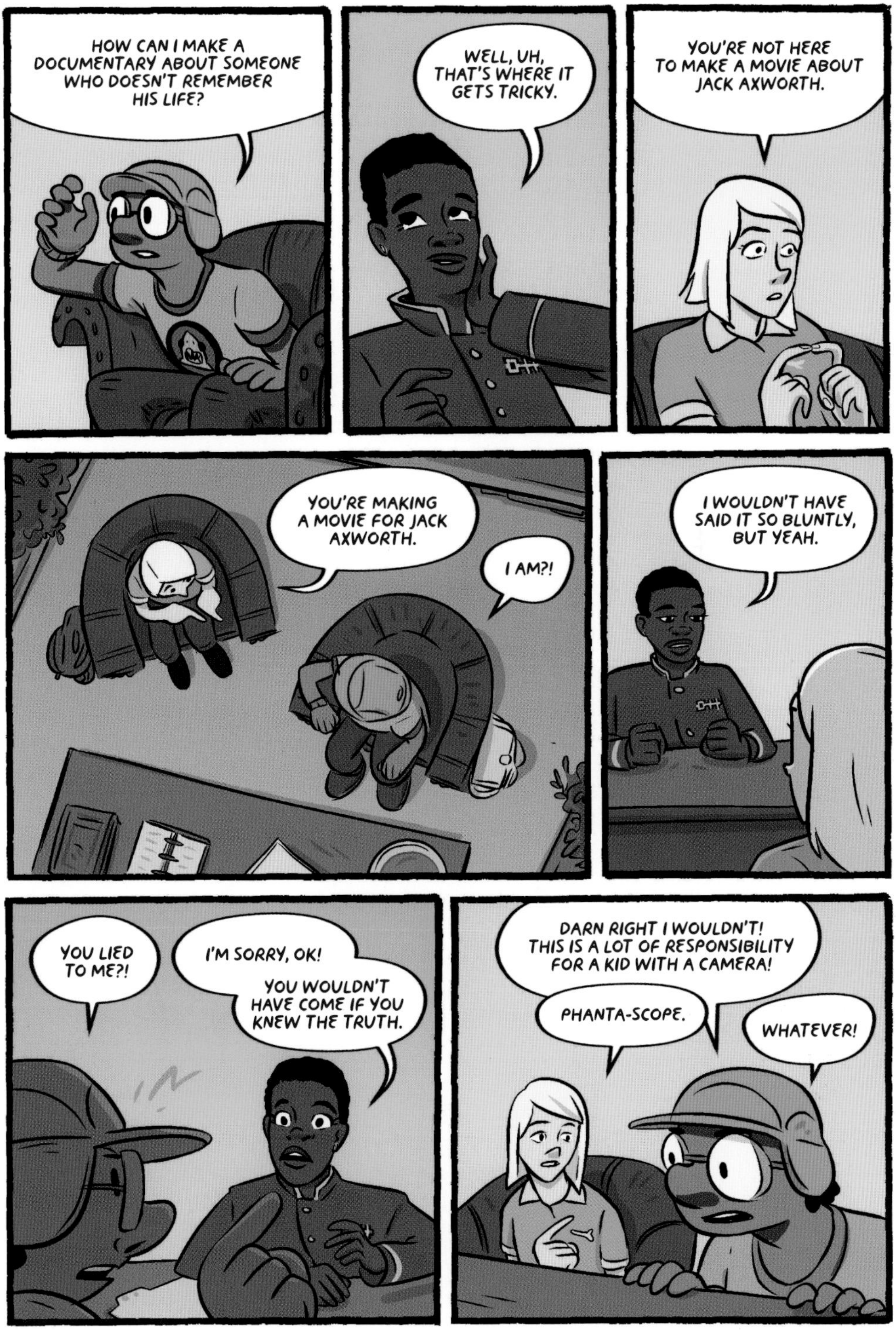
HOW CAN I MAKE A DOCUMENTARY ABOUT SOMEONE WHO DOESN'T REMEMBER HIS LIFE?
WELL, UH, THAT'S WHERE IT GETS TRICKY.
YOU'RE NOT HERE TO MAKE A MOVIE ABOUT JACK AXWORTH.
YOU'RE MAKING A MOVIE FOR JACK AXWORTH.
I AM?!
I WOULDN'T HAVE SAID IT SO BLUNTLY, BUT YEAH.
YOU LIED TO ME?!
I'M SORRY, OK!
YOU WOULDN'T HAVE COME IF YOU KNEW THE TRUTH.
DARN RIGHT I WOULDN'T! THIS IS A LOT OF RESPONSIBILITY FOR A KID WITH A CAMERA!
PHANTA-SCOPE.
WHATEVER!

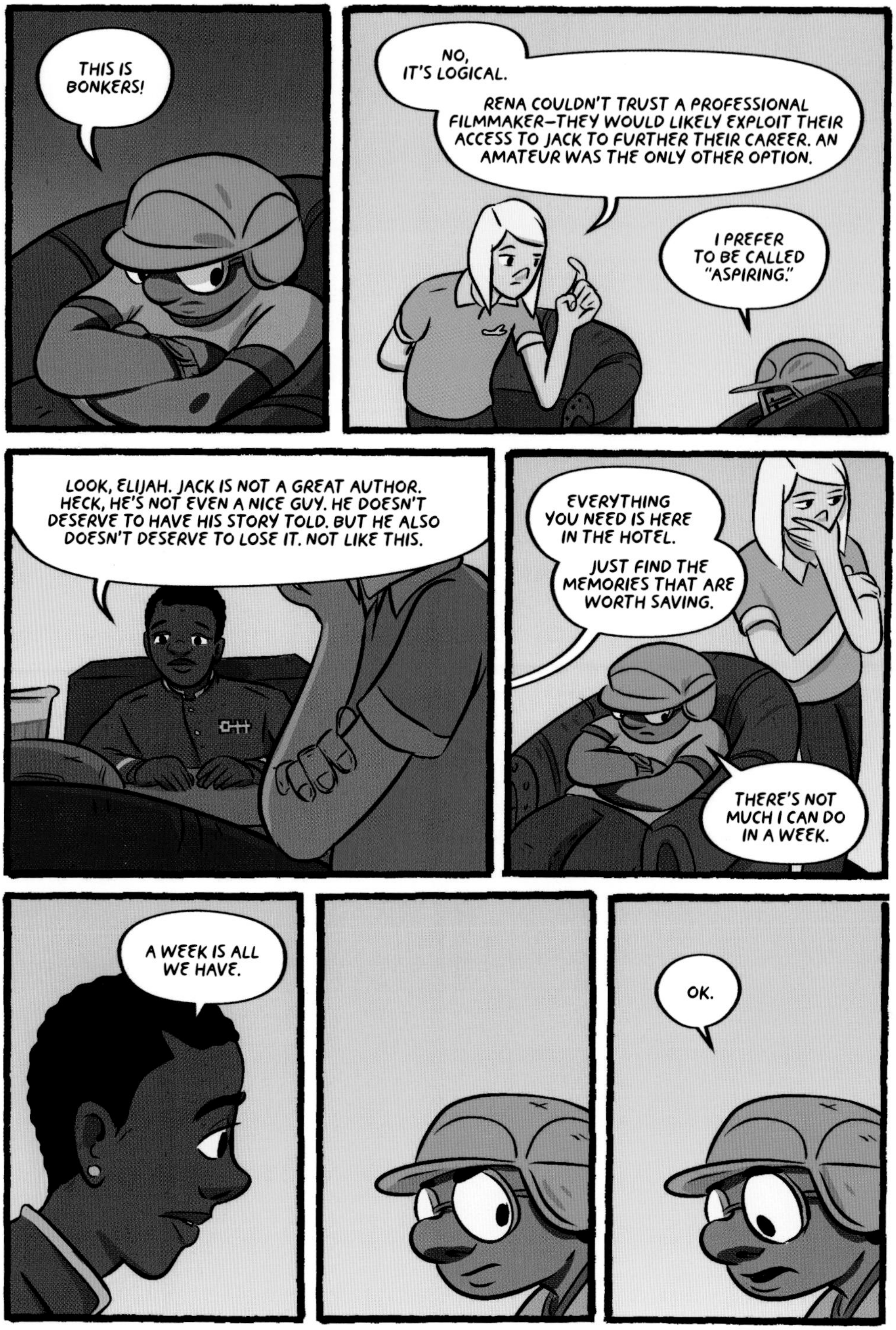
THIS IS BONKERS!
NO, IT'S LOGICAL.
RENA COULDN'T TRUST A PROFESSIONAL FILMMAKER—THEY WOULD LIKELY EXPLOIT THEIR ACCESS TO JACK TO FURTHER THEIR CAREER. AN AMATEUR WAS THE ONLY OTHER OPTION.
I PREFER TO BE CALLED "ASPIRING."
LOOK, ELIJAH. JACK IS NOT A GREAT AUTHOR. HECK, HE'S NOT EVEN A NICE GUY. HE DOESN'T DESERVE TO HAVE HIS STORY TOLD. BUT HE ALSO DOESN'T DESERVE TO LOSE IT. NOT LIKE THIS.
EVERYTHING YOU NEED IS HERE IN THE HOTEL.
JUST FIND THE MEMORIES THAT ARE WORTH SAVING.
THERE'S NOT MUCH I CAN DO IN A WEEK.
A WEEK IS ALL WE HAVE.
OK.

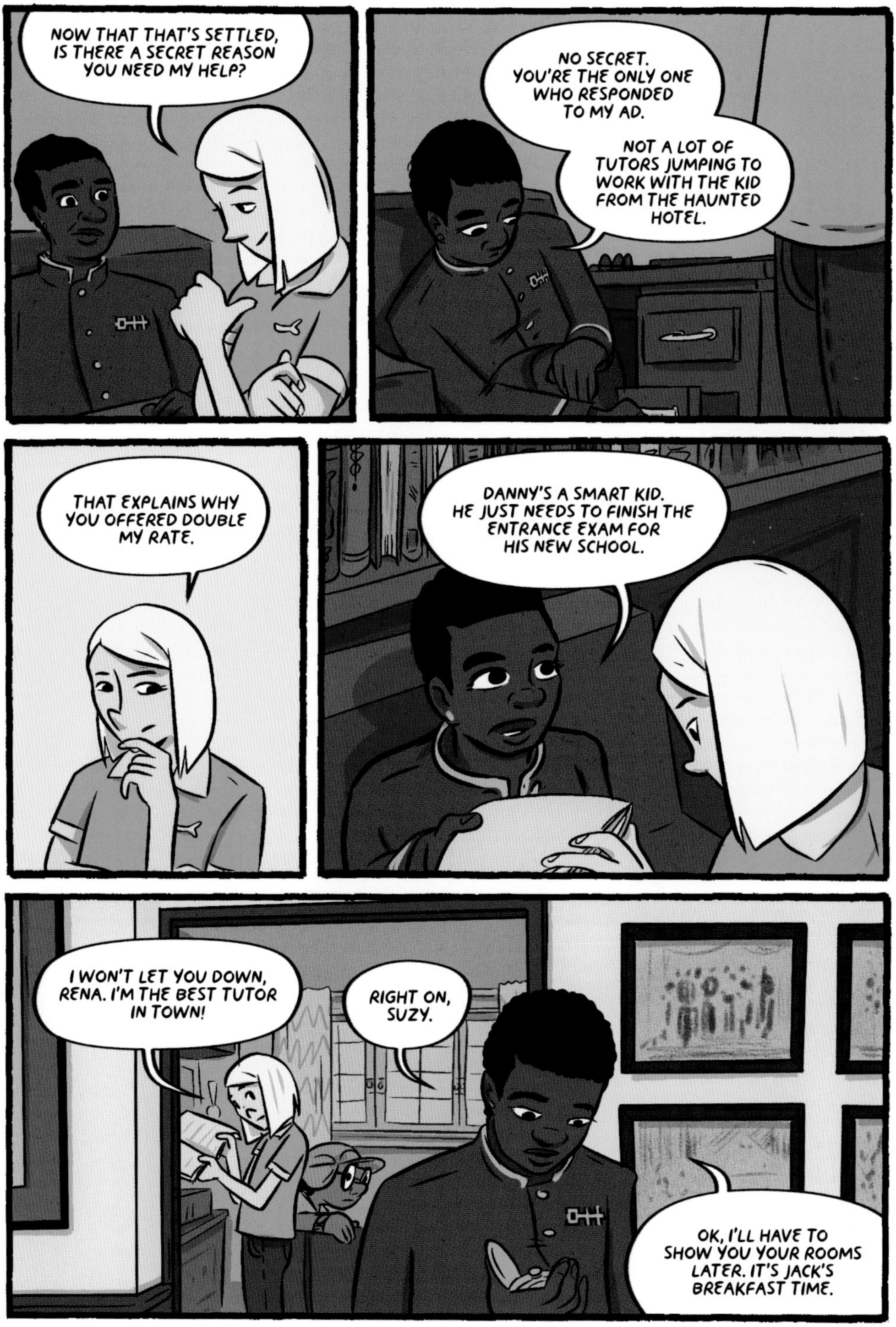
NOW THAT THAT'S SETTLED, IS THERE A SECRET REASON YOU NEED MY HELP?
NO SECRET. YOU'RE THE ONLY ONE WHO RESPONDED TO MY AD.
NOT A LOT OF TUTORS JUMPING TO WORK WITH THE KID FROM THE HAUNTED HOTEL.
THAT EXPLAINS WHY YOU OFFERED DOUBLE MY RATE.
DANNY'S A SMART KID. HE JUST NEEDS TO FINISH THE ENTRANCE EXAM FOR HIS NEW SCHOOL.
I WON'T LET YOU DOWN, RENA. I'M THE BEST TUTOR IN TOWN!
RIGHT ON, SUZY.
OK, I'LL HAVE TO SHOW YOU YOUR ROOMS LATER. IT'S JACK'S BREAKFAST TIME.

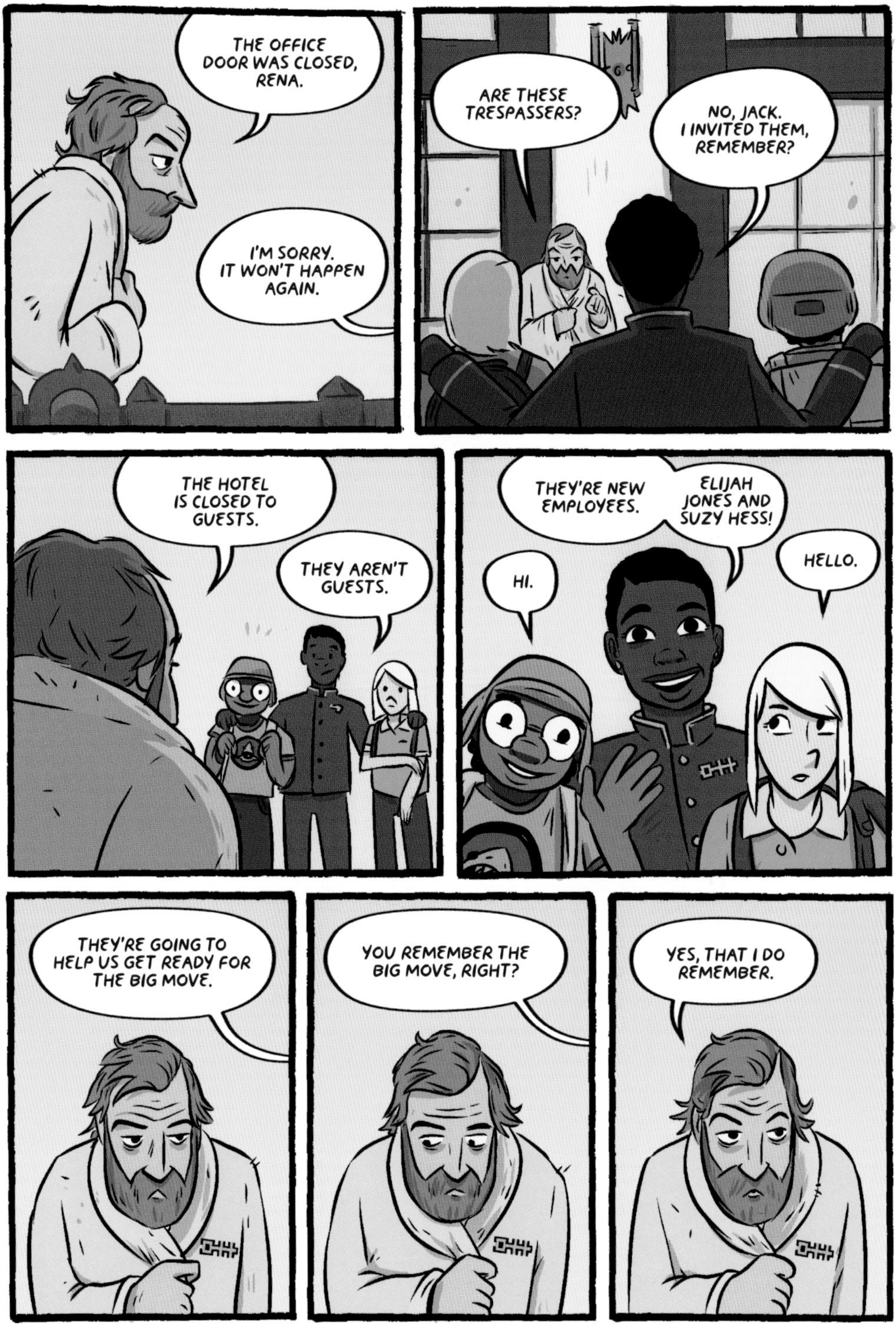
THE OFFICE DOOR WAS CLOSED, RENA.
I'M SORRY. IT WON'T HAPPEN AGAIN.
ARE THESE TRESPASSERS?
NO, JACK. I INVITED THEM, REMEMBER?
THE HOTEL IS CLOSED TO GUESTS.
THEY AREN'T GUESTS.
THEY'RE NEW EMPLOYEES.
ELIJAH JONES AND SUZY HESS!
HI.
HELLO.
THEY'RE GOING TO HELP US GET READY FOR THE BIG MOVE.
YOU REMEMBER THE BIG MOVE, RIGHT?
YES, THAT I DO REMEMBER.

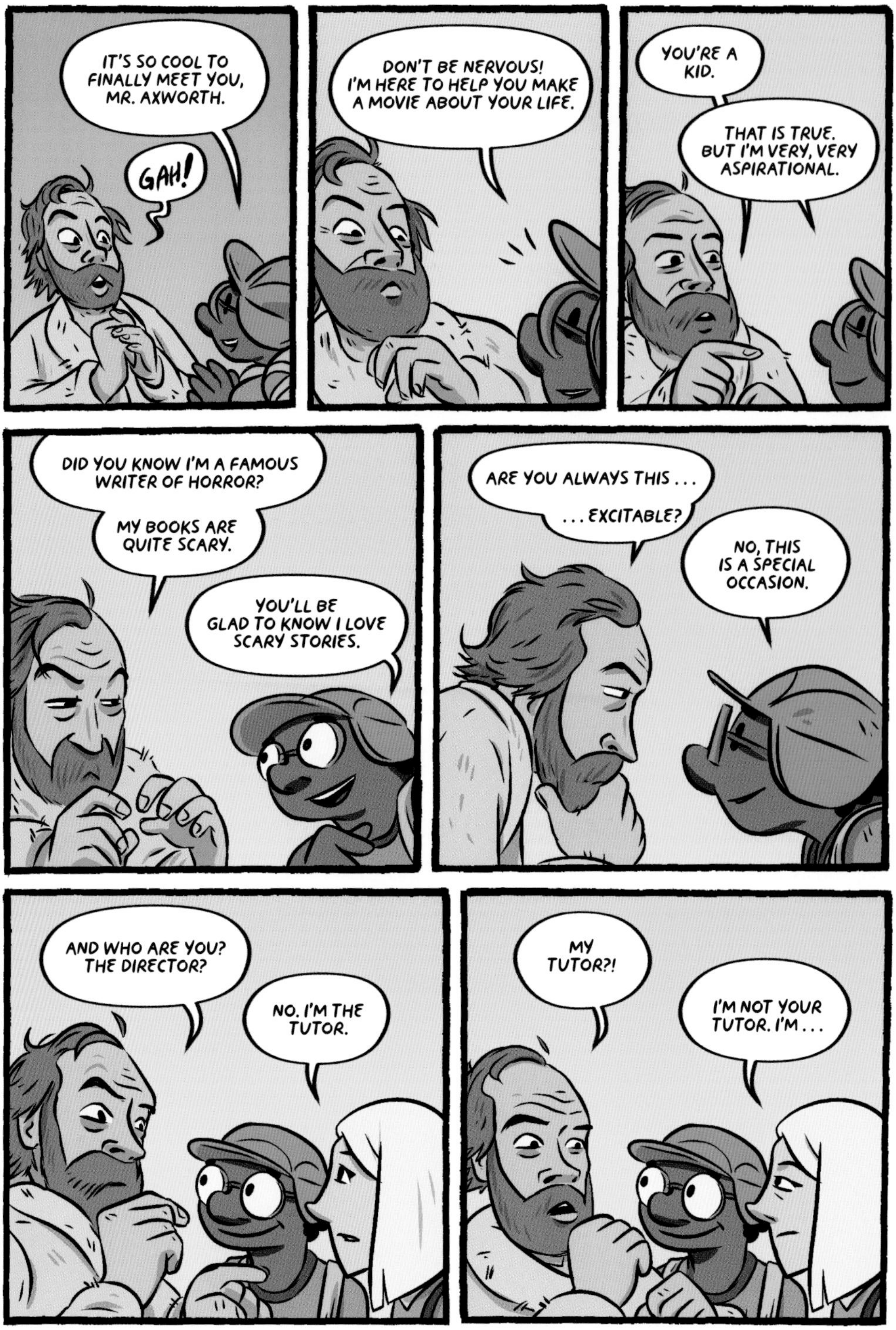
IT'S SO COOL TO FINALLY MEET YOU, MR. AXWORTH.
GAH!
DON'T BE NERVOUS! I'M HERE TO HELP YOU MAKE A MOVIE ABOUT YOUR LIFE.
YOU'RE A KID.
THAT IS TRUE. BUT I'M VERY, VERY ASPIRATIONAL.
DID YOU KNOW I'M A FAMOUS WRITER OF HORROR?
MY BOOKS ARE QUITE SCARY.
YOU'LL BE GLAD TO KNOW I LOVE SCARY STORIES.
ARE YOU ALWAYS THIS . . .
. . . EXCITABLE?
NO, THIS IS A SPECIAL OCCASION.
AND WHO ARE YOU? THE DIRECTOR?
NO. I'M THE TUTOR.
MY TUTOR?!
I'M NOT YOUR TUTOR. I'M . . .

DANNY
AXWORTH!

GET BACK
HERE!

HA! HA!
HA!

YOU'D BETTER HURRY.
IF HE GETS TO THE ELEVATOR,
YOU'LL NEVER CATCH HIM.

WHAT?

GO! GO! GO!

OK!

DANNY!

STOP BEING
CHILDISH!

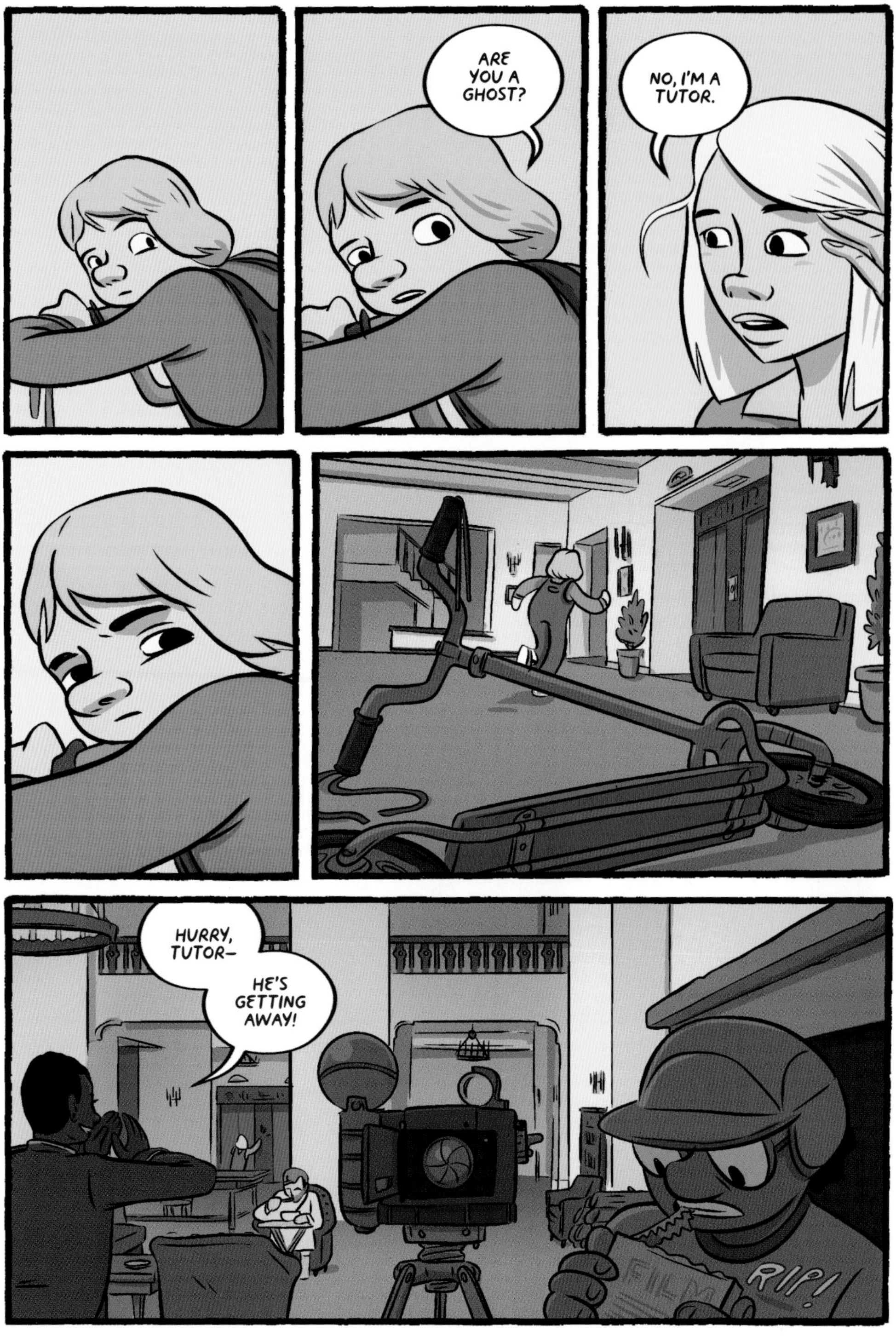
ARE YOU A GHOST?
NO, I'M A TUTOR.
HURRY, TUTOR–
HE'S GETTING AWAY!
RIP!

HELLO, DANNY.
I'M SUZY.

LET'S FIND A
PLACE TO TALK.

I DON'T NEED A TUTOR. I ACE ALL MY TESTS.

YOU CAN ASK RENA.

THUNK

AN ENTRANCE EXAM ISN'T JUST A TEST.

IT'S MORE LIKE AN ACADEMIC TRACK MEET.

OK.

SO WHAT?

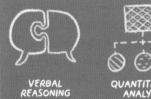
VERBAL
REASONING

QUANTITATIVE
ANALYSIS

APPLIED
MATHEMATICS

READING
COMPREHENSION

PERSONAL
ESSAY

83

WHAT GRADE IS THAT?

EIGHTH.

I HEARD ON THE NEWS THAT IT'S WINTER BREAK.

WE'RE GETTING OFF TOPIC, DANNY.

BUT DOESN'T A BREAK MEAN YOU KIDS ARE SUPPOSED TO, UM, TAKE A BREAK FROM SCHOOL STUFF?

YOU KIDS, HUH?

YEAH.

WELL, **THIS KID** IS USING HER BREAK TO EARN MONEY TOWARD SUMMER CAMP.

OH, SUMMER CAMP?! I'VE HEARD ABOUT THOSE! YOU GO SWIMMING AND HAVE CAMPFIRES AND TELL SCARY STORIES AND EAT THOSE S'MORES—

NO, NO, NO.

I GO TO **ENGINEERING** SUMMER CAMP.

AND IT'S VERY COMPETITIVE. THIS YEAR I'M DEFENDING MY TEAM'S STATE CHAMPIONSHIP.

SO FOR A BREAK FROM SCHOOL, YOU'RE WORKING . . .

. . . TO PAY FOR MORE SCHOOL?

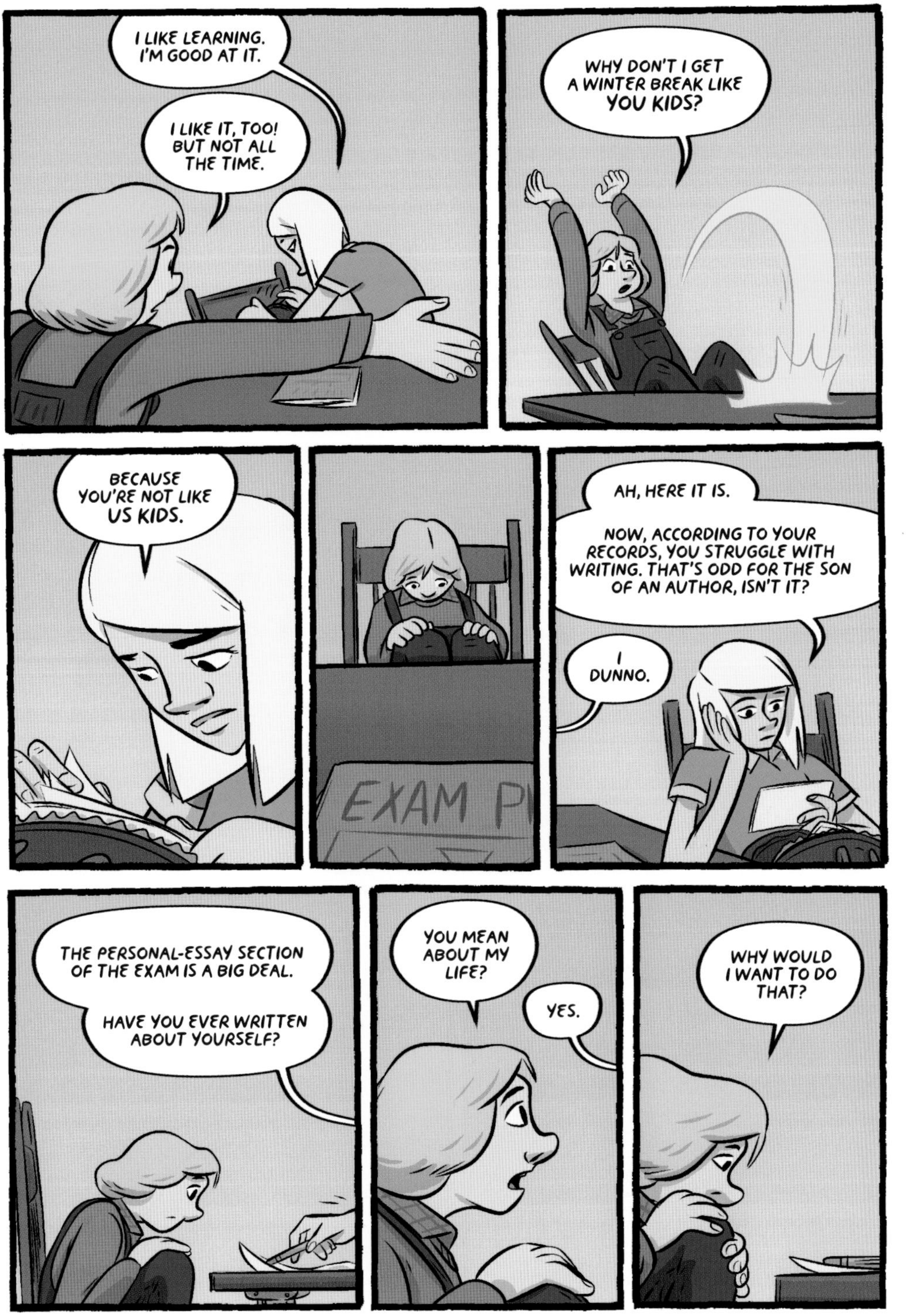
I LIKE LEARNING. I'M GOOD AT IT.
I LIKE IT, TOO! BUT NOT ALL THE TIME.
WHY DON'T I GET A WINTER BREAK LIKE YOU KIDS?
BECAUSE YOU'RE NOT LIKE US KIDS.
EXAM P
AH, HERE IT IS.
NOW, ACCORDING TO YOUR RECORDS, YOU STRUGGLE WITH WRITING. THAT'S ODD FOR THE SON OF AN AUTHOR, ISN'T IT?
I DUNNO.
THE PERSONAL-ESSAY SECTION OF THE EXAM IS A BIG DEAL.
HAVE YOU EVER WRITTEN ABOUT YOURSELF?
YOU MEAN ABOUT MY LIFE?
YES.
WHY WOULD I WANT TO DO THAT?

WHAT ARE YOU DOING, RENA?

STARTING A FIRE.

WITH JACK'S BOOKS?!

HE CALLS IT "CLEANSING."

SAY, WHAT'S THAT YOU GOT, MR. JONES?

OH, UH . . .

LOOKS LIKE A *FIRST EDITION* TO ME.

YEAH, THIS WAS MY DAD'S COPY.

I WAS HOPING YOU'D SIGN—

HEY!

GRAB!

NO YOU DON'T!

ELIJAH CAME ALL THIS WAY TO HELP YOU. SO PLAY NICE, JACK.

HMPH.

HE'S BEEN BUYING BACK EVERY COPY HE CAN GET HIS HANDS ON.

BETTER HOLD ON TO THIS. IT'S ABOUT TO BE ONE OF THE LAST ON EARTH.

WHOA.

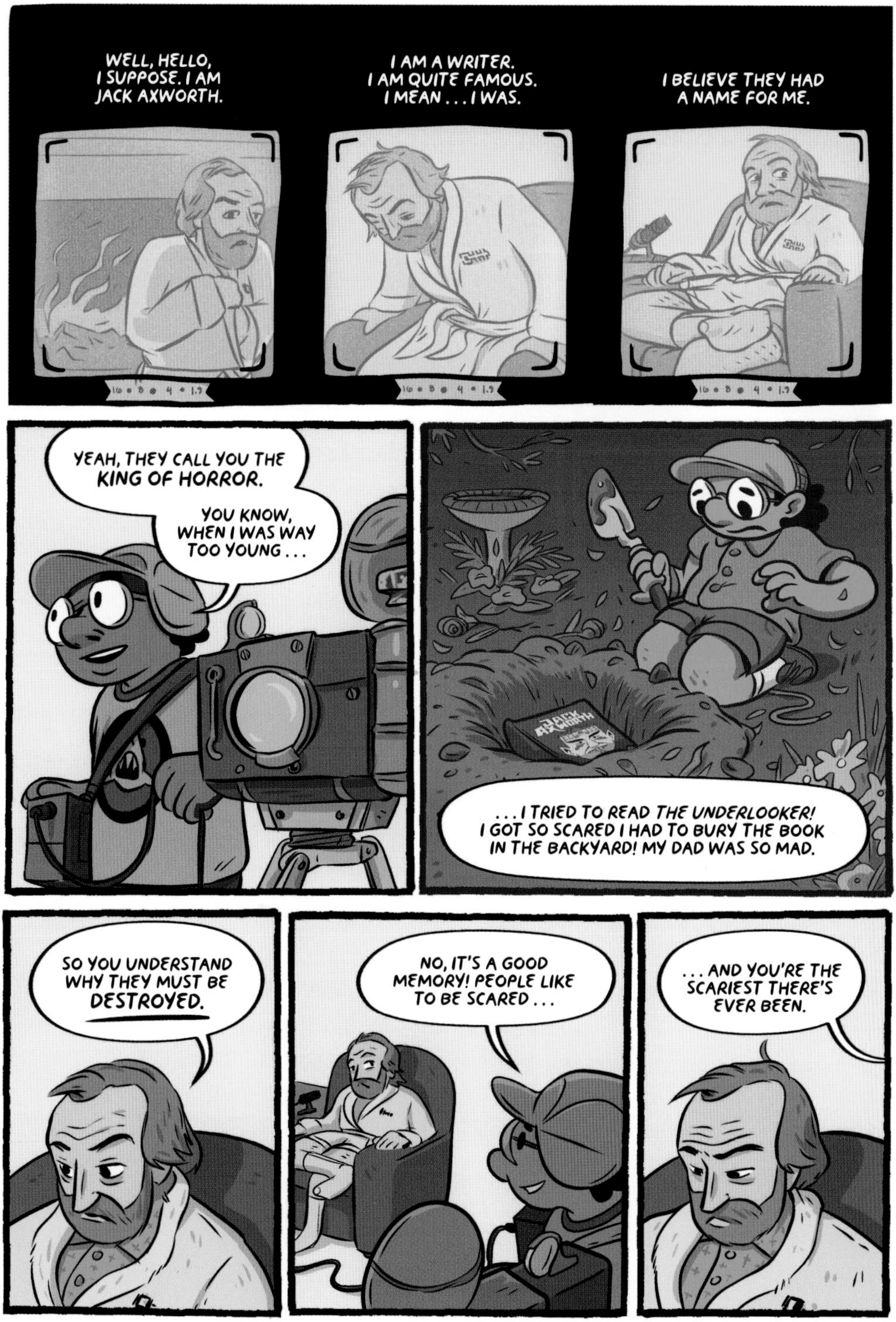
WELL, HELLO, I SUPPOSE. I AM JACK AXWORTH.
I AM A WRITER. I AM QUITE FAMOUS. I MEAN . . . I WAS.
I BELIEVE THEY HAD A NAME FOR ME.
YEAH, THEY CALL YOU THE KING OF HORROR.
YOU KNOW, WHEN I WAS WAY TOO YOUNG . . .
. . . I TRIED TO READ THE UNDERLOOKER! I GOT SO SCARED I HAD TO BURY THE BOOK IN THE BACKYARD! MY DAD WAS SO MAD.
SO YOU UNDERSTAND WHY THEY MUST BE DESTROYED.
NO, IT'S A GOOD MEMORY! PEOPLE LIKE TO BE SCARED . . .
. . . AND YOU'RE THE SCARIEST THERE'S EVER BEEN.

COME ON! YOU LIVE IN THE OH-SO-*INFAMOUS* UNDERLOOK HOTEL.

DON'T TELL ME YOU HAVE NOTHING TO WRITE ABOUT.

IT'S MY HOME.

I DON'T KNOW WHAT ELSE TO SAY.

TRUST ME, THERE ARE *PEOPLE* WHO'D LOVE TO KNOW WHAT'S IN YOUR LITTLE HEAD.

WHAT PEOPLE?

PECULIAR PEOPLE.

I DUNNO, SUZY. I'M JUST NOT A WRITER. THAT'S MY DAD'S THING.

ER, WAS MY DAD'S THING.

OH! UH . . .

DON'T TELL HIM I HAVE THAT, OK?

OOOOH! IS IT AS SCARY AS THEY SAY?

SCARY? NO, I FEEL BAD FOR THE VAMPIRE. HE HAD A HARD LIFE, YOU KNOW?

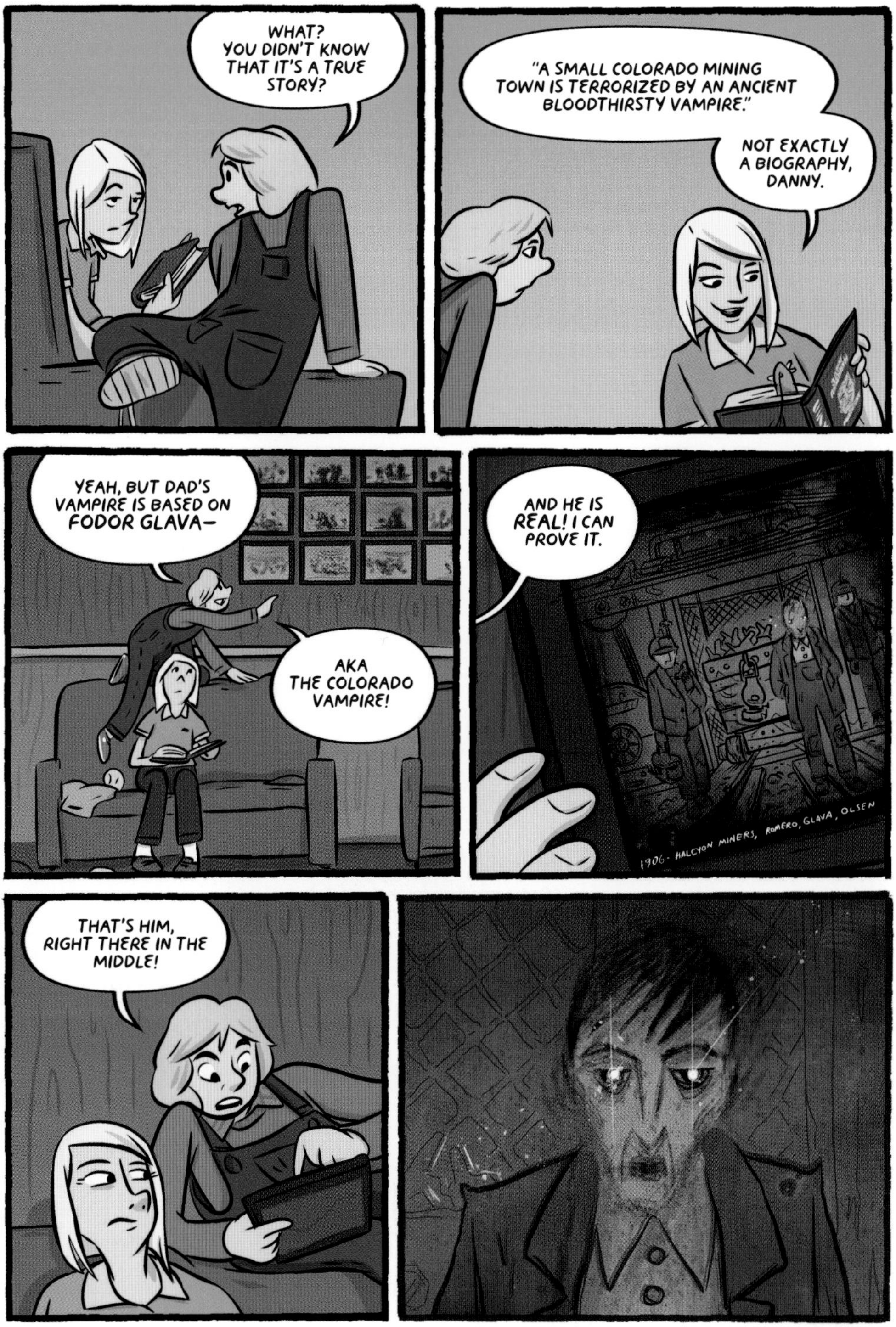
WHAT? YOU DIDN'T KNOW THAT IT'S A TRUE STORY?
"A SMALL COLORADO MINING TOWN IS TERRORIZED BY AN ANCIENT BLOODTHIRSTY VAMPIRE."
NOT EXACTLY A BIOGRAPHY, DANNY.
YEAH, BUT DAD'S VAMPIRE IS BASED ON FODOR GLAVA—
AKA THE COLORADO VAMPIRE!
AND HE IS REAL! I CAN PROVE IT.
1906- HALCYON MINERS, ROMERO, GLAVA, OLSEN
THAT'S HIM, RIGHT THERE IN THE MIDDLE!

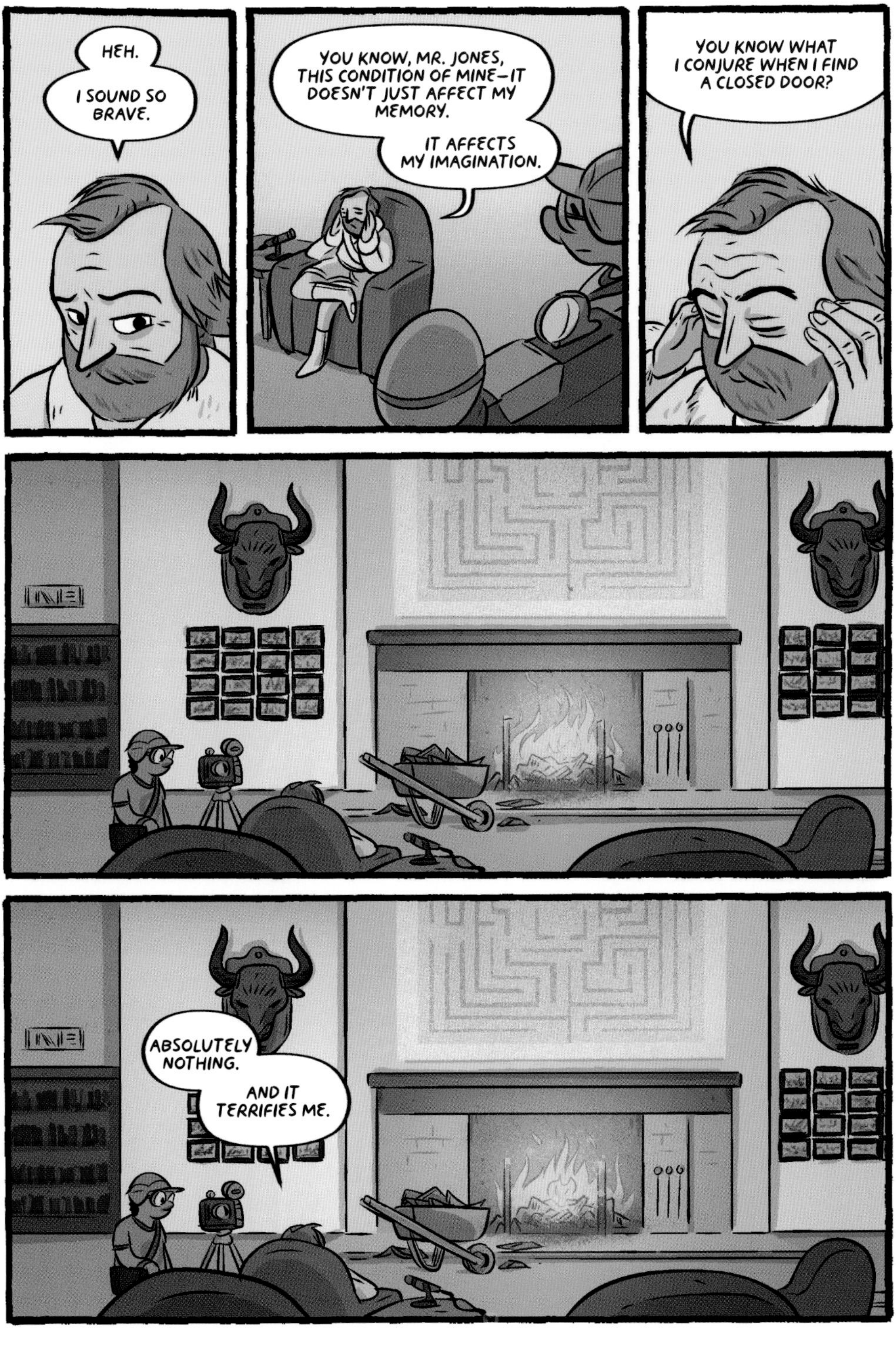
HEH.
I SOUND SO BRAVE.
YOU KNOW, MR. JONES, THIS CONDITION OF MINE—IT DOESN'T JUST AFFECT MY MEMORY.
IT AFFECTS MY IMAGINATION.
YOU KNOW WHAT I CONJURE WHEN I FIND A CLOSED DOOR?
ABSOLUTELY NOTHING.
AND IT TERRIFIES ME.

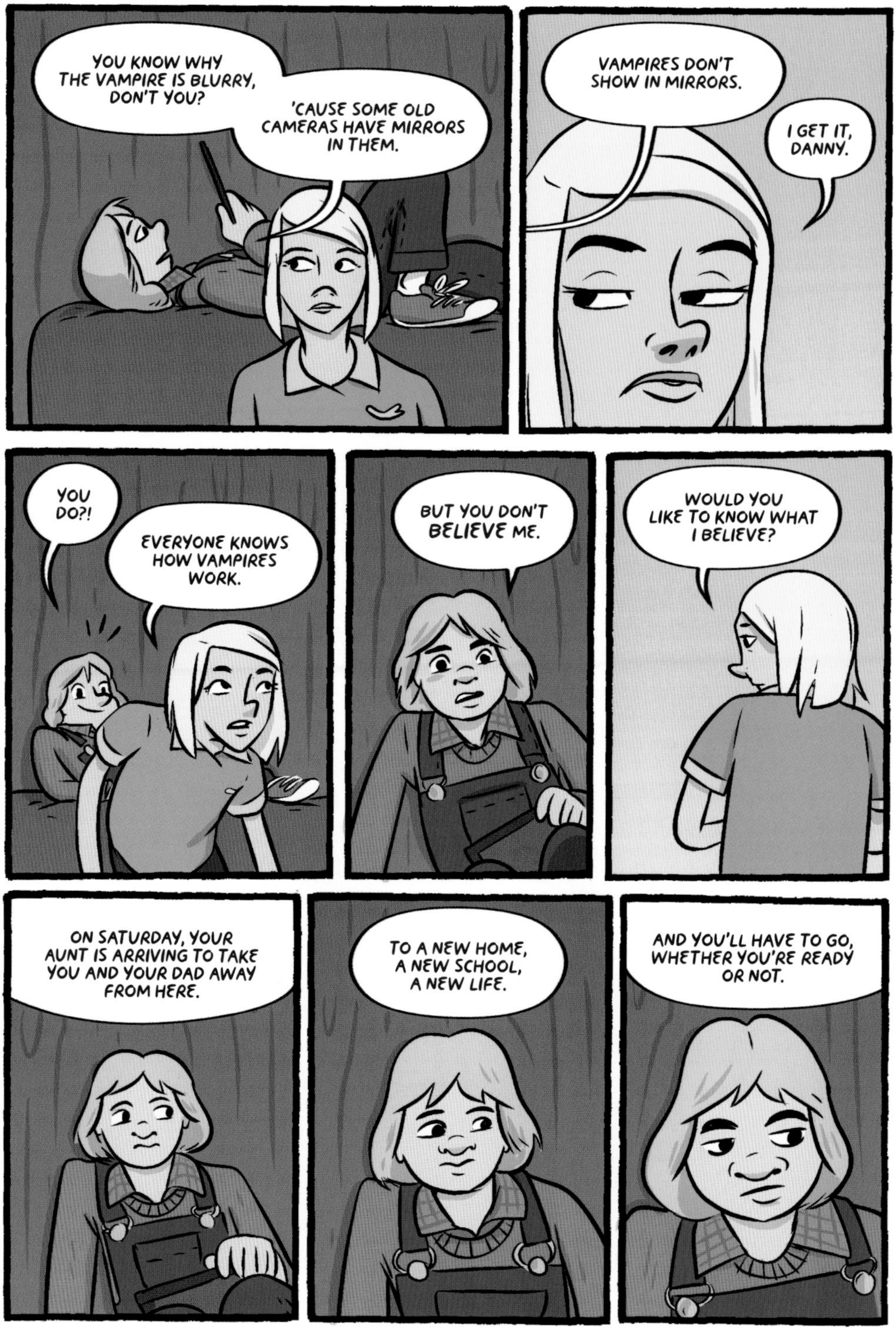
YOU KNOW WHY THE VAMPIRE IS BLURRY, DON'T YOU?
'CAUSE SOME OLD CAMERAS HAVE MIRRORS IN THEM.
VAMPIRES DON'T SHOW IN MIRRORS.
I GET IT, DANNY.
YOU DO?!
EVERYONE KNOWS HOW VAMPIRES WORK.
BUT YOU DON'T BELIEVE ME.
WOULD YOU LIKE TO KNOW WHAT I BELIEVE?
ON SATURDAY, YOUR AUNT IS ARRIVING TO TAKE YOU AND YOUR DAD AWAY FROM HERE.
TO A NEW HOME, A NEW SCHOOL, A NEW LIFE.
AND YOU'LL HAVE TO GO, WHETHER YOU'RE READY OR NOT.

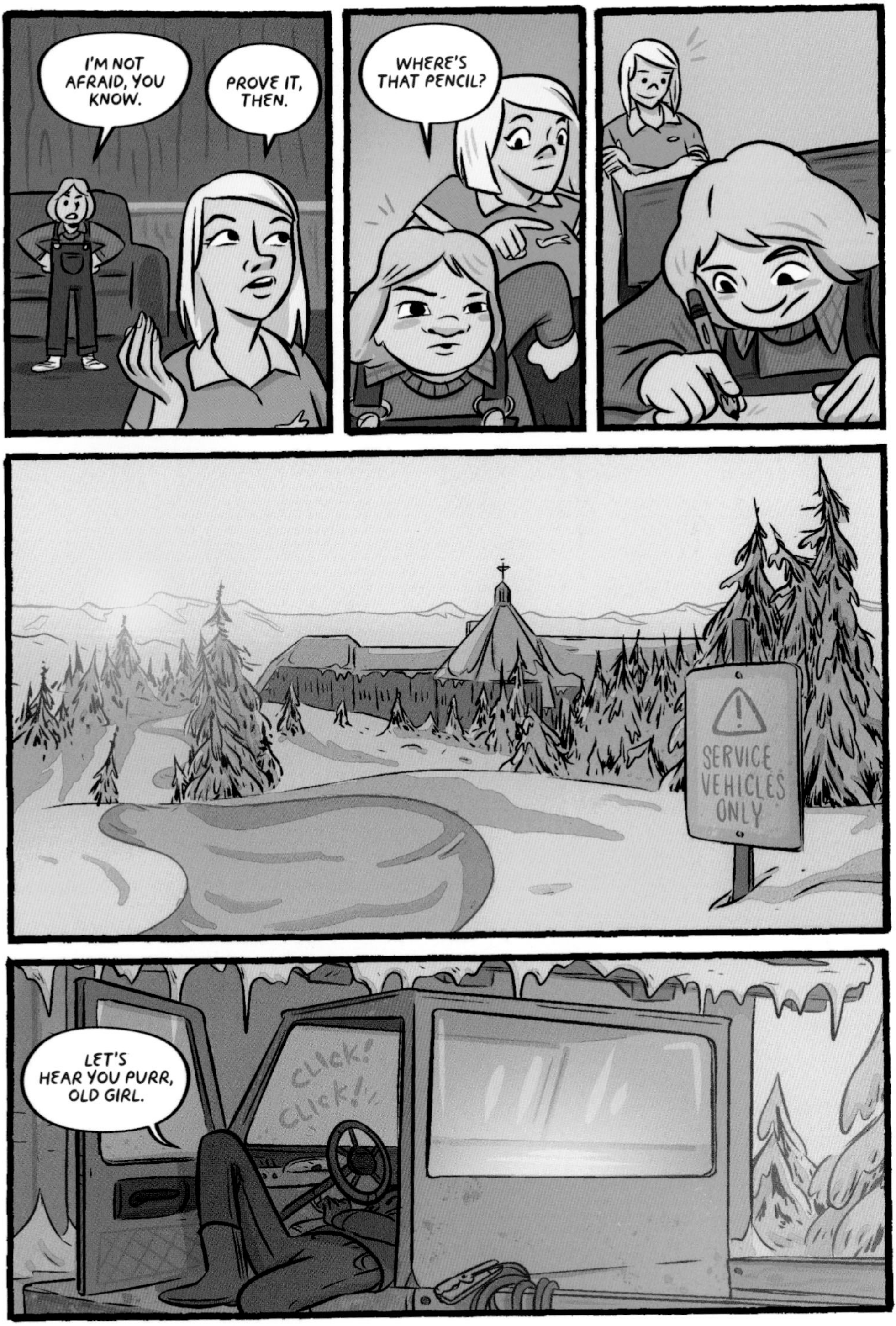
I'M NOT AFRAID, YOU KNOW.
PROVE IT, THEN.
WHERE'S THAT PENCIL?
SERVICE VEHICLES ONLY
LET'S HEAR YOU PURR, OLD GIRL.
CLICK! CLICK!

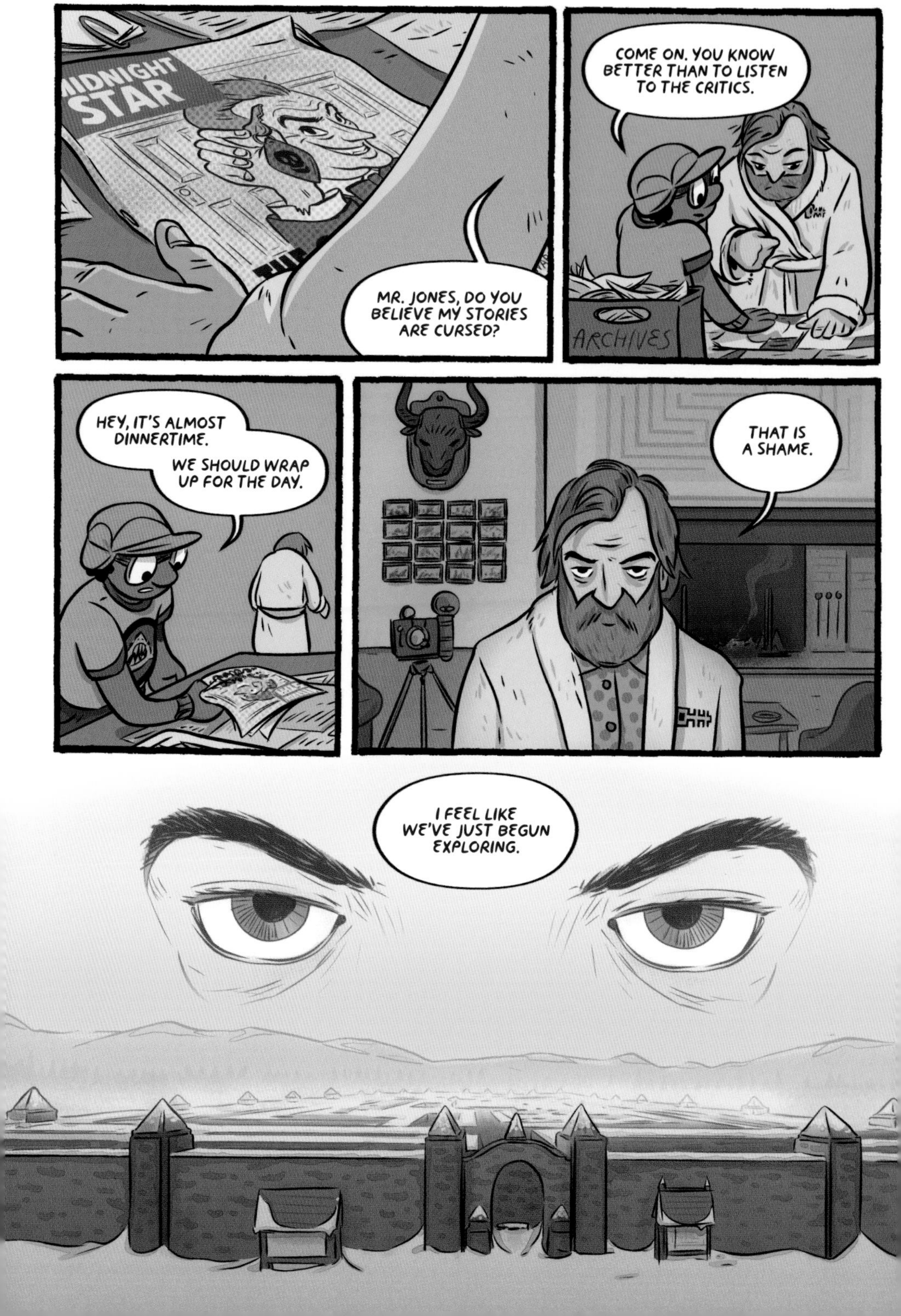
MIDNIGHT STAR
MR. JONES, DO YOU BELIEVE MY STORIES ARE CURSED?
COME ON. YOU KNOW BETTER THAN TO LISTEN TO THE CRITICS.
ARCHIVES
HEY, IT'S ALMOST DINNERTIME.
WE SHOULD WRAP UP FOR THE DAY.
THAT IS A SHAME.
I FEEL LIKE WE'VE JUST BEGUN EXPLORING.

DON'T WORRY, MR. AXWORTH.

WE CAN OPEN MORE DOORS TOMORROW!

BUT I DO WORRY, MR. JONES.

I WORRY SOME OF THESE DOORS CANNOT BE OPENED.

I'LL DO MY BEST, MR. AXWORTH. I PROMISE.

YES, I'M SURE YOU WILL.

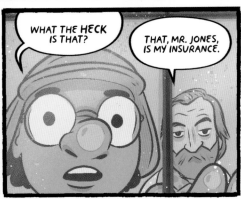

WHAT THE HECK IS THAT?

THAT, MR. JONES, IS MY INSURANCE.

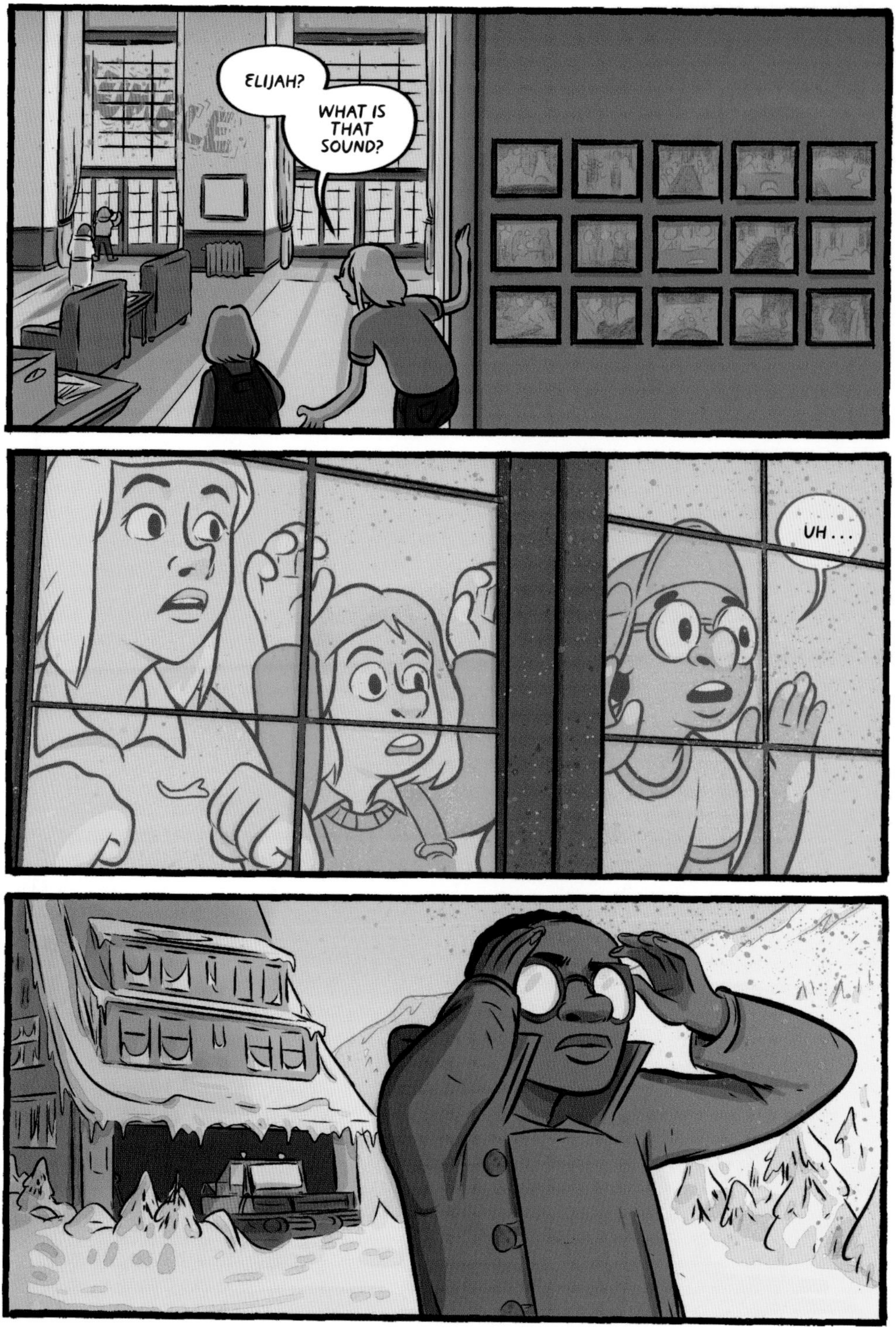
ELIJAH?
WHAT IS THAT SOUND?
UH . . .

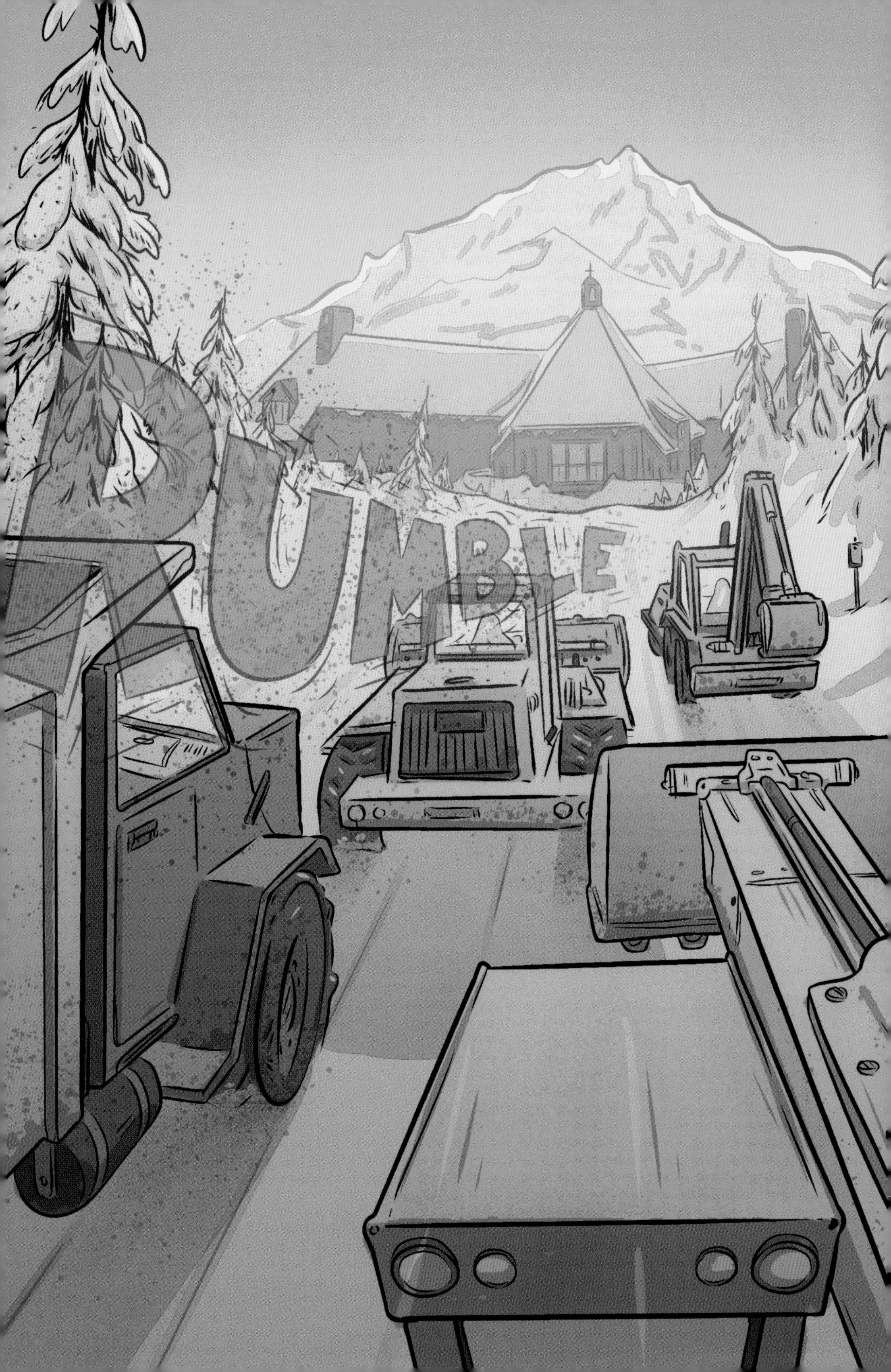
RUMBLE

THE UNDERLOOK HOTEL

ESTES PARK, COLORADO

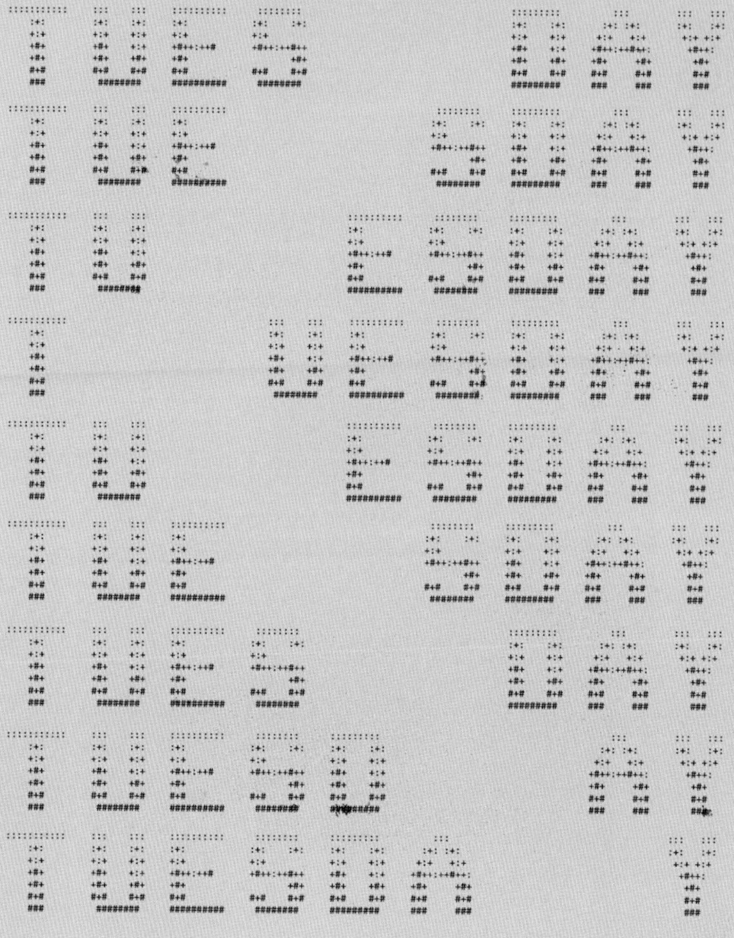
TUES DAY
TUE SDAY
TU ESDAY
T UESDAY
TU ESDAY
TUE SDAY
TUES DAY
TUESD AY
TUESDA Y

101

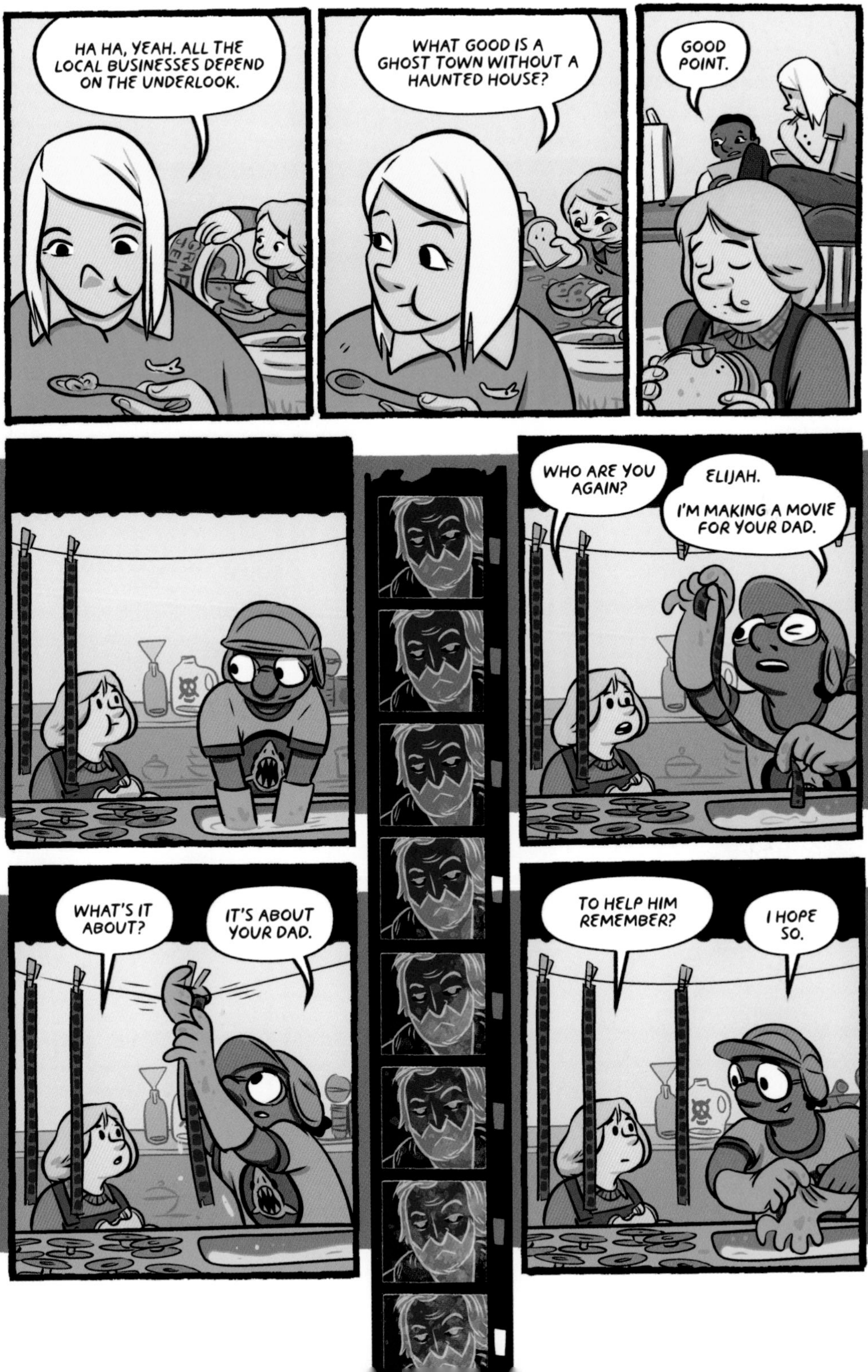
HA HA, YEAH. ALL THE LOCAL BUSINESSES DEPEND ON THE UNDERLOOK.
WHAT GOOD IS A GHOST TOWN WITHOUT A HAUNTED HOUSE?
GOOD POINT.
WHO ARE YOU AGAIN?
ELIJAH.
I'M MAKING A MOVIE FOR YOUR DAD.
WHAT'S IT ABOUT?
IT'S ABOUT YOUR DAD.
TO HELP HIM REMEMBER?
I HOPE SO.

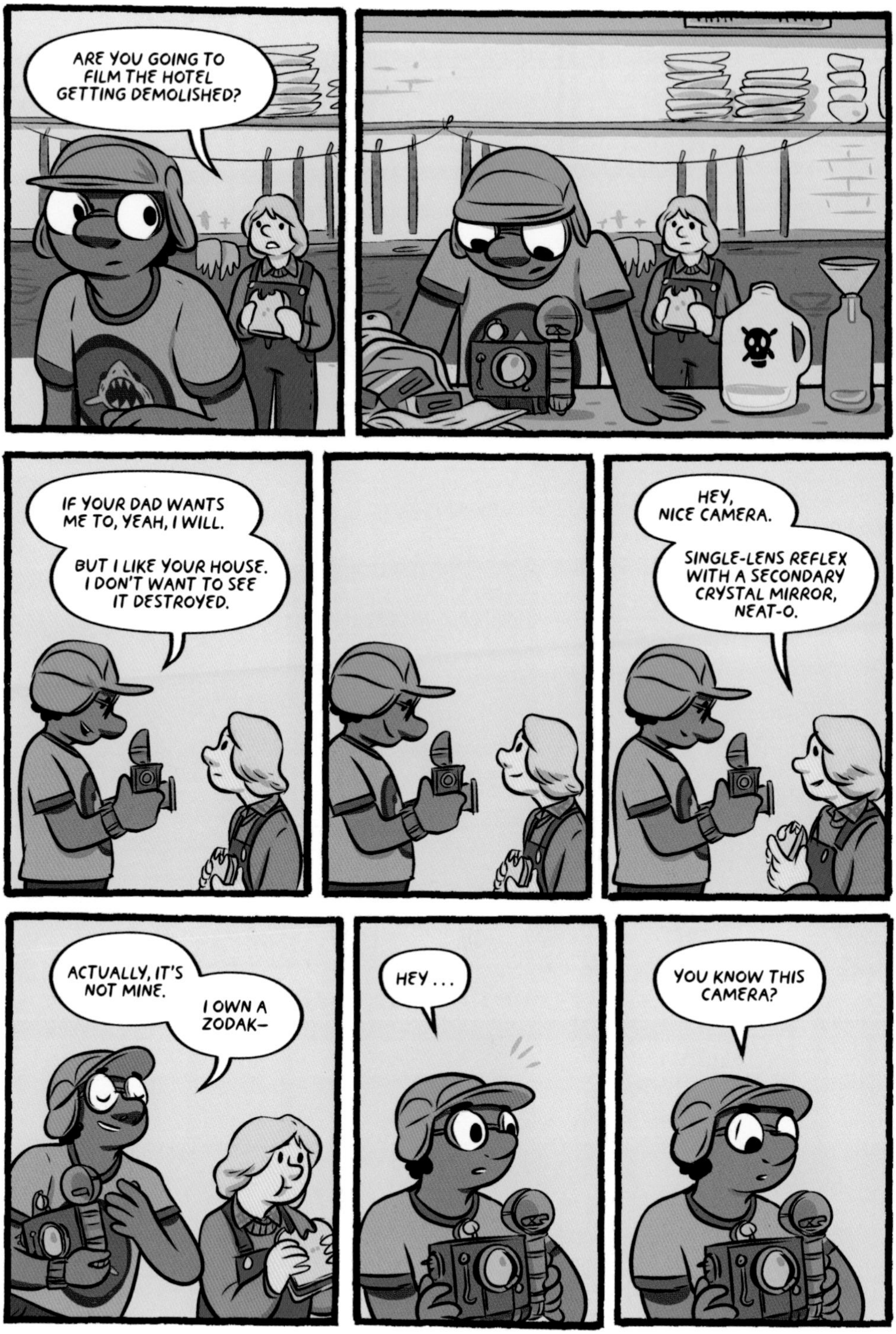

ARE YOU GOING TO FILM THE HOTEL GETTING DEMOLISHED?
IF YOUR DAD WANTS ME TO, YEAH, I WILL.
BUT I LIKE YOUR HOUSE. I DON'T WANT TO SEE IT DESTROYED.
HEY, NICE CAMERA.
SINGLE-LENS REFLEX WITH A SECONDARY CRYSTAL MIRROR, NEAT-O.
ACTUALLY, IT'S NOT MINE.
I OWN A ZODAK–
HEY . . .
YOU KNOW THIS CAMERA?

RENA, CAN DAD REALLY TEAR DOWN THE HOTEL?

ACCORDING TO HIS CONTRACT. HE'S BEEN PLANNING IT FOR A WHILE, APPARENTLY.

WHAT ABOUT HIS CONDITION?

WITHOUT A DOCTOR'S DIAGNOSIS, THE CONTRACT STANDS.

BUT WHY DESTROY OUR HOME?

I DON'T GET IT.

HE MUST HAVE AN OFFER ON THE LAND FROM A DEVELOPMENT COMPANY. THIS LOCATION IS WORTH A FORTUNE.

YOU THINK YOU'VE GOT THIS ALL FIGURED OUT DON'T YOU, MR. HOLMES?

BUT I SEE ALL HIS MAIL. HE'S HAD NO CORRESPONDENCE WITH LAND DEVELOPERS.

THIS ISN'T ABOUT MONEY. HE'S HIDING HIS REAL REASON.

HE'S NOT HIDING IT THAT WELL. I HAVE IT ON TAPE.

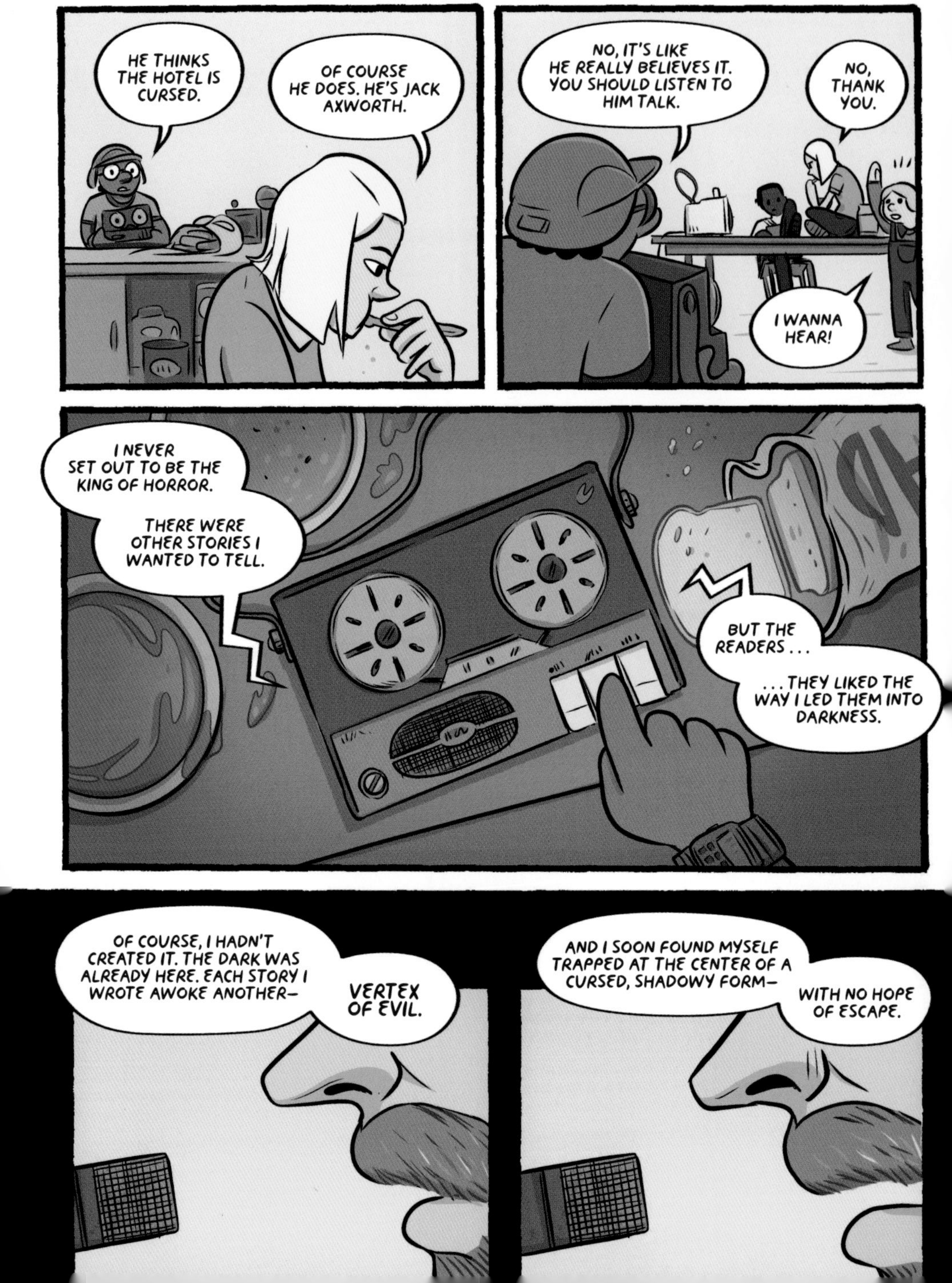
HE THINKS THE HOTEL IS CURSED.
OF COURSE HE DOES. HE'S JACK AXWORTH.
NO, IT'S LIKE HE REALLY BELIEVES IT. YOU SHOULD LISTEN TO HIM TALK.
NO, THANK YOU.
I WANNA HEAR!
I NEVER SET OUT TO BE THE KING OF HORROR.
THERE WERE OTHER STORIES I WANTED TO TELL.
BUT THE READERS . . .
. . . THEY LIKED THE WAY I LED THEM INTO DARKNESS.
OF COURSE, I HADN'T CREATED IT. THE DARK WAS ALREADY HERE. EACH STORY I WROTE AWOKE ANOTHER–
VERTEX OF EVIL.
AND I SOON FOUND MYSELF TRAPPED AT THE CENTER OF A CURSED, SHADOWY FORM–
WITH NO HOPE OF ESCAPE.

WHAT'S A **VORTEX** OF EVIL, ELIJAH?

IT MUST BE, LIKE, A WHIRLPOOL OR SOMETHING. SPINNING HIM AROUND AND AROUND INTO A BLACK HOLE OF TOTAL, ABSOLUTE DARKNESS!

GOD. PLEASE SPARE ME THE METAPHORS.

HE SOUNDS SO DEFEATED.

AND THEN I SAW THIS ON HIS DESK.

OK, SO JACK HAS BEEN READING UP ON HIMSELF—

TRYING TO FILL IN THE BLANKS, ELIJAH.

MIDNIGHT STAR

THE **CURSE** OF THE **UNDERLOOKER**

BY EDWARD BARLOW

107

WHAT IF HE BELIEVES THE CURSE IS REAL?

REAL ENOUGH TO DESTROY THE HOTEL?

COME ON.

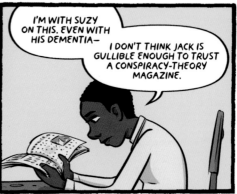

I'M WITH SUZY ON THIS. EVEN WITH HIS DEMENTIA—

I DON'T THINK JACK IS GULLIBLE ENOUGH TO TRUST A CONSPIRACY-THEORY MAGAZINE.

THE ARTICLE ISN'T ABOUT A CONSPIRACY THEORY. THIS IS ONE OF THE MOST INFAMOUS EVENTS IN FILMMAKING HISTORY.

"KING of HORROR"

JACK AXWORTH

AT THE PEAK OF JACK'S CAREER, *THE UNDERLOOKER* WAS ONE OF THE BESTSELLING BOOKS IN THE WORLD.

DIRECTOR

ANXIOUS TO CASH IN ON THE BOOK'S POPULARITY, GLOBAL STUDIOS BOUGHT THE FILM RIGHTS AND RUSHED A MOVIE INTO PRODUCTION.

THE TERRIFYING NO. 1 BESTSELLER

THE UNDERLOOKER

NOW A TERRIFYING MOTION PICTURE

IT WAS A HUGE SUCCESS. EVERYONE GOT RICH.

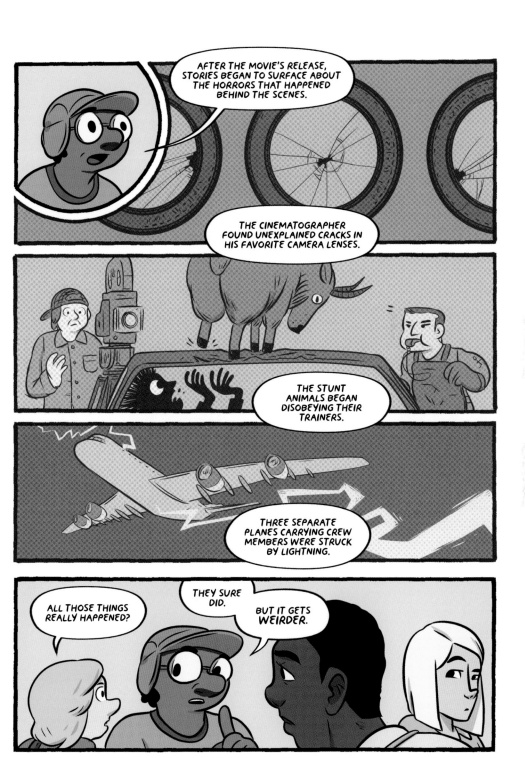

AFTER THE MOVIE'S RELEASE, STORIES BEGAN TO SURFACE ABOUT THE HORRORS THAT HAPPENED BEHIND THE SCENES.

THE CINEMATOGRAPHER FOUND UNEXPLAINED CRACKS IN HIS FAVORITE CAMERA LENSES.

THE STUNT ANIMALS BEGAN DISOBEYING THEIR TRAINERS.

THREE SEPARATE PLANES CARRYING CREW MEMBERS WERE STRUCK BY LIGHTNING.

ALL THOSE THINGS REALLY HAPPENED?

THEY SURE DID.

BUT IT GETS WEIRDER.

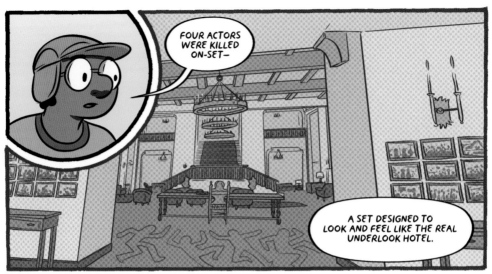

FOUR ACTORS WERE KILLED ON-SET—

A SET DESIGNED TO LOOK AND FEEL LIKE THE REAL UNDERLOOK HOTEL.

"THE EVIL EVOKED BY JACK AXWORTH'S WORDS WAS SO POWERFUL THAT IT CURSED A WHOLE MOVIE PRODUCTION."

JACK'S REALLY GOT A WAY WITH WORDS, HUH?

IT'S OBVIOUS THIS GLOBAL STUDIOS WAS IGNORING SAFETY PRECAUTIONS AND USING JACK AS A SCAPEGOAT.

PROBABLY. BUT THE MAGAZINE STILL SOLD A TON OF COPIES.

JACK WAS BLACKLISTED IN HOLLYWOOD, AND EVEN HIS PUBLISHER STOPPED PRINTING HIS BOOKS.

I CAN'T BELIEVE PEOPLE BELIEVE THIS JUNK.

COME ON, SUZY. EVERYONE IS SUPERSTITIOUS.

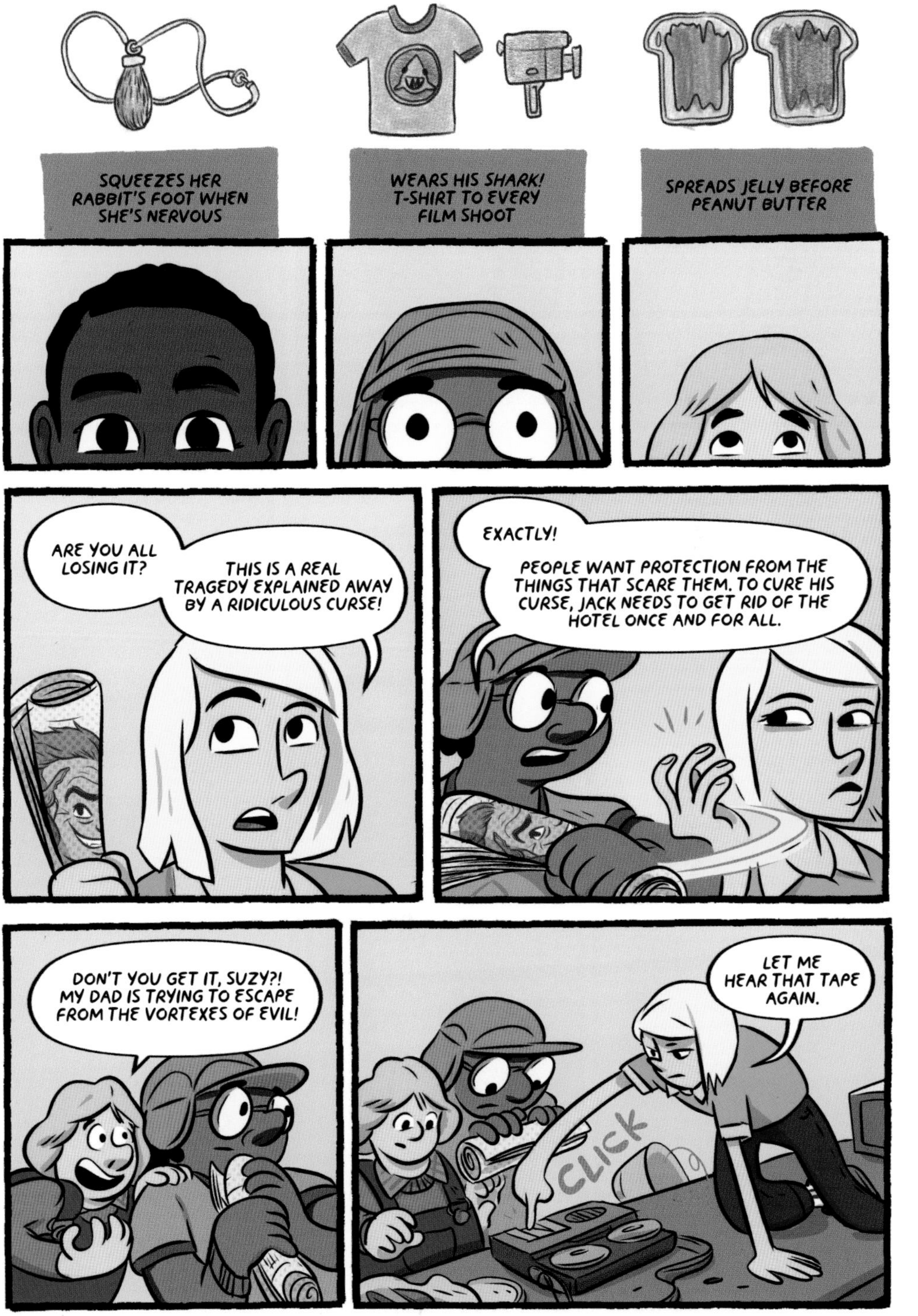
SQUEEZES HER RABBIT'S FOOT WHEN SHE'S NERVOUS
WEARS HIS SHARK! T-SHIRT TO EVERY FILM SHOOT
SPREADS JELLY BEFORE PEANUT BUTTER
ARE YOU ALL LOSING IT?
THIS IS A REAL TRAGEDY EXPLAINED AWAY BY A RIDICULOUS CURSE!
EXACTLY!
PEOPLE WANT PROTECTION FROM THE THINGS THAT SCARE THEM. TO CURE HIS CURSE, JACK NEEDS TO GET RID OF THE HOTEL ONCE AND FOR ALL.
DON'T YOU GET IT, SUZY?! MY DAD IS TRYING TO ESCAPE FROM THE VORTEXES OF EVIL!
LET ME HEAR THAT TAPE AGAIN.
CLICK

"AWOKE ANOTHER VERTEX OF EVIL—"

AH! THERE! HE'S NOT SAYING "VORTEX." HE'S SAYING "VERTEX."

CLICK

VERTEX, VORTEX.

SAME DIFFERENCE.

ACTUALLY, THERE'S A BIG DIFFERENCE.

VERTEX IS A MATHEMATICAL TERM.

HE MUST BE TALKING ABOUT THE VERTICES OF THE HALCYON TRIANGLE.

THE WHAT?

OH WOW. I THOUGHT YOU WERE A FAN, ELIJAH.

I COULD SHOW YOU ON A MAP, BUT—

OH!

I GOT ONE AT THE AIRPORT GIFT SHOP.

YETI'S MAP!

PERFECT.

YETI'S MAP!

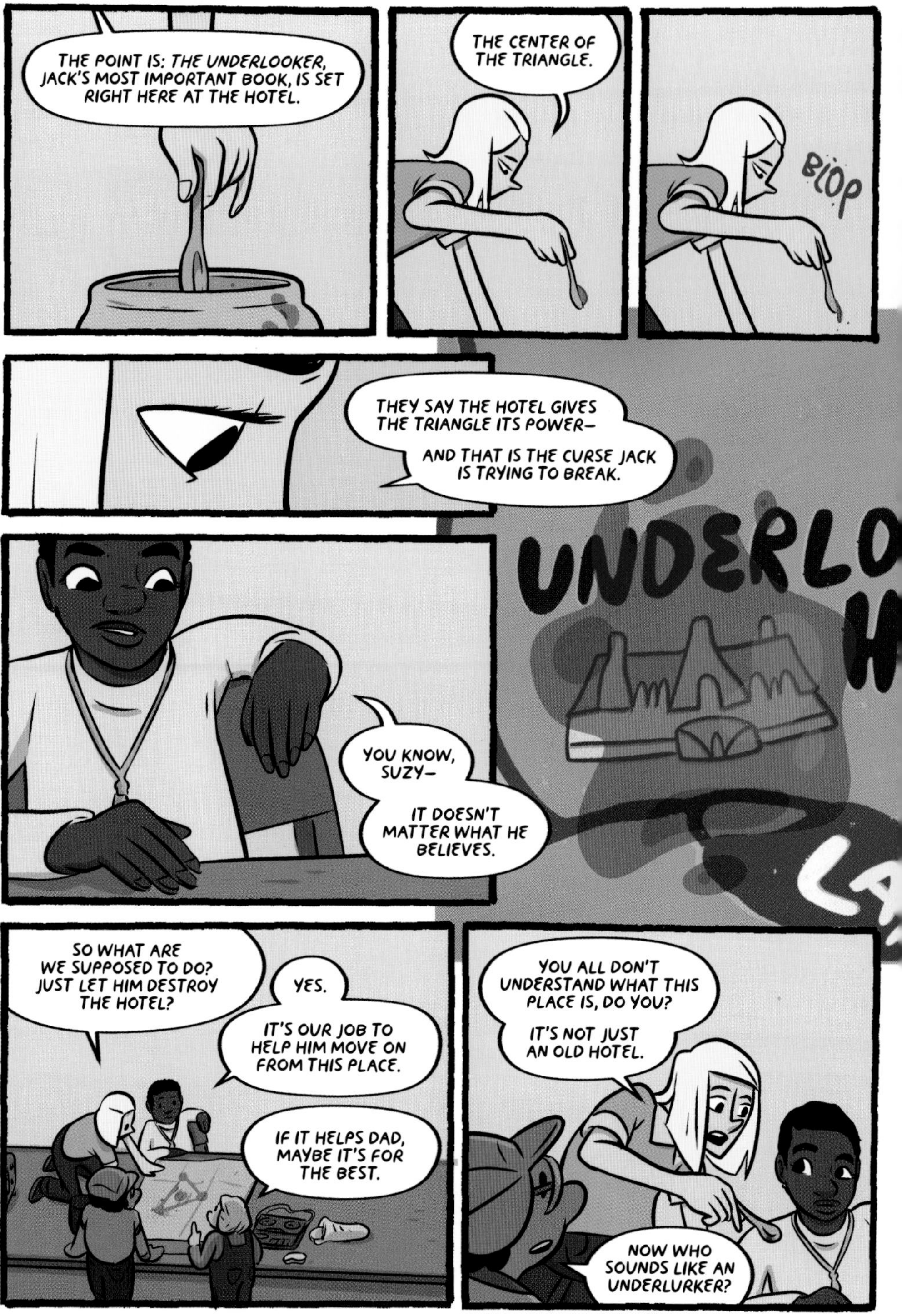
THE POINT IS: THE UNDERLOOKER, JACK'S MOST IMPORTANT BOOK, IS SET RIGHT HERE AT THE HOTEL.
THE CENTER OF THE TRIANGLE.
BLOP
THEY SAY THE HOTEL GIVES THE TRIANGLE ITS POWER—
AND THAT IS THE CURSE JACK IS TRYING TO BREAK.
UNDERLO
H
YOU KNOW, SUZY—
IT DOESN'T MATTER WHAT HE BELIEVES.
SO WHAT ARE WE SUPPOSED TO DO? JUST LET HIM DESTROY THE HOTEL?
YES.
IT'S OUR JOB TO HELP HIM MOVE ON FROM THIS PLACE.
IF IT HELPS DAD, MAYBE IT'S FOR THE BEST.
YOU ALL DON'T UNDERSTAND WHAT THIS PLACE IS, DO YOU?
IT'S NOT JUST AN OLD HOTEL.
NOW WHO SOUNDS LIKE AN UNDERLURKER?

THE HALCYON TRIANGLE GIVES THE UNDERLOOK A PURPOSE.

AN EVIL PURPOSE, BUT A PURPOSE.

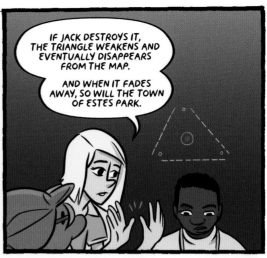

IF JACK DESTROYS IT, THE TRIANGLE WEAKENS AND EVENTUALLY DISAPPEARS FROM THE MAP.

AND WHEN IT FADES AWAY, SO WILL THE TOWN OF ESTES PARK.

YOU'RE WRONG, SUZY. PEOPLE WILL COME BACK FOR THE—

THE GREAT VIEW, YEAH? THE FISHING, THE SKIING, YEAH?

SO THAT MEANS YOU'LL BE BACK, RIGHT?

I DIDN'T THINK SO.

FRIEND.

YOU KNOW WHY I'M GOOD AT ENGINEERING?

IT'S NOT 'CAUSE I KNOW HOW TO PUT THINGS TOGETHER.

IT'S 'CAUSE I KNOW HOW THINGS FALL APART.

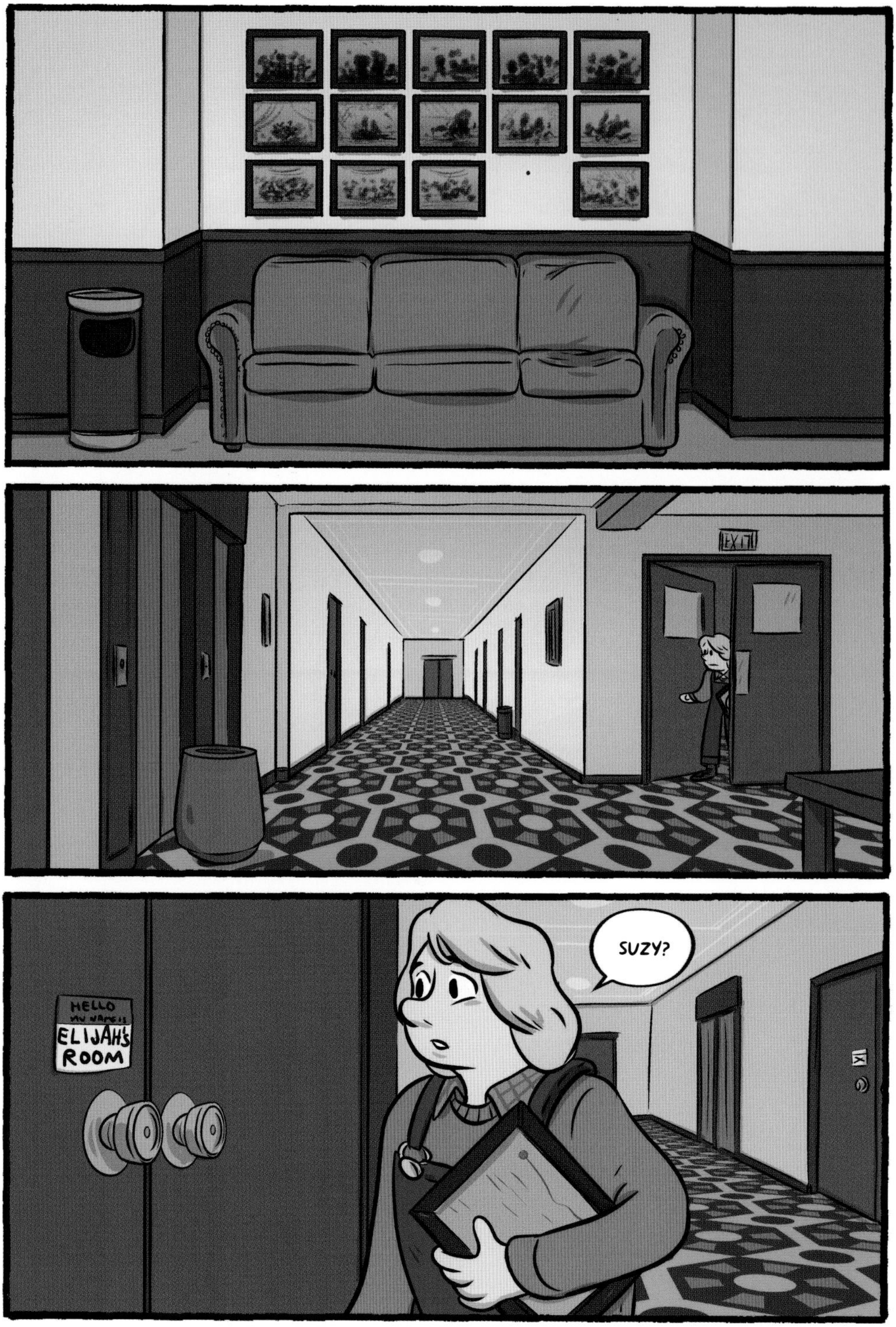
HELLO
ELIJAH'S ROOM
SUZY?

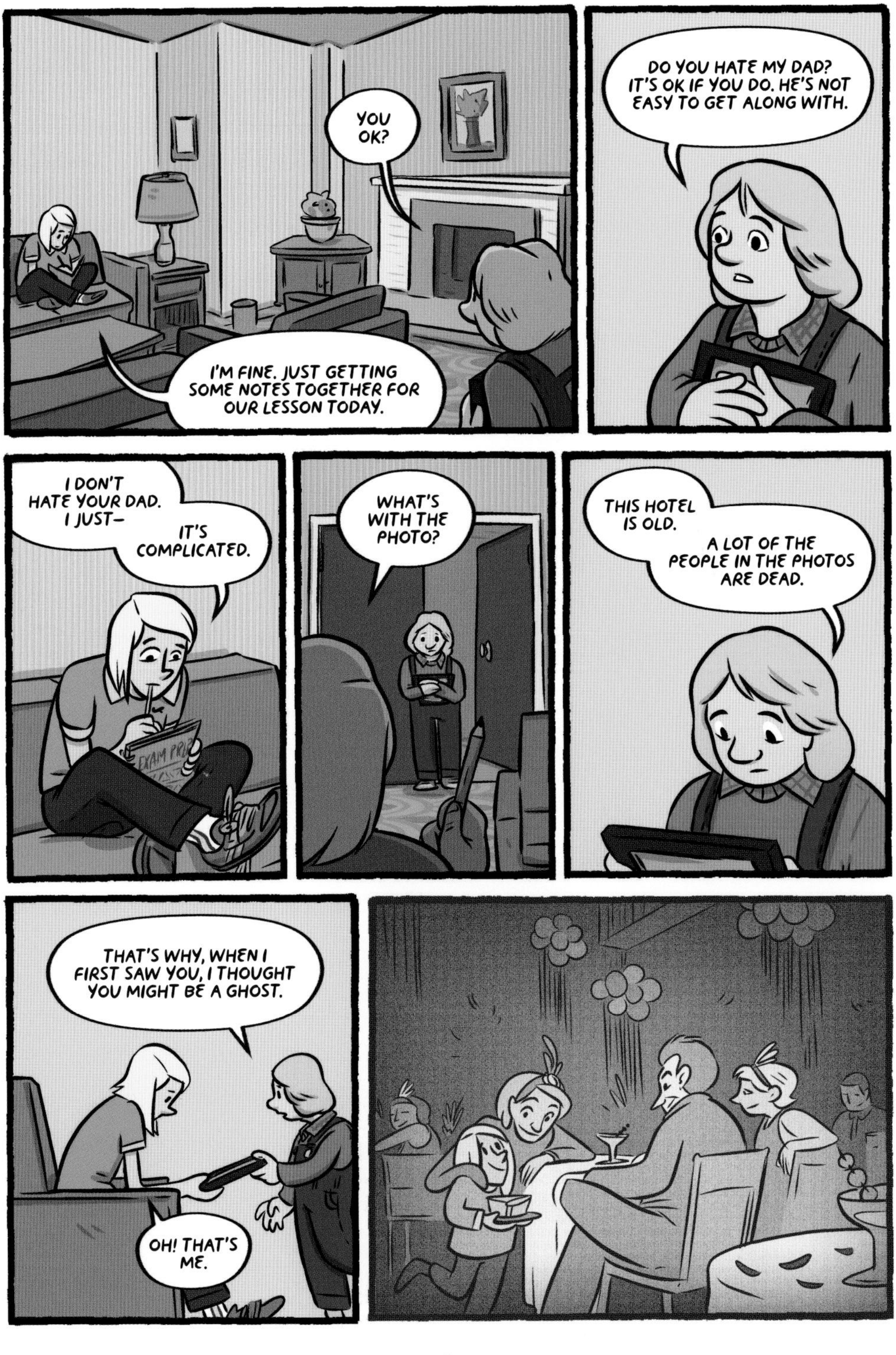
YOU OK?
I'M FINE. JUST GETTING SOME NOTES TOGETHER FOR OUR LESSON TODAY.
DO YOU HATE MY DAD? IT'S OK IF YOU DO. HE'S NOT EASY TO GET ALONG WITH.
I DON'T HATE YOUR DAD. I JUST—
IT'S COMPLICATED.
EXAM PREP
WHAT'S WITH THE PHOTO?
THIS HOTEL IS OLD.
A LOT OF THE PEOPLE IN THE PHOTOS ARE DEAD.
THAT'S WHY, WHEN I FIRST SAW YOU, I THOUGHT YOU MIGHT BE A GHOST.
OH! THAT'S ME.

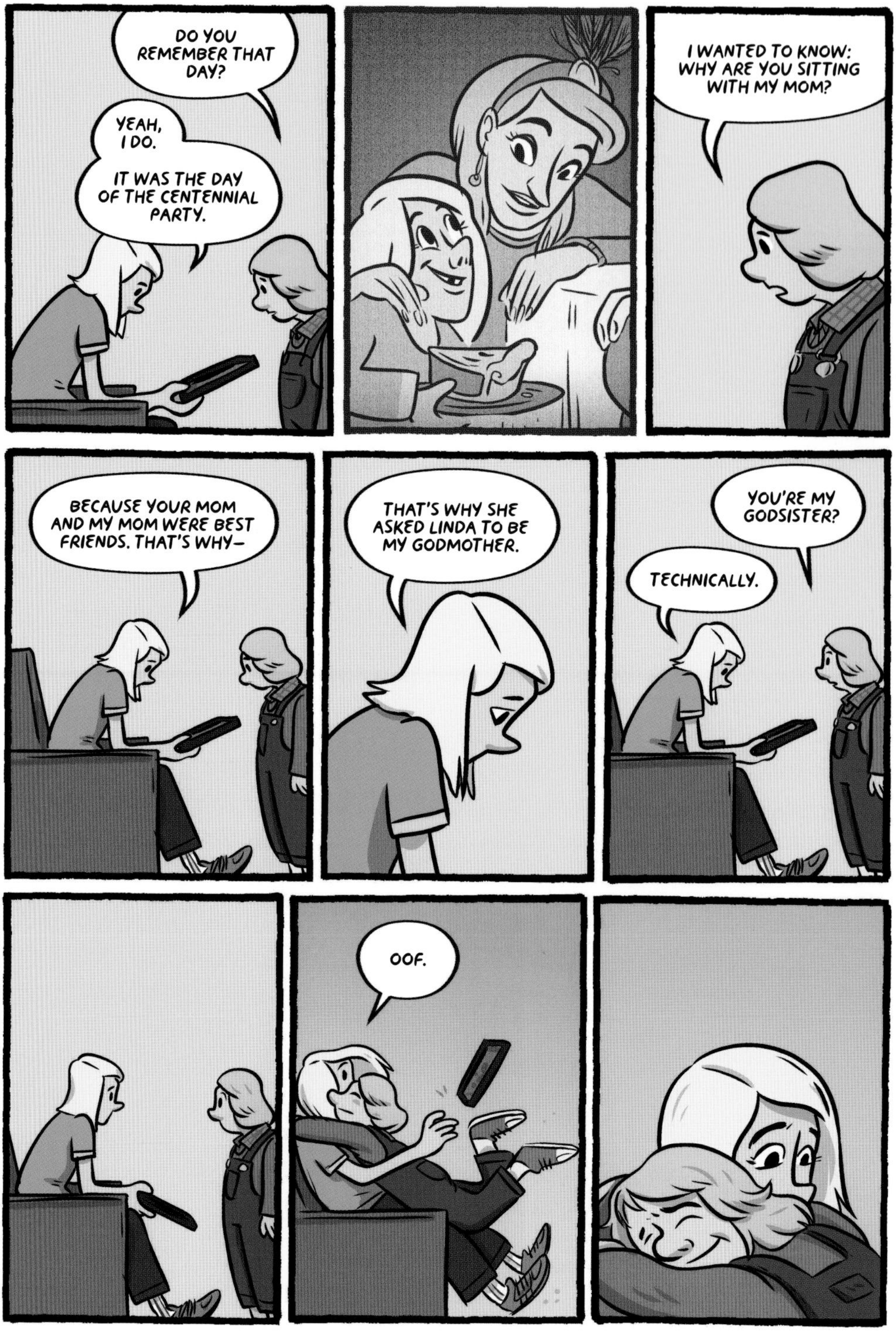
DO YOU REMEMBER THAT DAY?
YEAH, I DO.
IT WAS THE DAY OF THE CENTENNIAL PARTY.
I WANTED TO KNOW: WHY ARE YOU SITTING WITH MY MOM?
BECAUSE YOUR MOM AND MY MOM WERE BEST FRIENDS. THAT'S WHY—
THAT'S WHY SHE ASKED LINDA TO BE MY GODMOTHER.
YOU'RE MY GODSISTER?
TECHNICALLY.
OOF.

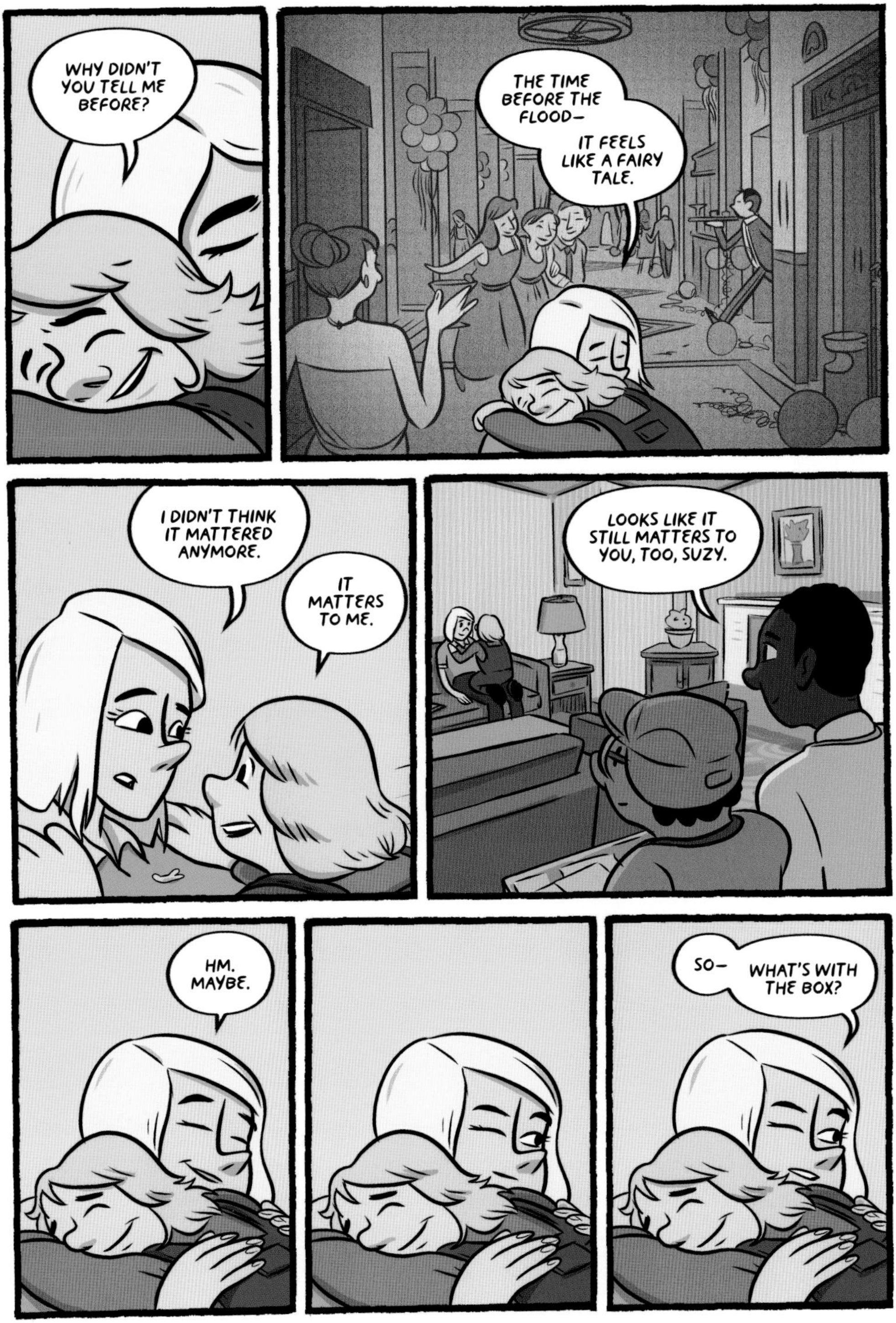
WHY DIDN'T YOU TELL ME BEFORE?
THE TIME BEFORE THE FLOOD—
IT FEELS LIKE A FAIRY TALE.
I DIDN'T THINK IT MATTERED ANYMORE.
IT MATTERS TO ME.
LOOKS LIKE IT STILL MATTERS TO YOU, TOO, SUZY.
HM. MAYBE.
SO—
WHAT'S WITH THE BOX?

YEAH, THE BOX—

AH, WE WERE DISCUSSING WHAT YOU SAID—

AND, UM, RENA?

WELL, IT JUST SO HAPPENS JACK'S BEEN GETTING A LOT OF MAIL LATELY . . .

. . . FROM PEOPLE WHO SHARE YOUR PARTICULAR CONCERN.

REALLY?

WHAT KIND OF PEOPLE?

PEOPLE WHO, UH, ARE INVESTED IN THE HOTEL'S HISTORY.

PEOPLE LIKE YOU.

HOLD ON . . .

THIS MAIL ISN'T FROM PEOPLE—

IT'S FROM **UNDERLURKERS.**

THAT'S TRUE.

AND NORMALLY THIS KIND OF MAIL GOES RIGHT INTO THE BOILER.

BUT YOU GOT ME THINKING, SUZY . . .

OOOH, CREEPY!

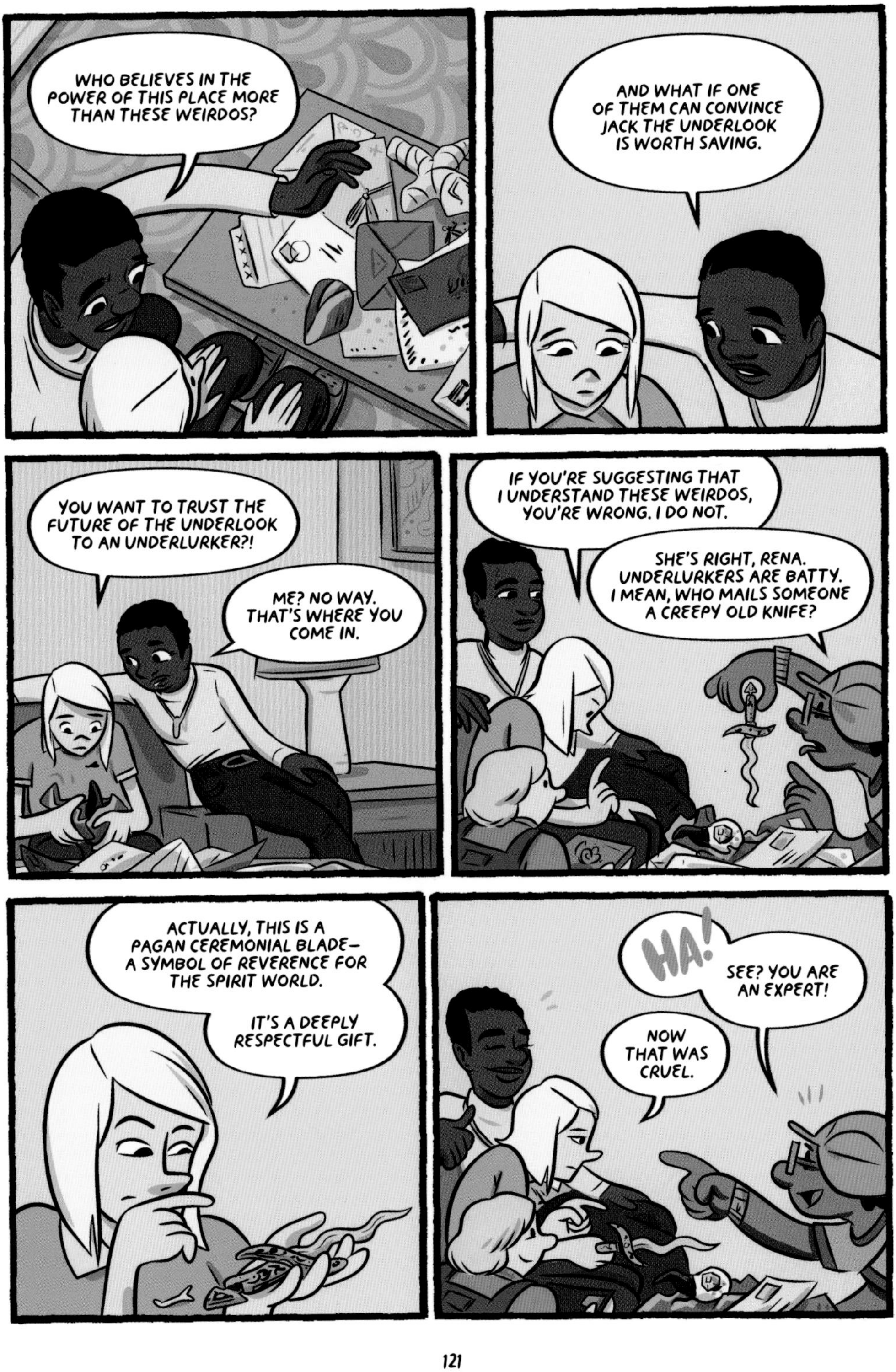
WHO BELIEVES IN THE POWER OF THIS PLACE MORE THAN THESE WEIRDOS?
AND WHAT IF ONE OF THEM CAN CONVINCE JACK THE UNDERLOOK IS WORTH SAVING.
YOU WANT TO TRUST THE FUTURE OF THE UNDERLOOK TO AN UNDERLURKER?!
ME? NO WAY. THAT'S WHERE YOU COME IN.
IF YOU'RE SUGGESTING THAT I UNDERSTAND THESE WEIRDOS, YOU'RE WRONG. I DO NOT.
SHE'S RIGHT, RENA. UNDERLURKERS ARE BATTY. I MEAN, WHO MAILS SOMEONE A CREEPY OLD KNIFE?
ACTUALLY, THIS IS A PAGAN CEREMONIAL BLADE—A SYMBOL OF REVERENCE FOR THE SPIRIT WORLD.
IT'S A DEEPLY RESPECTFUL GIFT.
HA!
SEE? YOU ARE AN EXPERT!
NOW THAT WAS CRUEL.

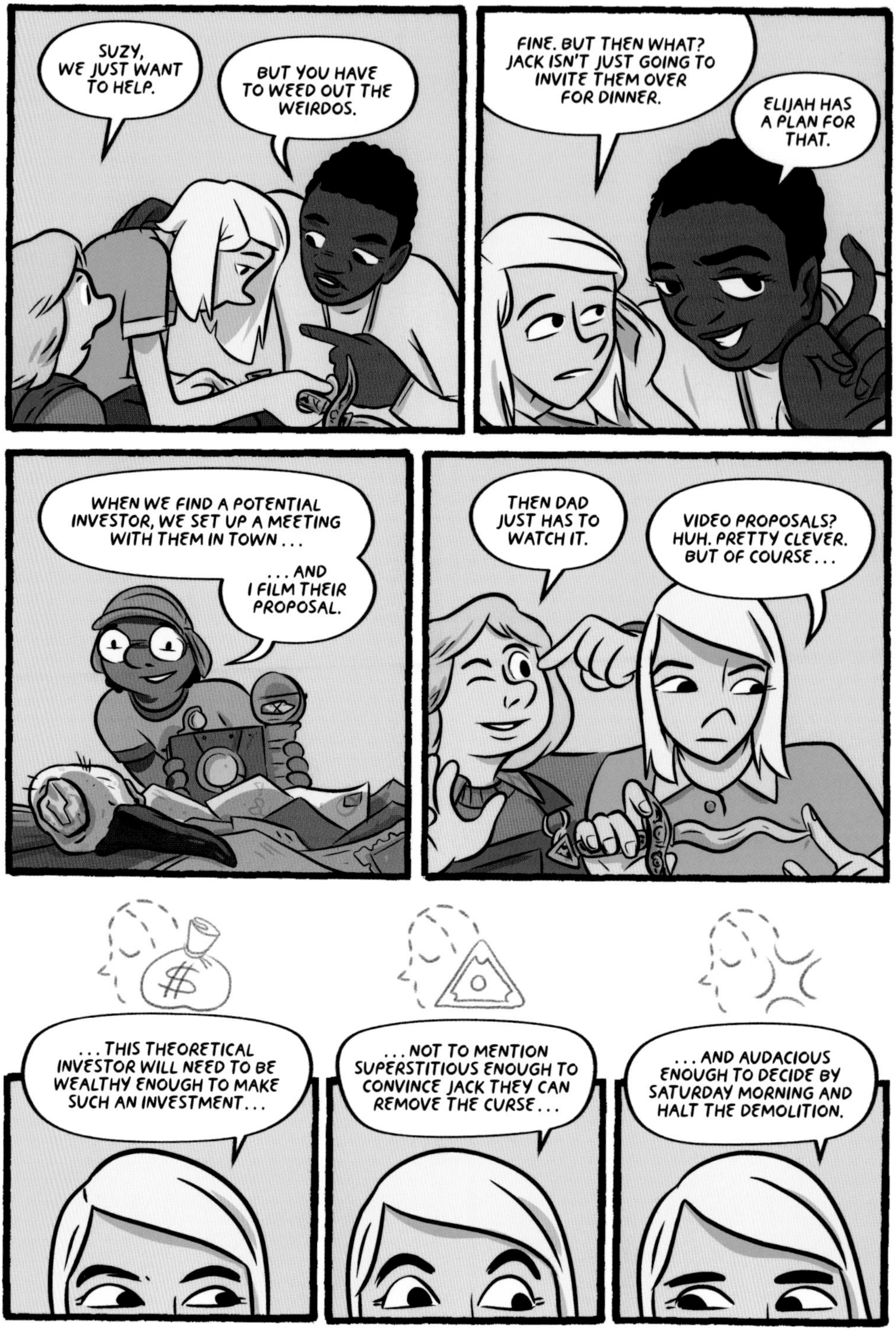
SUZY, WE JUST WANT TO HELP.
BUT YOU HAVE TO WEED OUT THE WEIRDOS.
FINE. BUT THEN WHAT? JACK ISN'T JUST GOING TO INVITE THEM OVER FOR DINNER.
ELIJAH HAS A PLAN FOR THAT.
WHEN WE FIND A POTENTIAL INVESTOR, WE SET UP A MEETING WITH THEM IN TOWN . . .
. . . AND I FILM THEIR PROPOSAL.
THEN DAD JUST HAS TO WATCH IT.
VIDEO PROPOSALS? HUH. PRETTY CLEVER. BUT OF COURSE . . .
. . . THIS THEORETICAL INVESTOR WILL NEED TO BE WEALTHY ENOUGH TO MAKE SUCH AN INVESTMENT . . .
. . . NOT TO MENTION SUPERSTITIOUS ENOUGH TO CONVINCE JACK THEY CAN REMOVE THE CURSE . . .
. . . AND AUDACIOUS ENOUGH TO DECIDE BY SATURDAY MORNING AND HALT THE DEMOLITION.

IMPROBABLE BUT NOT IMPOSSIBLE.

LET'S GET TO WORK.

WOOO! THIS IS GONNA BE SO—

NOT YOU.

YOU HAVE AN ESSAY TO WRITE.

CAN I AT LEAST OPEN ONE LITTLE LETTER?

NO.

COME ON, SUZY. DON'T BE DULL.

JUST ONE LITTLE LETTER, SUZY?

ARE YOU HIS TUTOR, ELIJAH? NO, YOU'RE NOT!

THANK YOU FOR YOUR TIME, MR. LUTHOR.

SO WHAT'D YOU THINK, SUZY?

THAT MAN IS PURE EVIL. AND NOT THE GOOD KIND.

HE OWNS A CASINO IN LAS VEGAS!

HE MUST HAVE THE MONEY TO SAVE A DOZEN UNDERLOOK HOTELS.

HE DOESN'T CARE ABOUT THE HOTEL. HE WANTS THE LAND. BEFORE WE KNOW IT, HE'LL BE BUILDING A CONVENTION CENTER OR CORPORATE RESORT OR EVEN AN AIRPORT.

TRUST ME, THAT IS NO UNDERLURKER.

127

APPARENTLY SHE'S THE CEO OF COOKIE CASTLE.

I LOVE COOKIE CASTLE!

RICH AND NOSTALGIC— GREAT COMBINATION.

LET'S HOPE SHE'S SENSIBLE, TOO—

WE'RE MEETING AT HER HOUSE.

TAXI!

HELLO AGAIN!

HEY, MOVIE KID. WHERE TO?

NINETEEN AVALON DRIVE.

I CAN SEE WHY MR. AXWORTH WOULD SEND YOU TO NEGOTIATE WITH ME.

WHAT A CUTE CREW Y'ALL ARE!

YEAH, JACK SURE TRUSTS US.

AW, I'M SURE Y'ALL LOVE HIS HOTEL.

HEH, I MEAN, WHO DOESN'T?

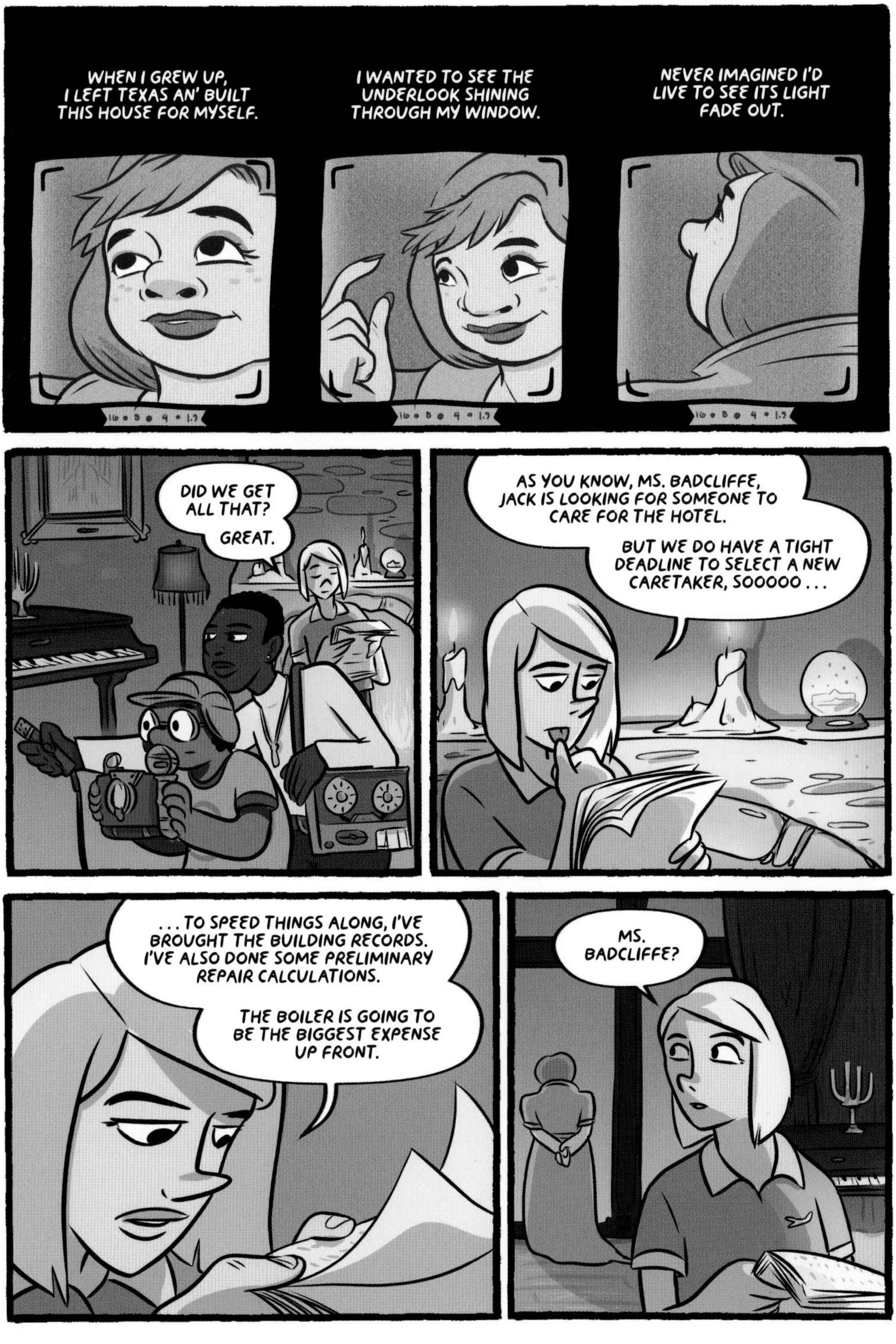
WHEN I GREW UP, I LEFT TEXAS AN' BUILT THIS HOUSE FOR MYSELF.
I WANTED TO SEE THE UNDERLOOK SHINING THROUGH MY WINDOW.
NEVER IMAGINED I'D LIVE TO SEE ITS LIGHT FADE OUT.
DID WE GET ALL THAT?
GREAT.
AS YOU KNOW, MS. BADCLIFFE, JACK IS LOOKING FOR SOMEONE TO CARE FOR THE HOTEL.
BUT WE DO HAVE A TIGHT DEADLINE TO SELECT A NEW CARETAKER, SOOOOO . . .
. . . TO SPEED THINGS ALONG, I'VE BROUGHT THE BUILDING RECORDS. I'VE ALSO DONE SOME PRELIMINARY REPAIR CALCULATIONS.
THE BOILER IS GOING TO BE THE BIGGEST EXPENSE UP FRONT.
MS. BADCLIFFE?

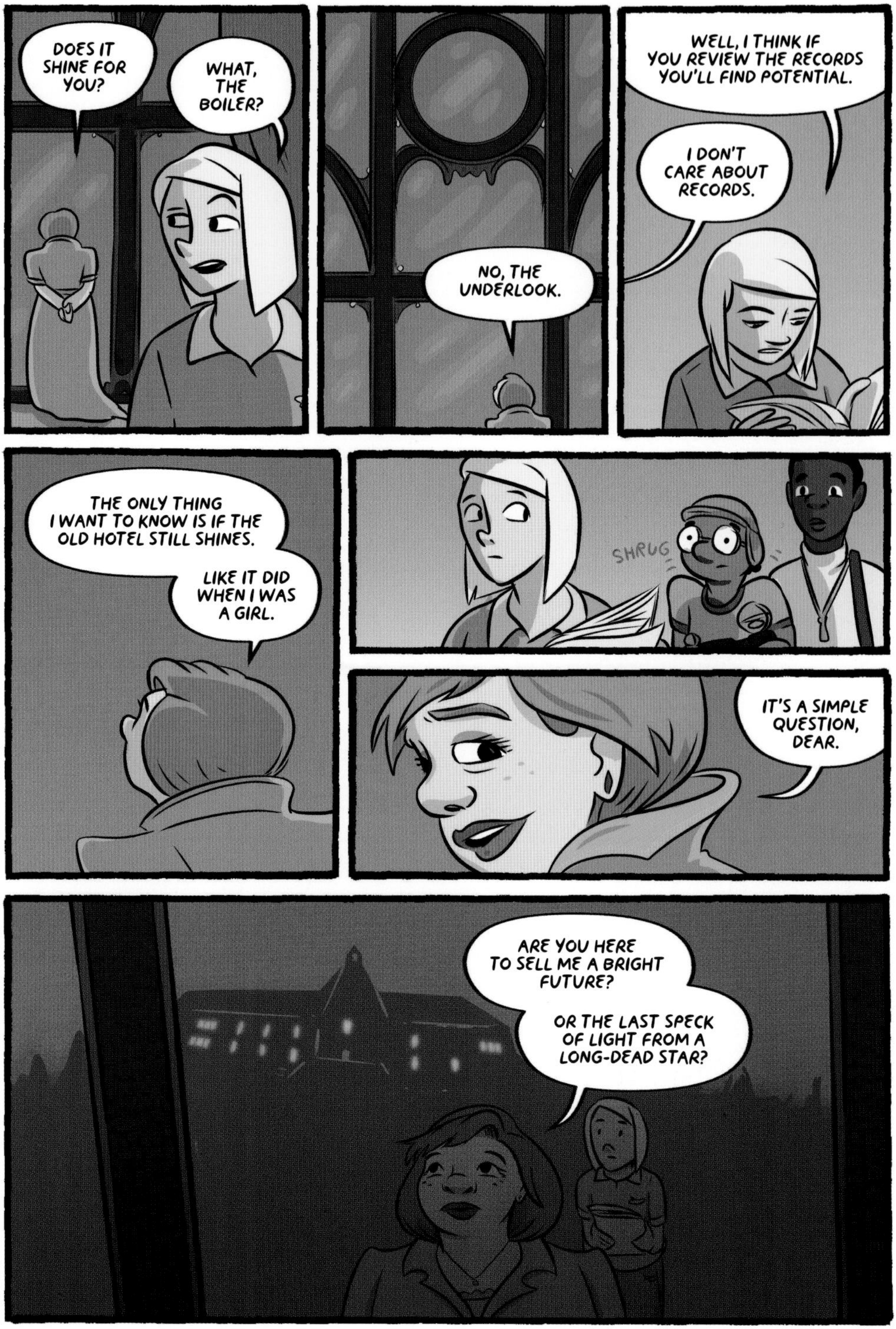

DOES IT SHINE FOR YOU?
WHAT, THE BOILER?
NO, THE UNDERLOOK.
WELL, I THINK IF YOU REVIEW THE RECORDS YOU'LL FIND POTENTIAL.
I DON'T CARE ABOUT RECORDS.
THE ONLY THING I WANT TO KNOW IS IF THE OLD HOTEL STILL SHINES.
LIKE IT DID WHEN I WAS A GIRL.
SHRUG
IT'S A SIMPLE QUESTION, DEAR.
ARE YOU HERE TO SELL ME A BRIGHT FUTURE?
OR THE LAST SPECK OF LIGHT FROM A LONG-DEAD STAR?

SUZY—

FORGET ABOUT THE COOKIE LADY.

BUT SHE'S RIGHT. THEY'RE ALL RIGHT!

NO MATTER HOW I DO THE MATH, THE HOTEL IS A HORRIBLE INVESTMENT.

WUMP!

CRUNCH

ANY REASONABLE PERSON WOULD BULLDOZE IT AND START OVER.

THEN WE FIND SOMEONE UNREASONABLE.

YOU KNOW THEY'RE OUT THERE.

WE JUST HAVE TO KEEP LOOKING.

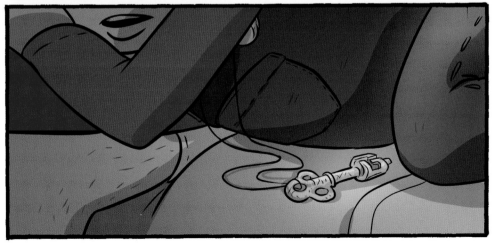

THE
UNDERLOOK HOTEL
ESTES PARK, COLORADO

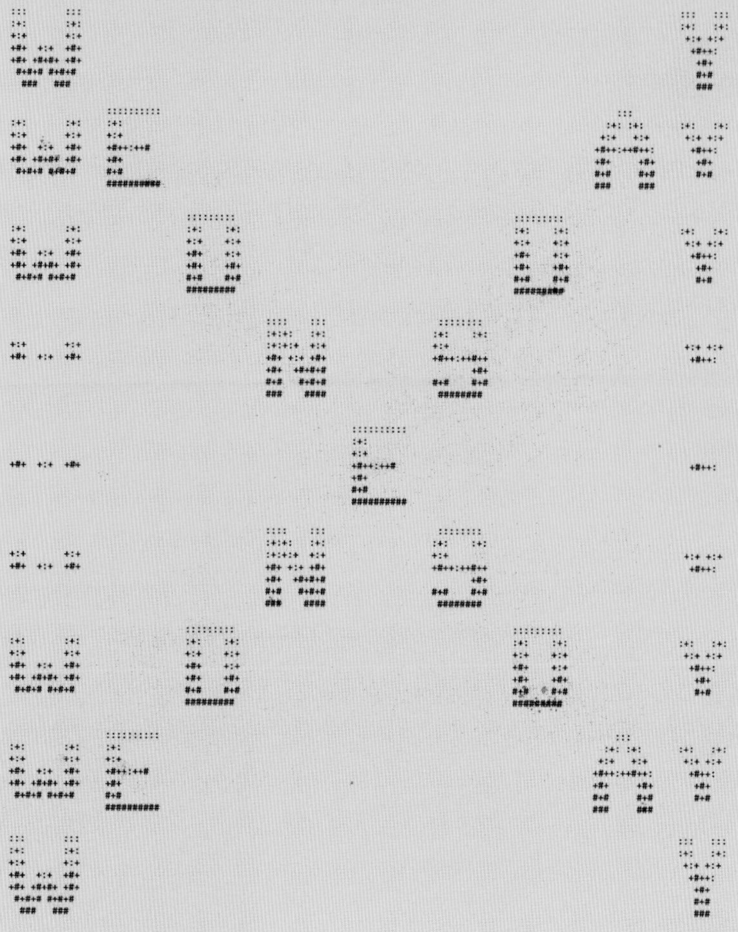

GOOD MORNING, TUTOR.

OR SHOULD I CALL YOU GOD-DAUGHTER?

DANNY TOLD YOU, I ASSUME?

HE DID.

I WAS HOPING THAT BEFORE YOU STARTED YOUR DAY, YOU'D HELP ME RECLAIM A MEMORY OF OUR TIME TOGETHER.

OK.

MAKE IT QUICK.

DID YOU AND I EVER WALK THE LABYRINTH TOGETHER?

YOU MEAN THE OLD HEDGE MAZE?

NOT A MAZE— A LABYRINTH.

16 • SAME DIFFERENCE.

NO.

16 • 8 • 4 • 1.7

A MAZE IS A LOGIC PUZZLE. A LABYRINTH IS SIMPLY A PATH; IT HAS NO SOLUTION.

16 • THEN WHAT'S THE POINT?

THE POINT IS TO WANDER.

16 • 8 • 4 • 1.7

NO, WE NEVER WANDERED TOGETHER.

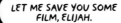

THANK GOD! I'M STARVING.

HOW'S IT GOING?

JUST FINISHED SORTING THE LATEST BATCH OF PROPOSAL LETTERS.

WEIRDER

WEIRDEST

TOO WEIRD

AND IT'S NOT IDEAL.

SUZY, I WANT TO LOOK AT THE LETTERS, TOO.

NOT UNTIL YOU FINISH YOUR ESSAY.

AND STOP EATING THOSE COOKIES.

HERE, HAVE A SANDWICH.

HOW AM I SUPPOSED TO WRITE ABOUT MYSELF . . .

VERY INSIGHTFUL, DR. RUBRIK. THANK YOU FOR YOUR TIME.

AFTER THE BREAK, WE WILL TALK WITH SOME SPIRITED LOCALS PLANNING THE BIGGEST PARTY ESTES PARK HAS SEEN IN YEARS.

MR. AXWORTH, IF YOU'RE LISTENING, PLEASE, IT IS IMPERATIVE THAT WE MEET. I'M STAYING AT THE DROWSY MOOSE—

NED! GO TO COMMERCIAL!

HE'S A GENIUS.

AHA! I KNEW I RECOGNIZED HIS NAME! LISTEN TO THIS:

"MR. AXWORTH, I AM ONCE AGAIN WRITING TO REQUEST AN OPPORTUNITY TO STUDY YOUR UNCANNY HOTEL.

"IF MY SUSPICIONS ARE TRUE, WE DO NOT HAVE MUCH TIME."

WELL, THAT'S OMINOUS.

RENA! THIS IS OUR GUY!

YOU THINK HE'LL WANT TO BUY THE HOTEL?

I DON'T KNOW. BUT HE'S THE ONLY ONE WHO CAN CURE IT.

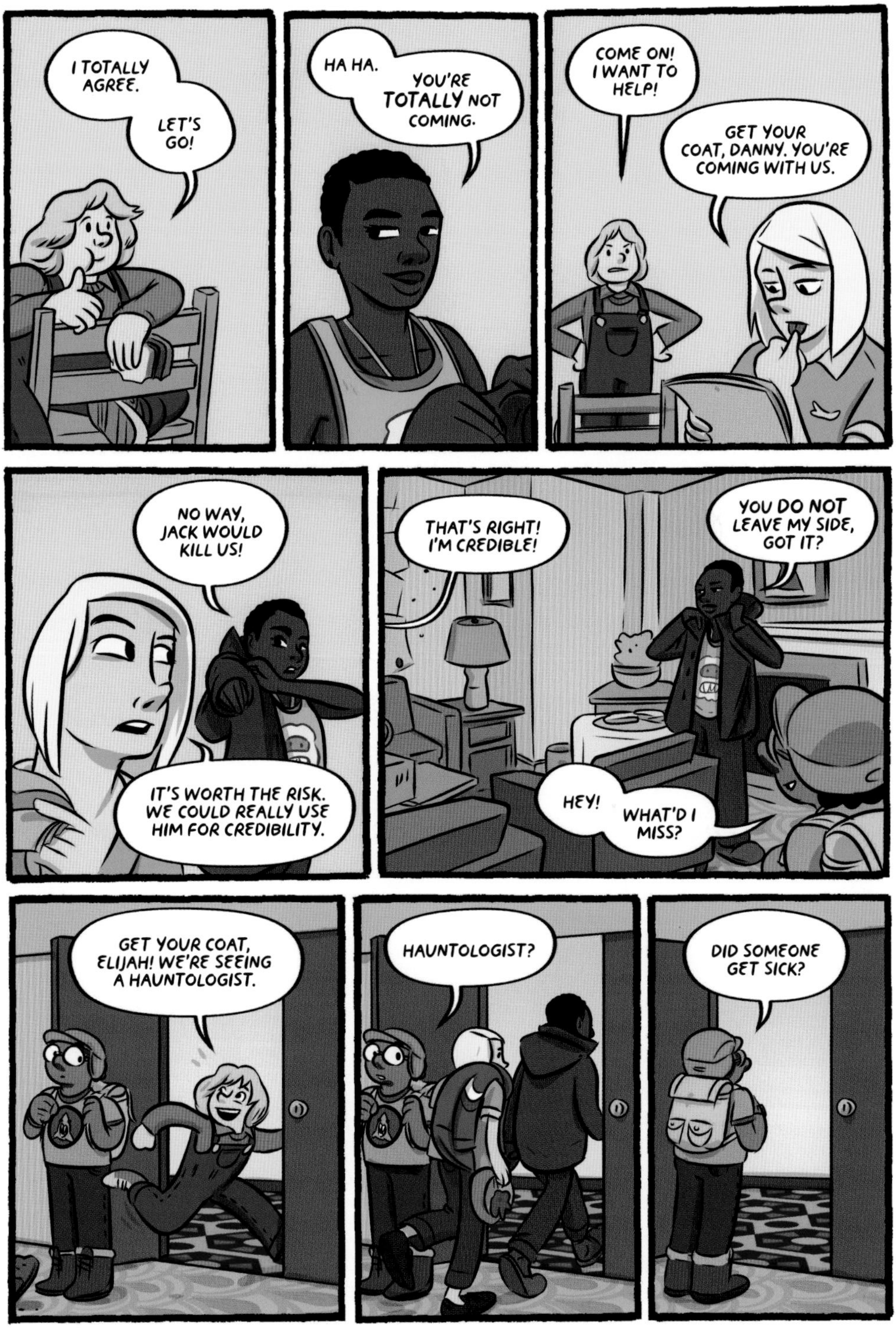
I TOTALLY AGREE.
LET'S GO!
HA HA.
YOU'RE TOTALLY NOT COMING.
COME ON! I WANT TO HELP!
GET YOUR COAT, DANNY. YOU'RE COMING WITH US.
NO WAY, JACK WOULD KILL US!
IT'S WORTH THE RISK. WE COULD REALLY USE HIM FOR CREDIBILITY.
THAT'S RIGHT! I'M CREDIBLE!
YOU DO NOT LEAVE MY SIDE, GOT IT?
HEY!
WHAT'D I MISS?
GET YOUR COAT, ELIJAH! WE'RE SEEING A HAUNTOLOGIST.
HAUNTOLOGIST?
DID SOMEONE GET SICK?

YES?

HELLO, DR. RUBRIK. I'M SUZY HESS. AND THIS IS ELIJAH, RENA, AND DANNY.

WE WANT TO TALK ABOUT THE UNDERLOOK.

DANNY AXWORTH?

HI!

PLEASE COME INSIDE.

THANK YOU.

LEGGO, RENA!

OOOH, TAXIDERMY! CREEPY.

TAXIDERMY! TAXIDERMY! TAXIDERMY! TAXIDERMY! YIDER TAXID

HA HA, I'M OK!

SAY HELLO TO OUR GUESTS, LENORE.

HELLO TO OUR GUESTS, LENORE.

NICE TO MEET YOU.

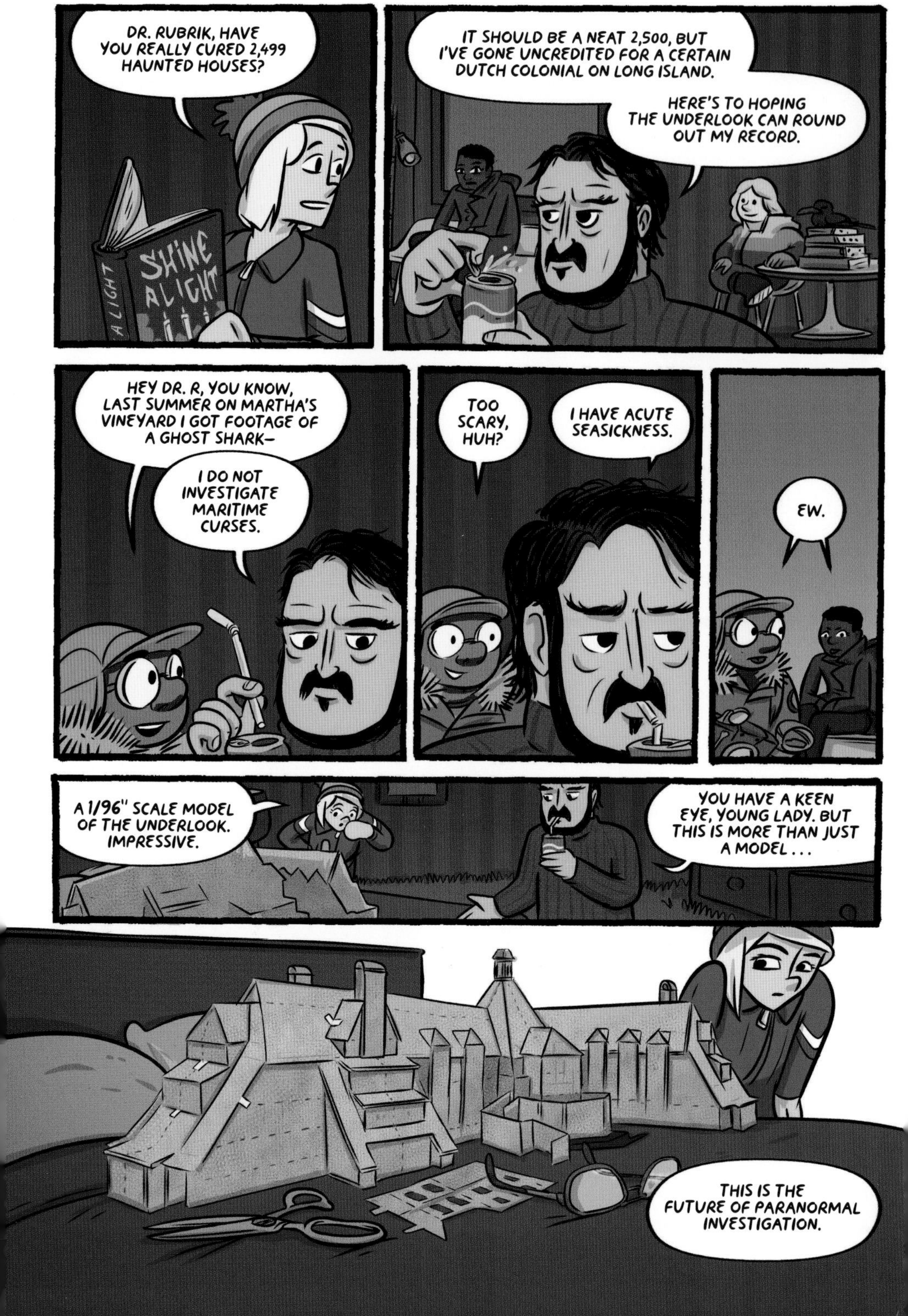
DR. RUBRIK, HAVE YOU REALLY CURED 2,499 HAUNTED HOUSES?
SHINE ALIGHT
IT SHOULD BE A NEAT 2,500, BUT I'VE GONE UNCREDITED FOR A CERTAIN DUTCH COLONIAL ON LONG ISLAND.
HERE'S TO HOPING THE UNDERLOOK CAN ROUND OUT MY RECORD.
HEY DR. R, YOU KNOW, LAST SUMMER ON MARTHA'S VINEYARD I GOT FOOTAGE OF A GHOST SHARK—
I DO NOT INVESTIGATE MARITIME CURSES.
TOO SCARY, HUH?
I HAVE ACUTE SEASICKNESS.
EW.
A 1/96" SCALE MODEL OF THE UNDERLOOK. IMPRESSIVE.
YOU HAVE A KEEN EYE, YOUNG LADY. BUT THIS IS MORE THAN JUST A MODEL . . .
THIS IS THE FUTURE OF PARANORMAL INVESTIGATION.

=FLICK=

149

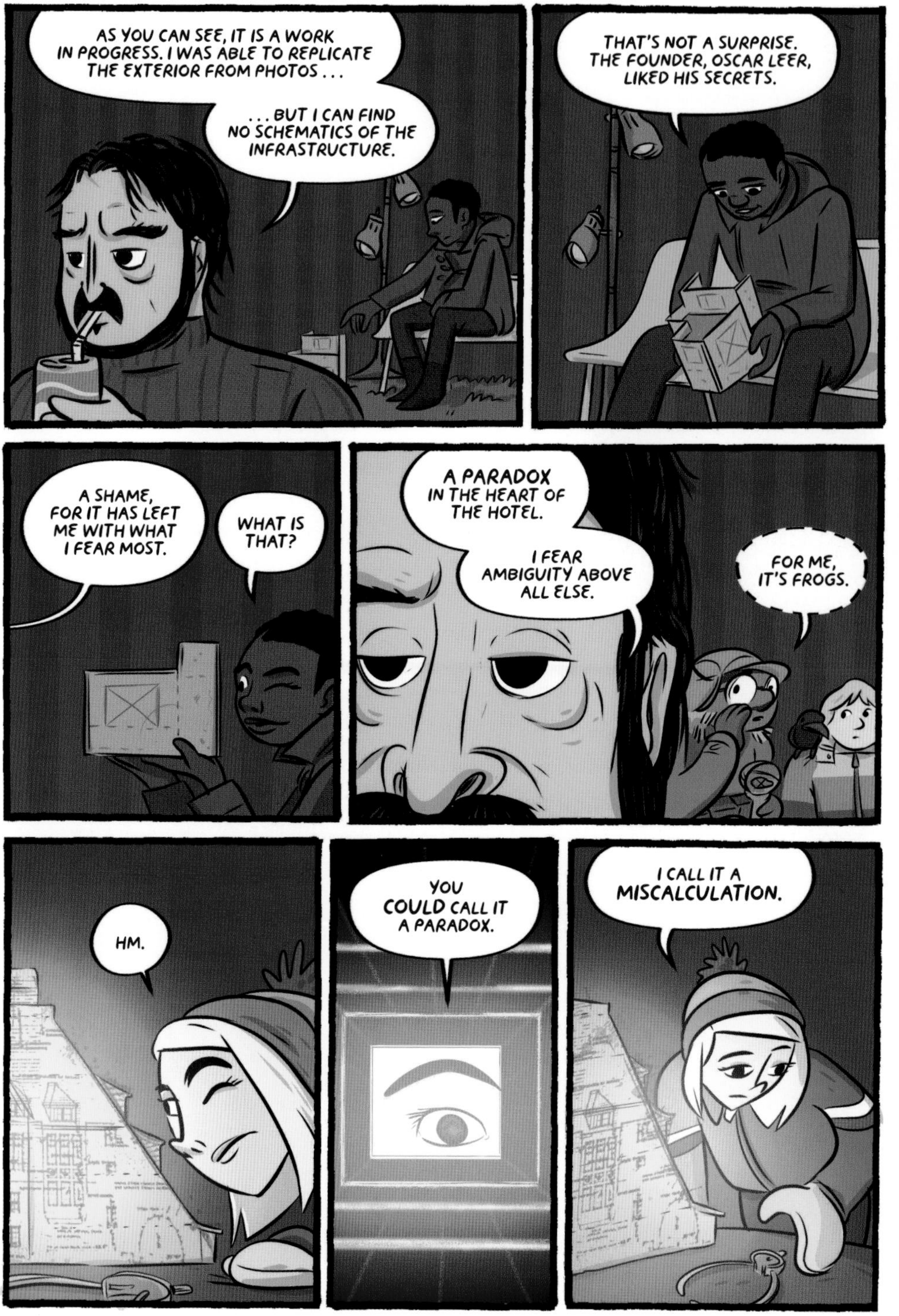
AS YOU CAN SEE, IT IS A WORK IN PROGRESS. I WAS ABLE TO REPLICATE THE EXTERIOR FROM PHOTOS . . .
. . . BUT I CAN FIND NO SCHEMATICS OF THE INFRASTRUCTURE.
THAT'S NOT A SURPRISE. THE FOUNDER, OSCAR LEER, LIKED HIS SECRETS.
A SHAME, FOR IT HAS LEFT ME WITH WHAT I FEAR MOST.
WHAT IS THAT?
A PARADOX IN THE HEART OF THE HOTEL.
I FEAR AMBIGUITY ABOVE ALL ELSE.
FOR ME, IT'S FROGS.
HM.
YOU COULD CALL IT A PARADOX.
I CALL IT A MISCALCULATION.

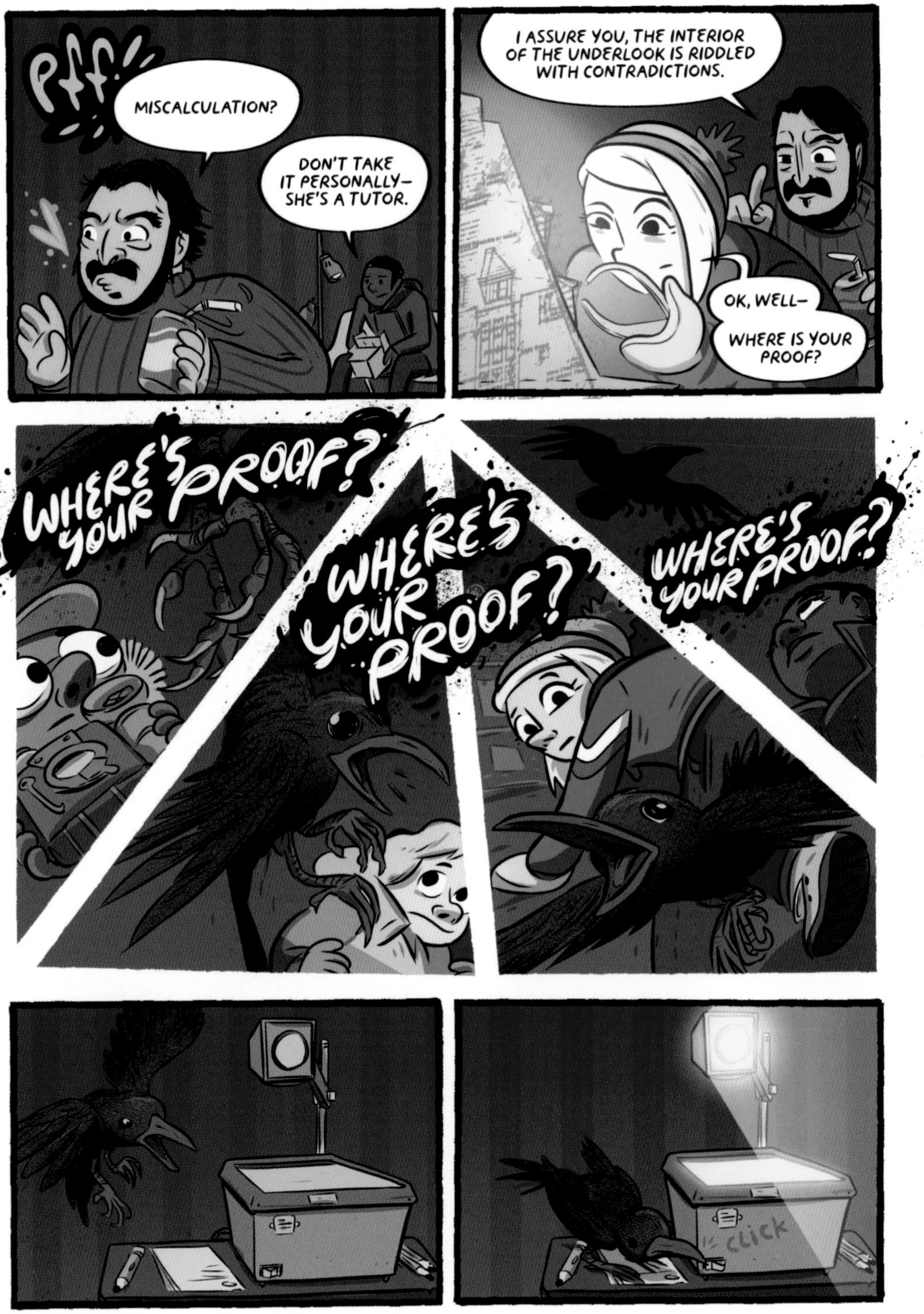
PFF!
MISCALCULATION?
DON'T TAKE IT PERSONALLY— SHE'S A TUTOR.
I ASSURE YOU, THE INTERIOR OF THE UNDERLOOK IS RIDDLED WITH CONTRADICTIONS.
OK, WELL—
WHERE IS YOUR PROOF?
WHERE'S YOUR PROOF?
WHERE'S YOUR PROOF?
WHERE'S YOUR PROOF?
CLICK

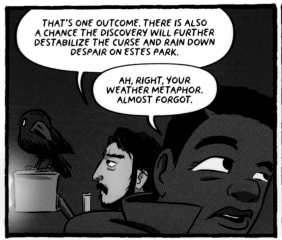

THAT'S ONE OUTCOME. THERE IS ALSO A CHANCE THE DISCOVERY WILL FURTHER DESTABILIZE THE CURSE AND RAIN DOWN DESPAIR ON ESTES PARK.

AH, RIGHT, YOUR WEATHER METAPHOR. ALMOST FORGOT.

THIS STORM THREATENS EVERYTHING YOU HOLD DEAR.

I MUST BE ALLOWED TO EXPLORE THE HOTEL IMMEDIATELY.

SURE YOU HAVEN'T BEEN THERE ALREADY?

WHAT ARE YOU IMPLYING?

OH, JUST CURIOUS . . . WHERE YOU GOT PHOTOS OF THE INSIDE OF THE HOTEL.

ESTES PARK HISTORICAL SOCIETY.

FUNNY. I HEARD THEIR ARCHIVES WERE DESTROYED IN THE BIG FLOOD.

I'LL BE BLUNT, MR. RUBRIK. YOU REALLY CREEP ME OUT.

I THINK YOU'RE A FRAUD WHO PREYS ON SMALL-TOWN SUPERSTITION.

BUT YOU'RE NOT THE ONE HE NEEDS TO CONVINCE, ARE YOU, RENA?

YOU'RE RIGHT, YOUNG LADY. THE ONLY ONE WHO HOLDS THE FATE OF THE UNDERLOOK HOTEL IS...

NOPE.

...DANNY AXWORTH.

ME?

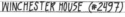

WINCHESTER HOUSE (#2497)

FRANKLIN CASTLE (#2498)

FALL RIVER INN (#2499)

BEHIND EVERY FAMOUS HAUNT I'VE ENCOUNTERED WAS A MYSTERY WAITING TO BE SOLVED.

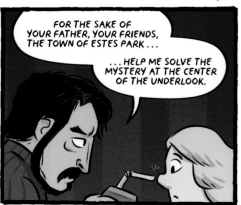

FOR THE SAKE OF YOUR FATHER, YOUR FRIENDS, THE TOWN OF ESTES PARK...

...HELP ME SOLVE THE MYSTERY AT THE CENTER OF THE UNDERLOOK.

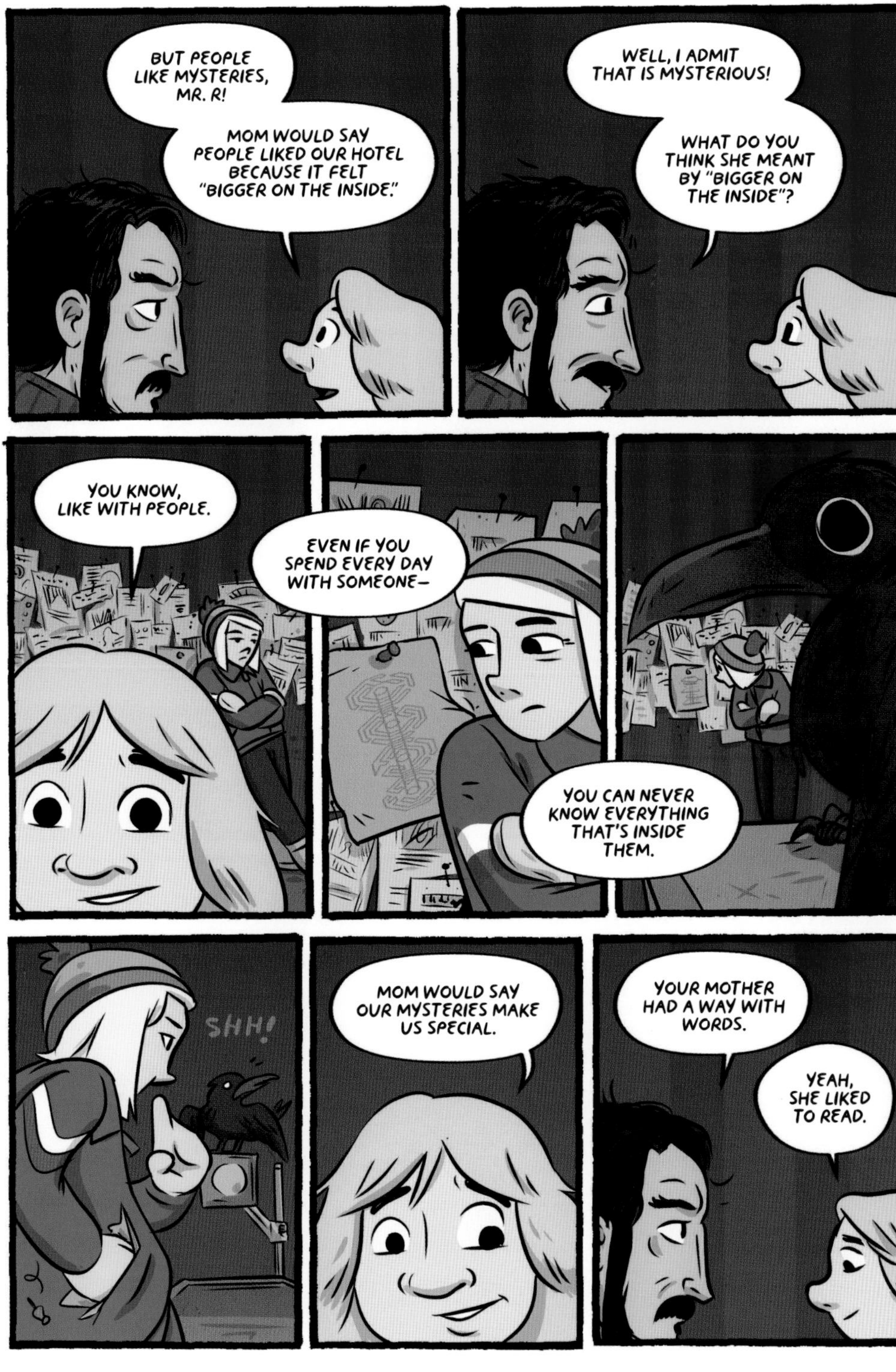
BUT PEOPLE LIKE MYSTERIES, MR. R!
MOM WOULD SAY PEOPLE LIKED OUR HOTEL BECAUSE IT FELT "BIGGER ON THE INSIDE."
WELL, I ADMIT THAT IS MYSTERIOUS!
WHAT DO YOU THINK SHE MEANT BY "BIGGER ON THE INSIDE"?
YOU KNOW, LIKE WITH PEOPLE.
EVEN IF YOU SPEND EVERY DAY WITH SOMEONE—
YOU CAN NEVER KNOW EVERYTHING THAT'S INSIDE THEM.
SHH!
MOM WOULD SAY OUR MYSTERIES MAKE US SPECIAL.
YOUR MOTHER HAD A WAY WITH WORDS.
YEAH, SHE LIKED TO READ.

YOUR DEARLY DEPARTED MOTHER, LINDA LEER, GREAT-GRANDDAUGHTER OF OSCAR LEER—SHE WAS THE RIGHTFUL HEIR TO THE HOTEL . . .

. . . AND ITS MYSTERIES.

AXWORTH

LEER

I DON'T KNOW IF MOM HAD ANSWERS TO THOSE MYSTERIES.

SHE DID HAVE A KEY, THOUGH.

KEY?

I MUST INSPECT THIS KEY.

NOW HOLD ON, DR. RUBRIK. THE DEAL IS YOU TALK TO THE CAMERA, NOT TO DANNY.

DON'T YOU SEE?

THE SECRET LIES WITH LINDA LEER.

OK, WE'RE DONE HERE.

IT'S NOT TOO LATE, DANNY BOY. YOU HAVE THE POWER TO SET HER FREE.

SHUT UP, BIRD!

SET HER FREE?

WE'RE GOING, SUZY

HEY, WAIT A SEC!

RUBRIK, I THINK—

SLAM!

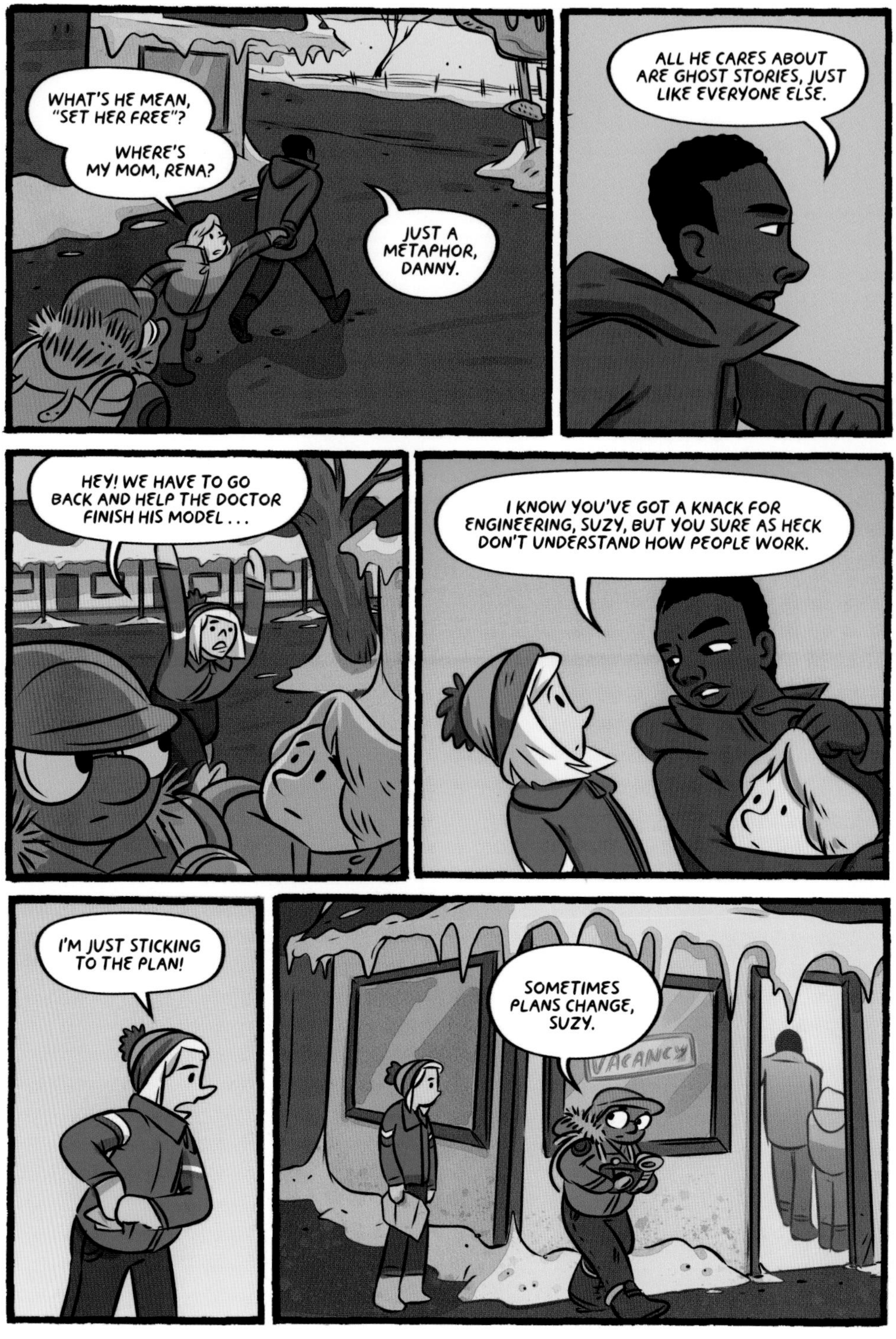
WHAT'S HE MEAN, "SET HER FREE"?
WHERE'S MY MOM, RENA?
JUST A METAPHOR, DANNY.
ALL HE CARES ABOUT ARE GHOST STORIES, JUST LIKE EVERYONE ELSE.
HEY! WE HAVE TO GO BACK AND HELP THE DOCTOR FINISH HIS MODEL . . .
I KNOW YOU'VE GOT A KNACK FOR ENGINEERING, SUZY, BUT YOU SURE AS HECK DON'T UNDERSTAND HOW PEOPLE WORK.
I'M JUST STICKING TO THE PLAN!
SOMETIMES PLANS CHANGE, SUZY.
VACANCY

HEY,
SUZY?

HM?

I WANT TO
SHOW YOU WHAT
MY KEY DOES.

LOOK, DANNY.

I WAS WRONG TO
BRING YOU WITH US
TODAY.

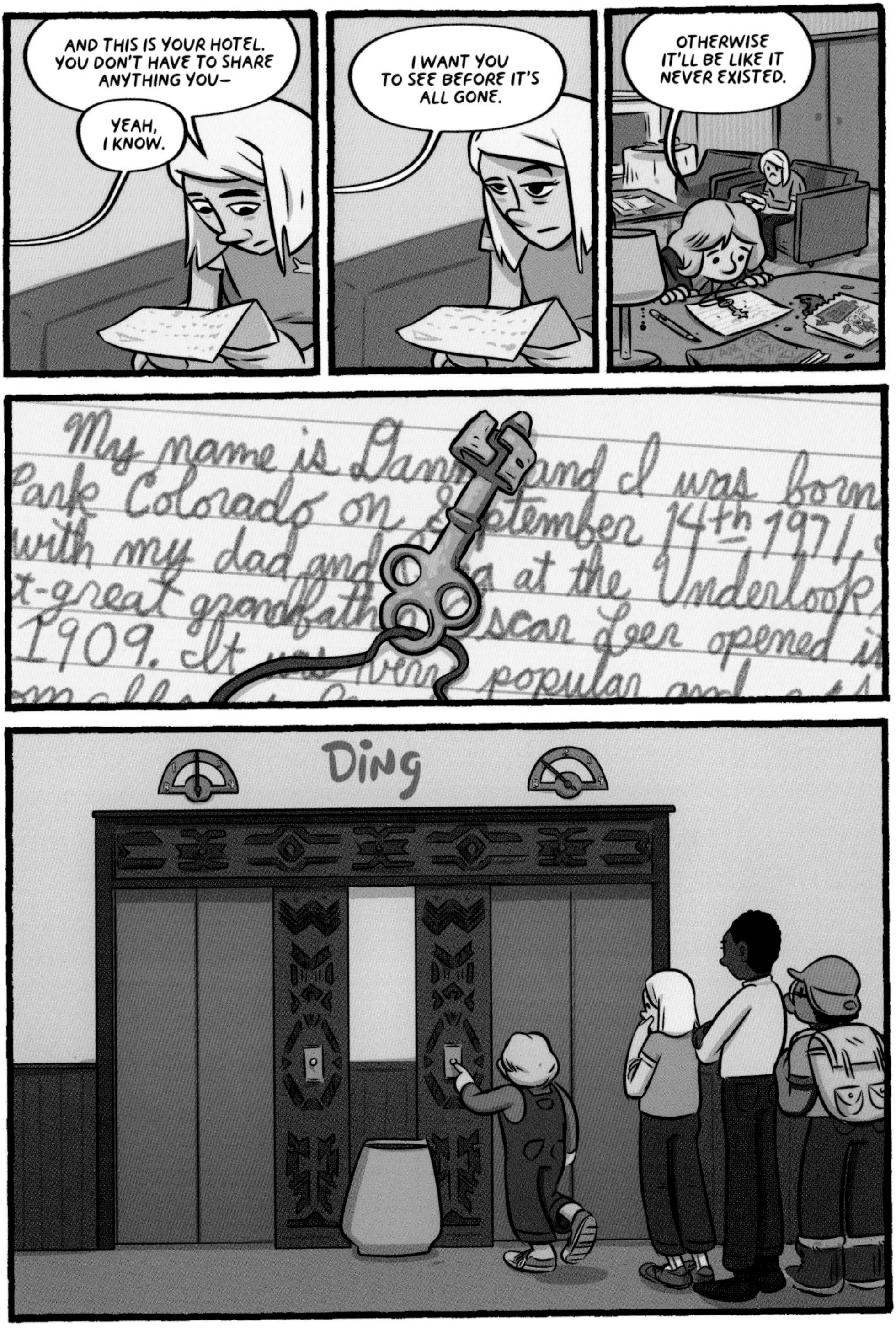
AND THIS IS YOUR HOTEL. YOU DON'T HAVE TO SHARE ANYTHING YOU—
YEAH, I KNOW.
I WANT YOU TO SEE BEFORE IT'S ALL GONE.
OTHERWISE IT'LL BE LIKE IT NEVER EXISTED.
My name is
and I was
Colorado on
with my dad
at the
1909. It
opened
popular
DING

READY?

CLONK

HALCYON MINING Co

WHAT?
I SAID READY!

DOES YOUR DAD KNOW ABOUT THIS?

NO WAY! ONLY MY KEY OPENS IT.

LOOK AT THIS OLD FILMMAKING EQUIPMENT.

IT'S MY GREAT-GREAT-GRANDPA'S STUFF.

THAT'S RIGHT. BEFORE BUILDING THE UNDERLOOK, OSCAR LEER MADE HIS FORTUNE SELLING FILM-PROCESSING TECHNOLOGY TO THE ZODAK COMPANY.

POP!

LIKE ALL INVENTORS, HE HAD LESSER-KNOWN EXPERIMENTS.

YEAH, IN THOSE DAYS, GHOST PHOTOGRAPHY WAS SUPER POPULAR!

LEER

SPIRIT·GRAPH

WANNA TRY IT?

WHAT? THIS THING WORKS?

GREAT-GREAT-GRANDPA USED TO MAKE MOVIES, TOO. THIS IS HIM AND HIS FILM CREW!

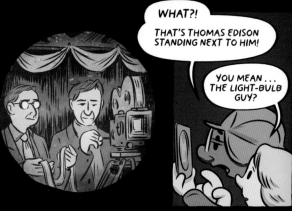

WHAT?! THAT'S THOMAS EDISON STANDING NEXT TO HIM!

YOU MEAN . . . THE LIGHT-BULB GUY?

EDISON STARTED ONE OF THE FIRST MOVIE STUDIOS.

FRANKENSTEIN 1910 Thomas A. Edison KINETOGRAM

Sweetheart, tonight my ambition will be accomplished when I am finished this shall return to claim you as my bride. Your devoted, Frankenstein

TWO YEARS LATER FRANKENSTEIN HAS DISCOVERED THE SECRET OF LIFE

INSTEAD OF A PERFECT HUMAN BEING THE EVIL IN FRANKENSTEIN'S MIND CREATES A MONSTER

OH MY GOD, THIS IS A PRINT OF EDISON'S ADAPTATION OF FRANKENSTEIN. DO YOU KNOW HOW RARE THIS IS?

NO.

THEN JACK CAN'T DESTROY IT.

RIGHT! IT'D BE, LIKE, AGAINST THE LAW.

DANNY! YOUR GREAT-GREAT-GRANDPA'S "STUFF" IS A PRICELESS COLLECTION OF AMERICAN FILM HISTORY.

OH.

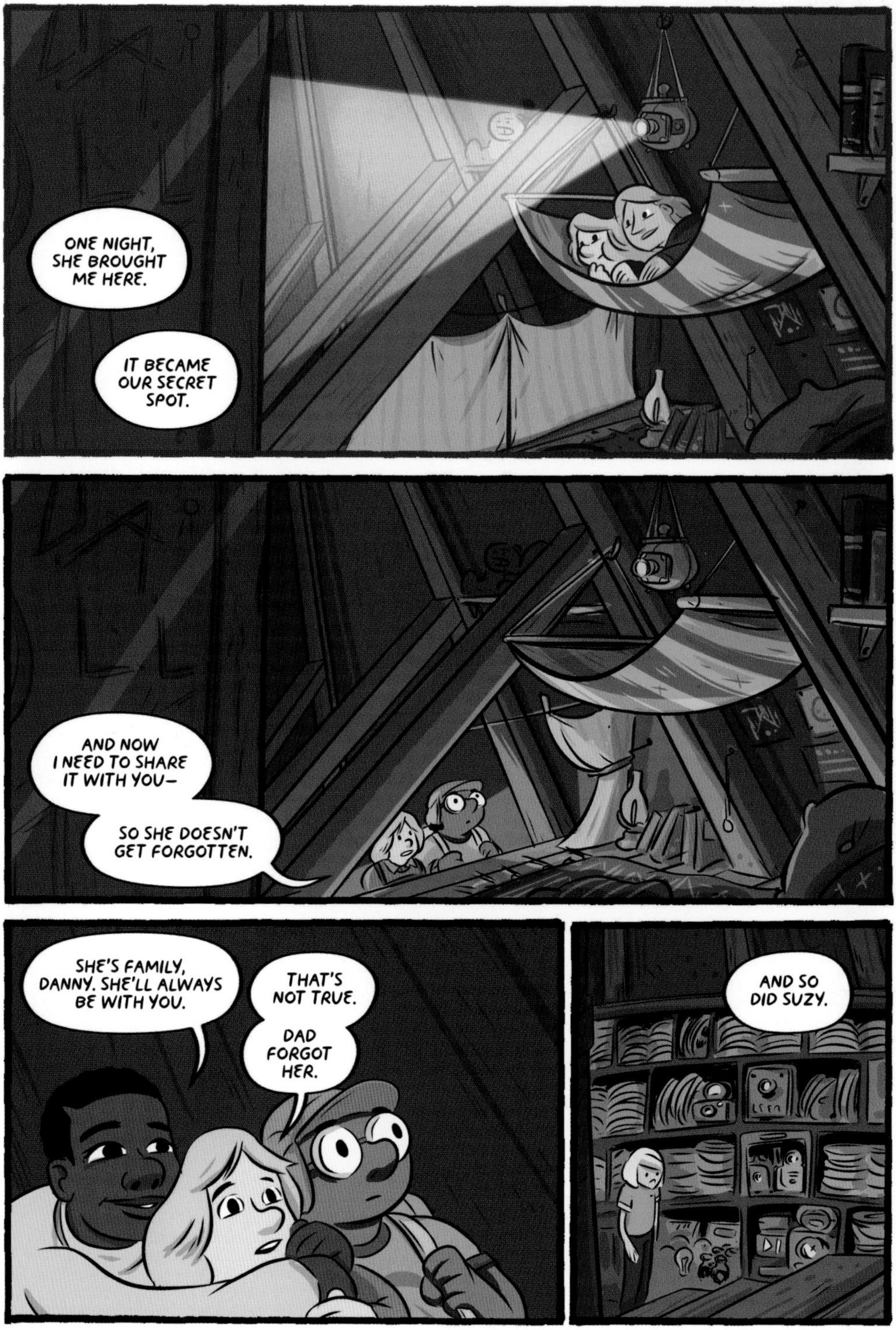

ONE NIGHT, SHE BROUGHT ME HERE.
IT BECAME OUR SECRET SPOT.
AND NOW I NEED TO SHARE IT WITH YOU—
SO SHE DOESN'T GET FORGOTTEN.
SHE'S FAMILY, DANNY. SHE'LL ALWAYS BE WITH YOU.
THAT'S NOT TRUE.
DAD FORGOT HER.
AND SO DID SUZY.

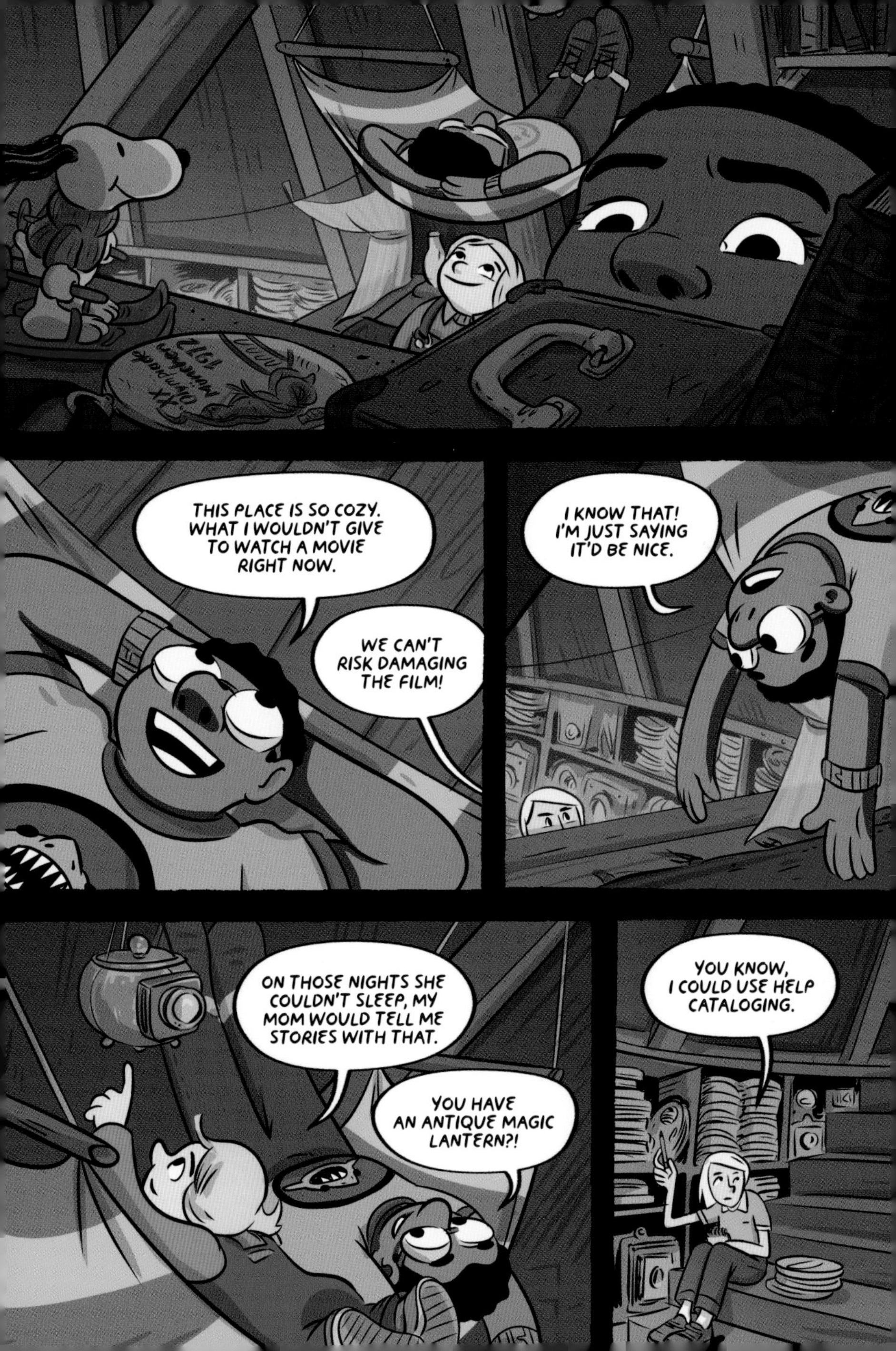
THIS PLACE IS SO COZY. WHAT I WOULDN'T GIVE TO WATCH A MOVIE RIGHT NOW.
WE CAN'T RISK DAMAGING THE FILM!
I KNOW THAT! I'M JUST SAYING IT'D BE NICE.
ON THOSE NIGHTS SHE COULDN'T SLEEP, MY MOM WOULD TELL ME STORIES WITH THAT.
YOU HAVE AN ANTIQUE MAGIC LANTERN?!
YOU KNOW, I COULD USE HELP CATALOGING.

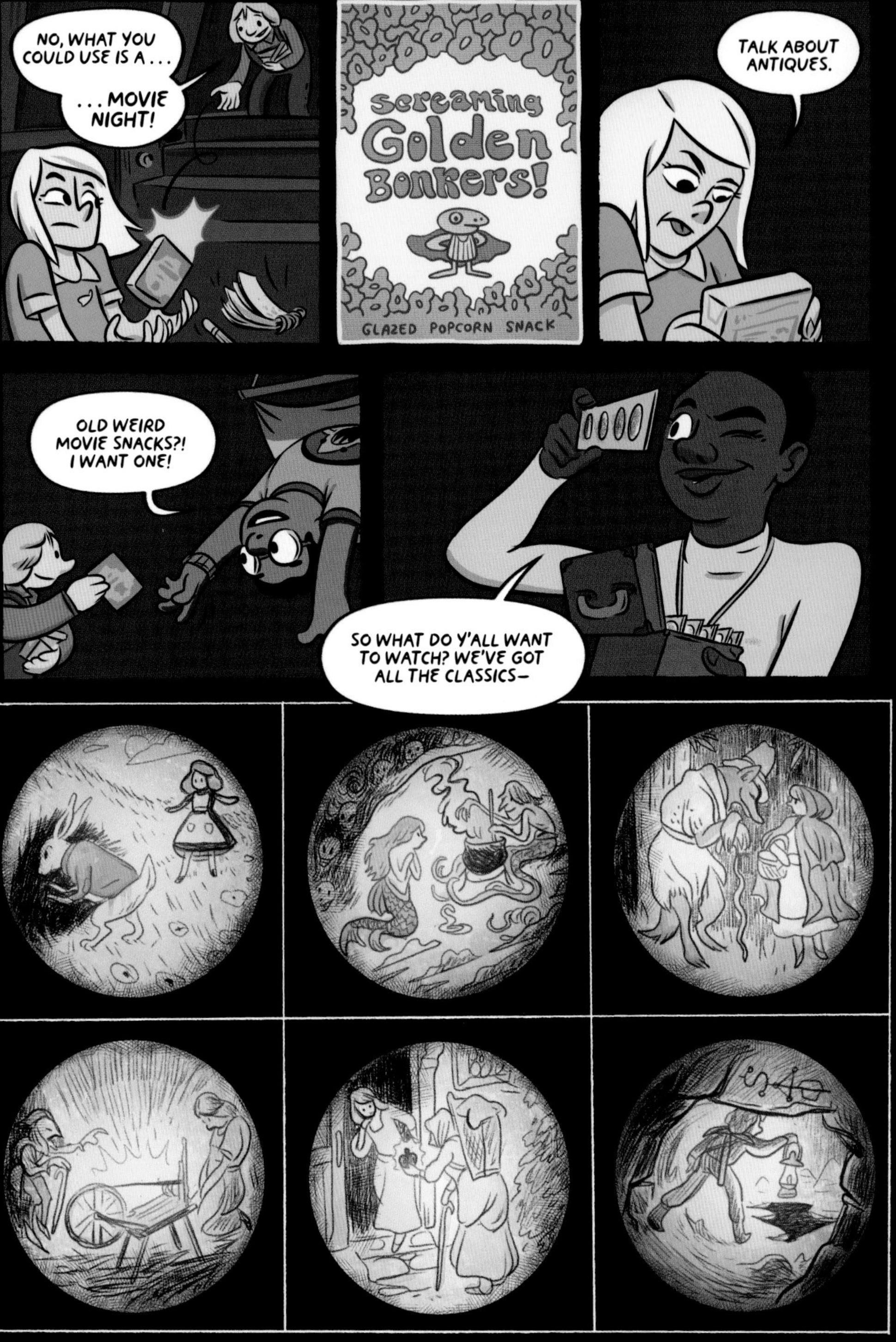
NO, WHAT YOU COULD USE IS A . . .
. . . MOVIE NIGHT!
Screaming Golden Bonkers!
GLAZED POPCORN SNACK
TALK ABOUT ANTIQUES.
OLD WEIRD MOVIE SNACKS?! I WANT ONE!
SO WHAT DO Y'ALL WANT TO WATCH? WE'VE GOT ALL THE CLASSICS–

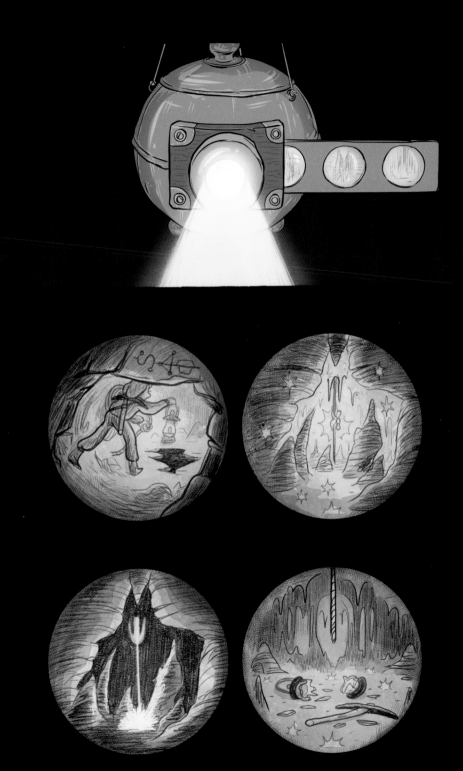

THE
UNDERLOOK HOTEL
ESTES PARK, COLORADO

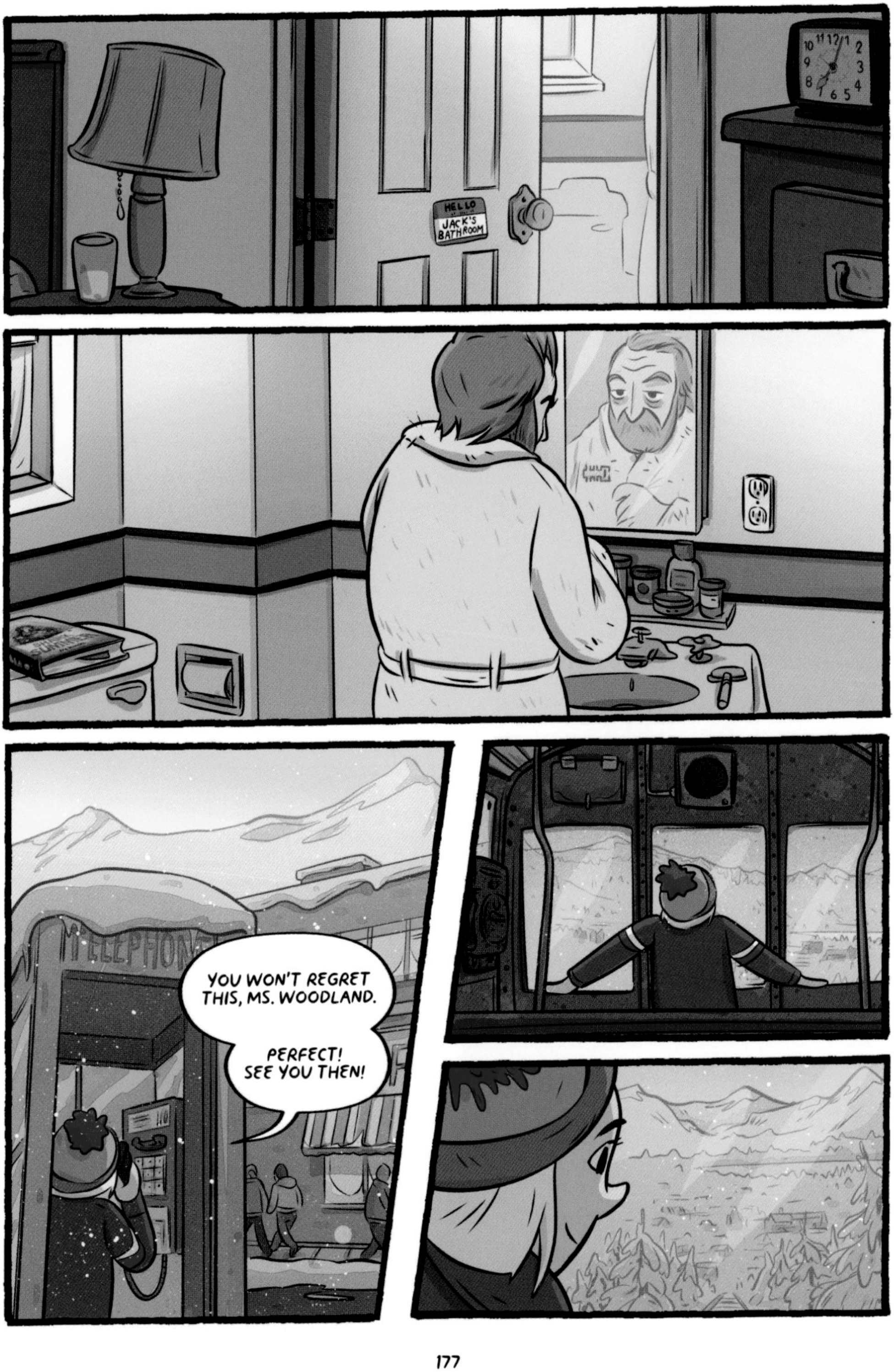
HELLO
JACK'S BATHROOM
TELEPHONE
YOU WON'T REGRET THIS, MS. WOODLAND.
PERFECT! SEE YOU THEN!

SUZY! YOU'RE ACTUALLY SMILING!

TELL ME YOU GOT SOMEONE ON THE PHONE?!

THE MUSEUM OF FILM PUT ME IN TOUCH WITH A CURATOR—THIS LADY, ANGELA WOODLAND.

SHE'S SAYS IF LEER'S COLLECTION IS HALF AS GOOD AS WE THINK, HER MUSEUM WILL SUBMIT THE HOTEL TO THE NATIONAL REGISTER OF HISTORIC PLACES!

BEST OF ALL, THERE'S NOTHING JACK AXWORTH CAN DO TO STOP IT.

WOODLAND'S DRIVING FROM DENVER TO VERIFY OUR CLAIM. WE NEED TO BE AT THE BIG HORN DINER AT FOUR O'CLOCK.

I CAN'T BELIEVE WE'RE GOING TO PULL THIS OFF.

FEELS GOOD TO BE ON THE WINNING TEAM FOR ONCE, HUH?

HA HA.

178

ELIJAH! DANNY!

WAIT TILL YOU HEAR THIS!

UH, WHAT'S WITH YOU TWO?

HELLO ELIJAH'S ROOM

AH, GOOD.

WE'RE ALL HERE.

JACK?

I'M SORRY TO INTERRUPT...

...BUT I HAVE LITTLE TIME LEFT HERE, AND THERE IS SOMEONE YOU MUST HELP ME SAY GOODBYE TO.

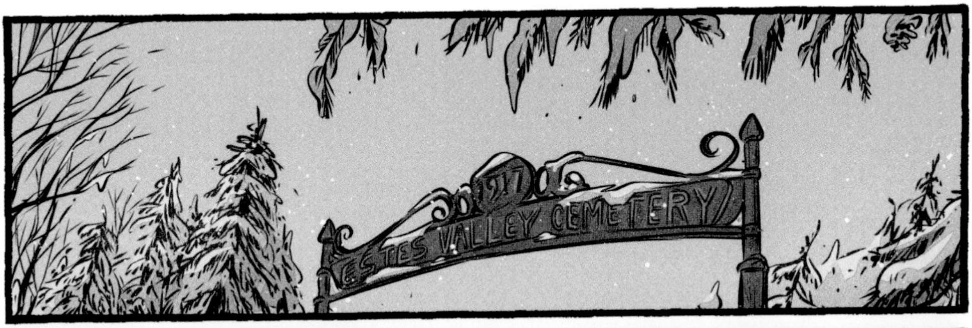
1917
ESTES VALLEY CEMETERY

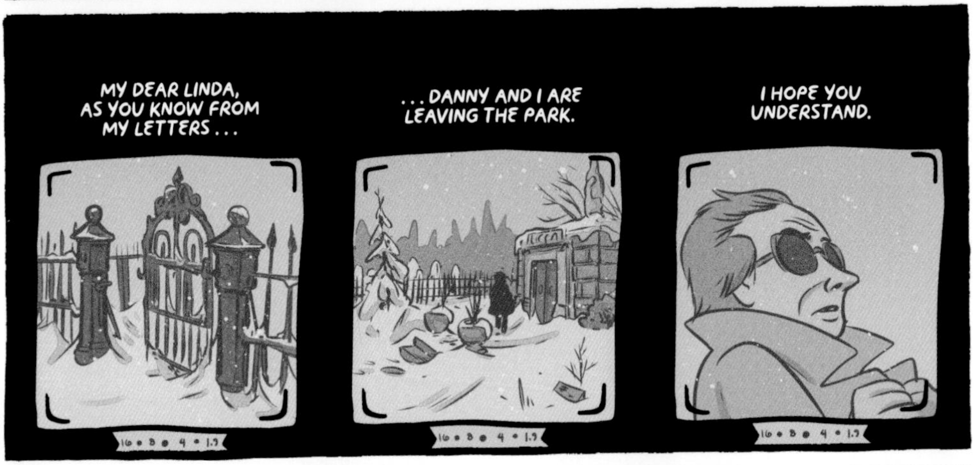
MY DEAR LINDA, AS YOU KNOW FROM MY LETTERS . . .
. . . DANNY AND I ARE LEAVING THE PARK.
I HOPE YOU UNDERSTAND.

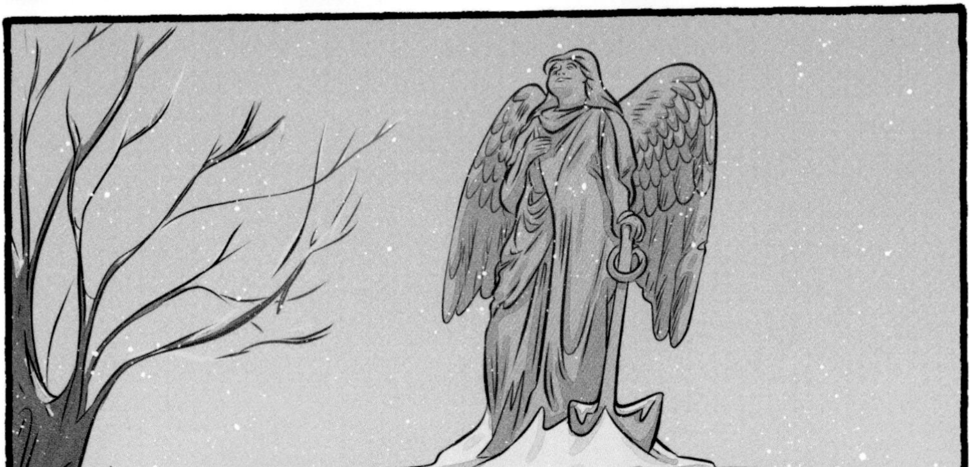
L. LEER

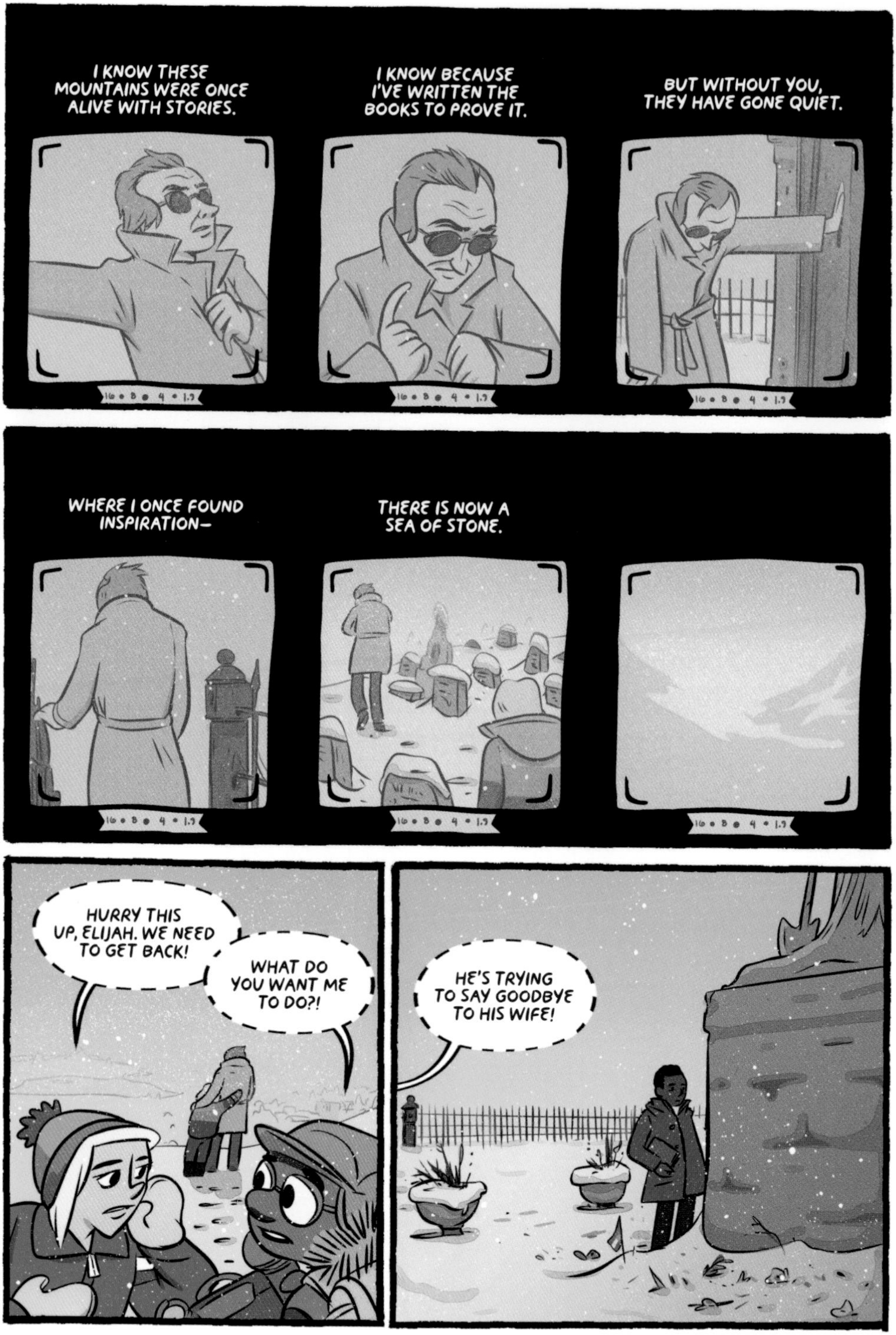
I KNOW THESE MOUNTAINS WERE ONCE ALIVE WITH STORIES.
I KNOW BECAUSE I'VE WRITTEN THE BOOKS TO PROVE IT.
BUT WITHOUT YOU, THEY HAVE GONE QUIET.
WHERE I ONCE FOUND INSPIRATION—
THERE IS NOW A SEA OF STONE.
HURRY THIS UP, ELIJAH. WE NEED TO GET BACK!
WHAT DO YOU WANT ME TO DO?!
HE'S TRYING TO SAY GOODBYE TO HIS WIFE!

"...LIVES IN ETERNITY'S SUNRISE."
—WILLIAM BLAKE

HEY, MS. LEER, JUST WANTED TO SAY—

I MISS WATCHING YOU SKI.

I WAS THINKING OF THE DAY OF YOUR OLYMPIC RUN.

LINDA LEER : USA

WE ALL GATHERED AT THE BIG HORN TO CHEER YOU ON.

YOU WERE LIKE A COMET.

NO ONE COULD TURN AWAY.

WHEN YOU MOVED BACK HOME, THE PARK WAS REJUVENATED.

OUR BELOVED QUEEN HAD RETURNED TO CLAIM HER KINGDOM.

SIXTY YEARS BEFORE, OSCAR LEER HAD COME HERE IN SEARCH OF A REMEDY FOR HIS FAILING LUNGS.

HE BUILT HIS CASTLE AMID THE COOL, HEALING AIR OF THE ROCKY MOUNTAINS.

BUT HE NEVER FOUND A CURE.

ALONG WITH HIS ESTATE, YOU INHERITED HIS CURSE.

WHEN YOU FELL SICK AND YOUR NIGHTS WERE RESTLESS, WE'D SIT TOGETHER READING POETRY.

I WOULD PRETEND NOT TO NOTICE YOUR WHEEZING BREATH—

OR YOUR BLOOD-SPECKLED HANDKERCHIEF.

YOU CAN CALL ME SUPERSTITIOUS, BUT I BELIEVE, WHEN SOMEONE'S GONE—

YOU CAN FIND THEM IN THE THINGS THEY LOVED.

I...

I REMEMBER THIS NIGHT.

LOS ANGELES. A PARTY HOSTED BY GLOBAL STUDIOS!

I WAS THERE TO TALK ABOUT ADAPTING MY LATEST BOOK.

THE STUDIO WAS COURTING LINDA, TOO. THEY WANTED TO MAKE A FILM ABOUT HER.

THIS IS THE DAY YOUR MOTHER AND I MET, DANNY. THE OLYMPIC ATHLETE AND THE HORROR WRITER.

WHAT A PAIR WE WERE!

SHE WON ME OVER BY RECITING A POEM. WHAT WAS IT CALLED?

"ETERNITY."

THE GREAT RED DRAGON AND THE WOMAN CLOTHED WITH THE SUN, 1805

THAT WAS BRAVE, RENA. YOU WERE SO—

—HONEST.

JACK AND MY DAD WERE BEST FRIENDS. I'VE KNOWN HIM SINCE I WAS DANNY'S AGE.

HE'S ALWAYS HAD A DARK CLOUD HANGING OVER HIM. I'M NOT SURE HE'LL EVER GET OUT FROM UNDER IT.

COME ON, LET'S GO. WE DON'T WANT TO MAKE WOODLAND WAIT FOR US.

HEY—

YOU COULDA SAID SOMETHING BACK THERE. YOU'RE A PART OF THE STORY, TOO, YOU KNOW.

IF WE DON'T GET BACK AND SAVE THE HOTEL, THERE WILL BE NO STORY!

GREAT. WHERE IS THAT KID?

DANNY!

188

WHAT THE HECK IS THIS?!

THE STREETS ARE QUICKLY FILLING WITH GHOULS, GHOSTS, AND HORROR FANS, HERE TO CELEBRATE THE LAST NIGHTS OF THE UNDERLOOK HOTEL.

13 KRKY

13 DONNA DUNKIN EYEWITNESS NEWS

BEEN A LONG WEEK OF WORRYIN' 'BOUT WHAT'S NEXT FOR THE PARK.

TONIGHT WE'RE GONNA JUST ENJOY WHAT WE GOT.

BOO.

MOM?

HELLO, ELIJAH.

AND RENA HALLORANN?! IT'S BEEN A MINUTE!

COOL LOOK, MS. HESS.

LIKE IT? I'M BUFFALO BILL.

WHAT'S LEFT OF HIM, ANYWAY.

EXCUSE ME, ARE YOU SUZY'S MOM?

DANNY?

YOU WON'T REMEMBER ME. I'M EDITH.

IT'LL SOUND STRANGE, BUT I'M YOUR—

I MISSED YOU, KIDDO.

OH. MY. GOD.

IT'S HIM!

COME ON, NED!

FOR CRYIN OUT—

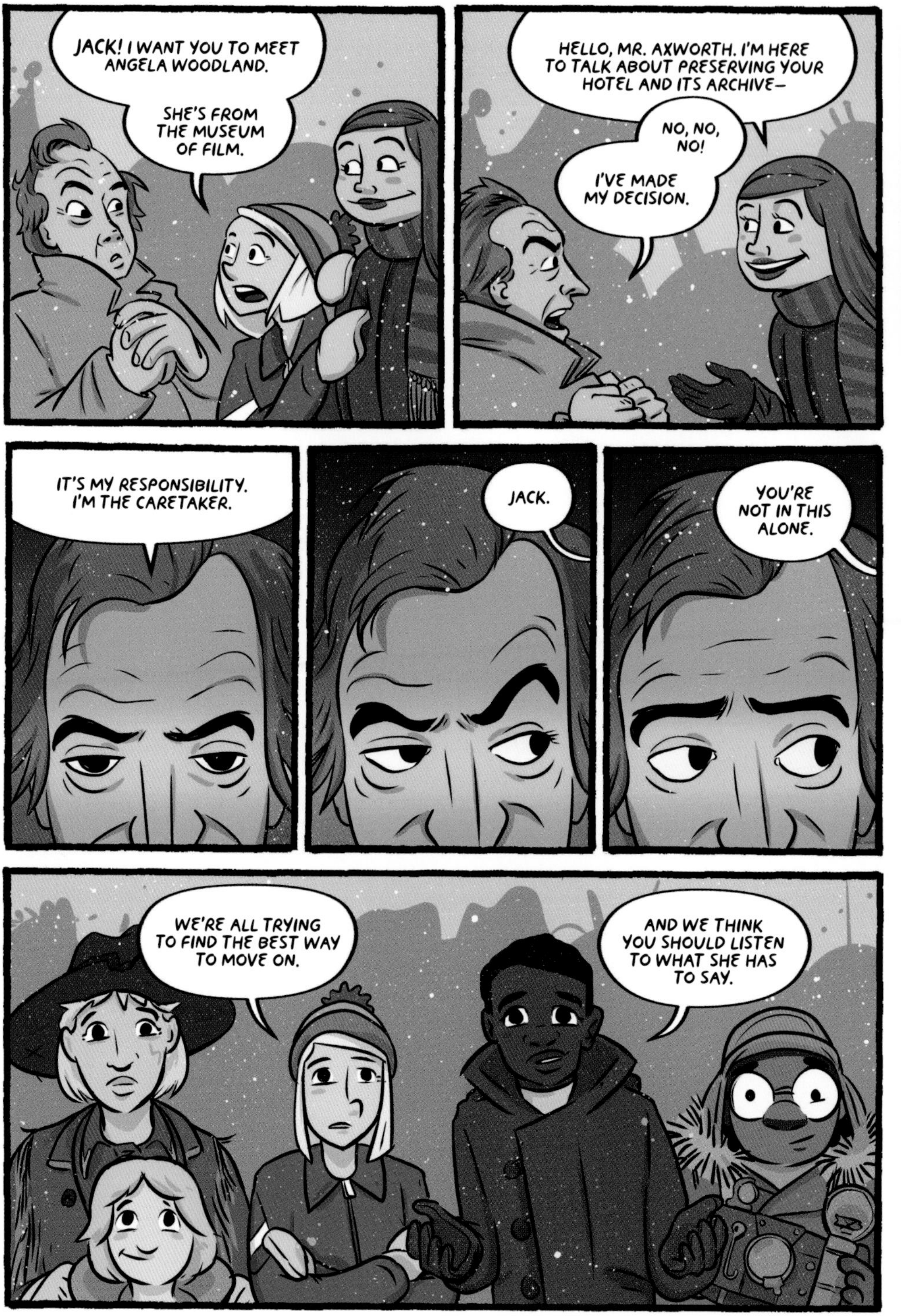
JACK! I WANT YOU TO MEET ANGELA WOODLAND.
SHE'S FROM THE MUSEUM OF FILM.
HELLO, MR. AXWORTH. I'M HERE TO TALK ABOUT PRESERVING YOUR HOTEL AND ITS ARCHIVE—
NO, NO, NO!
I'VE MADE MY DECISION.
IT'S MY RESPONSIBILITY. I'M THE CARETAKER.
JACK.
YOU'RE NOT IN THIS ALONE.
WE'RE ALL TRYING TO FIND THE BEST WAY TO MOVE ON.
AND WE THINK YOU SHOULD LISTEN TO WHAT SHE HAS TO SAY.

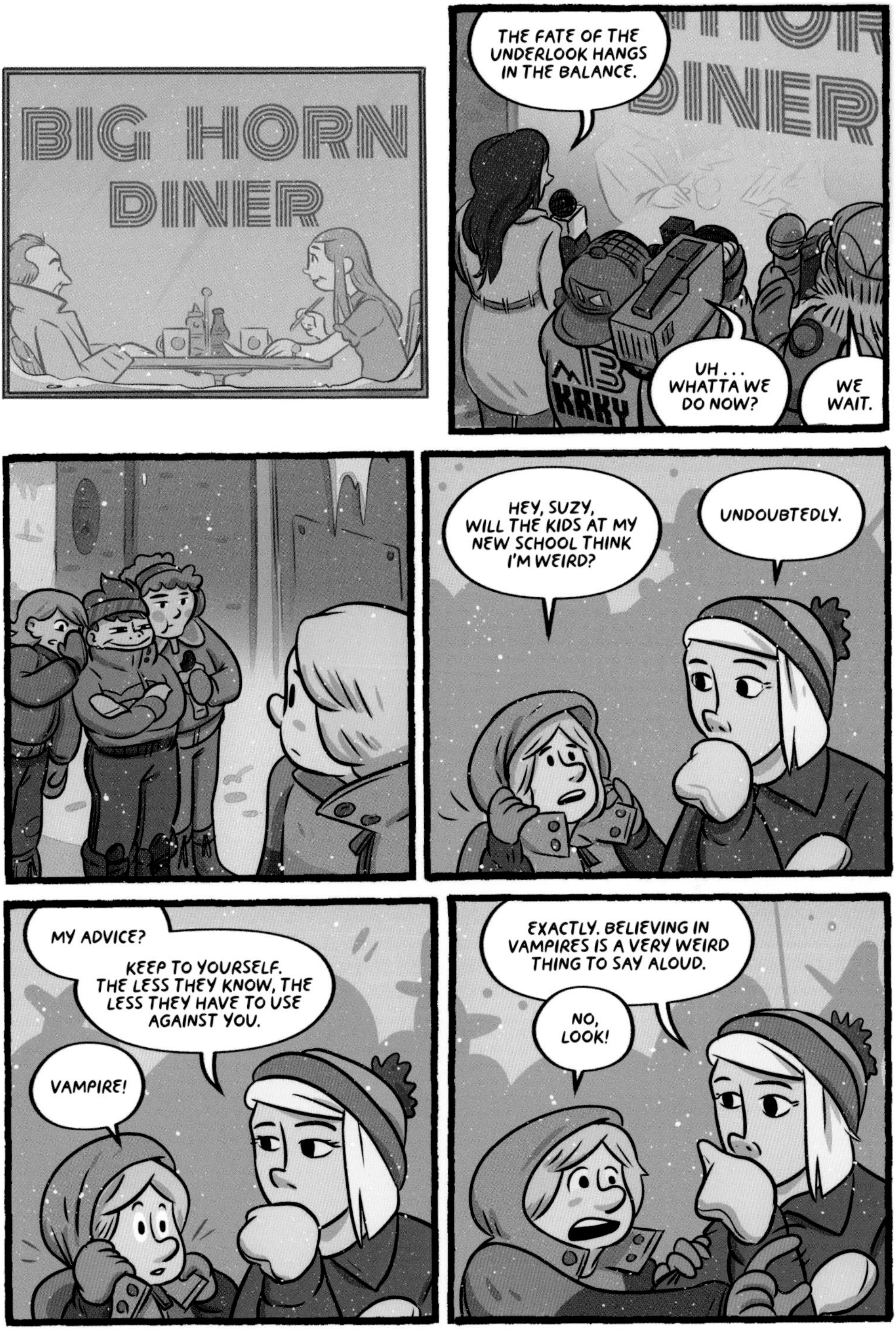
BIG HORN DINER
THE FATE OF THE UNDERLOOK HANGS IN THE BALANCE.
DINER
KRKY
UH . . . WHATTA WE DO NOW?
WE WAIT.
HEY, SUZY, WILL THE KIDS AT MY NEW SCHOOL THINK I'M WEIRD?
UNDOUBTEDLY.
MY ADVICE?
KEEP TO YOURSELF. THE LESS THEY KNOW, THE LESS THEY HAVE TO USE AGAINST YOU.
VAMPIRE!
EXACTLY. BELIEVING IN VAMPIRES IS A VERY WEIRD THING TO SAY ALOUD.
NO, LOOK!

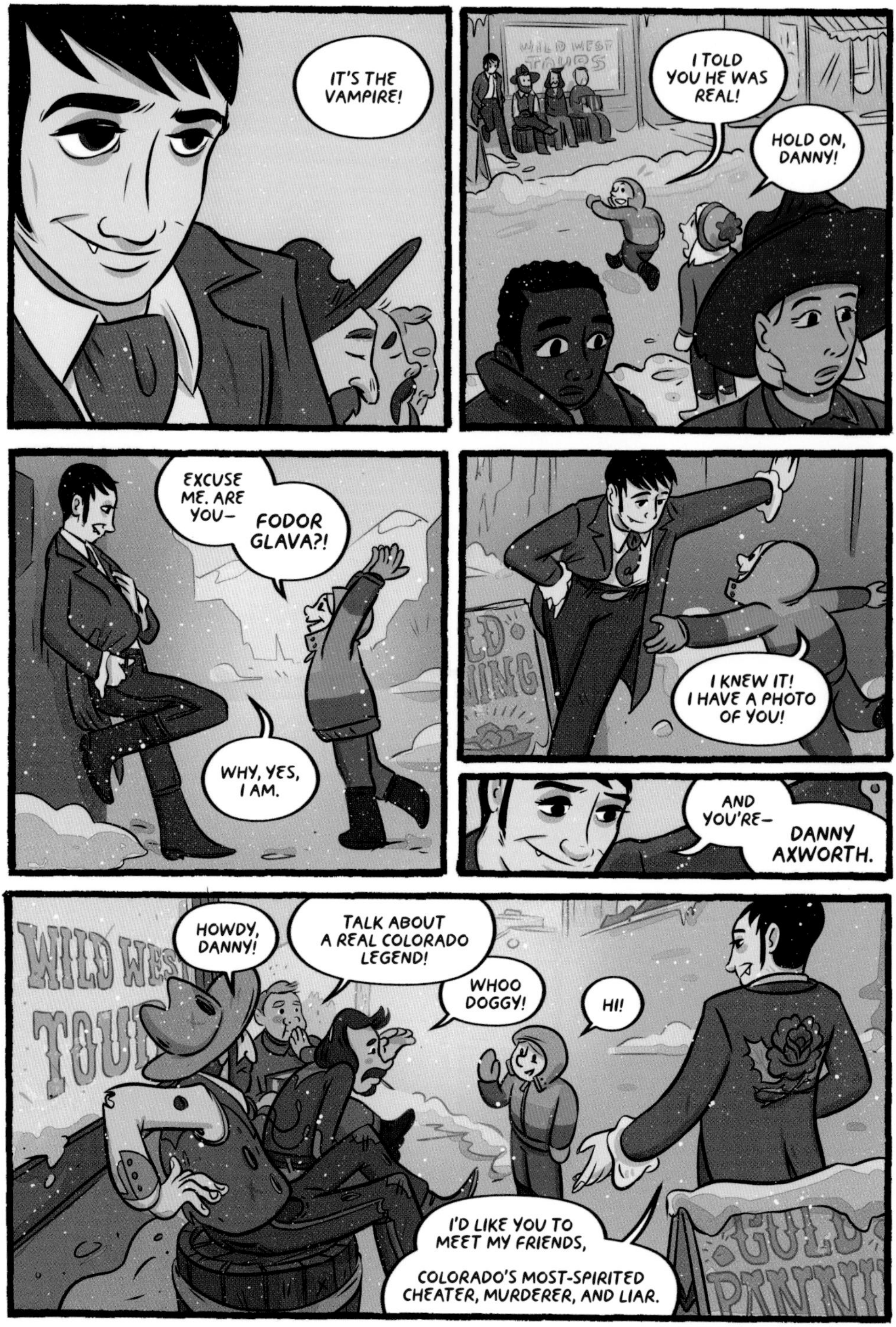

IT'S THE VAMPIRE!
I TOLD YOU HE WAS REAL!
HOLD ON, DANNY!
WILD WEST TOURS
EXCUSE ME. ARE YOU—
FODOR GLAVA?!
WHY, YES, I AM.
I KNEW IT! I HAVE A PHOTO OF YOU!
AND YOU'RE—
DANNY AXWORTH.
WILD WEST TOUR
HOWDY, DANNY!
TALK ABOUT A REAL COLORADO LEGEND!
WHOO DOGGY!
HI!
I'D LIKE YOU TO MEET MY FRIENDS,
COLORADO'S MOST-SPIRITED CHEATER, MURDERER, AND LIAR.

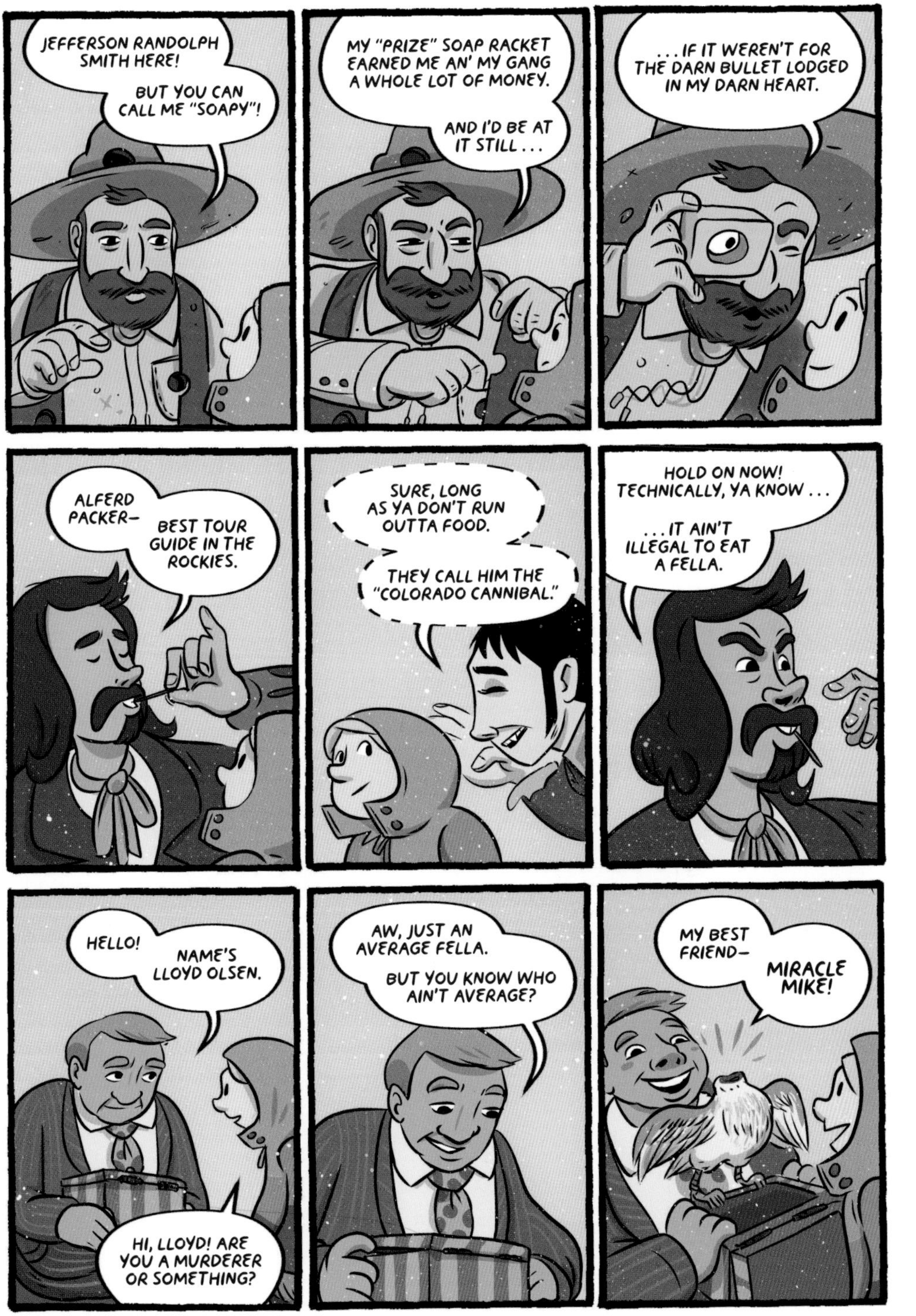
JEFFERSON RANDOLPH SMITH HERE!
BUT YOU CAN CALL ME "SOAPY"!
MY "PRIZE" SOAP RACKET EARNED ME AN' MY GANG A WHOLE LOT OF MONEY.
AND I'D BE AT IT STILL . . .
. . . IF IT WEREN'T FOR THE DARN BULLET LODGED IN MY DARN HEART.
ALFERD PACKER—
BEST TOUR GUIDE IN THE ROCKIES.
SURE, LONG AS YA DON'T RUN OUTTA FOOD.
THEY CALL HIM THE "COLORADO CANNIBAL."
HOLD ON NOW! TECHNICALLY, YA KNOW . . .
. . . IT AIN'T ILLEGAL TO EAT A FELLA.
HELLO!
NAME'S LLOYD OLSEN.
HI, LLOYD! ARE YOU A MURDERER OR SOMETHING?
AW, JUST AN AVERAGE FELLA.
BUT YOU KNOW WHO AIN'T AVERAGE?
MY BEST FRIEND—
MIRACLE MIKE!

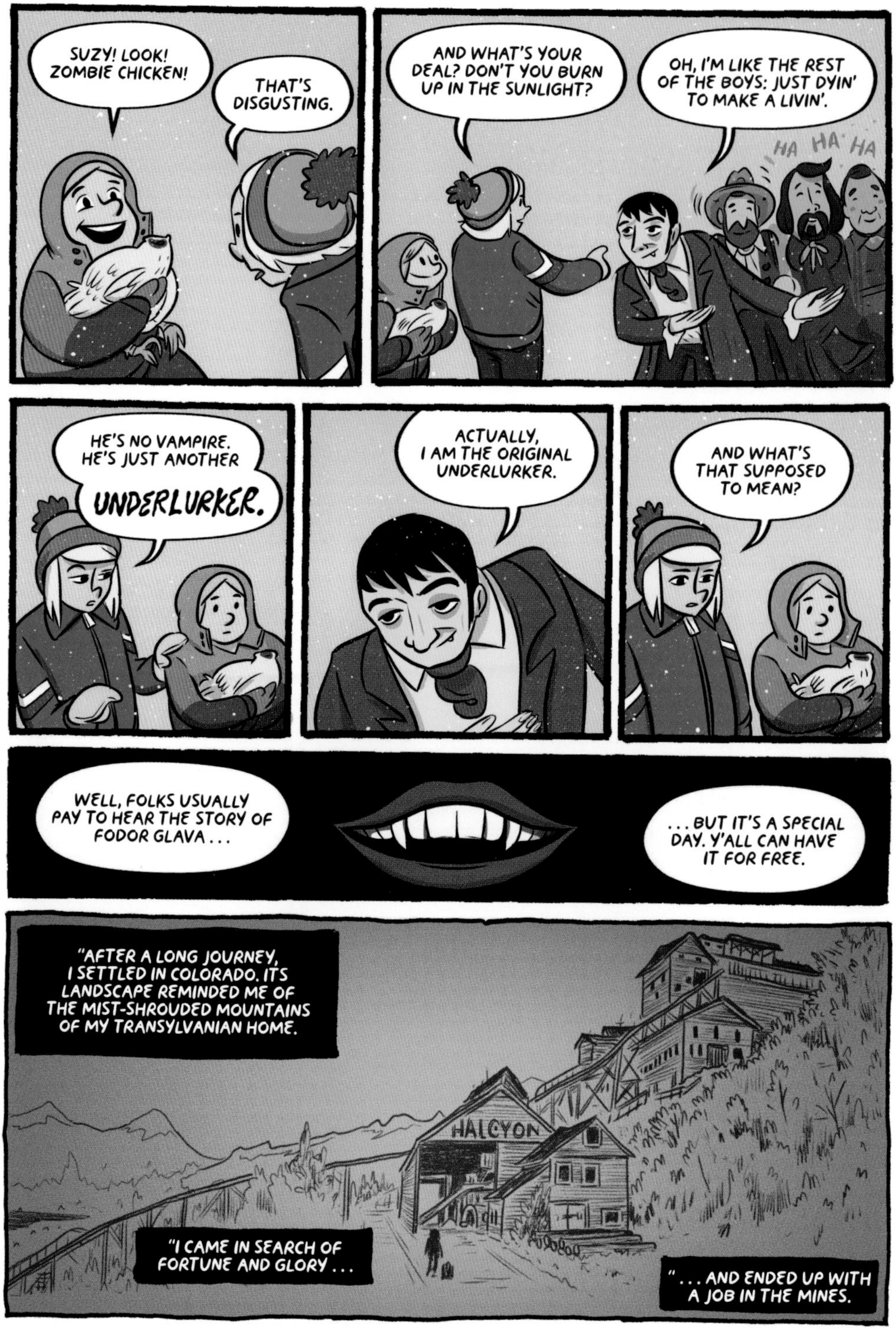
SUZY! LOOK! ZOMBIE CHICKEN!
THAT'S DISGUSTING.
AND WHAT'S YOUR DEAL? DON'T YOU BURN UP IN THE SUNLIGHT?
OH, I'M LIKE THE REST OF THE BOYS: JUST DYIN' TO MAKE A LIVIN'.
HA HA HA
HE'S NO VAMPIRE. HE'S JUST ANOTHER UNDERLURKER.
ACTUALLY, I AM THE ORIGINAL UNDERLURKER.
AND WHAT'S THAT SUPPOSED TO MEAN?
WELL, FOLKS USUALLY PAY TO HEAR THE STORY OF FODOR GLAVA . . .
. . . BUT IT'S A SPECIAL DAY. Y'ALL CAN HAVE IT FOR FREE.
"AFTER A LONG JOURNEY, I SETTLED IN COLORADO. ITS LANDSCAPE REMINDED ME OF THE MIST-SHROUDED MOUNTAINS OF MY TRANSYLVANIAN HOME.
HALCYON
"I CAME IN SEARCH OF FORTUNE AND GLORY . . .
". . . AND ENDED UP WITH A JOB IN THE MINES.

"I WORKED MY WAY UP THE RANKS FROM MINER TO UNDERLOOKER, SUPERVISING THE NIGHT-SHIFT OPERATION OF THE MINE'S DEEPEST TUNNELS.

"I'D BE SEEN WALKING HOME ALONE, COVERED IN SOOT, MELDING WITH THE LONG DARKNESS THAT COMES RIGHT BEFORE THE DAWN.

"TO THE TOWNSFOLK, I REMAINED A STRANGER FROM A DISTANT LAND, AND I DIED IN 1918 WITHOUT FRIENDS OR FAMILY TO MOURN ME.

"BUT THAT WAS NOT MY END, NOT BY A LONG SHOT.

"THAT WAS THE YEAR THE FLU PANDEMIC CAME TO TOWN AND STALKED THE STREETS OF ESTES PARK.

"AND TO THE FEARFUL AND SUPERSTITIOUS, DEATH LOOKED SUSPICIOUSLY LIKE ME.

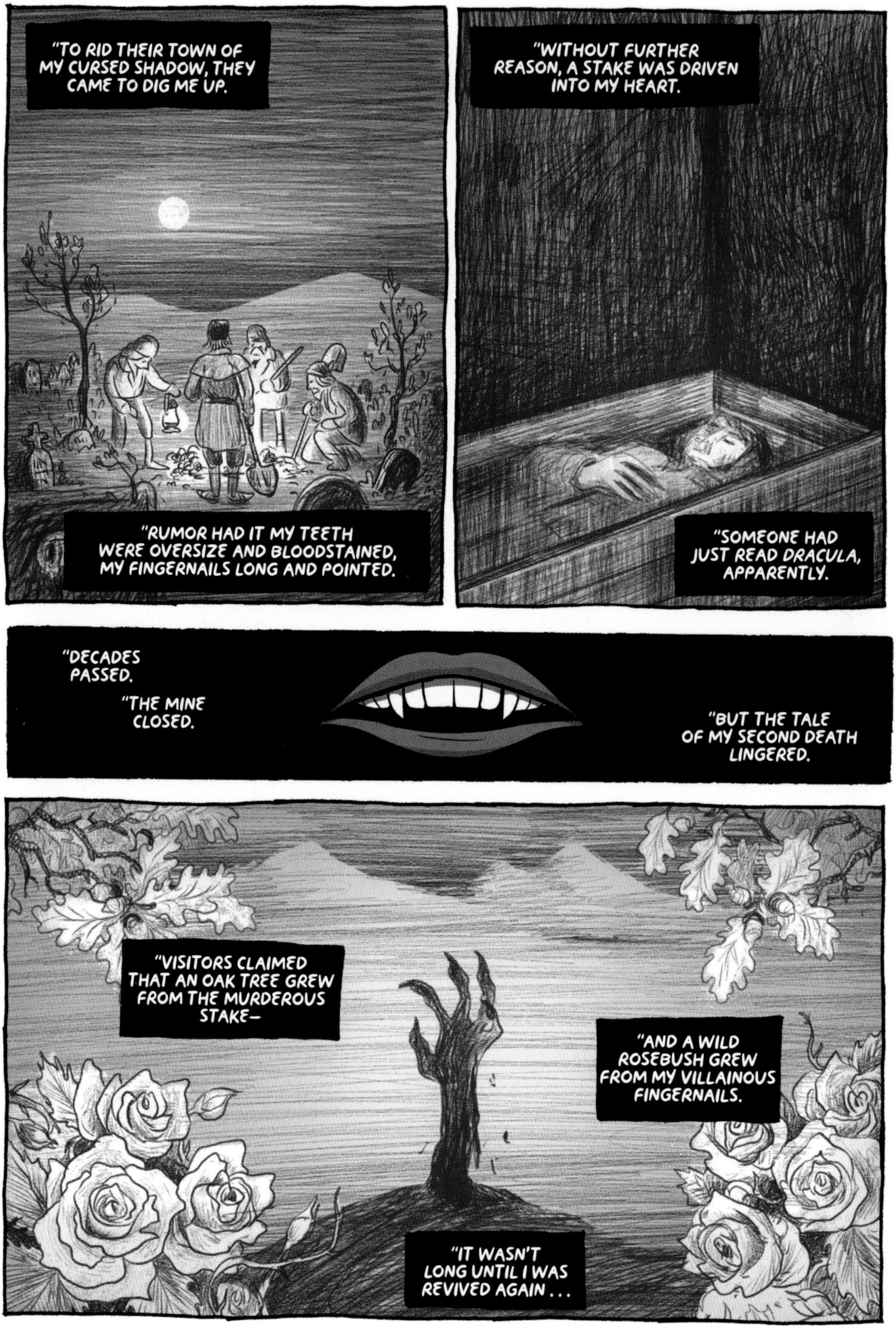
"TO RID THEIR TOWN OF MY CURSED SHADOW, THEY CAME TO DIG ME UP.
"RUMOR HAD IT MY TEETH WERE OVERSIZE AND BLOODSTAINED, MY FINGERNAILS LONG AND POINTED.
"WITHOUT FURTHER REASON, A STAKE WAS DRIVEN INTO MY HEART.
"SOMEONE HAD JUST READ *DRACULA*, APPARENTLY.
"DECADES PASSED.
"THE MINE CLOSED.
"BUT THE TALE OF MY SECOND DEATH LINGERED.
"VISITORS CLAIMED THAT AN OAK TREE GREW FROM THE MURDEROUS STAKE–
"AND A WILD ROSEBUSH GREW FROM MY VILLAINOUS FINGERNAILS.
"IT WASN'T LONG UNTIL I WAS REVIVED AGAIN . . .

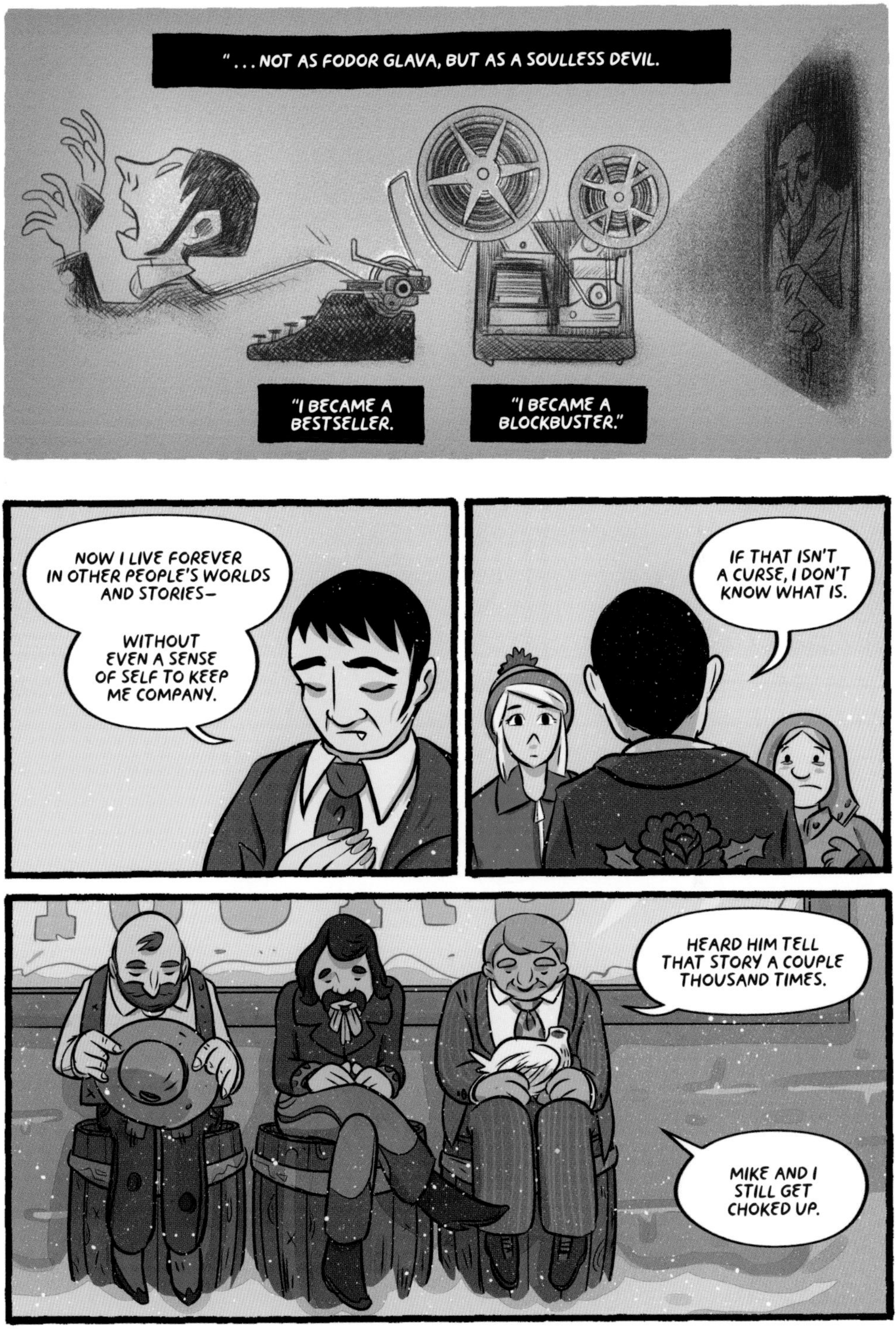
"... NOT AS FODOR GLAVA, BUT AS A SOULLESS DEVIL.
"I BECAME A BESTSELLER.
"I BECAME A BLOCKBUSTER."
NOW I LIVE FOREVER IN OTHER PEOPLE'S WORLDS AND STORIES—
WITHOUT EVEN A SENSE OF SELF TO KEEP ME COMPANY.
IF THAT ISN'T A CURSE, I DON'T KNOW WHAT IS.
HEARD HIM TELL THAT STORY A COUPLE THOUSAND TIMES.
MIKE AND I STILL GET CHOKED UP.

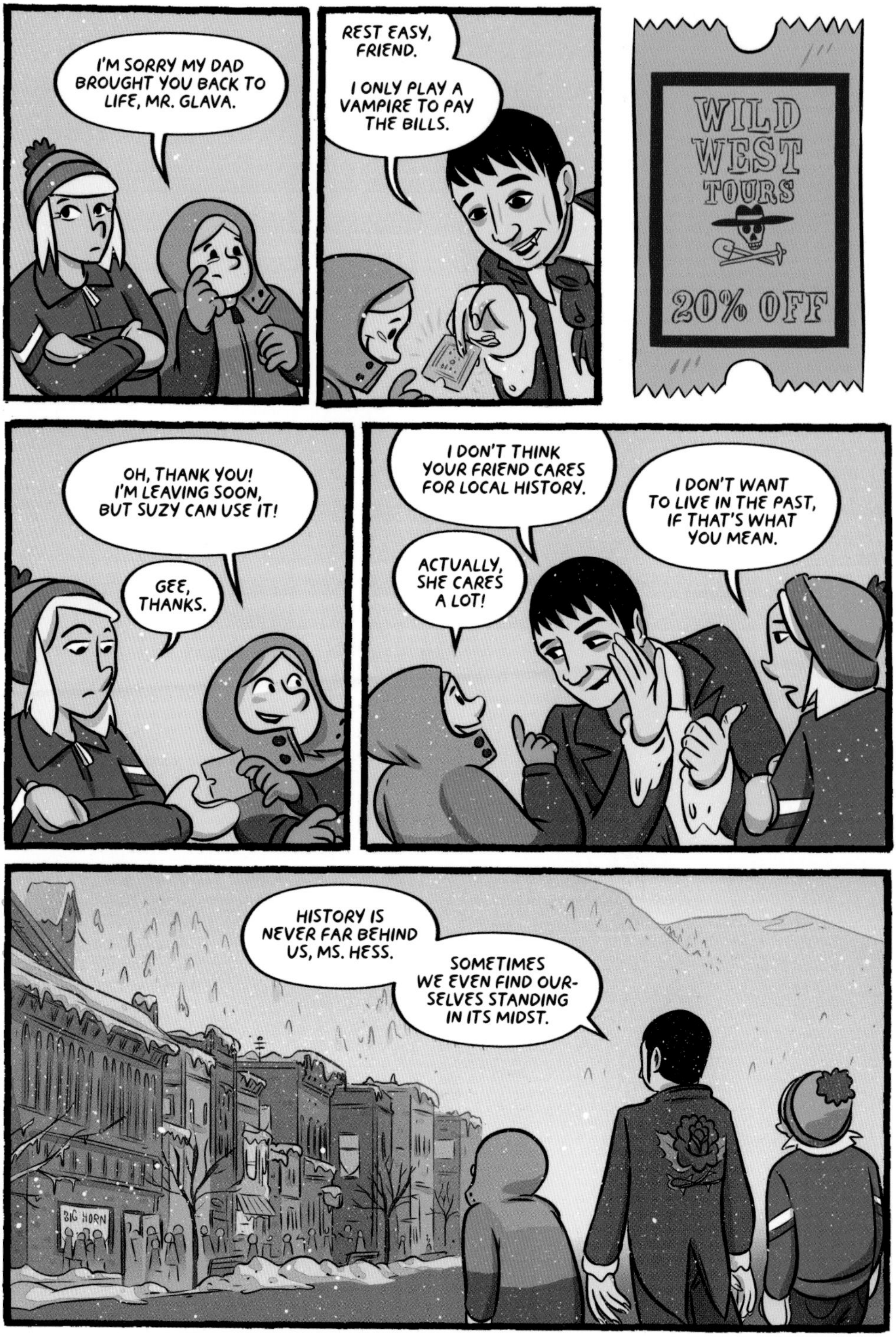
I'M SORRY MY DAD BROUGHT YOU BACK TO LIFE, MR. GLAVA.
REST EASY, FRIEND.
I ONLY PLAY A VAMPIRE TO PAY THE BILLS.
WILD WEST TOURS
20% OFF
OH, THANK YOU! I'M LEAVING SOON, BUT SUZY CAN USE IT!
GEE, THANKS.
I DON'T THINK YOUR FRIEND CARES FOR LOCAL HISTORY.
ACTUALLY, SHE CARES A LOT!
I DON'T WANT TO LIVE IN THE PAST, IF THAT'S WHAT YOU MEAN.
HISTORY IS NEVER FAR BEHIND US, MS. HESS.
SOMETIMES WE EVEN FIND OURSELVES STANDING IN ITS MIDST.
BIG HORN

I...

I'VE BEEN READING MY BOOKS THIS PAST WEEK.

IT SEEMS I'VE NEVER BEEN VERY GOOD WITH ENDINGS.

NONETHELESS, WE HAVE REACHED THE END OF OUR STORY TOGETHER, AND I'D LIKE TO SAY—

YEAH, YOUR ENDINGS STINK!

YOU TEARING DOWN OUR HOTEL OR WHAT?!

YEAH! JUST TELL US!

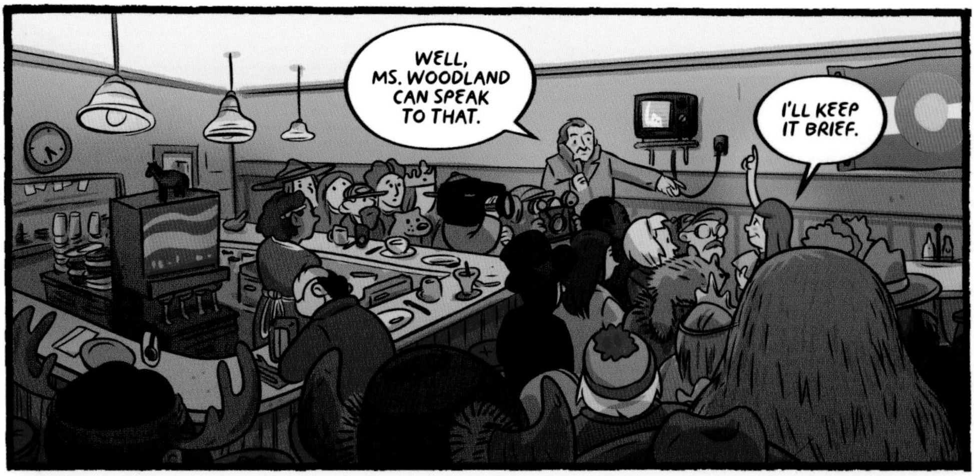
WELL, MS. WOODLAND CAN SPEAK TO THAT.
I'LL KEEP IT BRIEF.

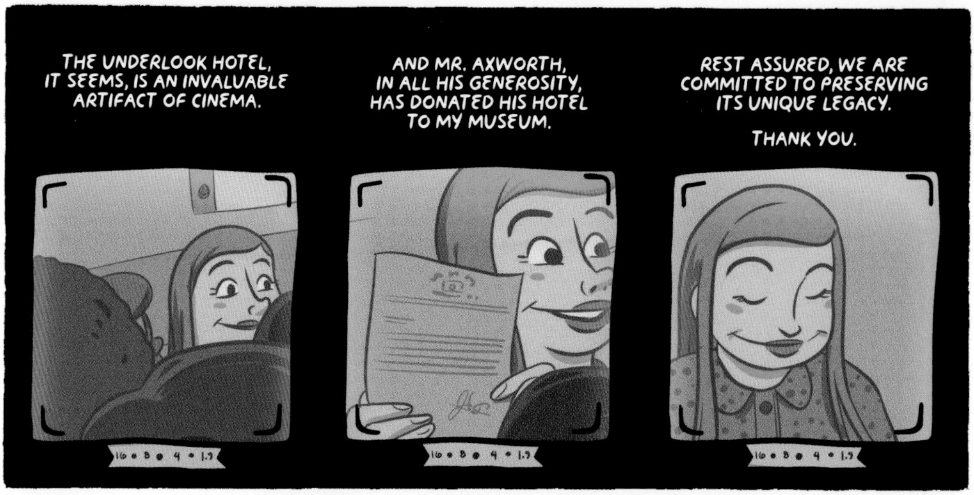
THE UNDERLOOK HOTEL, IT SEEMS, IS AN INVALUABLE ARTIFACT OF CINEMA.
AND MR. AXWORTH, IN ALL HIS GENEROSITY, HAS DONATED HIS HOTEL TO MY MUSEUM.
REST ASSURED, WE ARE COMMITTED TO PRESERVING ITS UNIQUE LEGACY.
THANK YOU.

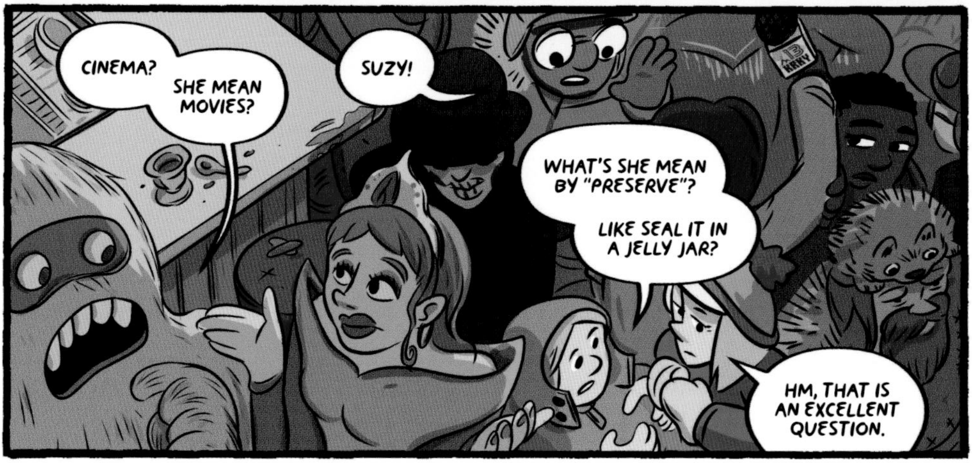
CINEMA?
SHE MEAN MOVIES?
SUZY!
WHAT'S SHE MEAN BY "PRESERVE"?
LIKE SEAL IT IN A JELLY JAR?
HM, THAT IS AN EXCELLENT QUESTION.

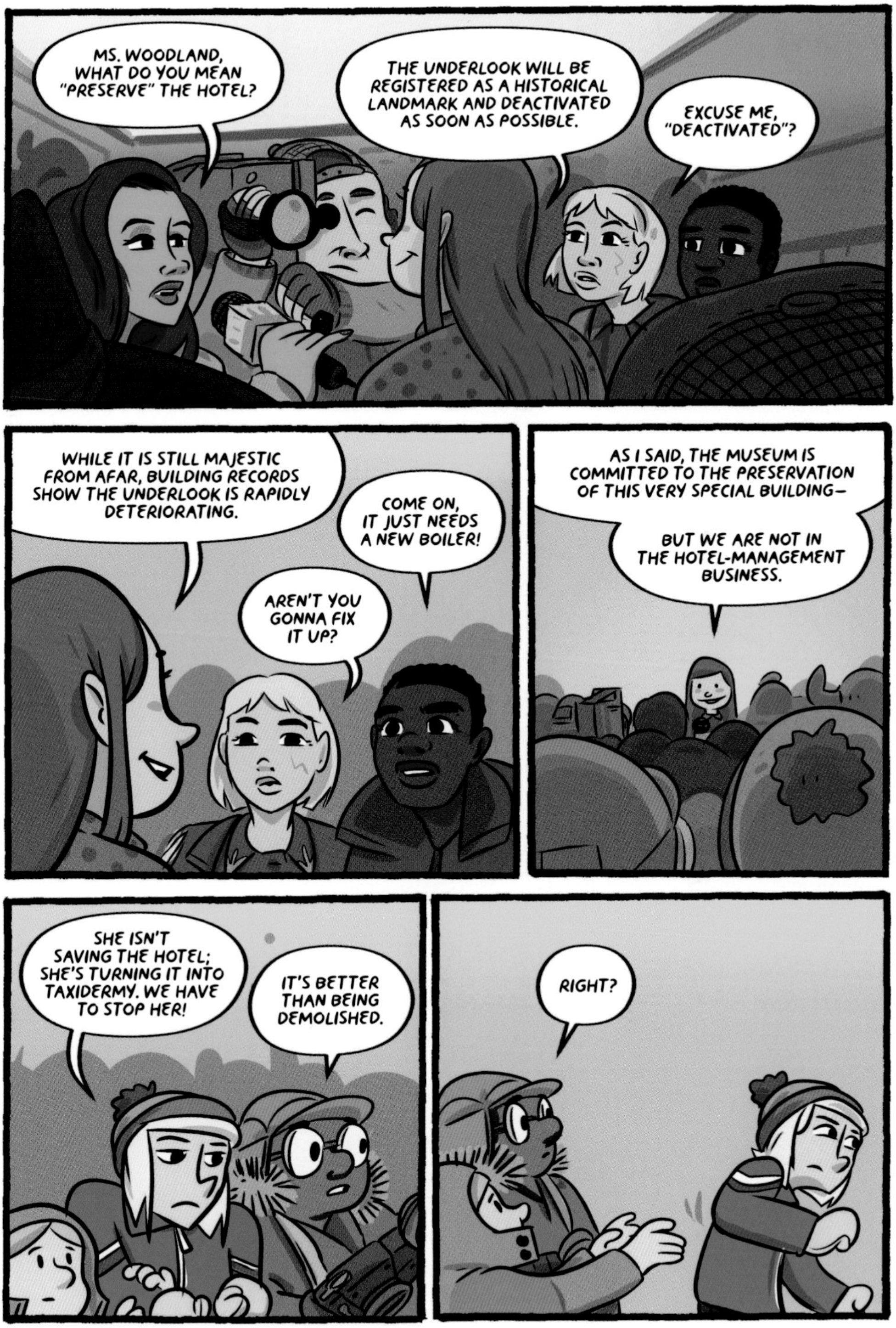
MS. WOODLAND, WHAT DO YOU MEAN "PRESERVE" THE HOTEL?
THE UNDERLOOK WILL BE REGISTERED AS A HISTORICAL LANDMARK AND DEACTIVATED AS SOON AS POSSIBLE.
EXCUSE ME, "DEACTIVATED"?
WHILE IT IS STILL MAJESTIC FROM AFAR, BUILDING RECORDS SHOW THE UNDERLOOK IS RAPIDLY DETERIORATING.
COME ON, IT JUST NEEDS A NEW BOILER!
AREN'T YOU GONNA FIX IT UP?
AS I SAID, THE MUSEUM IS COMMITTED TO THE PRESERVATION OF THIS VERY SPECIAL BUILDING—
BUT WE ARE NOT IN THE HOTEL-MANAGEMENT BUSINESS.
SHE ISN'T SAVING THE HOTEL; SHE'S TURNING IT INTO TAXIDERMY. WE HAVE TO STOP HER!
IT'S BETTER THAN BEING DEMOLISHED.
RIGHT?

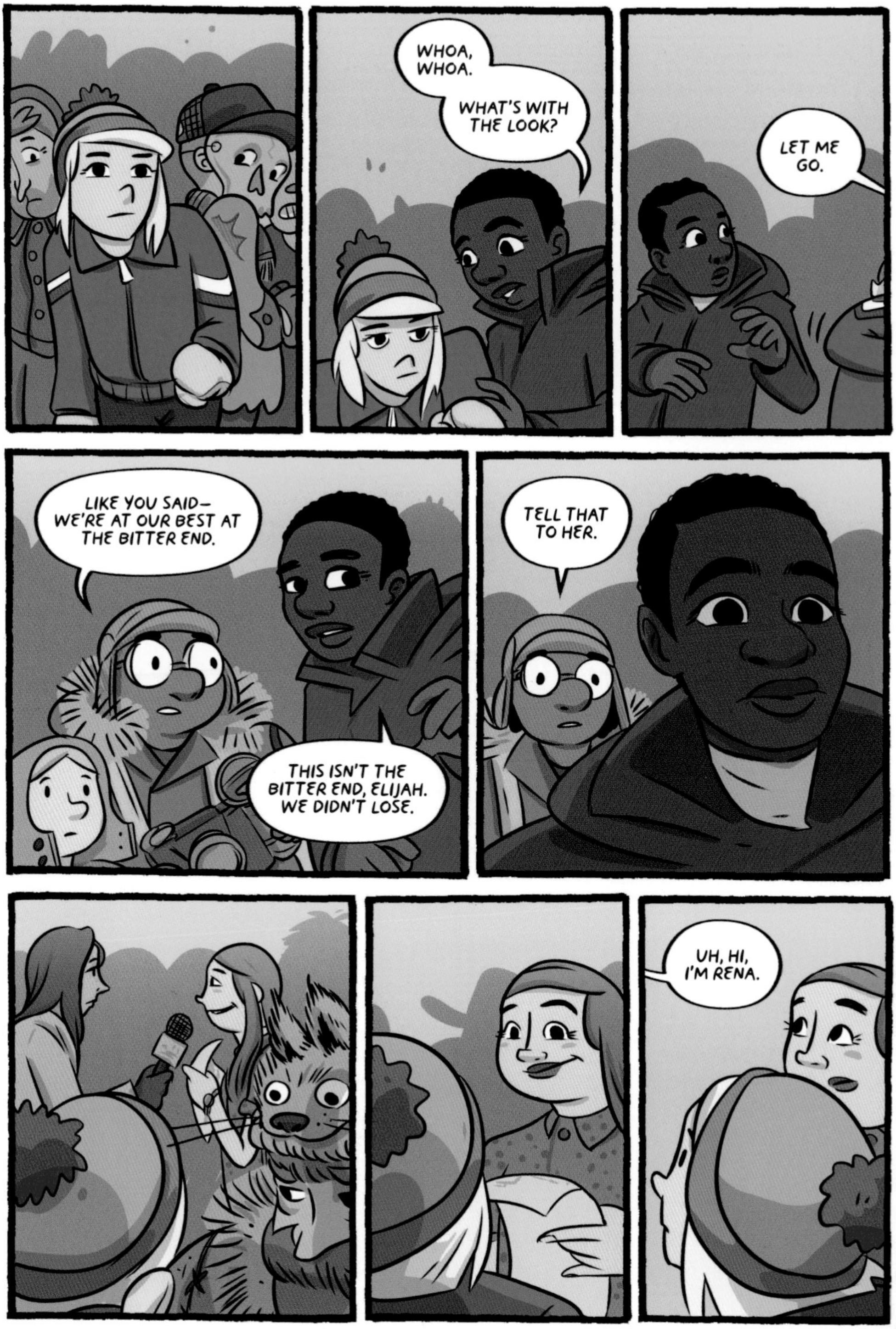
WHOA, WHOA.
WHAT'S WITH THE LOOK?
LET ME GO.
LIKE YOU SAID— WE'RE AT OUR BEST AT THE BITTER END.
THIS ISN'T THE BITTER END, ELIJAH. WE DIDN'T LOSE.
TELL THAT TO HER.
UH, HI, I'M RENA.

I USED TO PLAY FOR THE PARK.

STOMP 'EM, YETIS!

HA HA, YEAH.

MY GREAT-GREAT-GRANDPA HELPED BUILD LEER'S BIG, FANCY HOTEL.

HALF A CENTURY LATER, MY DAD WAS RUNNING THE KITCHEN.

THERE ARE A MILLION STORIES LIVING IN THAT OLD PLACE.

I KNOW MINE'S ONE OF THEM.

I'LL TELL YA, I'M SCARED THEY'RE ALL ABOUT TO DISAPPEAR—

AND NO DOUBT SOME OF THEM WILL.

BUT I DON'T THINK TODAY SHOULD BE ABOUT SAYING GOODBYE.

208

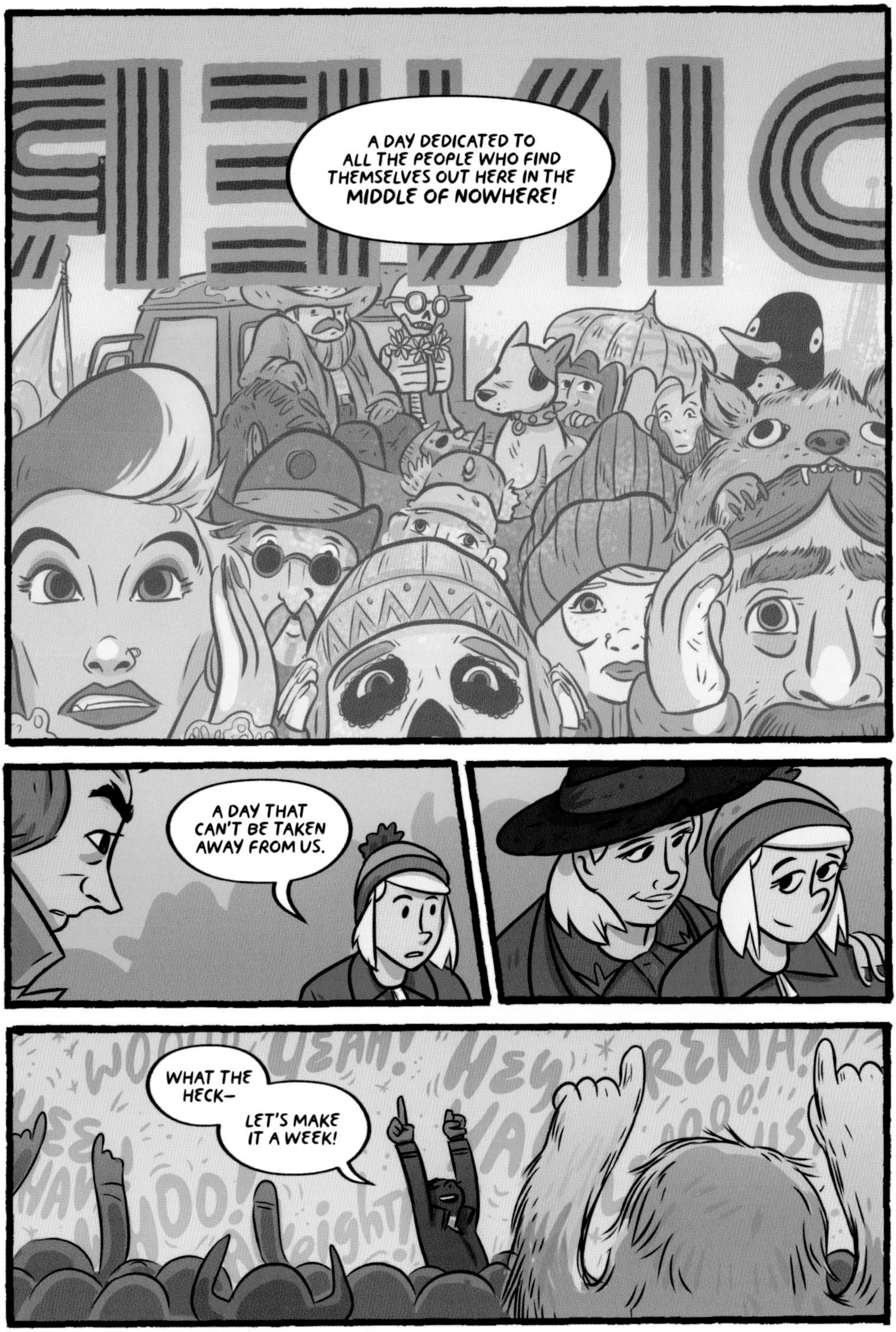
A DAY DEDICATED TO ALL THE PEOPLE WHO FIND THEMSELVES OUT HERE IN THE MIDDLE OF NOWHERE!
A DAY THAT CAN'T BE TAKEN AWAY FROM US.
WHAT THE HECK–
LET'S MAKE IT A WEEK!

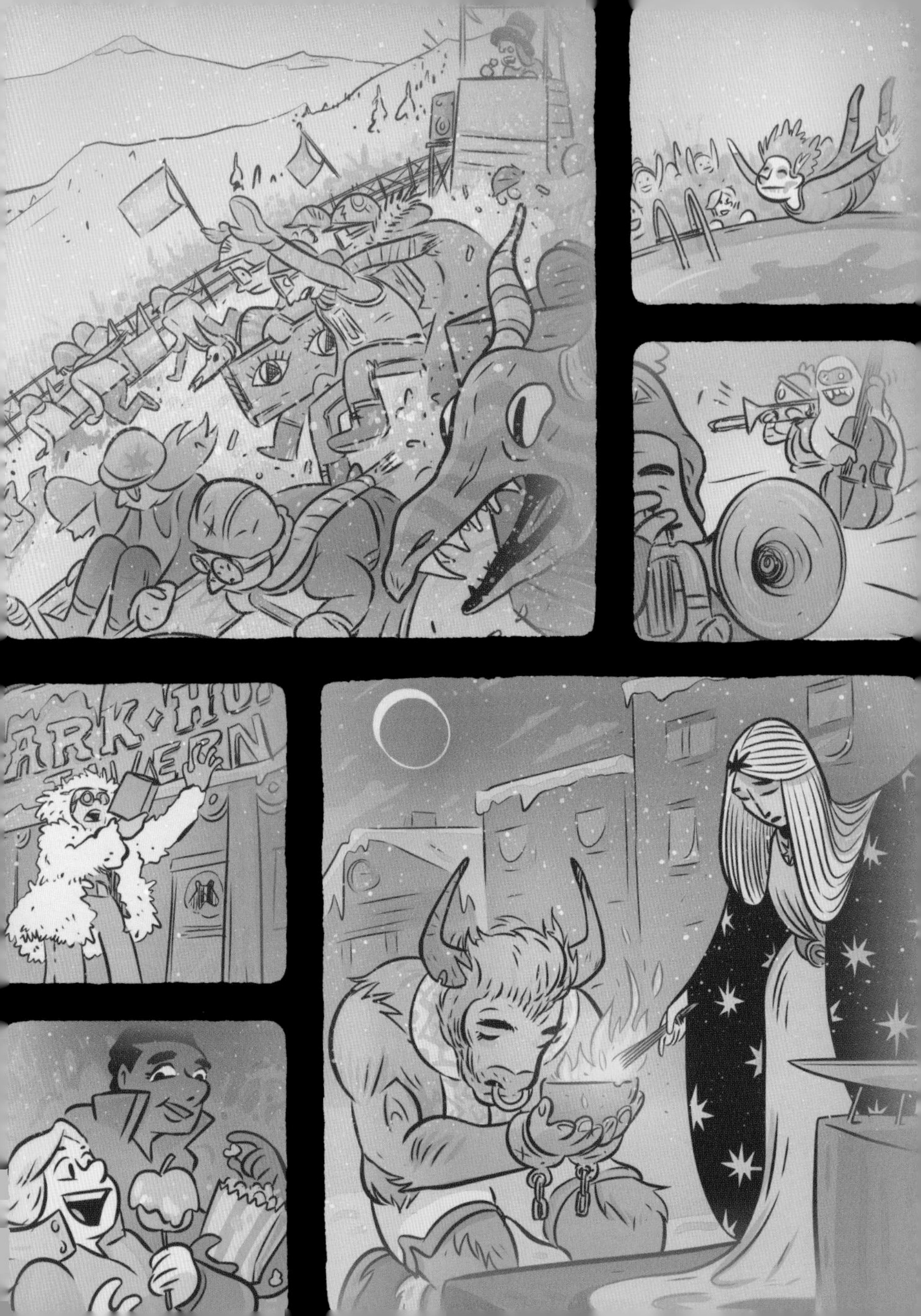

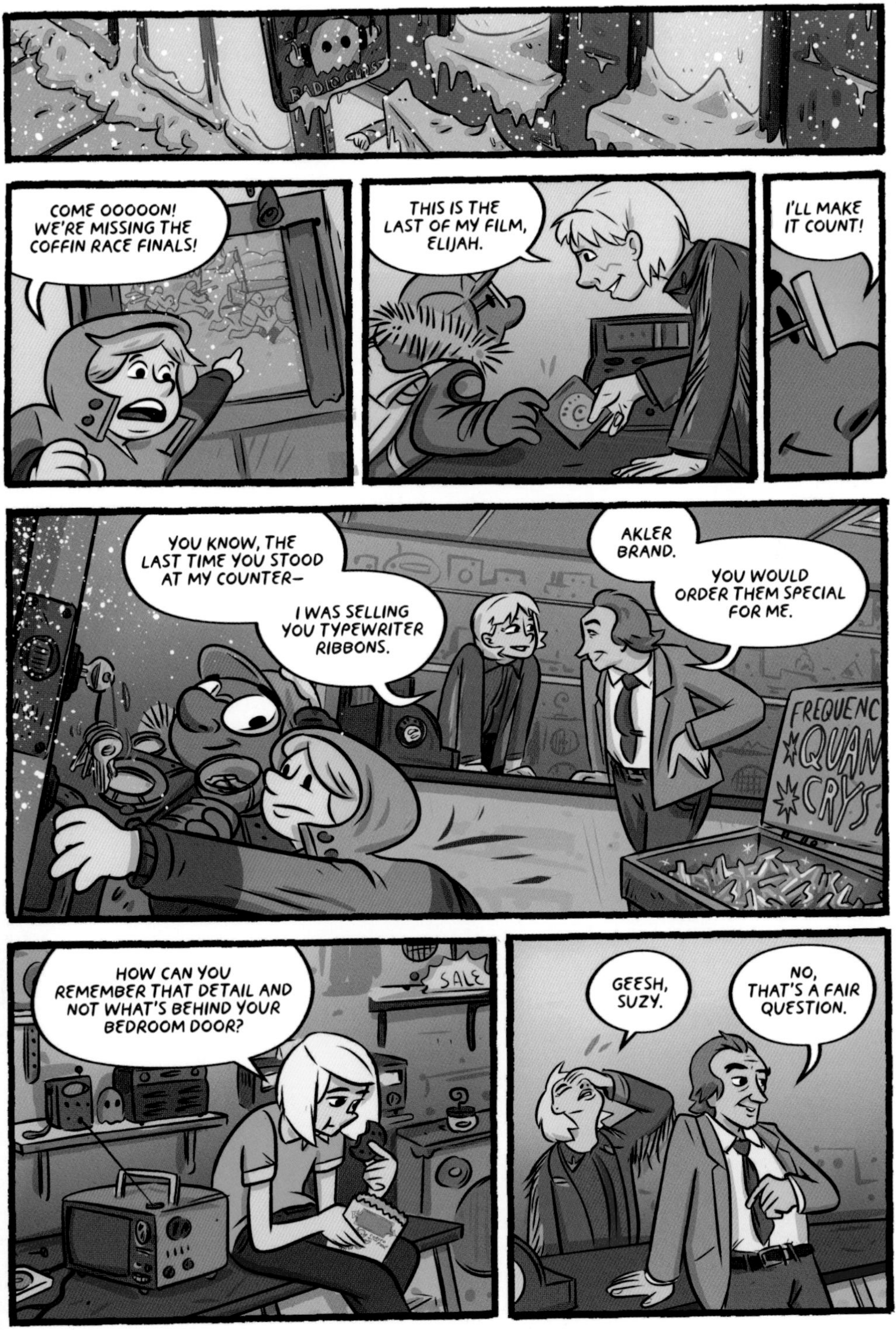
RADIO GHOST
COME OOOOON! WE'RE MISSING THE COFFIN RACE FINALS!
THIS IS THE LAST OF MY FILM, ELIJAH.
I'LL MAKE IT COUNT!
YOU KNOW, THE LAST TIME YOU STOOD AT MY COUNTER—
I WAS SELLING YOU TYPEWRITER RIBBONS.
AKLER BRAND.
YOU WOULD ORDER THEM SPECIAL FOR ME.
HOW CAN YOU REMEMBER THAT DETAIL AND NOT WHAT'S BEHIND YOUR BEDROOM DOOR?
SALE
GEESH, SUZY.
NO, THAT'S A FAIR QUESTION.

MY TYPEWRITER.

WHAT HAVE YOU DONE TO IT?

I JAZZED IT UP. YOU KNOW, FOR THE...

...TOURISTS.

YES, YES, BUT WHAT DOES IT DO?

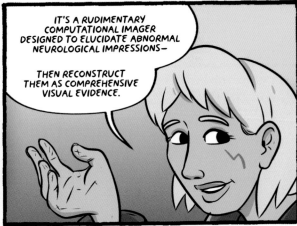

IT'S A RUDIMENTARY COMPUTATIONAL IMAGER DESIGNED TO ELUCIDATE ABNORMAL NEUROLOGICAL IMPRESSIONS—

THEN RECONSTRUCT THEM AS COMPREHENSIVE VISUAL EVIDENCE.

I CALL IT THE GHOST WRITER.

DING!

WHAT DO YOU SAY, MR. AXWORTH?

WANT TO KNOW WHAT THE CREEPY VOICES IN YOUR HEAD HAVE TO SAY?

HM, WELL, I AM THE KING OF HORROR.

THAT'S THE SPIRIT.

DON'T BE SCARED. I'LL EXPLAIN HOW IT WORKS.

FIRST, THE NEURAL PICKUPS IN THE HEADBAND TRANSMIT ELECTRICAL PULSES FROM YOUR BRAIN'S NERVE CELLS.

TABLE SURFACE

THEN THE SIGNALS PASS THROUGH A HEAT-SENSITIVE METAL FILAMENT, ERODING HOLES IN A PHOTOSENSITIVE CYLINDER.

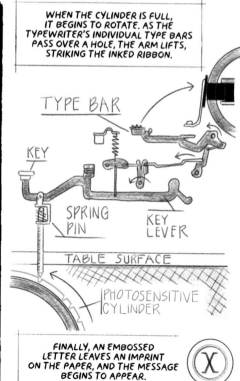

WHEN THE CYLINDER IS FULL, IT BEGINS TO ROTATE. AS THE TYPEWRITER'S INDIVIDUAL TYPE BARS PASS OVER A HOLE, THE ARM LIFTS, STRIKING THE INKED RIBBON.

TYPE BAR

KEY

SPRING PIN

KEY LEVER

TABLE SURFACE

PHOTOSENSITIVE CYLINDER

FINALLY, AN EMBOSSED LETTER LEAVES AN IMPRINT ON THE PAPER, AND THE MESSAGE BEGINS TO APPEAR.

X

CLEVER, THOUGH NOT VERY SUPERNATURAL.

THAT'S WHERE MOM'S CUSTOM AMPLIFIER COMES INTO PLAY.

COME ON, YOU'RE RUINING THE ILLUSION!

IT FILTERS OUT ERRANT SIGNALS.

ERRANT SIGNALS?

IT'S HER SPOOKY TERM FOR "UNIDENTIFIABLE STRAY NOISE."

YOU REALLY ARE NO FUN, SUZY.

HOLD ON, JACK. I'M GOING TO TRY TO TUNE IN TO A BESTSELLER.

WOOOOOO

IT'S A JOKE! SEE, I CAN BE FUN!

YOU DON'T THINK MUCH OF ME, DO YOU?

ACTUALLY—

I'VE THOUGHT ABOUT YOU A LOT.

I JUST DON'T UNDERSTAND YOU.

MECHANICAL SYSTEMS, COMPUTATIONAL STUFF— IT CLICKS FOR ME.

BUT THE WAY YOUR STORIES WORK... IT'S TOO ABSTRACT. YOUR BOOKS ARE LIKE READING A MATHEMATICAL PROOF.

YOU KNOW WHAT I MEAN?

NO, I DO NOT.

A PROOF STARTS WITH A CONCLUSION, SOMETHING THE MATHEMATICIAN BELIEVES TO BE TRUE.

HALCYON TRIANGLE

RED MOUNTAIN

UNDERLOOK

MT. OLYMPUS

GLACIER CREEK

LET'S SAY...

...A PARTICULAR GEOMETRIC SHAPE.

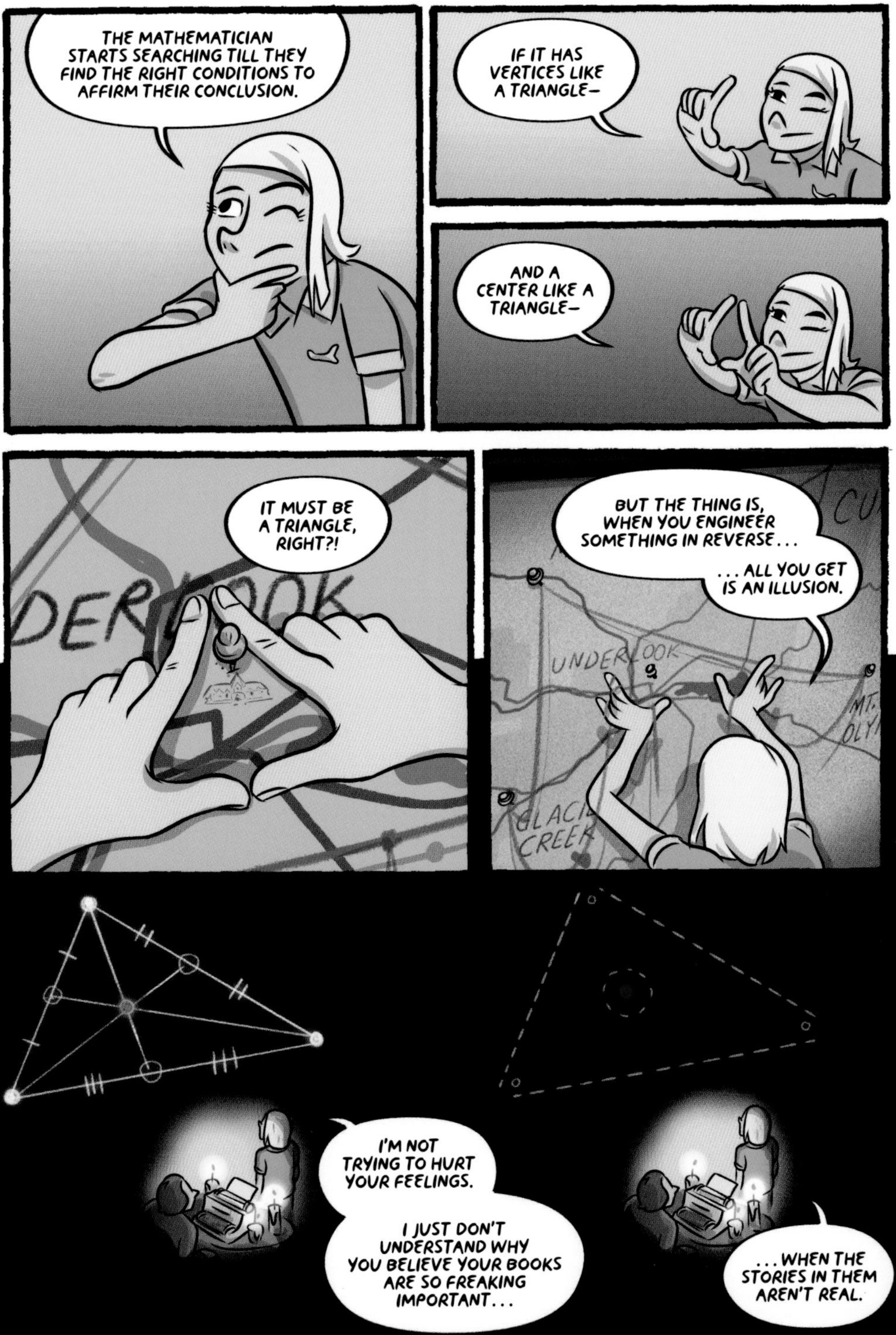
THE MATHEMATICIAN STARTS SEARCHING TILL THEY FIND THE RIGHT CONDITIONS TO AFFIRM THEIR CONCLUSION.
IF IT HAS VERTICES LIKE A TRIANGLE—
AND A CENTER LIKE A TRIANGLE—
IT MUST BE A TRIANGLE, RIGHT?!
DER OOK
BUT THE THING IS, WHEN YOU ENGINEER SOMETHING IN REVERSE . . .
. . . ALL YOU GET IS AN ILLUSION.
UNDERLOOK
GLACI CREEK
I'M NOT TRYING TO HURT YOUR FEELINGS.
I JUST DON'T UNDERSTAND WHY YOU BELIEVE YOUR BOOKS ARE SO FREAKING IMPORTANT . . .
. . . WHEN THE STORIES IN THEM AREN'T REAL.

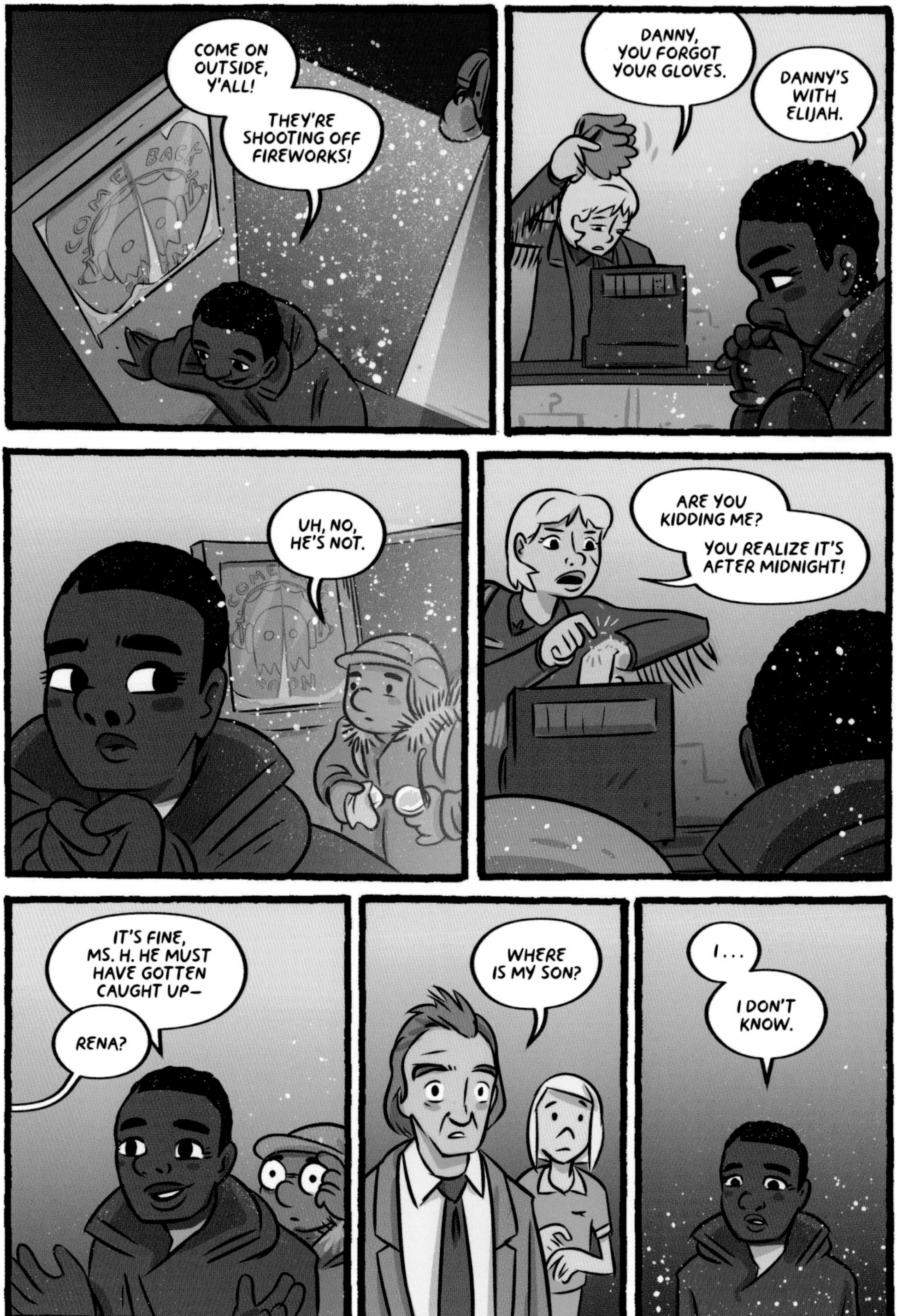
COME ON OUTSIDE, Y'ALL!
THEY'RE SHOOTING OFF FIREWORKS!
DANNY, YOU FORGOT YOUR GLOVES.
DANNY'S WITH ELIJAH.
UH, NO, HE'S NOT.
ARE YOU KIDDING ME?
YOU REALIZE IT'S AFTER MIDNIGHT!
IT'S FINE, MS. H. HE MUST HAVE GOTTEN CAUGHT UP—
RENA?
WHERE IS MY SON?
I . . .
I DON'T KNOW.

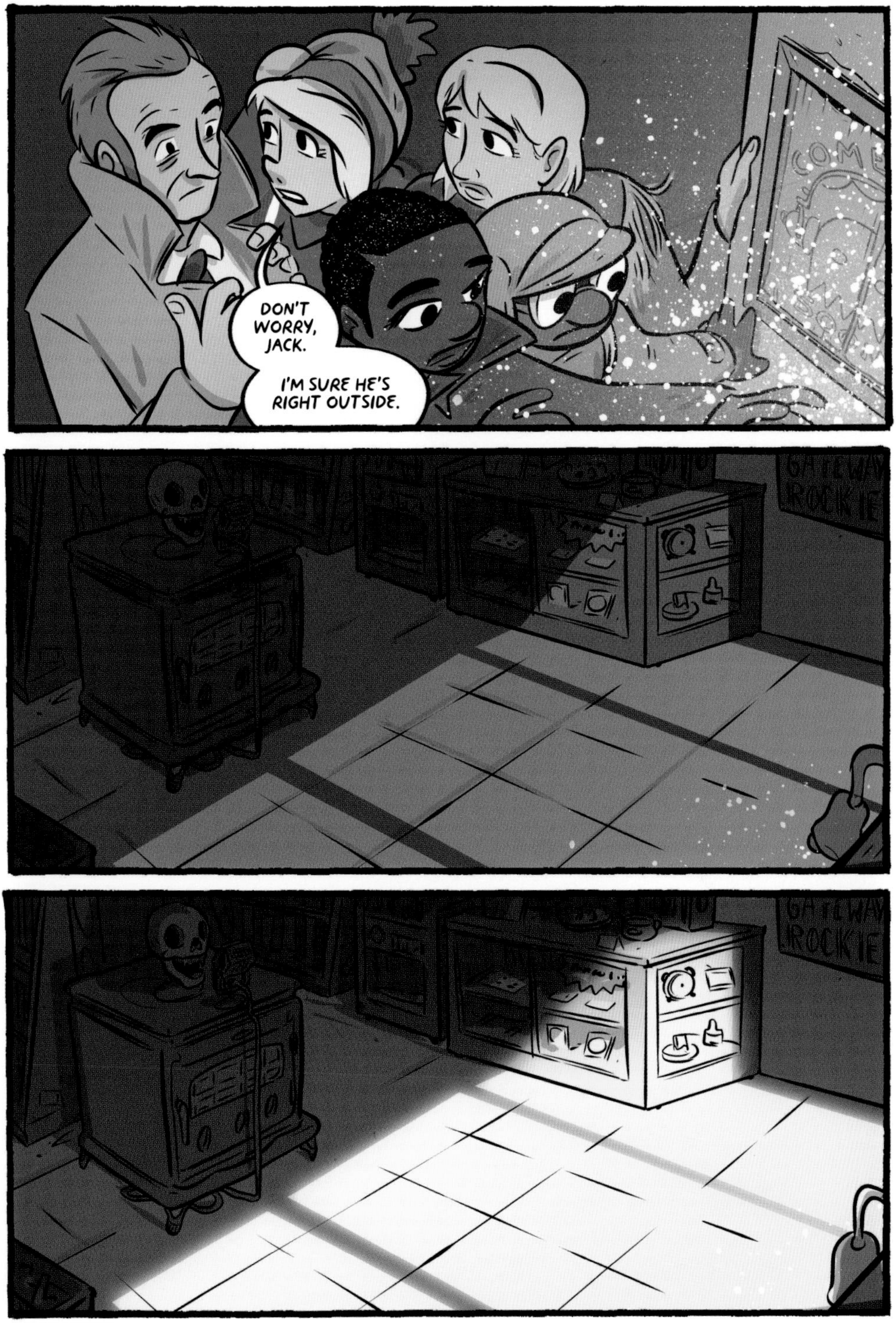
DON'T WORRY, JACK.
I'M SURE HE'S RIGHT OUTSIDE.

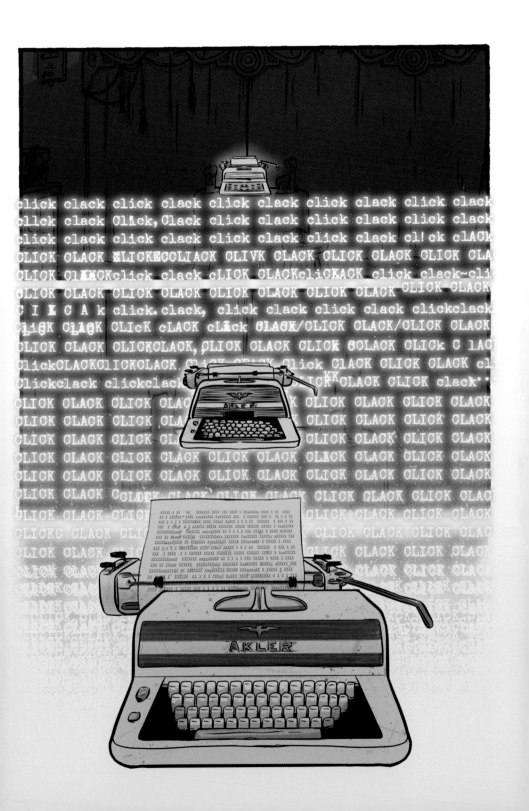

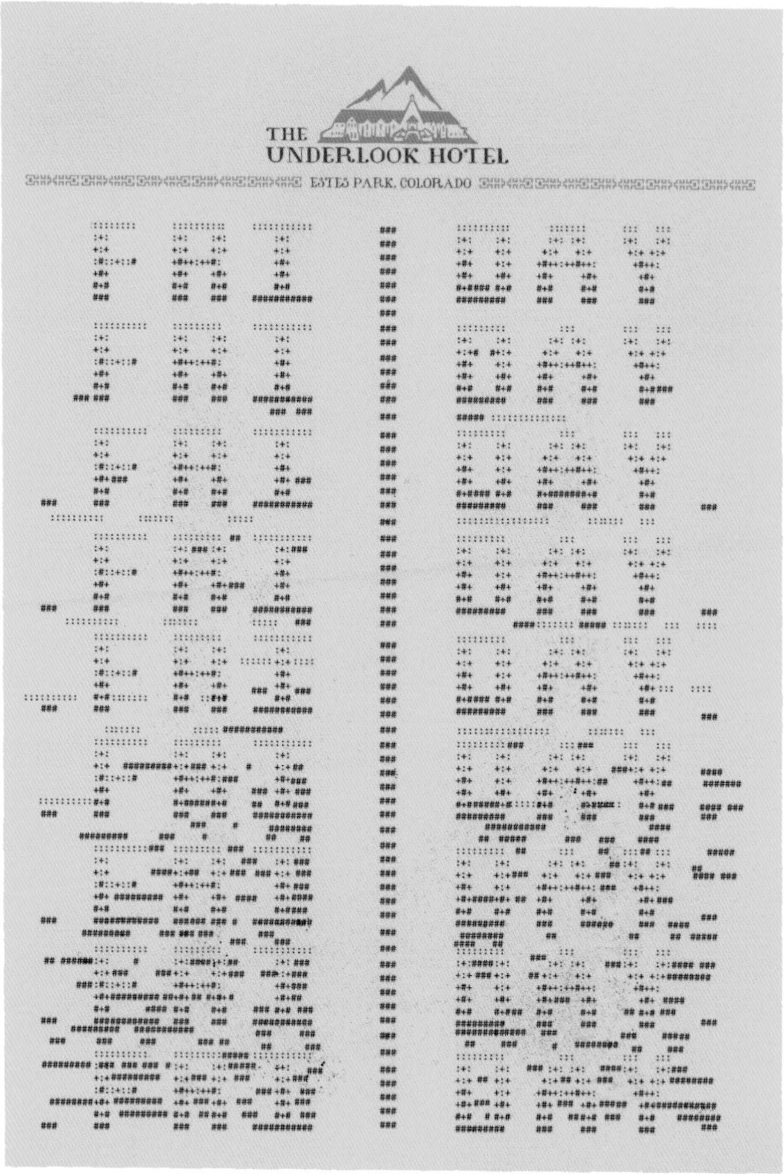
THE
UNDERLOOK HOTEL
ESTES PARK, COLORADO

HEY, CHUCK! UNLOCK THE BACK!

YOU KIDDING ME, SUZ? THIS ISN'T A JOY RIDE.

TRUST US, HON. WE'RE ON IT.

MOM!

WE HAVE TO FOLLOW THEM.

WHERE'S ELIJAH? WE NEED HIS CRABBY TAXI GUY.

ELIJAH!

DID YOU SEE THOSE TIRES? NO TAXI IS GETTING UP THAT ROAD.

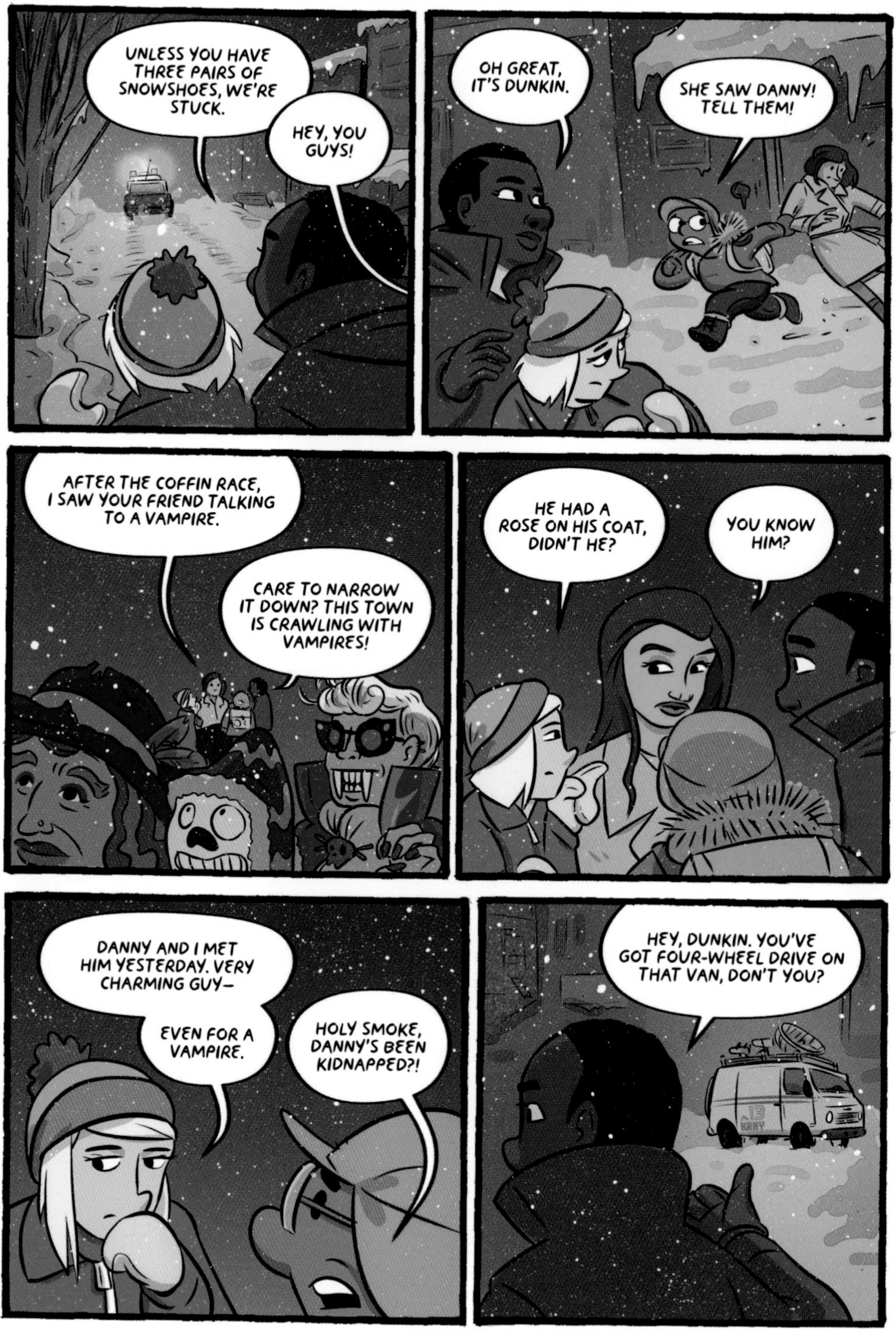
UNLESS YOU HAVE THREE PAIRS OF SNOWSHOES, WE'RE STUCK.
HEY, YOU GUYS!
OH GREAT, IT'S DUNKIN.
SHE SAW DANNY! TELL THEM!
AFTER THE COFFIN RACE, I SAW YOUR FRIEND TALKING TO A VAMPIRE.
CARE TO NARROW IT DOWN? THIS TOWN IS CRAWLING WITH VAMPIRES!
HE HAD A ROSE ON HIS COAT, DIDN'T HE?
YOU KNOW HIM?
DANNY AND I MET HIM YESTERDAY. VERY CHARMING GUY—
EVEN FOR A VAMPIRE.
HOLY SMOKE, DANNY'S BEEN KIDNAPPED?!
HEY, DUNKIN. YOU'VE GOT FOUR-WHEEL DRIVE ON THAT VAN, DON'T YOU?

FORGET IT.

I DON'T GO ANYWHERE WITHOUT A CAMERAMAN.

SMILE!

MOVE OVER, DUNKIN.

NO ONE KNOWS THAT ROAD LIKE I DO.

A MOBILE EDITING BAY!

SOOOO COOL!

HEY! DON'T YOU TOUCH THAT!

click! *click!*

229

CAN I SEE THE FOOTAGE FROM YOUR INTERVIEW?

HOW DARE YOU TRY TO SCOOP MY STORY!

WHERE'S YOUR JOURNALISTIC INTEGRITY?

I'M NOT SCOOPING!

I'M LOOKING FOR CLUES!

CLUES?!

THIS IS A NEWS VAN! IT'S NOT THE MYSTERY MACHINE!

STOP!

SKREECH

OOF!

CAN YOU STOP DOING THAT?!

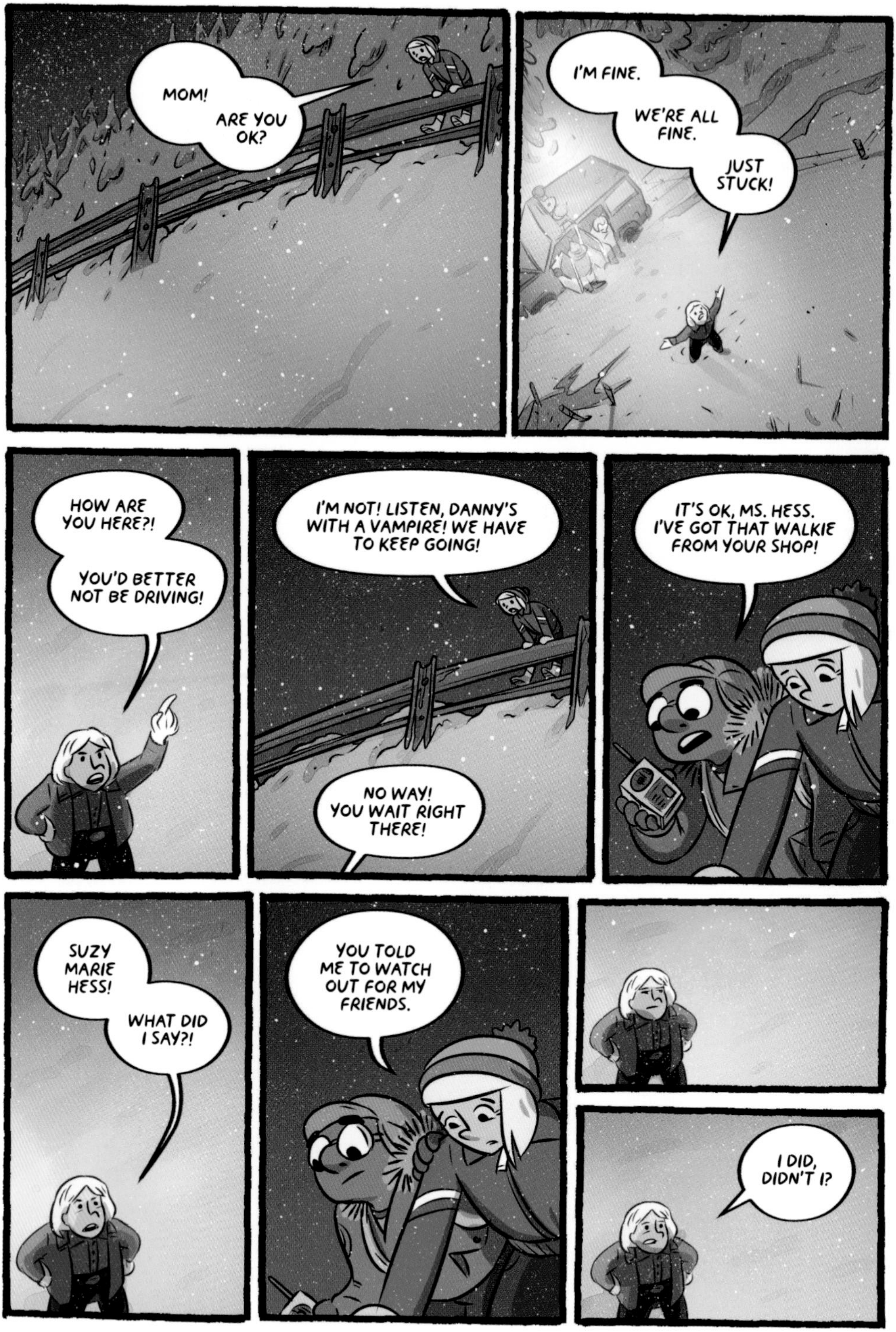
MOM!
ARE YOU OK?
I'M FINE.
WE'RE ALL FINE.
JUST STUCK!
HOW ARE YOU HERE?!
YOU'D BETTER NOT BE DRIVING!
I'M NOT! LISTEN, DANNY'S WITH A VAMPIRE! WE HAVE TO KEEP GOING!
NO WAY! YOU WAIT RIGHT THERE!
IT'S OK, MS. HESS. I'VE GOT THAT WALKIE FROM YOUR SHOP!
SUZY MARIE HESS!
WHAT DID I SAY?!
YOU TOLD ME TO WATCH OUT FOR MY FRIENDS.
I DID, DIDN'T I?

HERE WE GO.

HOLD ON.

WE'RE NOT GOING ANYWHERE UNTIL WE CAN TRUST EACH OTHER.

FINE.

I'LL LET YOU SEE MY FOOTAGE...

...IF YOU LET ME INTO THE UNDERLOOK.

DEAL.

AND I WANT AN EXCLUSIVE INTERVIEW WITH JACK AXWORTH—

VROOM

DON'T PUSH IT.

THERE'S A CERTAIN BEAUTY TO THESE MOUNTAINS.

IT DRAWS PEOPLE TO THEM.

SOMETIMES PEOPLE MISTAKE THAT BEAUTY FOR GENEROSITY.

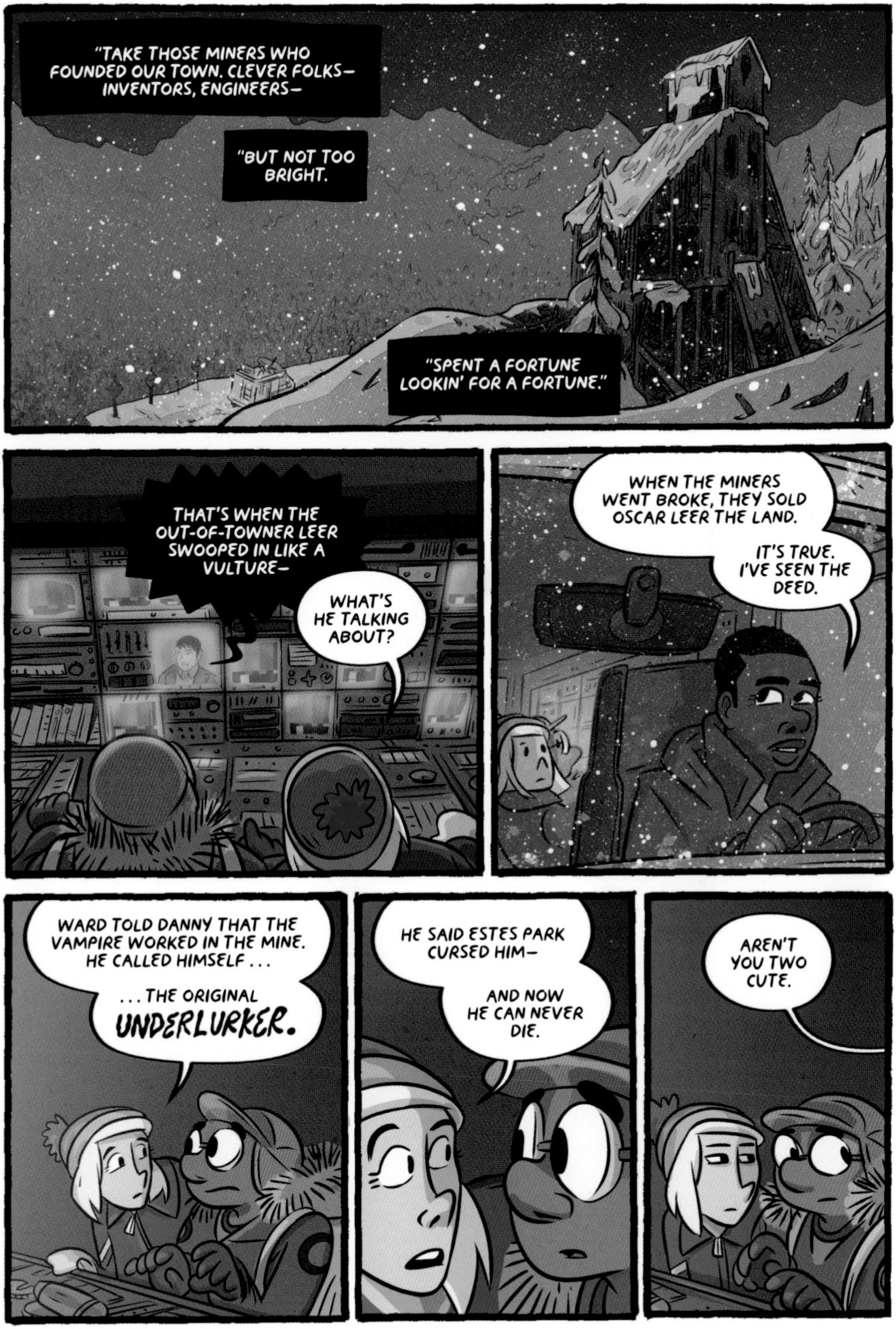
"TAKE THOSE MINERS WHO FOUNDED OUR TOWN. CLEVER FOLKS—INVENTORS, ENGINEERS—
"BUT NOT TOO BRIGHT.
"SPENT A FORTUNE LOOKIN' FOR A FORTUNE."
THAT'S WHEN THE OUT-OF-TOWNER LEER SWOOPED IN LIKE A VULTURE—
WHAT'S HE TALKING ABOUT?
WHEN THE MINERS WENT BROKE, THEY SOLD OSCAR LEER THE LAND.
IT'S TRUE. I'VE SEEN THE DEED.
WARD TOLD DANNY THAT THE VAMPIRE WORKED IN THE MINE. HE CALLED HIMSELF . . .
. . . THE ORIGINAL UNDERLURKER.
HE SAID ESTES PARK CURSED HIM—
AND NOW HE CAN NEVER DIE.
AREN'T YOU TWO CUTE.

DEDUCTIVE REASONING IS NOT CUTE!

CREEPING EACH OTHER OUT WITH AN OLD-TIME FOLKTALE? IT'S CUTE.

HEY, WHAT FOLKTALE?

"THE GIRL IN THE CAVE"—

OF COURSE.

WHAT?!

OK, YOU TWO ARE CUTE, BUT THIS IS ADORABLE.

BUT WHERE DOES THIS STORY COME FROM?!

YOU DON'T KNOW?

IT'S A CAUTIONARY TALE. BEEN AROUND FOREVER.

PARENTS USE IT TO SCARE KIDS FROM WANDERING INTO ABANDONED MINESHAFTS.

OF COURSE! THE CAVE IS A MINE! HOW DID I NOT FIGURE THAT OUT?!

DON'T WORRY, SHERLOCK. WE WON'T TELL ANYONE.

HUH. YOU GAVE THE GIRL A HAPPY ENDING.

WHAT'S WRONG WITH A HAPPY ENDING?

WELL, IT RUINS THE LESSON.

THE KID HAS TO DIE—

OR THE STORY IS POINTLESS.

OK, THAT'S ENOUGH STORY TIME.

LET'S HUNT A VAMPIRE.

237

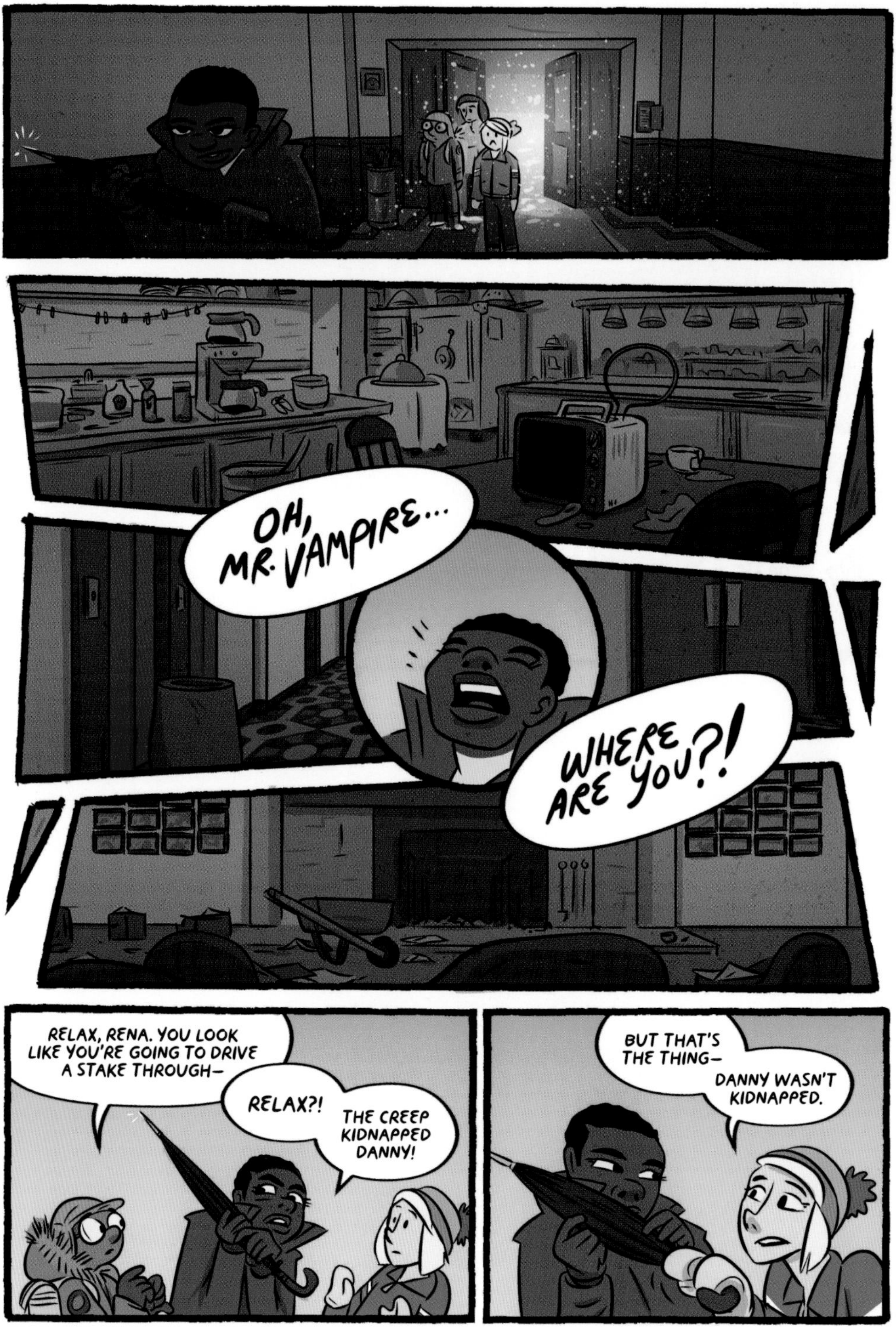
OH, MR. VAMPIRE...
WHERE ARE YOU?!
RELAX, RENA. YOU LOOK LIKE YOU'RE GOING TO DRIVE A STAKE THROUGH—
RELAX?!
THE CREEP KIDNAPPED DANNY!
BUT THAT'S THE THING—
DANNY WASN'T KIDNAPPED.

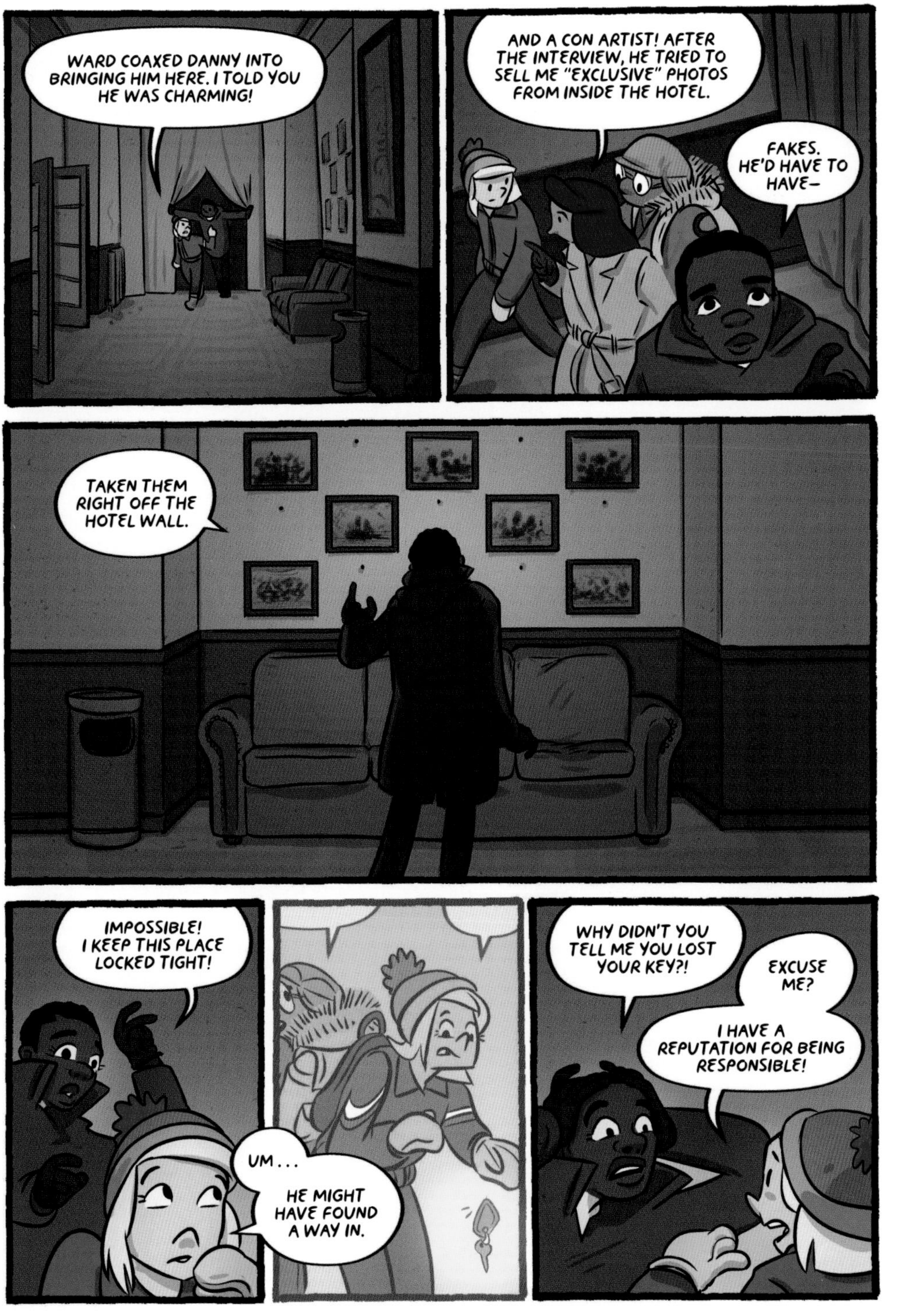
WARD COAXED DANNY INTO BRINGING HIM HERE. I TOLD YOU HE WAS CHARMING!
AND A CON ARTIST! AFTER THE INTERVIEW, HE TRIED TO SELL ME "EXCLUSIVE" PHOTOS FROM INSIDE THE HOTEL.
FAKES. HE'D HAVE TO HAVE—
TAKEN THEM RIGHT OFF THE HOTEL WALL.
IMPOSSIBLE! I KEEP THIS PLACE LOCKED TIGHT!
UM...
HE MIGHT HAVE FOUND A WAY IN.
WHY DIDN'T YOU TELL ME YOU LOST YOUR KEY?!
EXCUSE ME?
I HAVE A REPUTATION FOR BEING RESPONSIBLE!

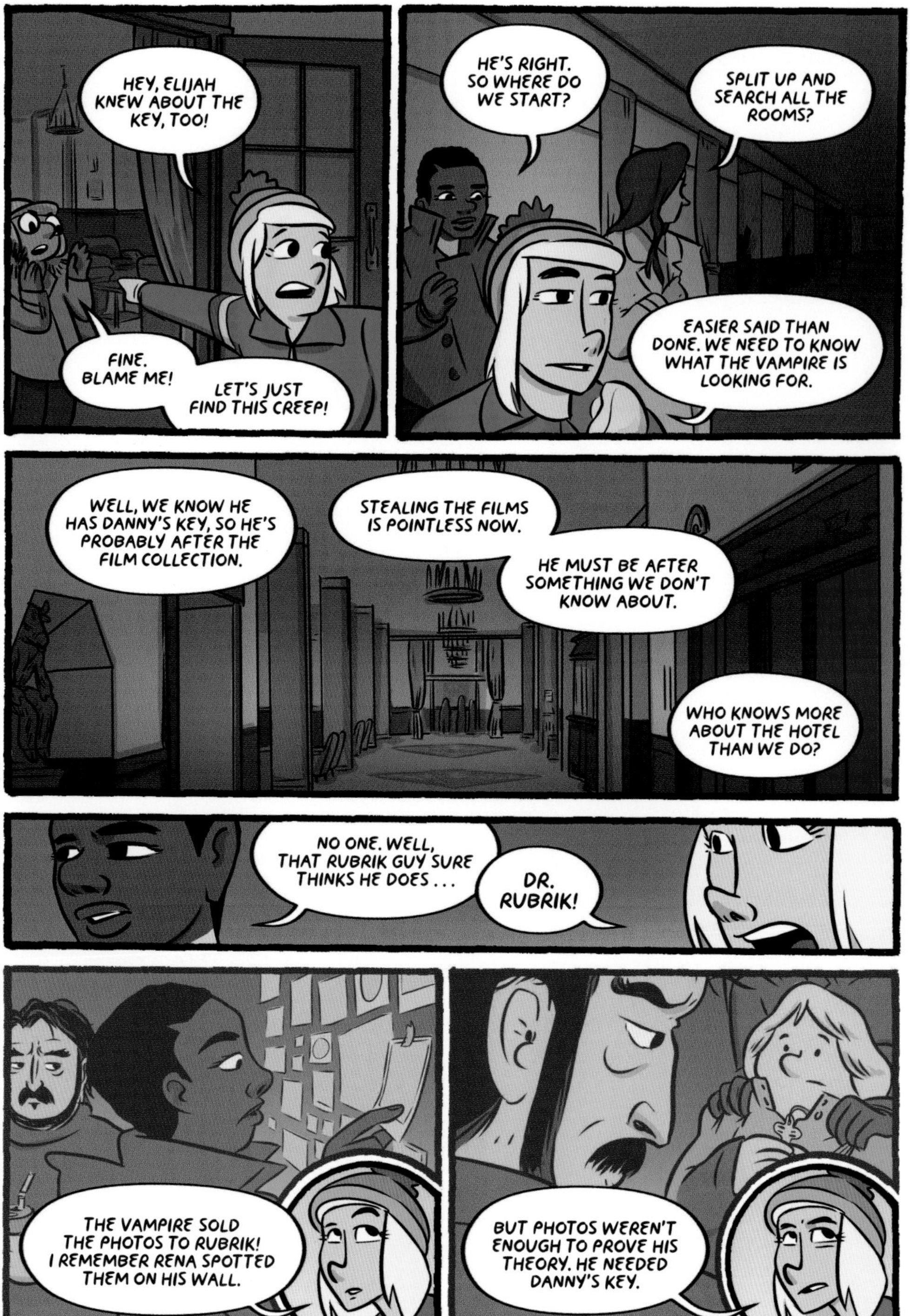

HEY, ELIJAH KNEW ABOUT THE KEY, TOO!
FINE. BLAME ME!
LET'S JUST FIND THIS CREEP!
HE'S RIGHT. SO WHERE DO WE START?
SPLIT UP AND SEARCH ALL THE ROOMS?
EASIER SAID THAN DONE. WE NEED TO KNOW WHAT THE VAMPIRE IS LOOKING FOR.
WELL, WE KNOW HE HAS DANNY'S KEY, SO HE'S PROBABLY AFTER THE FILM COLLECTION.
STEALING THE FILMS IS POINTLESS NOW.
HE MUST BE AFTER SOMETHING WE DON'T KNOW ABOUT.
WHO KNOWS MORE ABOUT THE HOTEL THAN WE DO?
NO ONE. WELL, THAT RUBRIK GUY SURE THINKS HE DOES . . .
DR. RUBRIK!
THE VAMPIRE SOLD THE PHOTOS TO RUBRIK! I REMEMBER RENA SPOTTED THEM ON HIS WALL.
BUT PHOTOS WEREN'T ENOUGH TO PROVE HIS THEORY. HE NEEDED DANNY'S KEY.

RIGHT BEFORE WE LEFT, RUBRIK SAID TO US—

"DON'T YOU SEE? THE SECRET LIES WITH LINDA LEER!"

1974

HER KEY UNLOCKS MORE THAN A ROOM OF OLD MOVIES—

AND THE VAMPIRE KNOWS IT.

ZOINKS!

ALL WE NEED IS A TALKING GREAT DANE TO SOLVE THE MYSTERY, RIGHT, GANG?!

YOU HAVE ALL THE LEER FAMILY RECORDS, RIGHT?

YEAH, THEY'RE IN MY OFFICE.

OH, WHAT, Y'ALL ARE TOO COOL FOR CARTOONS?

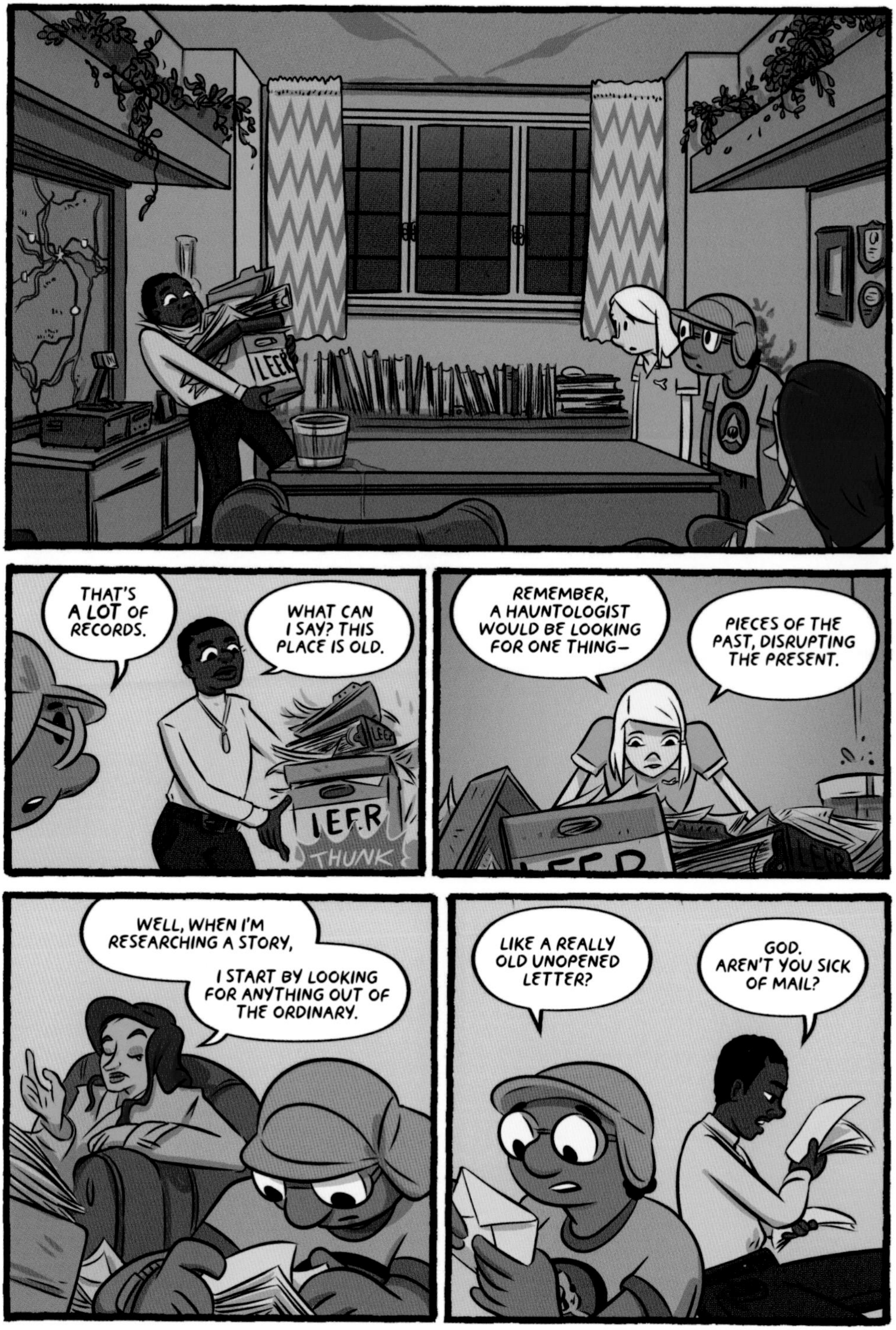

THAT'S A LOT OF RECORDS.
WHAT CAN I SAY? THIS PLACE IS OLD.
LEEF
LEER
THUNK
REMEMBER, A HAUNTOLOGIST WOULD BE LOOKING FOR ONE THING—
PIECES OF THE PAST, DISRUPTING THE PRESENT.
WELL, WHEN I'M RESEARCHING A STORY,
I START BY LOOKING FOR ANYTHING OUT OF THE ORDINARY.
LIKE A REALLY OLD UNOPENED LETTER?
GOD. AREN'T YOU SICK OF MAIL?

WHY WOULD THE HALCYON MINING COMPANY SEND A LETTER TO . . .

. . . ITSELF?

LET ME SEE THAT.

WHAT YOU HAVE HERE IS A PATENT- APPLICATION LETTER.

WHEN APPLYING FOR A PATENT, YOU MAIL YOURSELF A COPY OF THE SCHEMATIC AS A BACKUP RECORD.

SCHEMATIC?

LET ME SEE THAT.

IT'S SOME KIND OF MINING HOIST . . .

. . . AND I'VE SEEN IT BEFORE.

SUZY, WHAT THE HECK?!

LOOK!

THEY REALLY BUILT IT!

1906 - HALCYON MINERS; ROMERO, GLAVA, OLSEN

AND THIS GUY? THIS IS FODOR GLAVA. HE WORKED FOR THE MINE. HIS JOB TITLE WAS **UNDERLOOKER.**

WHY'S HE BLURRY?

tap tap tap

SOME OLD CAMERAS HAVE MIRRORS!

VAMPIRES DON'T SHOW UP IN MIRRORS!

SO YOU THINK THE VAMPIRE CAME BACK TO THE HOTEL . . .

. . . BECAUSE HE WANTS HIS OLD JOB BACK?

AN UNDERLOOKER'S JOB WAS TO MANAGE THE MINE.

HE WOULD KNOW EVERYTHING THAT'S DOWN THERE.

SO . . . WHAT'S DOWN THERE?

THE GIRL IN THE CAVE . . .

THE EVIL SPIRIT GUARDS A TREASURE.

THAT'S A STORY. IT ISN'T REAL.

RIGHT.

BUT WHAT IF WARD BARLOW THINKS IT IS?

WE FIND THIS TREASURE, WE FIND DANNY.

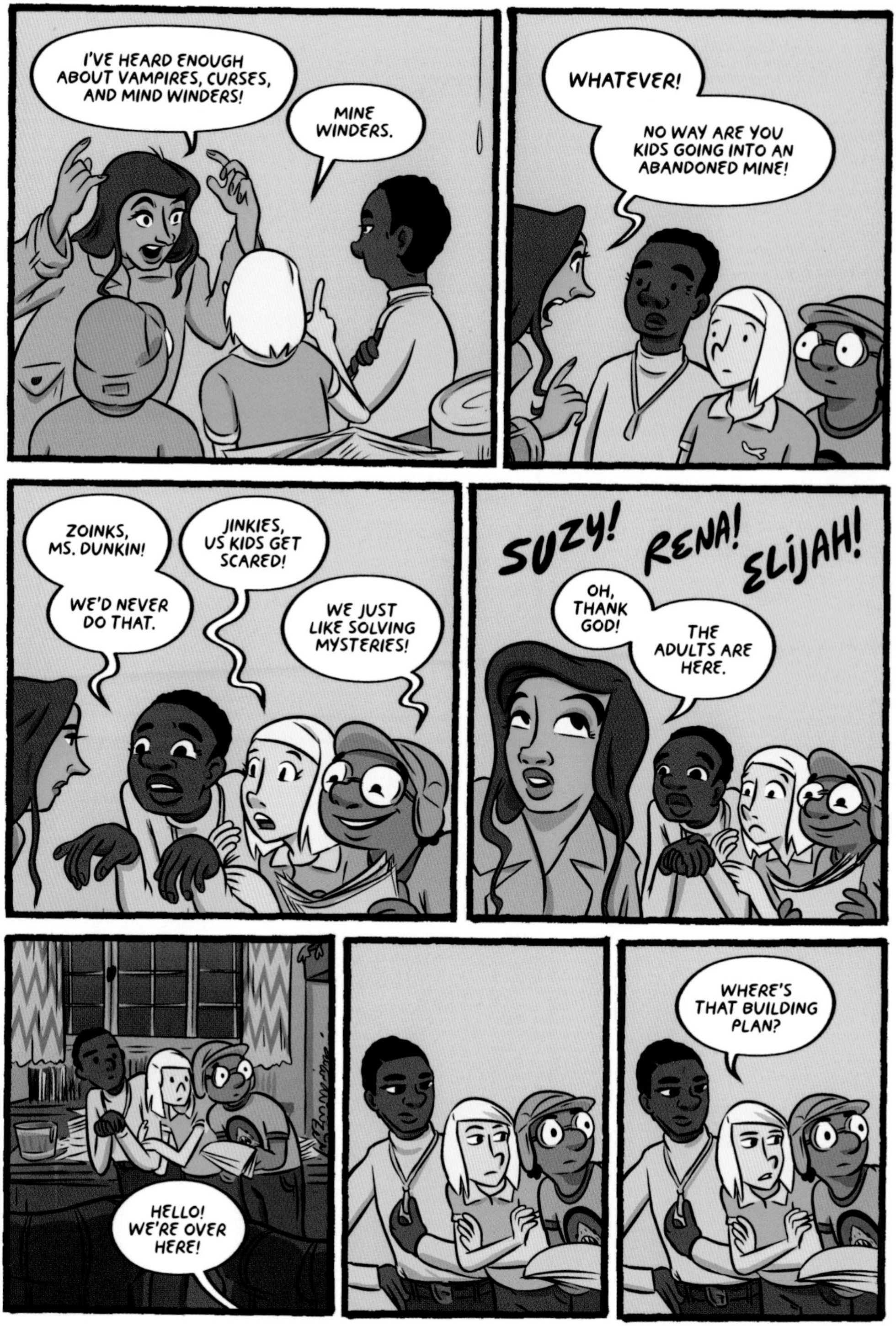
I'VE HEARD ENOUGH ABOUT VAMPIRES, CURSES, AND MIND WINDERS!
MINE WINDERS.
WHATEVER!
NO WAY ARE YOU KIDS GOING INTO AN ABANDONED MINE!
ZOINKS, MS. DUNKIN!
WE'D NEVER DO THAT.
JINKIES, US KIDS GET SCARED!
WE JUST LIKE SOLVING MYSTERIES!
SUZY!
RENA!
ELIJAH!
OH, THANK GOD!
THE ADULTS ARE HERE.
HELLO! WE'RE OVER HERE!
WHERE'S THAT BUILDING PLAN?

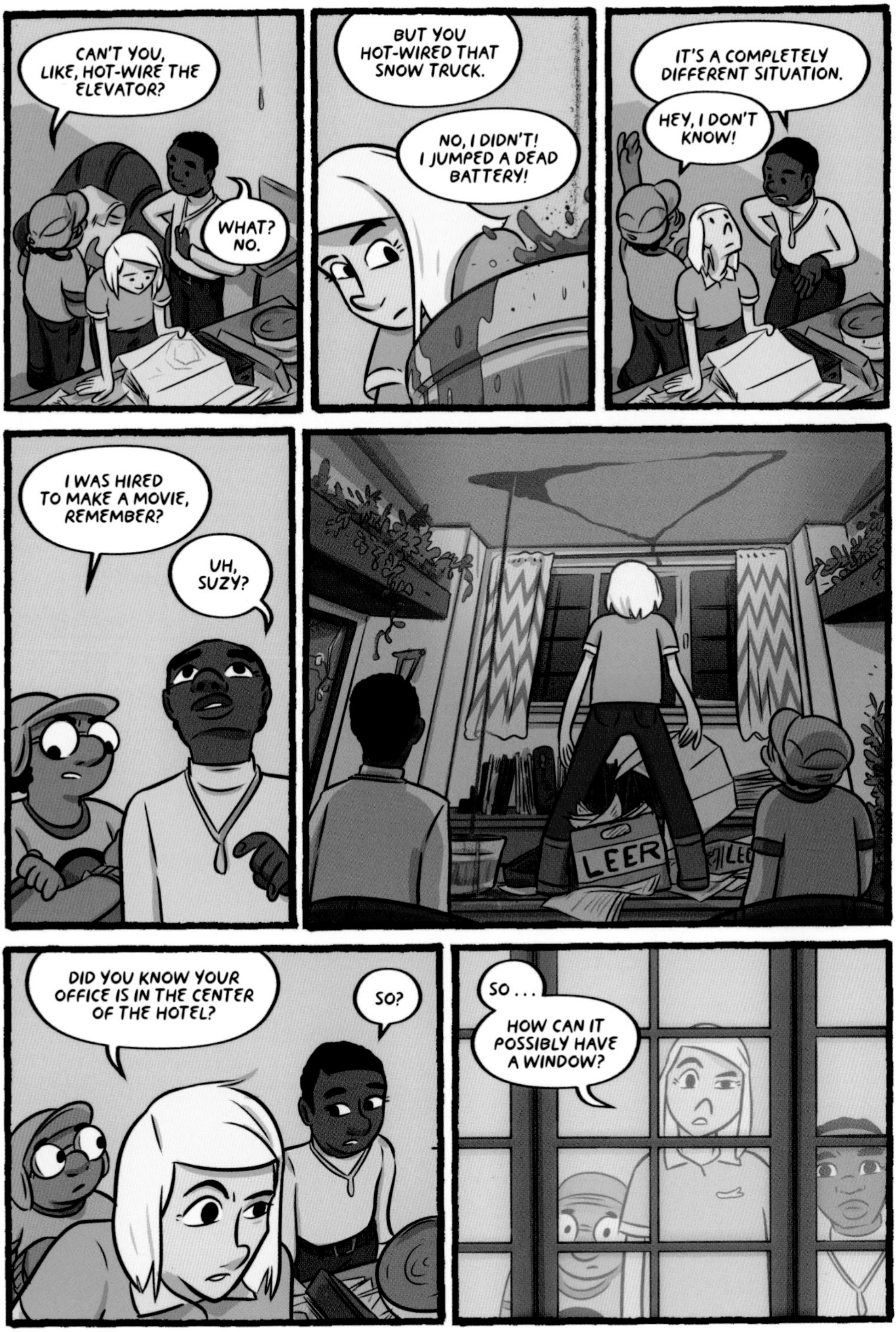
CAN'T YOU, LIKE, HOT-WIRE THE ELEVATOR?
WHAT? NO.
BUT YOU HOT-WIRED THAT SNOW TRUCK.
NO, I DIDN'T! I JUMPED A DEAD BATTERY!
IT'S A COMPLETELY DIFFERENT SITUATION.
HEY, I DON'T KNOW!
I WAS HIRED TO MAKE A MOVIE, REMEMBER?
UH, SUZY?
LEER
DID YOU KNOW YOUR OFFICE IS IN THE CENTER OF THE HOTEL?
SO?
SO . . .
HOW CAN IT POSSIBLY HAVE A WINDOW?

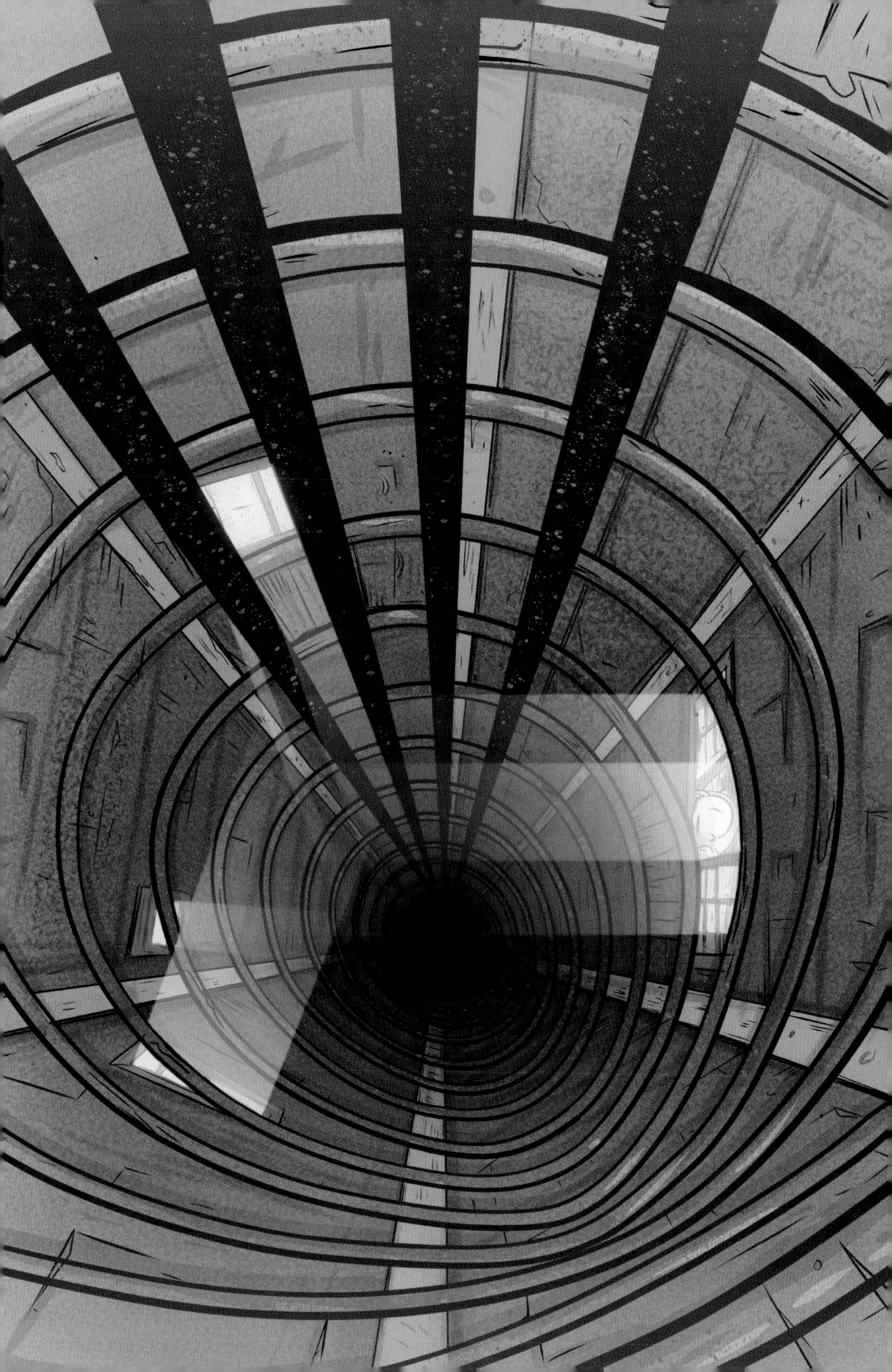

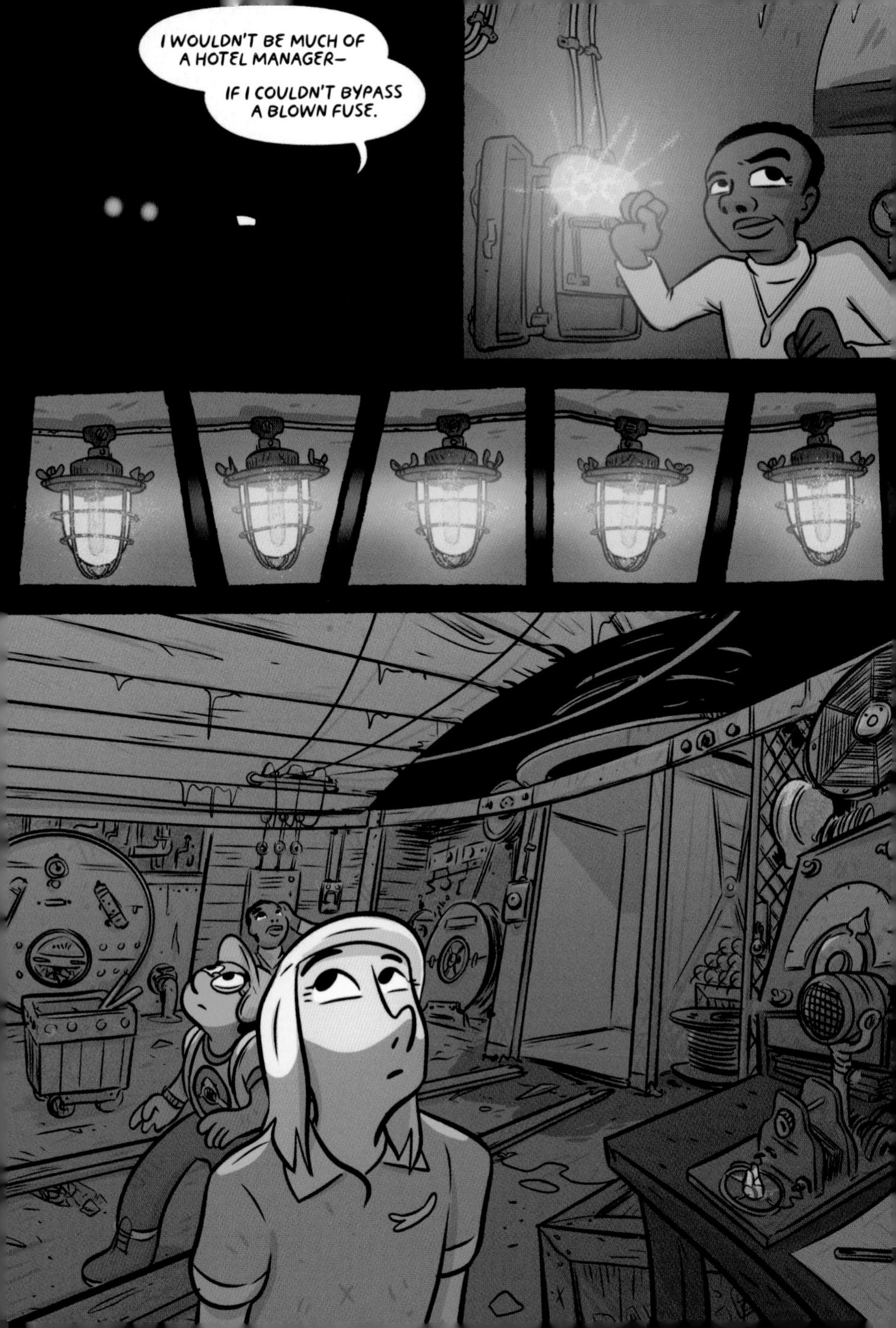
I WOULDN'T BE MUCH OF A HOTEL MANAGER–
IF I COULDN'T BYPASS A BLOWN FUSE.

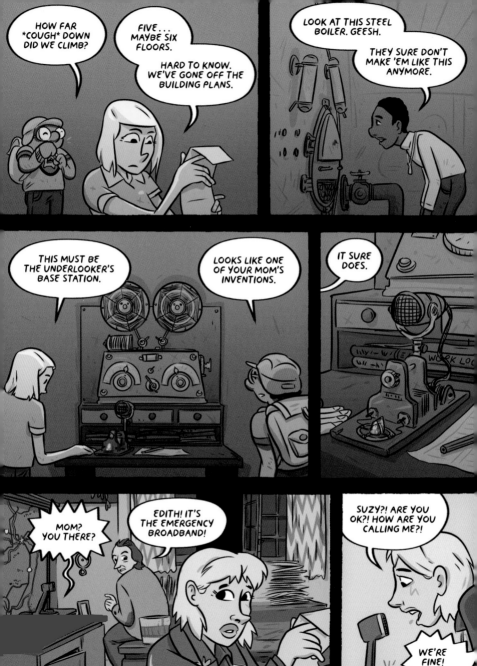

THROUGH HERE.

DID YOU KNOW THAT SIX GOLD MINES WERE DISCOVERED WITHIN 100 MILES OF ESTES PARK? WHY CAN'T WE HAVE ONE?!

NO ONE'S SAYING IT'S NOT POSSIBLE.

BUT YOU'VE DONE YOUR PART, DANNY. GO BACK WITH RENA.

I WANT TO STAY AND HELP!

NO.

IT'S TIME TO MOVE ON.

WHAT ABOUT YOU?

I'LL BE RIGHT BEHIND YOU.

ELIJAH—

I'M NOT LEAVING WITHOUT HER.

WE'LL BE WAITING AT THE ELEVATOR.

MAKE IT QUICK.

YOU LOOK LIKE YOU HAVE SOMETHING ON YOUR MIND, MS. HESS.

I WAS JUST THINKING HOW YOU'RE NOT THE FIRST TO TRY TO SAVE THE PARK.

LINDA LEER BELIEVED IN THE GOLD, TOO.

SHE CAME DOWN HERE FOR THE FIRST TIME WHEN SHE WAS A LITTLE KID.

AND SHE WOULD HAVE DIED DOWN HERE . . .

. . . IF SHE HADN'T HAD HER BEST FRIEND WITH HER.

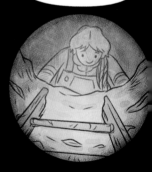

EDIE? WAS THAT YOU?

I HAD NO IDEA SHE KNEW THAT STORY.

THE ACCIDENT TRANSFORMED LINDA.

SHE BECAME AN INSPIRATION.

A COMET!

SHE BECAME FEARLESS IN EVERYTHING SHE SET HER MIND TO ACHIEVING.

AFTER THE FLOOD, SHE LED THE EFFORT TO REBUILD OUR PARK.

SHE WAS MY HERO.

AND SHE KNEW IT, TOO.

SHE SPENT HER FAMILY FORTUNE TRYING TO HELP US.

BUT IT WASN'T ENOUGH.

THAT'S WHEN THE GIRL RETURNED TO THE CAVE.

FOR YEARS I WAS ABLE TO BURY THE MEMORY OF THAT DARK DAY.

BUT NOW IT'S ALL I SEE.

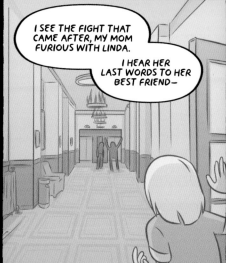

I SEE THE FIGHT THAT CAME AFTER, MY MOM FURIOUS WITH LINDA.

I HEAR HER LAST WORDS TO HER BEST FRIEND—

"STAY AWAY FROM MY DAUGHTER."

AND SHE DID.

I NEVER SAW MY GODMOTHER AGAIN.

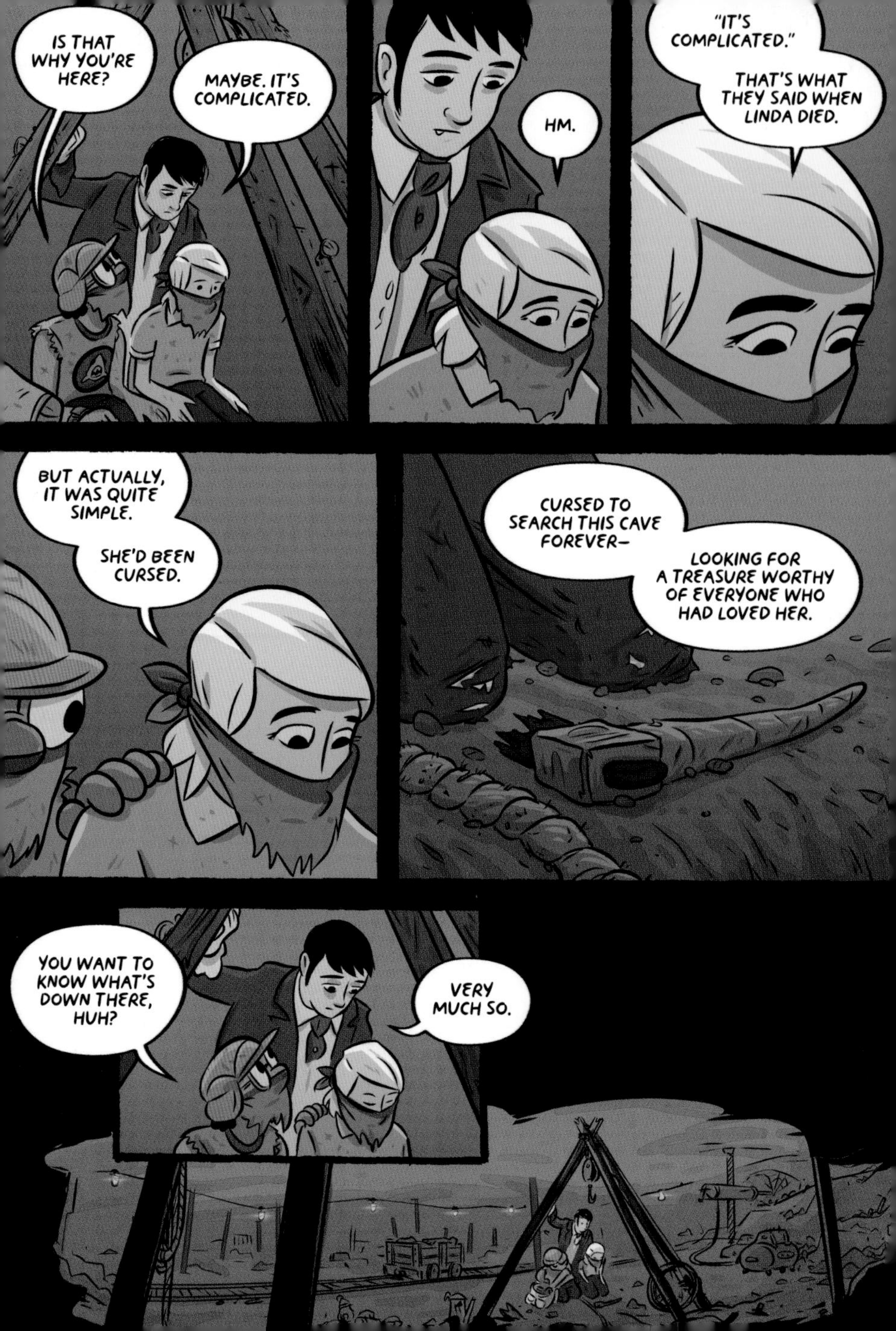
IS THAT WHY YOU'RE HERE?
MAYBE. IT'S COMPLICATED.
HM.
"IT'S COMPLICATED."
THAT'S WHAT THEY SAID WHEN LINDA DIED.
BUT ACTUALLY, IT WAS QUITE SIMPLE.
SHE'D BEEN CURSED.
CURSED TO SEARCH THIS CAVE FOREVER–
LOOKING FOR A TREASURE WORTHY OF EVERYONE WHO HAD LOVED HER.
YOU WANT TO KNOW WHAT'S DOWN THERE, HUH?
VERY MUCH SO.

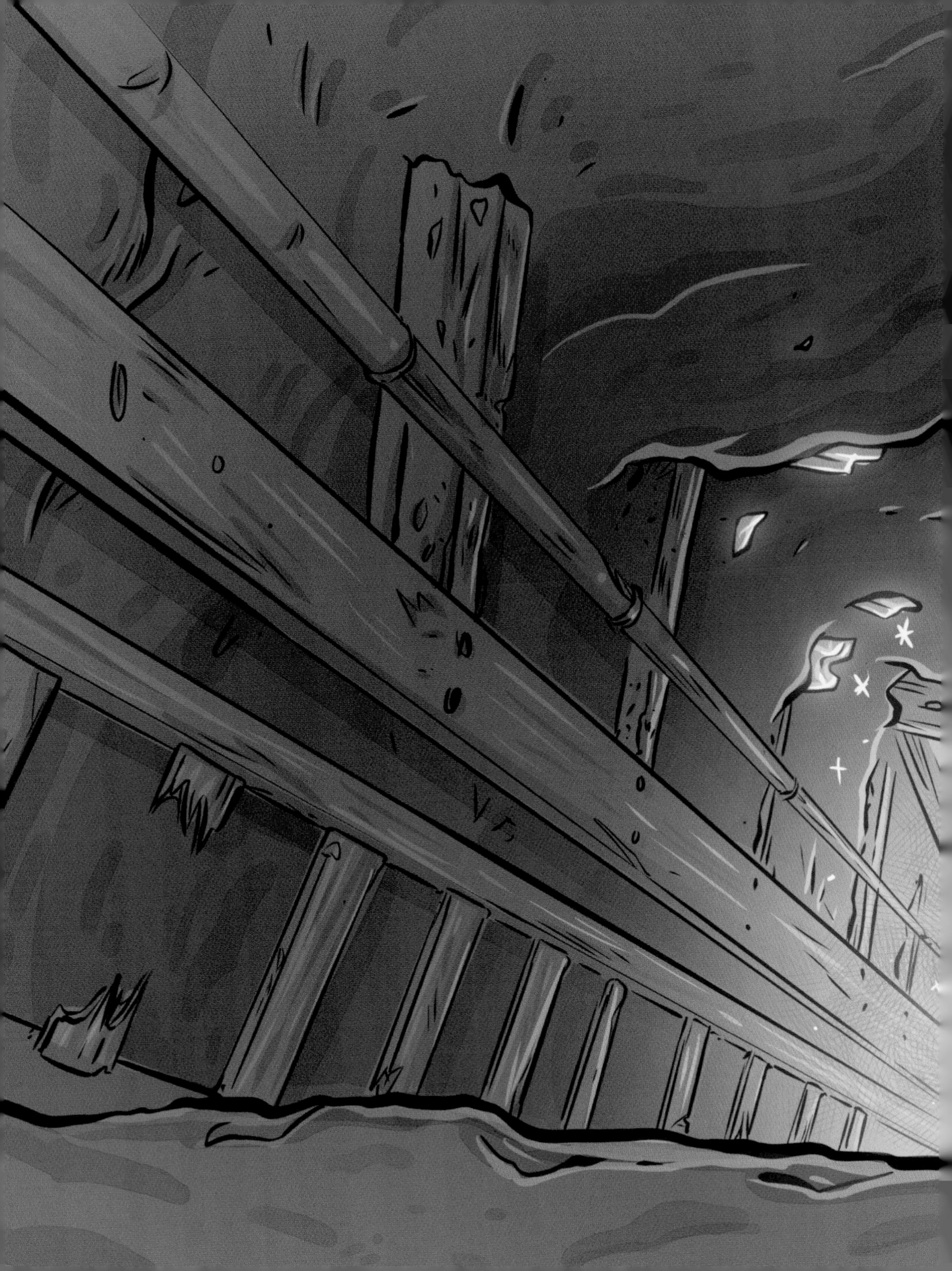

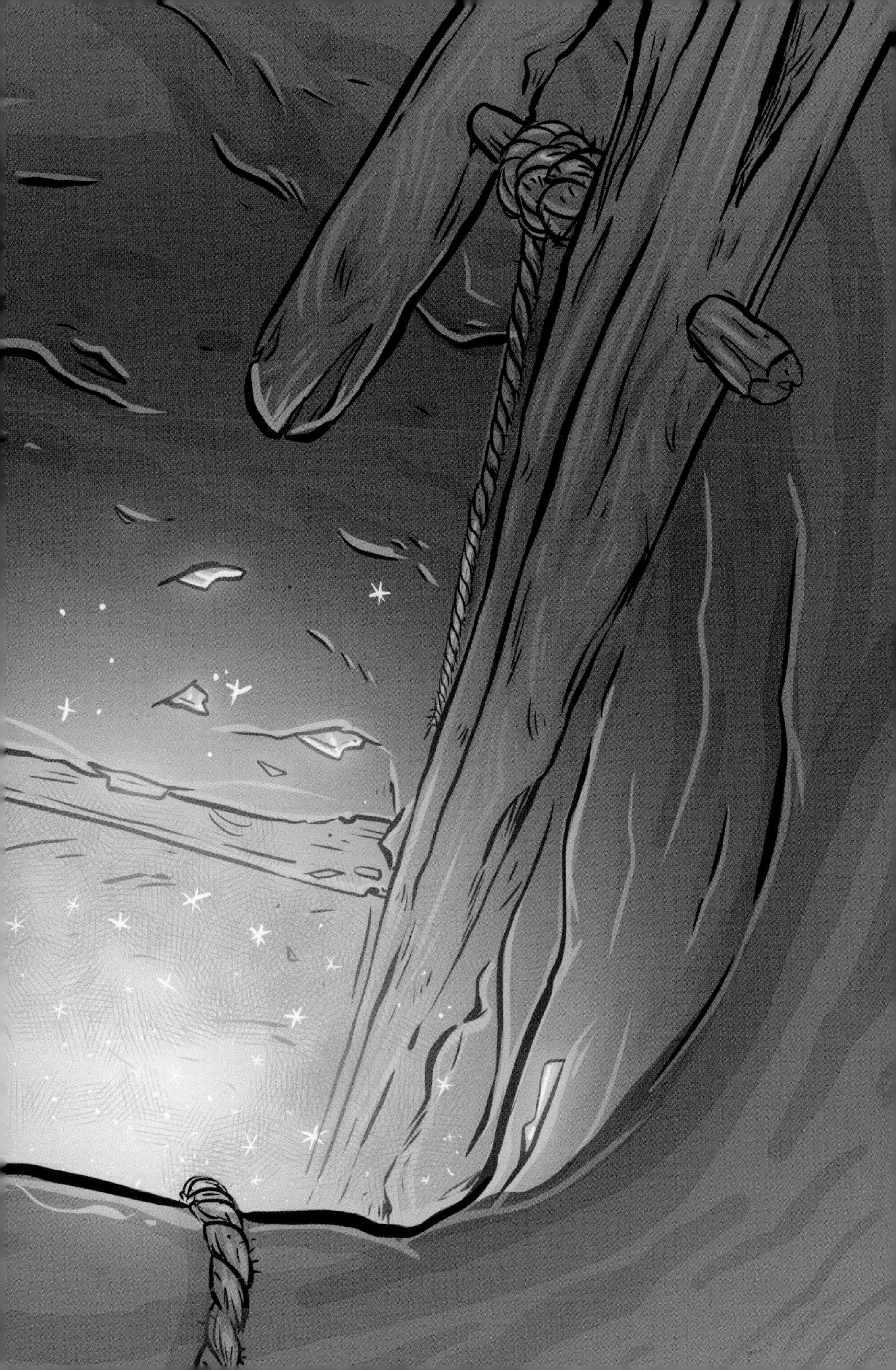

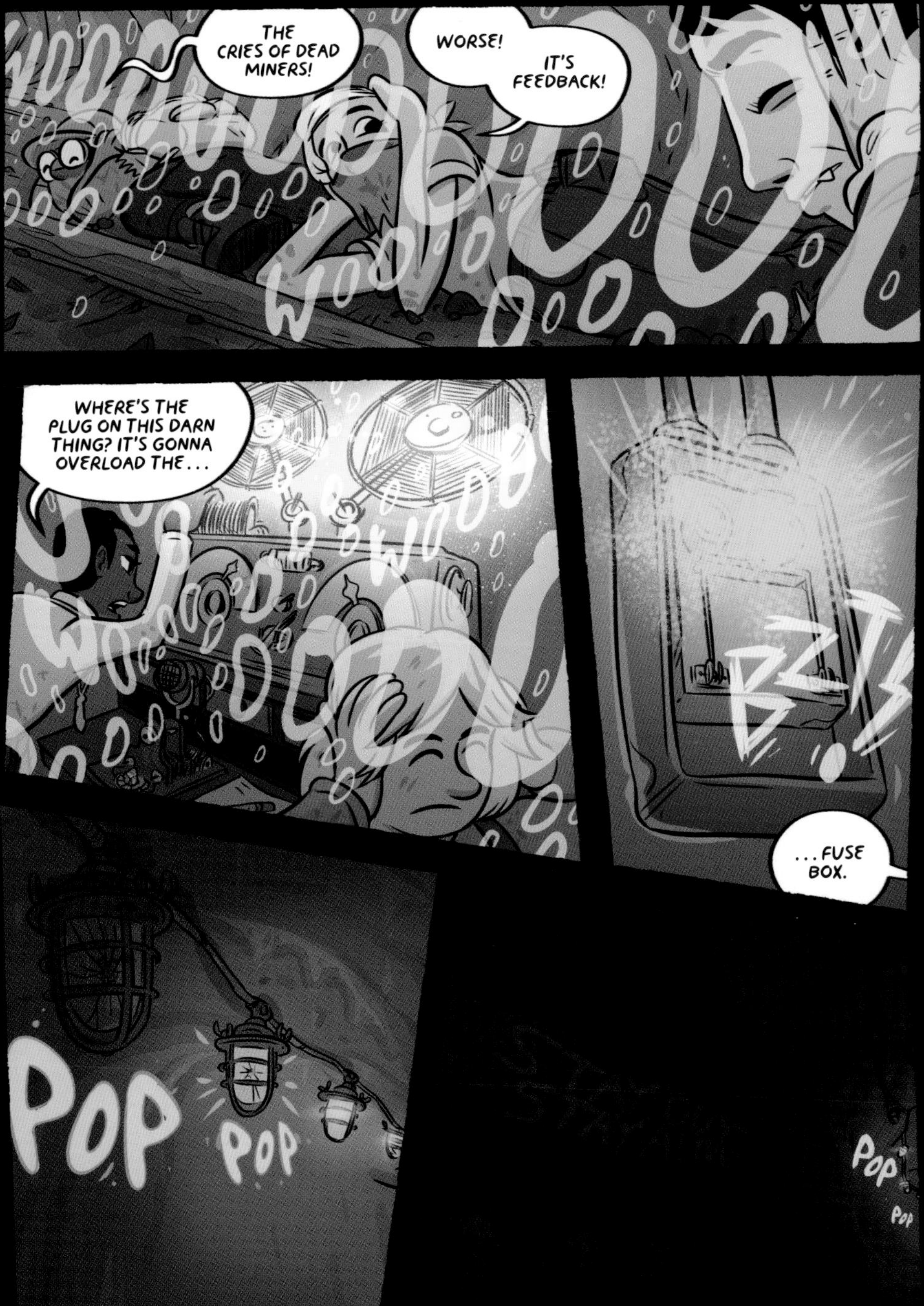
THE CRIES OF DEAD MINERS!
WORSE!
IT'S FEEDBACK!
WHERE'S THE PLUG ON THIS DARN THING? IT'S GONNA OVERLOAD THE . . .
. . . FUSE BOX.
POP
POP
POP
POP

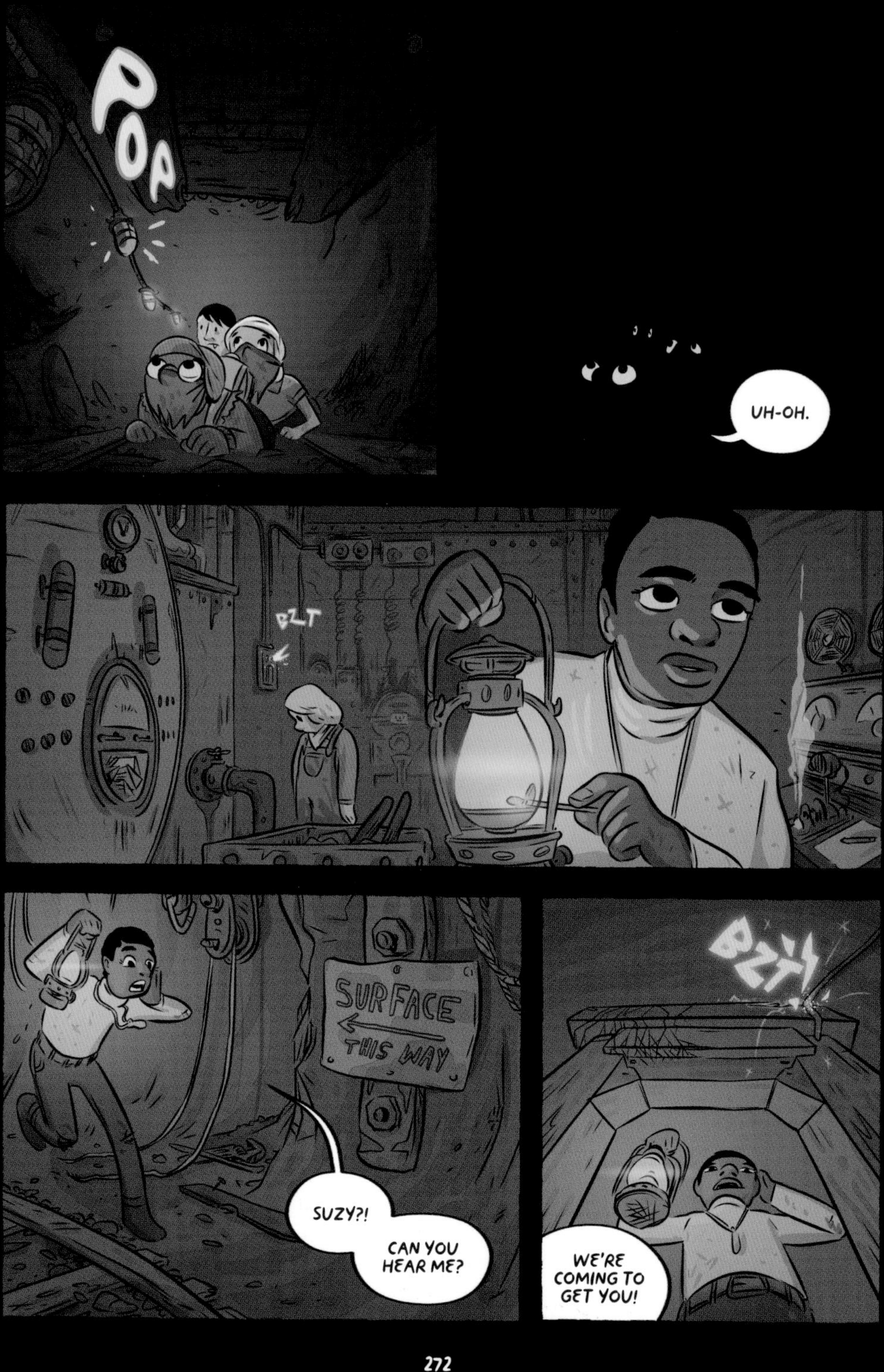
POP
UH-OH.
BZZT
SURFACE
THIS WAY
SUZY?!
CAN YOU HEAR ME?
BZZT
WE'RE COMING TO GET YOU!

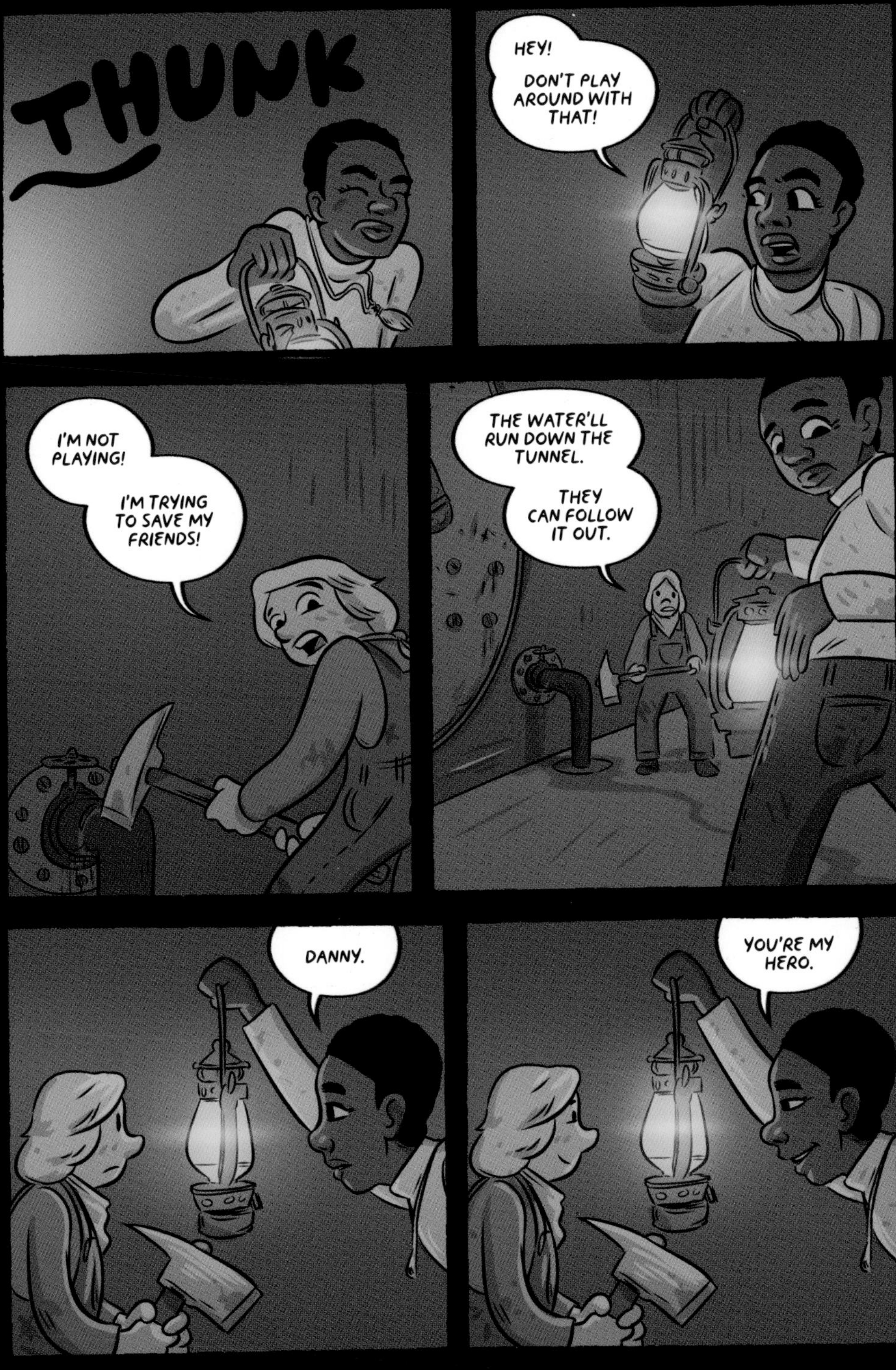
THUNK
HEY!
DON'T PLAY AROUND WITH THAT!
I'M NOT PLAYING!
I'M TRYING TO SAVE MY FRIENDS!
THE WATER'LL RUN DOWN THE TUNNEL.
THEY CAN FOLLOW IT OUT.
DANNY.
YOU'RE MY HERO.

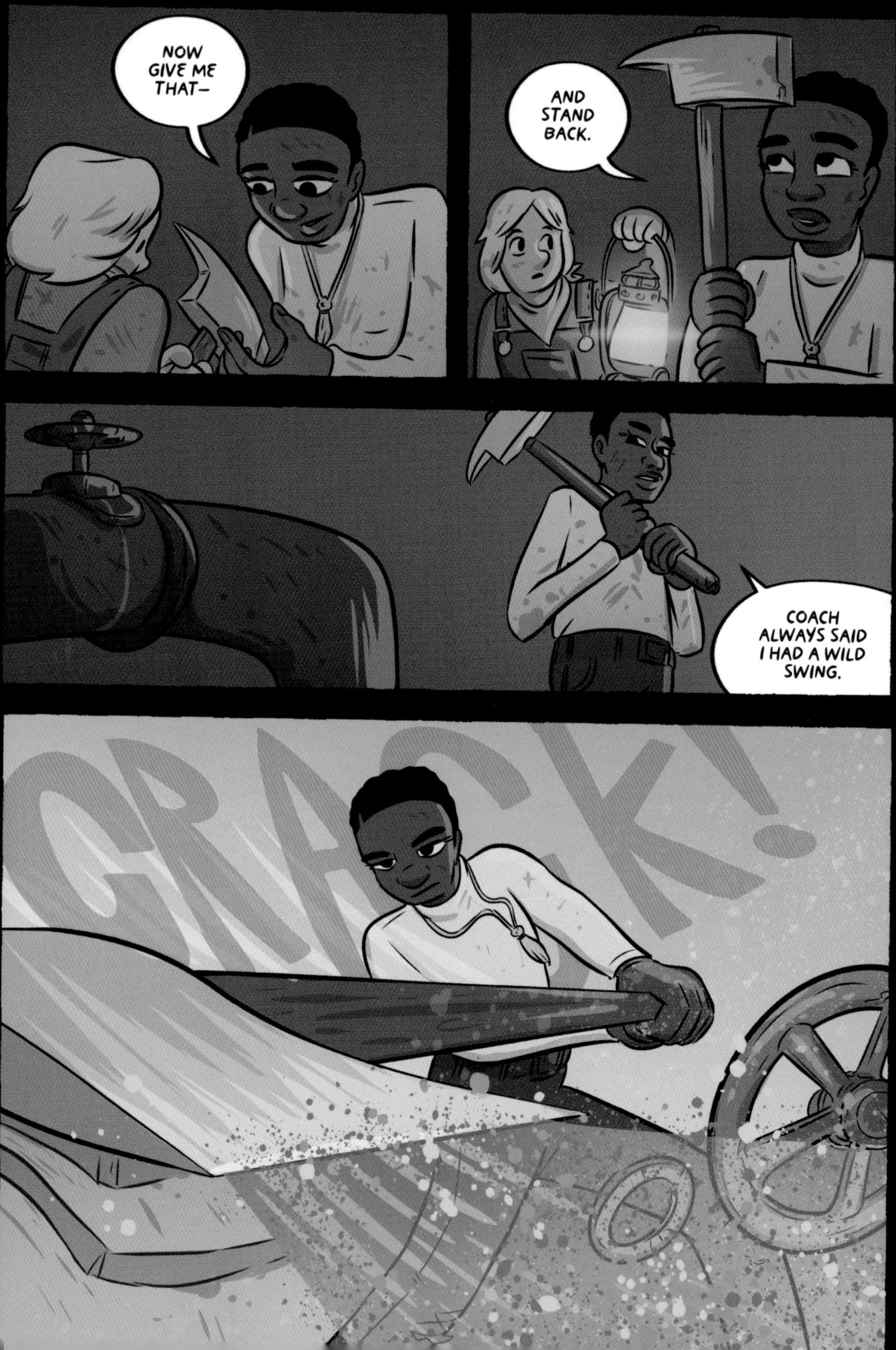
NOW GIVE ME THAT—
AND STAND BACK.
COACH ALWAYS SAID I HAD A WILD SWING.
CRACK!

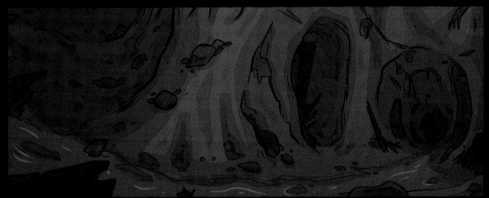

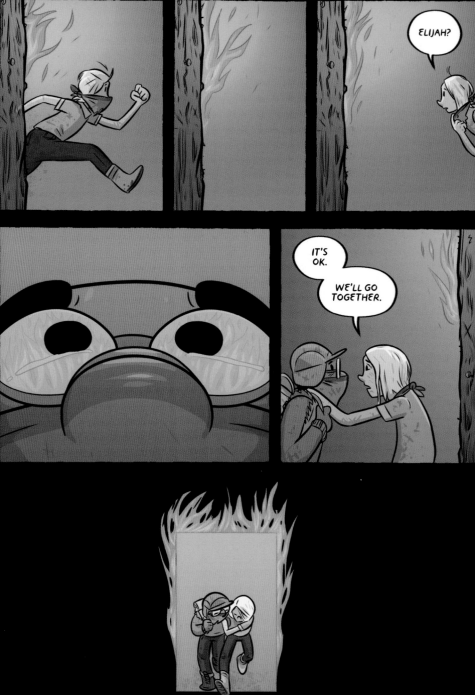

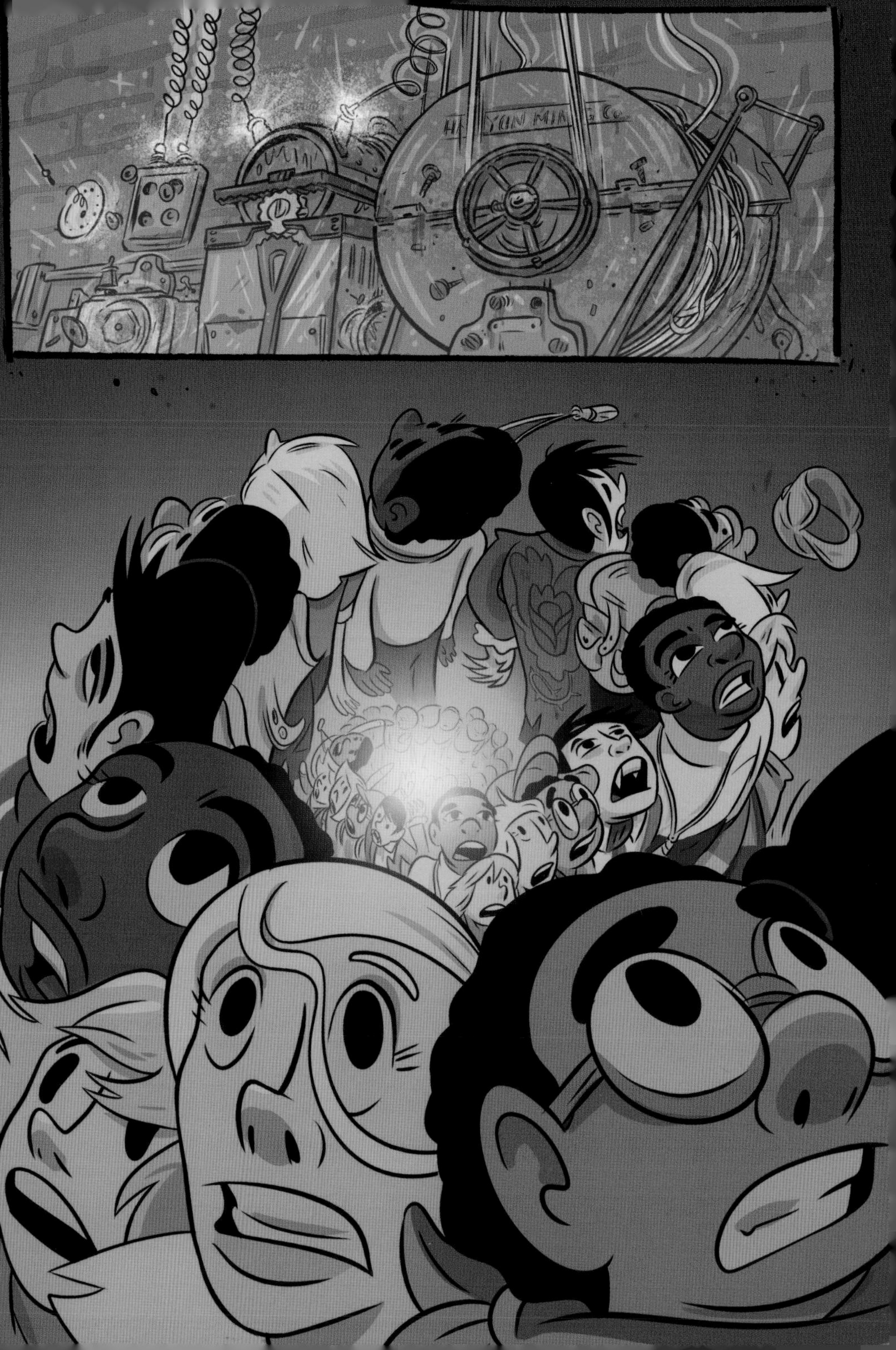

H YON MIN G Co.

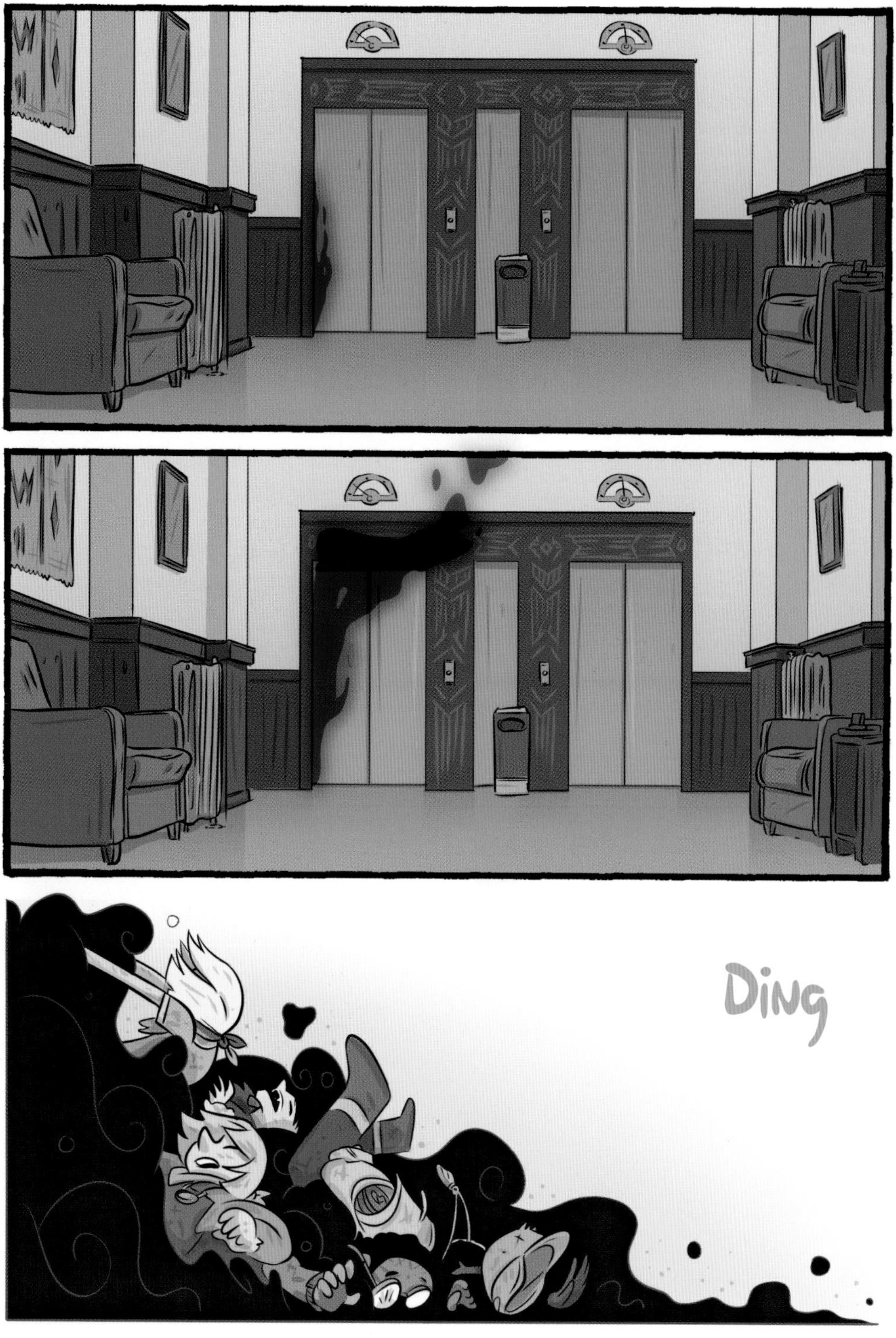
Ding

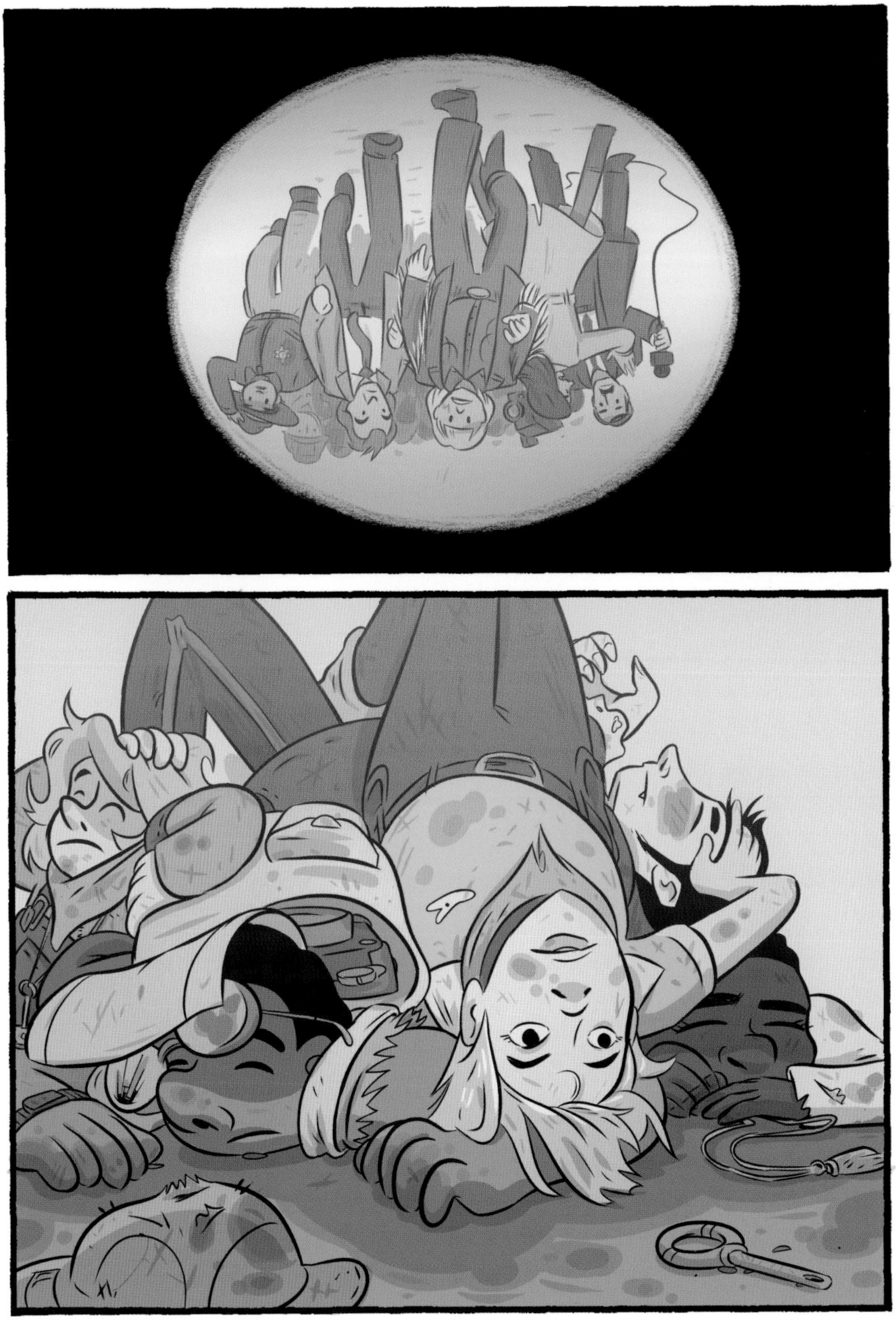

THE
UNDERLOOK HOTEL
ESTES PARK, COLORADO

```
 ::::::::   :::    :::  :::    :::    :::    ::::::::   ::::::::::   :::    :::    :::   :::
 :+:   :+:  :+:    :+:  :+:    :+:    :+:   :+:    :+:  :+:    :+:   :+:    :+:   :+:   :+:
 +:+        +:+    +:+  +:+    +:+    +:+   +:+         +:+    +:+   +:+    +:+   +:+ +:+
 +#++:++#++ +#++:++#++  +#+    +#+    +#+   +#++:++#    +#++:++#:    +#+    +#+    +#++:
        +#+ +#+    +#+  +#+    +#+    +#+          +#+  +#+    +#+   +#+    +#+    +#+
 #+#   #+#  #+#    #+#  #+#    #+#    #+#   #+#    #+#  #+#    #+#   #+#    #+#    #+#    #+#
 ########   ###    ###  ###    ###    ###    ########   ###    ###   ########   ###    ###
```

"All small towns have their secrets," he said. "You will no longer be one of them."

With those words, he pushed the stake through the vampire's heart. The monster fell dead. For the last time.

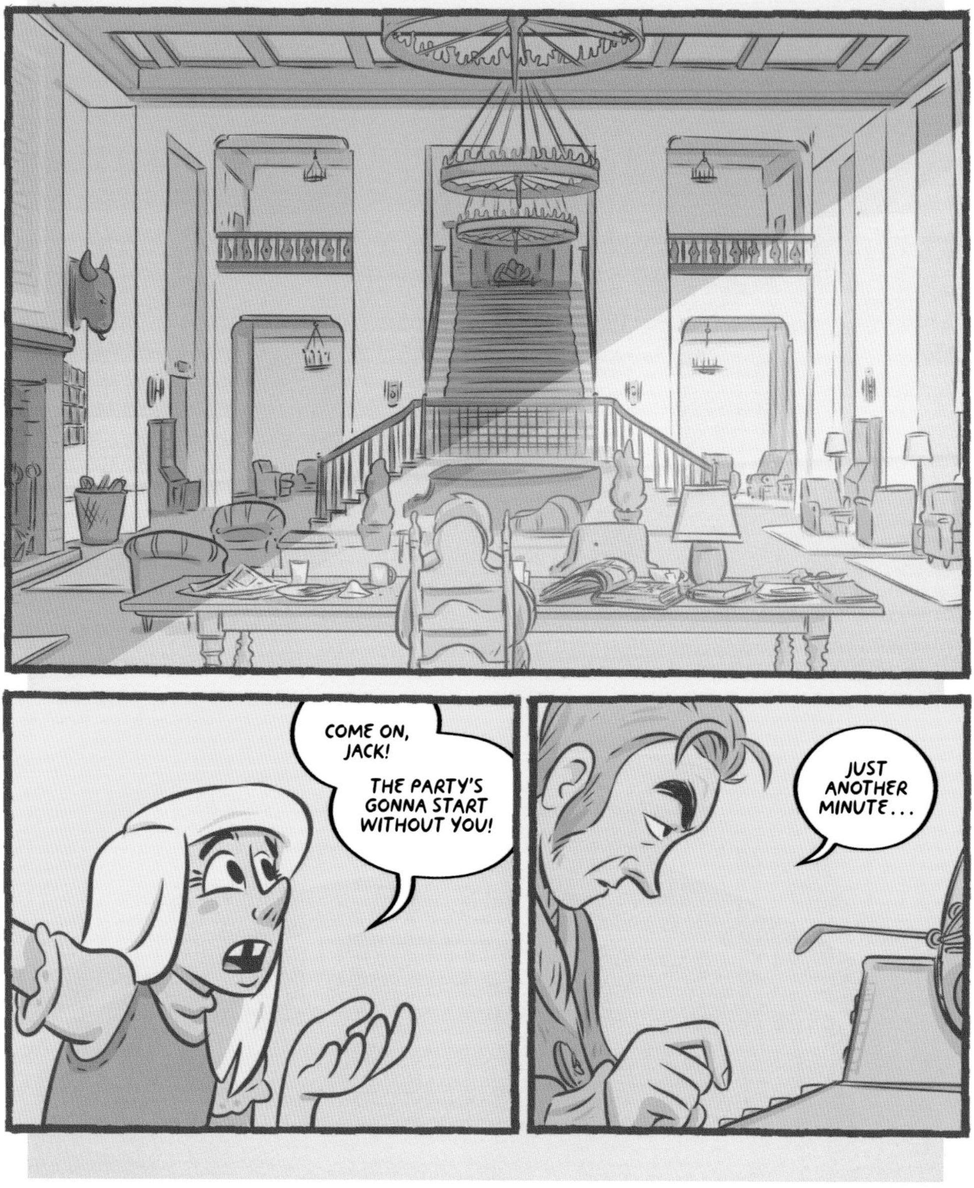
COME ON, JACK!
THE PARTY'S GONNA START WITHOUT YOU!
JUST ANOTHER MINUTE...

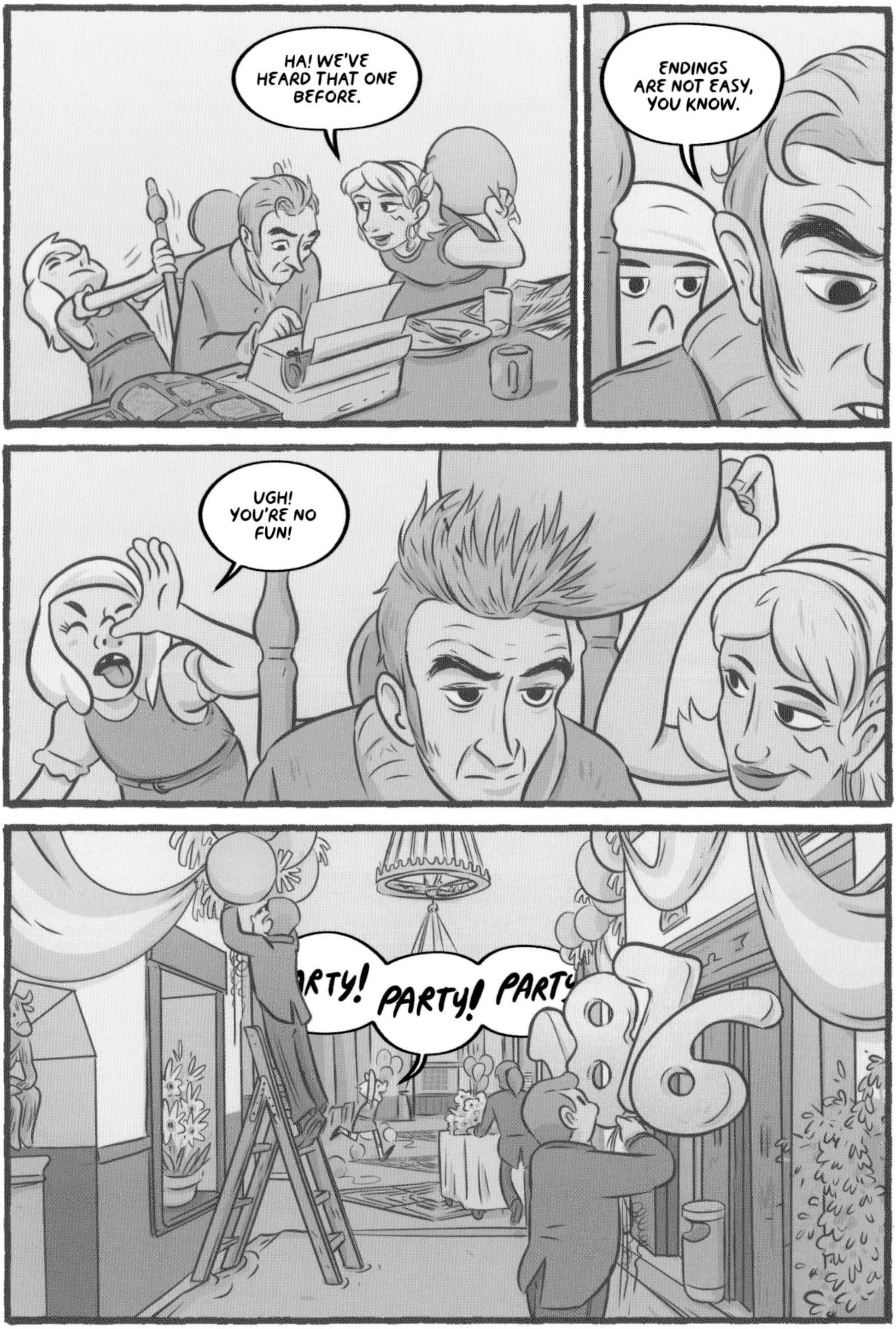
HA! WE'VE HEARD THAT ONE BEFORE.
ENDINGS ARE NOT EASY, YOU KNOW.
UGH! YOU'RE NO FUN!
ARTY! PARTY! PARTY

287

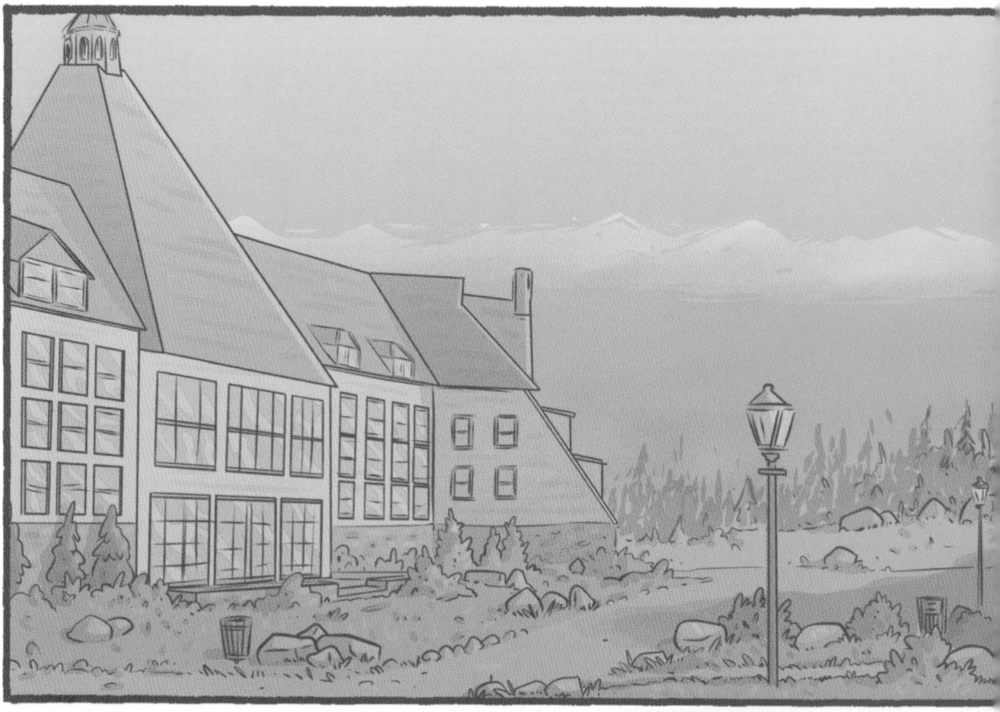

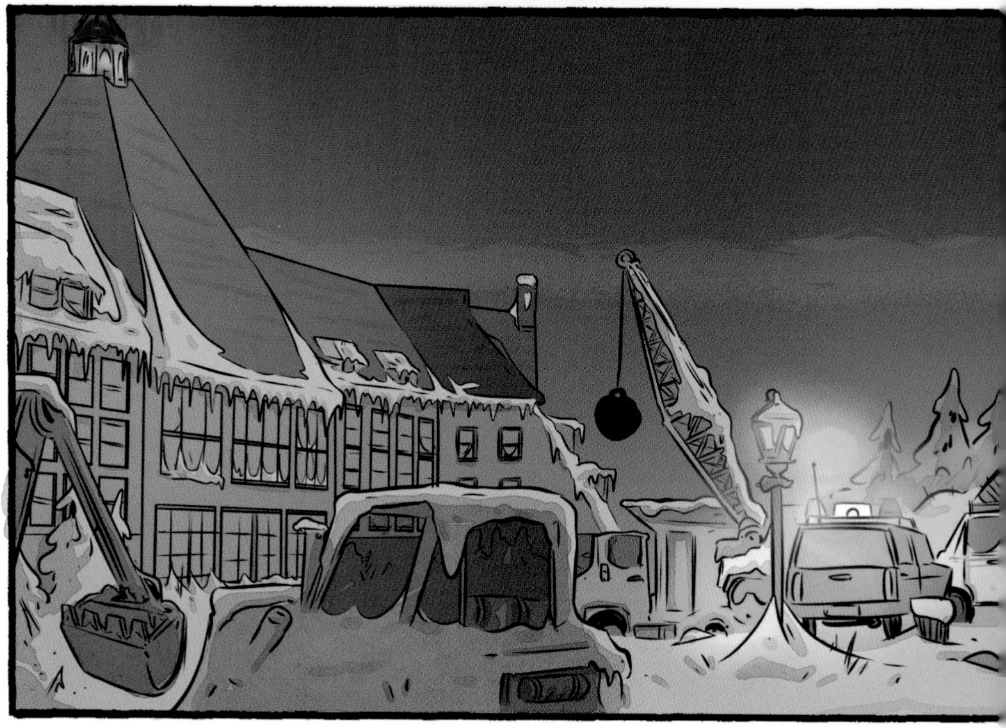

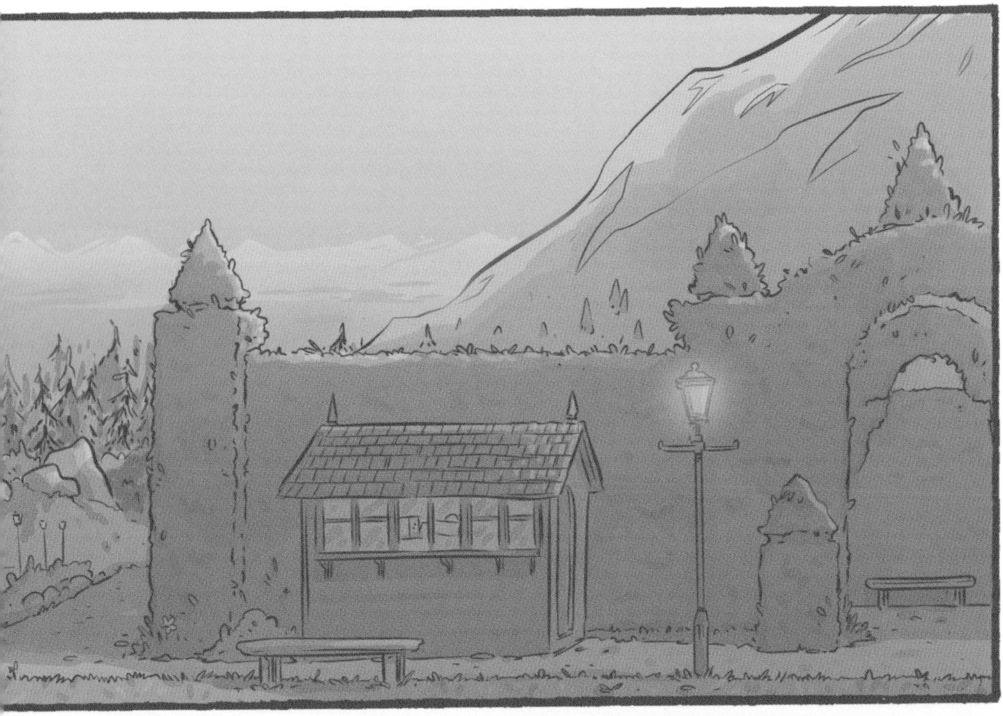

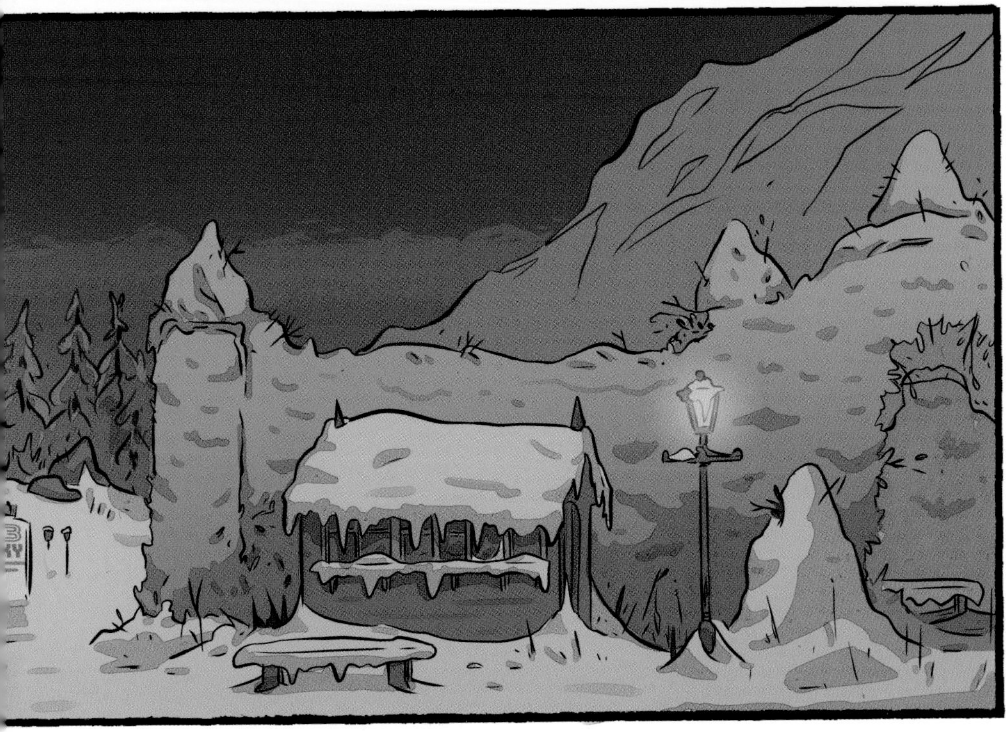

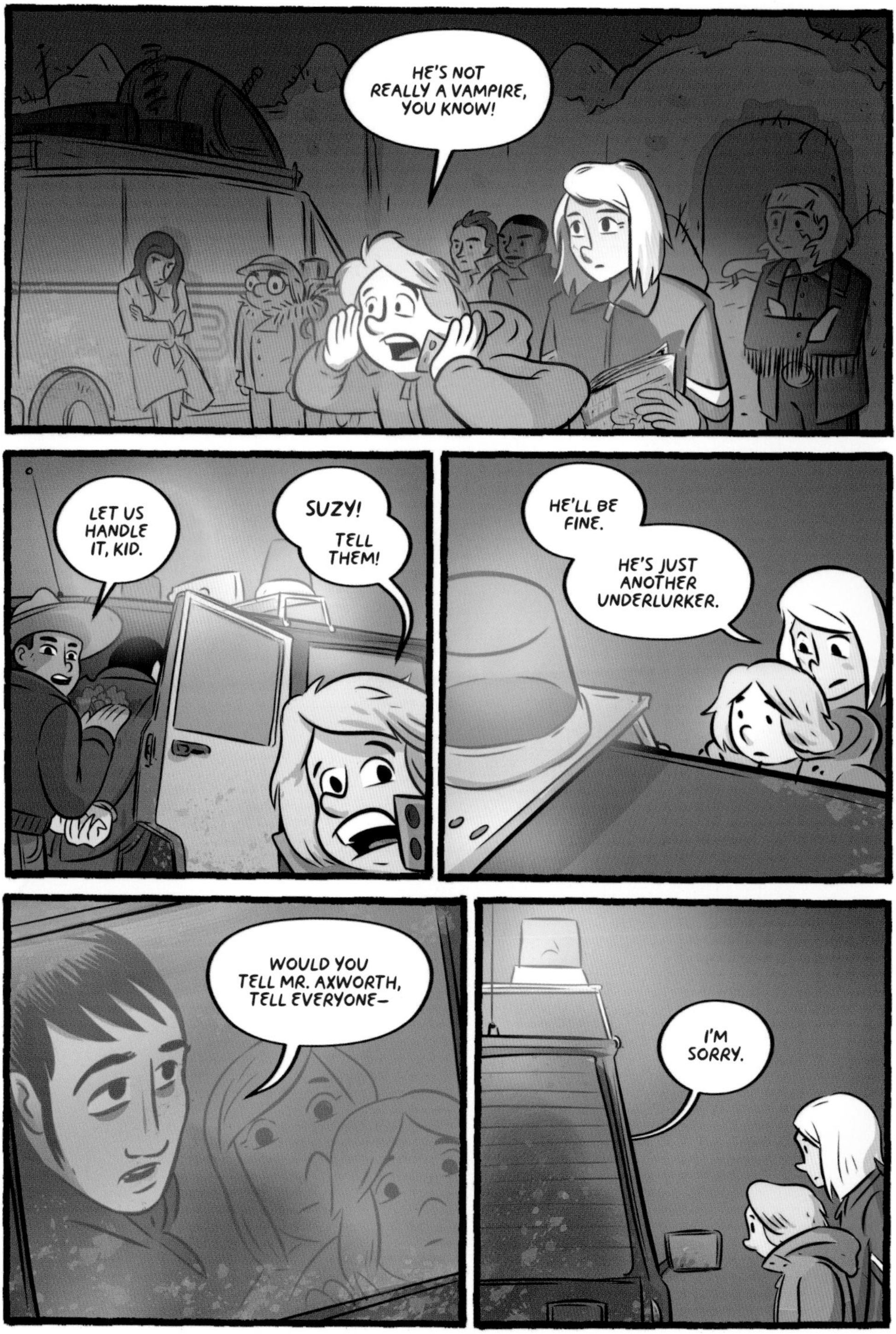
HE'S NOT REALLY A VAMPIRE, YOU KNOW!
LET US HANDLE IT, KID.
SUZY!
TELL THEM!
HE'LL BE FINE.
HE'S JUST ANOTHER UNDERLURKER.
WOULD YOU TELL MR. AXWORTH, TELL EVERYONE—
I'M SORRY.

MIDNIGHT STAR

THE CURSE OF THE UNDERLOOKER
BY EDWARD BARLOW

RLOOKEK
BY EDWARD BARLOW

YOU'RE KIDDING ME, SUZ!

WARD, THE VAMPIRE TOUR GUIDE...

...IS THE JOURNALIST EDWARD BARLOW?!

HE BLAMED HIMSELF FOR RUINING JACK'S CAREER.

I SHOULD HAVE FIGURED IT OUT BEFORE!

I COULD HAVE HELPED HIM!

SUZ, IT'S NOT UP TO YOU TO SAVE OUR TOWN.

IT'S OK TO JUST BE A KID SOMETIMES.

YOU REALIZE YOU'RE THE ONLY ONE WHO GOT THE WHOLE STORY?

YEAH.

AND YOU'RE JUST GOING TO LET IT GO? JUST LIKE THAT?

YEAH.

THAT'S INTEGRITY.

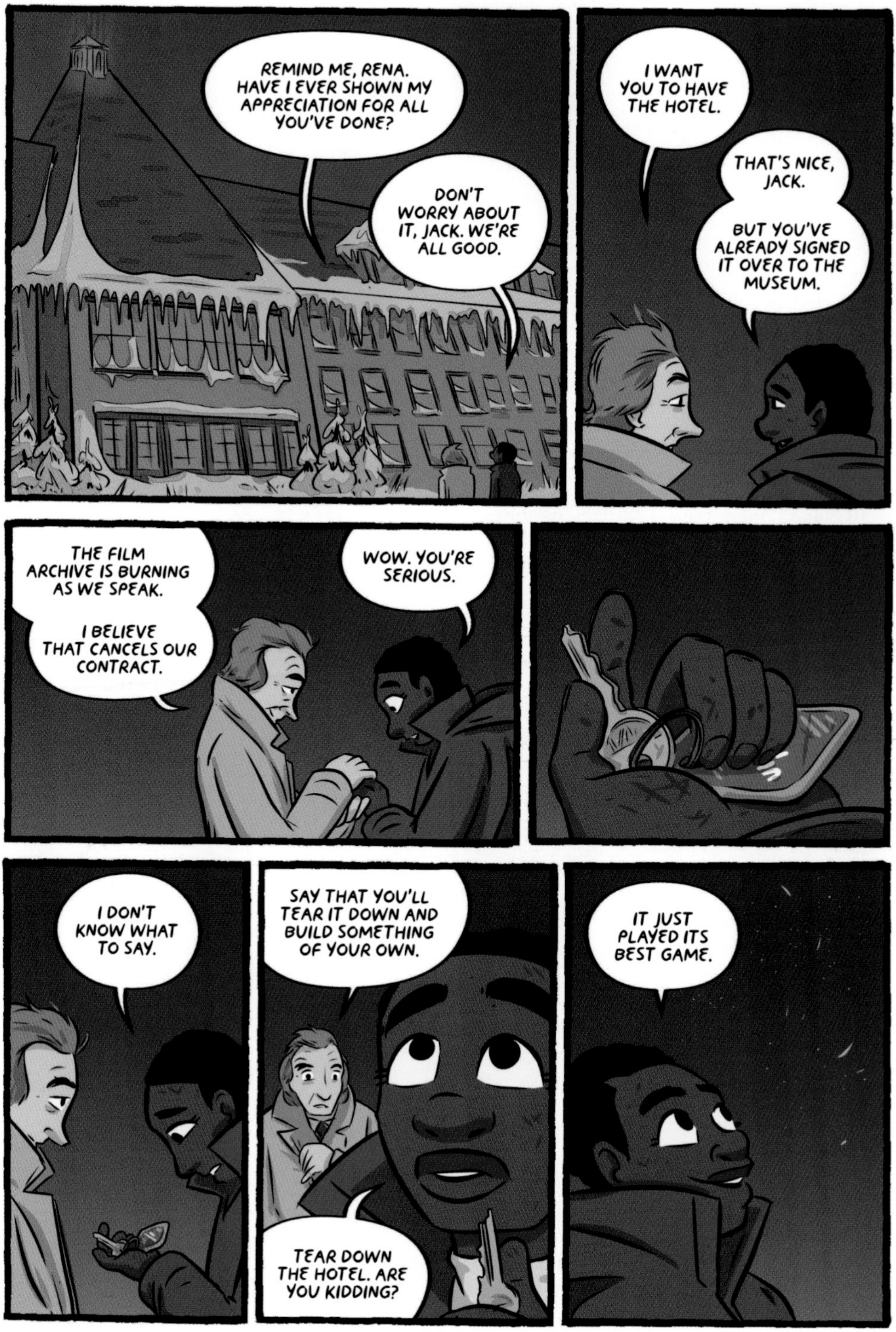
REMIND ME, RENA. HAVE I EVER SHOWN MY APPRECIATION FOR ALL YOU'VE DONE?
DON'T WORRY ABOUT IT, JACK. WE'RE ALL GOOD.
I WANT YOU TO HAVE THE HOTEL.
THAT'S NICE, JACK.
BUT YOU'VE ALREADY SIGNED IT OVER TO THE MUSEUM.
THE FILM ARCHIVE IS BURNING AS WE SPEAK.
I BELIEVE THAT CANCELS OUR CONTRACT.
WOW. YOU'RE SERIOUS.
I DON'T KNOW WHAT TO SAY.
SAY THAT YOU'LL TEAR IT DOWN AND BUILD SOMETHING OF YOUR OWN.
TEAR DOWN THE HOTEL. ARE YOU KIDDING?
IT JUST PLAYED ITS BEST GAME.

I DON'T THINK JACK
NEEDS TO REMEMBER
THIS PART, ELIJAH.

THIS
PART ISN'T
FOR HIM.

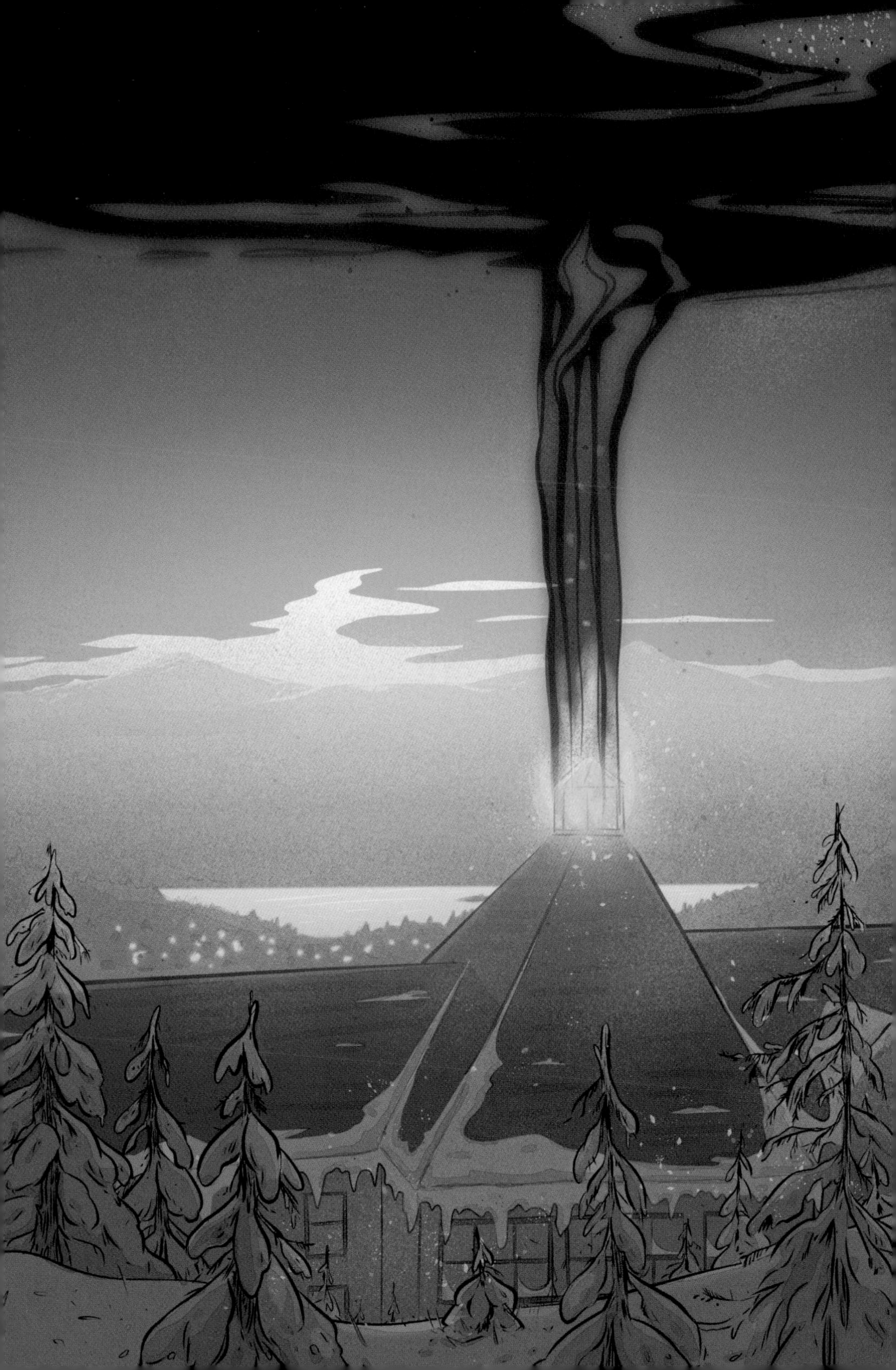

ACKNOWLEDGMENTS

THE BIGGEST THANK-YOU TO ANDREA COLVIN
FOR WANDERING WITH ME THROUGH THE ~~MAZE~~ LABYRINTH
THAT EVENTUALLY BECAME THIS BOOK.

THANK YOU TO MEGAN, JAKE, ADDISON, AND ARIA
FOR ALL THEIR HARD WORK AND TALENT.
SPECIAL THANKS TO ADRIANN FOR KEEPING
AN EYE ON EVERYTHING.

AND A FOREVER THANK-YOU TO DOTTIE AND MAURA,
WHO ARE ALWAYS UP FOR AN AFTERNOON WALK;
GARVEY, WHO IS ALWAYS HUNGRY WHEN WE GET HOME;
AND RESTY, WHO IS ALWAYS WITH US ♥

ABOUT THE AUTHOR

IRA MARCKS IS A CARTOONIST AND THE AUTHOR-ILLUSTRATOR OF *SHARK SUMMER* AND *SPIRIT WEEK*. HE LIVES IN UPSTATE NEW YORK WITH HIS WIFE, A CAT, A DOG, AND LOTS OF BOOKS HE'S BEEN MEANING TO READ.